THE OUTLANDS

TYLER EDWARDS

THE PATRIARCH

THE NIGHTLINGS

Copyright © 2019 by Tyler Edwards

Dedication

For my son Rowan: you bring more joy into our lives than you will ever know.

Message to readers:

I am so excited you are checking out the Outlands. This is my first novel and one I am hoping to turn into a series. I'd like to ask you a small favor. If you enjoy the book would you consider rating and reviewing it on Amazon and or Goodreads? Reviews are one the best ways to support an independent author and help build an audience for their work. If you are willing to do that, I would greatly appreciate it. Thank you so much, hope you enjoy: The Outlands.

TABLE OF CONTENTS

CHAPTER ONE

The black silhouette of a vulture circles overhead, its large dark shape contrasting with the bright afternoon sky. It flaps its outstretched wings a few times before returning to its casual drift, hovering in circles far above the city as if weightless. Its flight looks almost effortless. What a sweet freedom that would be.

"Come on!" Victor shouts, shoving a large sack into my arms. The light stubble that covers his square jaw makes his expression even more pronounced. He's not messing around. His voice is loud and forceful. Time seems to slow down. I am too lost in thought to really process what's happening. Instead of running, I freeze. It's stupid. Here I am standing around awkwardly, twiddling my thumbs, holding a bag of stolen goods. Seems like a good time to move. Instead, I am acting like a lawn ornament.

Despite his forceful shove, I remain frozen, holding tightly to the sack he'd just handed me. I look down at it and then back up at him. I can hear the sounds of angry voices and the thumping of boots against pavement getting closer. Victor may have gotten away with the prize, but he brought some unwanted guests. I can see it now. No, officer. I don't know where this bag came from. I was just doing my famous statue impersonation, and it showed up. Oh, I'm going to the Justice Block? Awesome.

"Jett! Come on!" Victor pulls at my arm.

My legs spring to motion. Nothing like a little adrenaline to ruin a perfectly good daydream. My cargo makes running awkward. Victor shouts for me to run faster, and I look over my shoulder. Three men in black uniforms with red accents on the shoulders and collar are charging after us, their heads covered with the traditional red beret of the city guard.

"Stop! Thief!" they shout. The sound of their approach encourages me to speed up.

Victor slides to a stop in front of me, nearly causing me to crash into him. At the end of the alley, I see two more guards with their bright red berets. We are boxed in. The guards in front of us turn to face us, blocking our escape. There's no time to think. The shadows of the guards behind us are looming closer with every moment.

"We're heaped," Victor mutters.

"There." I point, my brain finally joining the party.

About thirty yards before the end of the street is an intersection. I dig my feet into the ground and launch my body forward as hard as I can, propelling myself toward the side-alley, our only means of escape. There's no choice, no talking our way out. Either we escape or we become the newest residents of the Outlands.

The guards, who we call Red Caps, stare for a moment, apparently stunned to see thieves rushing toward them instead of away. That provides just enough of a distraction to keep them from noticing the side-alley. By the time they do, it's too late. We are halfway there when they move to intercept us.

I reach the turn first, but I need to buy some time. I scan the area. An empty crate lies at the corner of the building. I kick it as hard as I can in the direction of the approaching Red Caps. The crate flies between them, striking one on the shoulder and ricocheting, hitting the other one squarely in the stomach. I tell myself that's what I was going for. I just hope it slows them down long enough. Victor passes me and takes the lead.

A hand grasps my shoulder; one of the Red Caps caught up. His approach is too quick to control, so now it's time to fight back. I roll my shoulder, loosening his grip, and drop my body down. The Red Cap's momentum carries him forward. I trip him up with my foot and shove him in the back as he stumbles past me, sending his off-balance body into the two Red Caps approaching from the front.

That should buy us some time. Not risking a glance back, I sprint off down the street after Victor.

A door swings open in front of me, nearly taking me out. I sidestep, barely missing it. The rapid direction change, combined with my full sprint, knocks me off balance. I make quick friends with a wall that, thankfully, prevents me from face planting into the ground. Pushing off the wall as hard as I can, I scrape my hands against rough stone. At least I am able to steady myself and keep moving.

We navigate our way through a labyrinth of alleys. After a few minutes, convinced we have evaded our pursuers, we turn into a dark alleyway behind a shop and wait. I slide the bag carefully to the ground and clutch my knees as I catch my breath. The adrenaline surging through my body, making my heart pound violently, takes much longer to subside. Victor stands at the end of the alley, peeking his head out just past the stone wall to see if anyone followed us. After a few minutes, he seems satisfied that we evaded our pursuers.

"What's with you?" he asks with a snarl. If he's attempting to hide his frustration, he is doing a poor job. Even though we're close, there is still something intimidating about him when he's angry. Victor is bigger than I am, maybe six feet tall with a strong, athletic physique. His muscles are toned and hard. His dark brown eyes are accented with natural golden-yellow flecks, giving him the look of a predator searching for prey.

"Me? How was I supposed to know you were going to turn me into your bag man?" I said.

"You lagged! If I didn't know better, I would think you had never stolen anything before."

He knows that's not true. This is how we survive. We are thieves. Not the bad kind of thieves; we have principles. We don't steal things of personal value. We don't steal things we don't need. Most importantly, we don't steal from people who need it more than we do. Unfortunately, there aren't many of those. It's not like we chose this life. We steal because it's the only way for people like us to live.

We are orphans. In Dios that means we don't belong. We don't fit into the city's organized caste system. We also can't get a job—jobs are for citizens who belong to one of the three classes. Anyone born outside of that caste system is unable to find employment since the Patriarch assigns everyone their job.

Our options are limited to stealing or sitting on a street corner with a tattered old hat, begging. No thank you. Beggars are just thieves who are too lazy to do the work. Plus, you have to worry about beggar gangs. Beg on the wrong corner and, instead of credits, you get an energy blade to the back. Beggar gangs are bad enough when you aren't trying to encroach on their territory. I'll take my chances with the Red Caps.

"We got away, didn't we?" I say.

Victor shakes his head. "You got sloppy. It shouldn't have been that close. If they'd have had tracker darts, all of this would have been for nothing." He looks at me, his expression shifting from angry to concerned.

I nod in compliance. Victor is right. Victor is always right. He's annoying that way.

"Jett, we have to—"

Victor is interrupted by the sound of blaring trumpets all around us. The daily broadcast has begun. Every window on every building in the Market flashes with a faint purple glow. The image of an attractive woman with dark hair in a fancy suit appears from some unseen device. The sky transforms into one enormous projection, the sun replaced by the attractive woman's face. She begins with a warm, perfect smile.

Her teeth an unnatural white. Her eyes are bright but hollow and lifeless.

"Good evening, beloved citizens of the great city of Dios. May the blessings of the Great Bealz shine upon you."

She says it with a strange excitement. How she manages to pull off the same energy for the same sentence every day, I will never know. She goes over what she claims to be important city announcements: shift changes at the mine, a few new policies for conducting business in the Market, things no one in their right mind cares about. Everyone pretends to be listening for fear of what might happen should anyone discover what they are actually doing: ignoring her.

"I'm Barbra Boone. Today, we have a special guest with us," she begins. I look at Victor who rolls his eyes, resisting a chuckle. "Today is the two-hundredth anniversary of the reign of the Patriarch!" the woman announces with more charisma than any of her previous statements, which is impressive. "So, P1 News is proud to present the High Father of Dios, His Pontiff, Gregory Ignatius." The High Father is the supreme leader of Dios and the head of both the Patriarch and The Order.

The camera pans over to a regal man in long, flowing, white robes wearing an impressively large, square hat. Impractically large, unless its intent was to function as an umbrella—which the High Father wouldn't ever need. He stays in the Temple Sector; they don't make it rain there. Like his hat, his clothes are trimmed with gold. The High Father's elderly face looks sickly with his sunken eyes and wrinkled skin. His voice, once deep and commanding, is now hoarse, weathered, and weak. "Blessings upon you, citizens of Dios."

Even Victor has stopped fidgeting with the data-pad on his wrist. We knew what the High Father looked like. He was plastered on poster ads all over the city. For as long as I could remember, the only public appearances he ever made were for the weekly Chapel service. He never uses the media like this.

"On behalf of all of us in the Temple District, it is my honor to speak to you on this truly auspicious occasion. Today is a day we celebrate, for it marks the day we, the chosen people of Dios, were saved by the Great Bealz, who delivered us into this haven. After all we have endured—the trials, the struggles, and the joys—we have been formed into what we are today, a loving family."

"Loving family?" I scoff. "I bet he has never stepped foot out of the Temple Sector."

Victor puts his finger up to his lips and gestures subtly with his head. Two Red Caps walk past the alley we are in. We smile casually as they glance over. Nothing to see here, just a couple of Undesirables watching the daily broadcast. I close my mouth and stare back to the image projected in the sky.

"Today," he continues, opening his arms wide as if inviting the city in for a hug. He's so old his feeble arms shake in the process. "We celebrate the anniversary of our deliverance. Dios, our home, our hope, our salvation!" He lifts his arms up to the sky, tilting his head back as if speaking to the heavens. "Our salvation came at a cost. In the World That Was, differences were celebrated. Until those differences became divisions. From division, conflict. From conflict, fall. It was our differences that nearly led to our destruction. So, the Order was formed. that we may be protected from those dangerous divisions. For as the Sacred Texts teach, 'we are one when we are the same. When we are one, we are safe.' My people, you have risen to this challenge. You have conquered your differences. As a result, we have found peace and harmony in our sameness." The crowds repeat in unison with him, "Expression is arrogance. Duty is devotion. Conformity is virtue." This is the mantra of The Order and the spiritual method of systemic subjugation. "Today, we honor you, citizens of Dios, for your hard work and sacrifice in making our home the paradise it is—." His eyes return to us. "I declare, for the remainder of the day, all Market purchases will be tax-free and the sugar allotment will be doubled for the next month. Praise Bealz!" The Market Square fills with shouts of celebration before quieting down a moment later.

The camera pans back to the dark-haired woman in the suit. She smiles again, thanking the High Father for honoring us with his message. "It's we who should be thanking you, High Father, for your tireless work in keeping our city safe." Turning back to the camera, she speaks with a stern expression. "Remember, citizens of Dios, that without the laws of the Patriarch to provide us with order, we would surely fall into another Great Collapse. Lawbreakers risk the safety of us all. If you see someone breaking the law and you say nothing, you are helping them destroy our city." Her face warms up again, returning to its normal, unnatural levity, "Okay, citizens, let's show our support and appreciation for the men and women of the City Guard and to our benevolent rulers for their hard work in protecting us from the dangers of the Outlands. Let's observe a moment of silence in their honor."

An entire market full of people with better things to do stand around looking nervously at the ground, waiting for her to sign off and give them permission to go back to their lives. I swear I can hear the heartbeats across the Market Square. Finally, Barbra Fakesmile wraps up with her token conclusion, "I'm Barbra Boone. On behalf of all of us here at P1 News, I wish you a peaceful evening. Sleep well, citizens of Dios, knowing that you are safe and free thanks to the constant efforts of the Patriarch. Goodnight."

Safe and free? She says it with such natural ease; it's almost like she doesn't know. If she had seen what we have, I doubt she'd be able to smile so convincingly.

"You look like you just got nicked by a surprise inspection," Victor said. "What's going on in that head of yours?"

"Nothing."

"Jett, how long have we known each other?"

"A long time."

Thirteen years to be precise. We'd been best friends since before my parents were killed. There's no point in trying to keep secrets from

Victor. Victor knows me better than anyone. Sometimes he seems to know me better than I know myself.

"Do you think I can't tell when something is wrong?" Victor pauses, putting his hand on my shoulder.

I avoid making eye contact with him, moving my gaze to the ground. There's something about Victor's eyes; when you look into them, it's like he can peer into your essence. He was there for the most traumatic experience of my life.

"Parents again?" he guesses.

My memory plays like a moving picture. I see myself, a scrawny six-year-old kid, too young to understand what was happening but old enough to remember it all in vivid detail. My mother is lying motionless on the kitchen floor, warm blood pooling from her back. I'm holding her in my arms, crying as I call out to her as if my voice could somehow summon her back. Her breathing is faint, and she's coughing as she tries to speak, trying to tell me something that I can't hear over my own anguish.

I close my eyes to try and block out the memory, but the images barrage my thoughts with even greater clarity. Her dark brown hair lays disheveled across her shoulders and back, the ends soaking in her own blood. I don't know why she doesn't respond to my screams, why she just lies there. Well, I didn't know then. I know now. My father lies next to her on his stomach, his eyes closed almost as if he is sleeping. Standing above them is a man, his face hidden by shadow. I try to remember, to picture some identifying mark of the man who killed my parents. It's as if his face is covered by a dark cloud. There's only one thing I can truly tell: he is young.

Victor snaps his fingers in front of my face.

I blink and nod to answer his question. "What if it—"

"It wasn't," Victor interrupts me before I finish.

"But maybe I could—"

"You couldn't." Victor shakes my shoulder, and I meet his gaze. "It was not your fault, Jett."

"Those self-righteous Pharisites!" I curse. The more I try to understand what happened, the more I get lost in my rage. Maybe it's best to just forget about it and move on. Shaking the thoughts out of my head, I decide I'm done thinking about it. "Do you think we got enough?"

"Let's hope so," Victor says. "We better get going. Don't want to get stuck here after curfew."

I nod. A couple of Undesirables hanging out in an alley with a bag full of food is risky. One random Red Cap inspection and we are heaped. If the Red Caps didn't find us, the beggar gangs would. I like potatoes as much as the next guy, but I'm not sure I want my throat slit for them.

Victor pulls up the sleeve of his shirt, revealing his dark, smooth skin. His portable screen projects from the small data-pad on his wrist. He rubs his fingers on his temple, and the image on the screen begins to change. His fingers barely move to slide between electronic pages of information until he stops on a blueprint of the Market. He taps his temple twice, and a luminescent green arrow projects from his wrist down the street. We follow it through the alleys into the Market Square. The Square gets the most traffic. The further one moves out from the Square, the less crowded it gets. Shops further from the Square tend to be lower quality, lower prices, or just appealing to a more selective audience. The crowds provide great cover. Easy to get lost in them. One nice thing about being an Undesirable—no one really looks too closely unless they have a good reason. In a crowd, we are all but invisible.

The Market Square is the central location in the city, surrounded by four circular sectors with a designated train taking patrons to each. The North Train goes to the Temple Sector. It is highly restricted, Patriarch personnel only. The other trains travel out to the three sectors, transporting citizens to and from the Market.

9

Surrounding the Market, Sector A forms the smallest ring and is for Prime Citizens: upper class nobility. They have more credits than they know what to do with. Sector B is for the Artisans. As middle-class citizens, they are educated and have jobs that don't require much physical labor. The largest circle around the Market Square is Sector C, home to the Plebs. They are working class miners, farmers, and factory workers who make just enough to get by.

Those born without a class have to live in the Rim along the outer wall of the city. It's not a pleasant place. It's a slum. The Rim is an overcrowded dump of run-down, towering buildings on the verge of collapse as well as tents and make-shift homes. It houses the poorest, lowliest people in all of Dios. Thanks to the lack of proper sanitation, it may actually hold more infections than it does people. It is more like a prison than anything else. It's still better than the Outlands, but sometimes it's hard to imagine how.

We make our way to the Market Square, heading west toward our train. Victor freezes. A group of men walk past dressed in bright white robes, their uniforms trimmed with gold, designed to imitate the High Father's. Each man's hair is combed perfectly. Around their wrists they each have a golden data-pad that looks like a bracer. Around their waists, a golden belt with an attachment for their thrasher. Covering their right eyes are opaque, gold-tinted, square lens monocles. They move in unison. Twelve men, one footstep.

As one, they stop. The man in the front points. He doesn't say a word. Two Red Caps grab a boy who'd stopped in their path. The boy cries out. The Red Caps pull him away, nodding to the men in white who then continue their synchronized march. I wonder how long they practiced that. Good use of time, I'm sure. I hear a loud cracking sound, and the boy screams. The Red Caps are whipping him—five lashes for stopping in the wrong spot.

"Levites," Victor growls. He runs his fingers through his short black hair.

The name makes the hair on my neck stand up. Red Caps are bad but reasonable. Usually. Levites are something else.

"We need to split up," Victor says. "We'll look less suspicious. I'll take the potatoes. You take the bread. Meet you on the train."

Ever the big brother, Victor chooses the heavier, more noticeable item, knowing that if we get caught, it will give me a better chance of escaping. We don't have time to argue, so I do as he suggests. I remove the single strap of my busted up, dark brown pack from over my head and sling it to the ground. I open the flap and tuck the bread in securely before slinging it back over my shoulder. By the time I look up, Victor has already gone. I see him heading into the Market and toward the train. Of course, he takes the riskier route.

I pull the hood of my coat over my head and make my way down the west street until it opens up to Street One. Either side of the street is lined with stores built entirely of dark grey stone or cement. Most have beautiful glass windows that serve as moving picture screens for advertisements and messages from the Patriarch. Street One is the most highly trafficked of the streets, but it's still much less occupied than the Market Square itself.

"Well, well, well, what do we have here?"

Standing in front of me, blocking my path is a short, stout man with patchy facial hair and a large scar running across his neck. He's wearing a brown cloak that drapes over his body, concealing his arms and torso. On his cloak is a white emblem depicting a howling wolf's head inside a flaming circle. The Fire Wolves are one of the more aggressive beggar gangs. I recognize him—Bill Sonder, beggar gang enforcer. Bill pokes my shoulder, stepping closer to me. Victor and I did a job with them a few months back. The take was considerably less than they swore it would be. "You've been working in our nest again."

"Is it yours?" I say. "I can never keep track. Maybe you guys should post signs. I'm sure the Patriarch would love that."

He sneers. "Always the Lumegrin. You still owe us from that transport job. Debt's come due."

"You got your cut. Stop trying to shake us down for more."

"Last warning. We're watching you. If you don't bring us what you owe, there will be consequences."

"Thanks for the domes-up." I take a step forward, trying to push past him. He puts his hand on my chest to stop me.

"You don't pay, you're gonna end up on our prey list."

I shrug off the threat and walk past him, trying to pretend it didn't get to me. Victor can figure out how to handle this. Last thing we need is a beggar gang stalking our every move. The looming threat makes me a feel a little paranoid. I'm constantly looking over my shoulder as I try to get my nerves under control. Street Eight is surprisingly crowded. Usually by now it would be halfway to ghost town.

Out of the corner of my eye, I notice him—a Prime citizen in a black uniform with a light grey sash walking past me, trying to sound all superior and important, ranting to someone on the other end of his digi-call. I notice he didn't secure his data-pad, which is weird. Everyone in Dios has one. They contain access to all our personal information, credit accounts as well as any important information we choose to store in them. It's pretty much our entire digital identity and maybe the most important and valuable thing we own. Data-pads are secured digitally but very hackable if you know the right people. A Prime data-pad would be worth a stupid amount of credits. When someone loses a data-pad, they report it, the Patriarch issues them a new one, it's not a big loss, just an inconvenience. Normally we don't go for them because they are risky. A few missing data-pads and the Patriarch deploys a bunch of extra Red Caps. More Red Caps make it harder to steal anything. Just one shouldn't draw any extra attention.

This opportunity is too good to pass up. I move casually, looking around slowly and making sure no one is watching. I carefully slip the data-pad off his wrist as he passes by, slide it into my bag and duck around the first alley I come to. I've got to make sure I'm not in sight when he notices it's missing. He doesn't. Rich snobs have no awareness. Obliviousness must be a luxury of the wealthy. This was just what I needed to shake my nerves after my encounter with Bill.

"You there," comes a commanding voice blaring from behind me. It's a crowded street; no reason to assume it's meant for me. For some reason though, I know it is. I don't turn around and pretend I don't hear the voice.

"Undesirable!"

Still, there are tons of Undesirables in the Market. No reason to incriminate myself by turning around. There is no way anyone saw me swipe the card; the streets are too crowded.

A hand grabs my arm forcefully, pulling me to a stop and spinning me around. Standing in front of me is a man in a black uniform with red on the tops of the shoulders. He isn't city guard. He is also wearing a red sash over his right shoulder. On the sash is a black and white patch of a creepy lidless eye inside a triangle that's inside a circle, indicating he works for the Patriarch. On the shoulders of his uniform are the three black bars.

He's a commander. What is a commander doing here? Commanders do not police the streets. That's a job for common Red Caps. Commanders stay in the barracks or in their outposts, issuing orders from behind a desk. This is not good.

Using his forearm, he slams me into the stone wall of the shop behind me. The crash stings, sending little needles of pain up my back. I wince.

"ID," the commander barks out aggressively.

He is surprisingly strong. His hold on me seems effortless. Even with his uniform, I can see he is thick like the trunk of a tree. His shoulders stretch out wide atop his torso like an upside-down triangle. His face looks rough—a squared jaw covered in a soft shadow of stubble, eyes wild like a beast. There's a sense of cruelty and hatred in them. He slides the data-pad on his left over mine.

"2413985-U," I respond instinctively.

The "U" at the end of my number indicates I am an Undesirable. Anyone born without a caste is classified as one. It should be obvious enough; the Undesirables are the only people in Dios who don't wear a uniform—a black suit with a solid-colored sash that indicates one's class and occupation. It's the Patriarch's way of reminding us we are little more than garbage. No sense in trying to make worthless people look like they have value, I suppose.

The commander looks at the screen projected from his data-pad. I can see my picture through the transparent screen. "Jett Lasting. Age 18. Caucasian male. Hair brown. Eyes green." He glances up at me to confirm what he is reading on my bio. "Weight 165 pounds. Orphaned age 6. Taken in by the Karr family. Karr family branded as Heretics. No known occupation. No recorded criminal history. No recorded residence. No recorded class." He exhaled and flicked his wrist. The projected screen disappeared. "Another Undesirable street rat defiling the city with your filth. Every time I think we are too harsh with your kind, I am proven wrong." He chuckled to himself. "You don't respect the law, the system, the structure of society that keeps us safe. Your flagrant disregard for order and base human decency is a scourge upon this great city. I doubt this is your first offense. Tell me, rodent, do you know what the punishment is for theft?"

For a city that boasts about justice, punishments are a bit of a mixed bag. Every sector of the city has a Justice Block where all accused criminals stand trial. Two years ago, I saw a Prime get drunk and beat a man to death in front of a crowd. He was arrested and let go a week later with a "note on his record." For people like me, people who don't fit so neatly into the structure of Dios, an infraction as insignificant as say, bumping into someone of importance can result in a month in stocks. That's a Patriarch favorite: it's uncomfortable and humiliating, and it helps break your spirit. If they are in a bad mood or the Levite officiate doesn't like how you look, you're more likely to get a flogging. The worst part of it all is, any offense, gets your name entered into the Lottery.

In Dios, anyone who is convicted of a crime receives two punishments. The first is the penalty for the crime. The second is the criminal ID, which is a ten-digit number assigned to your name. For every offense you get an entry into the Lottery, where one lucky winner will get to an extra punishment voted on by the citizens of Dios. Or sometimes they are given a choice between execution or exile to the Outlands. Most choose execution. It's a much faster death.

The commander glares at me. He looks young, way too young to be a commander. I've never even heard of a commander being under fifty. This guy looks like he's thirty at best. Either he was born into a Class A family or he is very good at his job. I think it may be the latter, presently. His face is close enough to mine that I can smell his breath.

"Ugh, speaking of Undesirable," I blurt out.

It's not the smartest thing to do, but his breath is awful. It smells like he ate a bag full of overused socks. I turn away, trying to spare my nostrils from the assault.

He grumbles. "Perhaps twenty lashes will remind you of your place."

My eyes widen. Twenty is the maximum penalty for theft. Forty is considered a death sentence. My mind races. Excuses. Justifications. Bargaining. Escape. That's a bad idea. Trying to escape a high-ranking officer would definitely result in getting sent to the Outlands. Just thinking about it makes my skin crawl.

I'm so distracted I didn't even hear the other soldiers come running up. "Commander Stone!" one of them shouts.

Mental note: always avoid Commander Stone. I can't hear what they are saying to him. Something about a theft on Street Four. Something else about a briefing. Stone curses, and I feel his forearm push against my throat. I can't breathe. My arms flail helplessly as I try to pull myself free out of instinct. Is he going to choke me to death right here on the street? I can feel my heart racing, panic flooding my mind.

Release. I feel my body slump to the ground as my lungs gasp for air. Each breath burning like I'm inhaling flames.

His boots move. I look up, and he's running off with a small group of soldiers. A minute later, there's Victor. He helps me to my feet and holds me up.

"Good thing I came back to check on you," he says.

I straighten myself up and nod, finally regaining my breath. "How did you—?"

Victor smiles and waves his hand dismissively. "Oh, you know, whisper something to the right merchant. Rumors spread. Red Caps react. Before you know it, there's a whole lot to do about nothing."

I shake my head, and we make our way to the train, careful not to draw any more unnecessary attention to ourselves.

We reach the station a few minutes later. The train hovers several feet over the track. The familiar humming of the magnetic field is comforting after my encounter with Commander Stone and the beggar gangs. Underneath the train is a glowing green light indicating the train is boarding. In just a few minutes the doors will close, the green light will turn red, and we will hover our way home. The glorious life of a thief.

CHAPTER TWO

The hover train doors slide closed and seal with a sucking of air. The train car is almost empty—a refreshing change. Most the time the lower-class train cars are so packed with people the air you're breathing in is the air they just breathed out. You end up smooshed against a half-dozen strangers so tightly you start sweating all over each other. It's unpleasant.

We are leaving late. Most everyone has already made their way home, so our train is nearly empty. The free space feels like we got upgraded to Class A. Unfortunately, the train car still smells like a sweaty sock.

Victor sits down across from me with his arms stretched out over the empty seats on either side of him. It's almost luxurious having this much personal space.

I reach into my bag and pull out a book one of the shop owners lent me. The cover read The Collapse of the World that Was, and the Rise of the New World Order. Catchy title. There's something about quality scholarship that often lacks good salesmanship. The World that Was—life before the Great Collapse—has always fascinated me. Most books on the World that Was are strictly forbidden. The Patriarch doesn't allow for any version of history beyond their own. Good thing most of the shops have a back room for contraband. I flip the book open, scanning to where I left off.

Before the Great Collapse, when the end was drawing near, a group of scientists and government leaders joined forces and built five massive cities surrounded by massive walls. The cities were protected by a biodome that not only kept the toxic air out but gave them control of the weather conditions all throughout the dome. The domes were huge, around 20,000 square miles in diameter. Each dome was linked by an underground subway system that only the leaders could access. When the World that Was collapsed, only those five cities remained, becoming the last hope for humanity. There is Pargos, the strongest; Marthon, the wealthiest; Solis, the largest and most secure; Ragnor, nothing was really known about Ragnor; and Dios. Each city, fearing the others would try to take their resources, built massive walls around their territories. In order to avoid another Great Collapse, the five cities formed a council of elders. Two officials from each city would preside over issues that could affect all of the cities.

My attention suddenly diverts as a small potato thumps against my chest. Victor smiles, head tilted up on the back of his headrest. "Tell me, what's new about the magical World that Was?"

I close the book and lean forward. "Did you know, before the Great Collapse, there was so much food that entire countries were overweight? They had huge stores filled just with food, and you could buy all you wanted, no restrictions." Victor slowly moves, leaning forward and raising an eyebrow. I nod. "Get this, their struggle wasn't finding enough food to eat. It was deciding where they were going to eat because they had so many options, they couldn't make up their minds."

"Sounds like a Tod tale."

"Could you imagine a world with food everywhere? Not having to sleep through a rumbling stomach a couple of times a week?" Victor shook his head. "No one telling you what to wear, where to live, what to do. No Patriarch. No Levites. You could just be whoever you wanted to be. Do whatever you wanted to do. You could live instead of just trying not to die."

Victor sighs, cutting off my verbal daydream. "Sounds too good to be true. Makes you wonder what they fought about."

The train car gets suddenly bright. We are passing through the farming sector. It's always sunny in the farming sector. In order to grow enough food for everyone in the city, crops were planted in single-acre plots. Each plot is stacked three deep and is rotated every eight hours to get adequate sunlight.

I open the book again, but Victor reaches out and covers the page with his hand. "Why do you keep reading about the World that Was? You know it's never going to be like that again, right?"

I nod. "I know. Knowing what has been helps shape what can be. There has to be more to this life that just fitting in, staying off the radar, and surviving another day. When we aren't avoiding beggar gangs, we're running from the Red Caps. Or hiding from Levites. That's not a life." I exhale, letting myself calm down a little. Victor just looks at me. I can't tell if it is pity or appreciation I'm seeing in his eyes.

"Hope is a powerful thing. But be mindful. It's only as good as the object you place it in. Hope can bring you through the darkest night. When that hope is in an impossible dream, it will bring only despair." With that warning, Victor leans back in his seat and closes his eyes. We sit in silence for the rest of the ride.

The sun is setting when the train finally comes to a stop. The doors unlock, making a sound like pulling the top of a sealed container. We grab our bags and start the walk home. The train station, like most of the buildings in Sector C, is designed to reflect its community. Hardy. Plain. Uninspired. It's made entirely of concrete. Unpainted. No fancy architecture. Not even splashes of color like the Market Sector. It's just four big walls broken up by a few doors and windows. The windows are simple, unadorned. Advertisements flash over them constantly anyway. Despite its lack of design, the station is impressive in its size.

Sector C boasts the largest population of any of the classes. They are the only class that outnumber us Undesirables.

The crowds are moving in two clumsy but organized streams. Those flooding off the train pour down the right side, moving from the open track into the building to be scanned on their way home. Those flooding onto the train to go to the Market or another stop in Sector C flow to the left. We manage to push our way through both currents. At the edge of the track are two Red Caps holding rifles. They pace back and forth, watching, inspecting, looking for anything or anyone out of place.

A few years back, we discovered several of the Red Caps in the Education Wing of the Class C Sector were less rigid in their application of the law. The Patriarch rarely ventured so far from the Temple Sector, which gives us some wiggle room. You learn very quickly which Red Caps to avoid and which to work with.

We make our way to the edge of the platform toward the road leading home. Two Red Caps are standing at the edge of the stone steps between the railings, blocking our path. I recognize one of them, a younger Red Cap; he seems pretty laid back most of the time. That's good.

Victor pulls out a pocket watch from his jacket. Must have snagged it when we were separated. He smiles and casually walks over to the young Red Caps. I notice the young Red Cap has a small scar over his right eyebrow. Based on the look of it, I'm guessing he had a bottle cracked over his head.

Victor slides the watch into the Red Cap's hand, and he casually deposits it into his back pocket with a nod. Victor motions for me to follow as he starts down the steps. The other Red Cap, the one I didn't recognize, is a burly-looking man—much taller with broader shoulders than the other. He has a thick black beard that completely hides his neck. He looks out of place in the formal uniform with his rough, leathered-looking skin. The burly Red Cap steps in front of Victor. His uniform is a little different. Same color, black with red trimmings, but the style is more suited to his heavyset frame.

"You look familiar." His voice is gravely and harsh, and he gives Victor a suspicious stare.

Victor shakes his head, but I can't hear what he says. The young Red Cap with the scar casually puts his hand on the other Red Cap's shoulder. The burly Red Cap steps back, opening the path. That's a relief. I keep my head down as I walk past them, not wanting to give them any other reason to stop us.

We descend the stairs and walk down the street at a hurried pace. I feel eyes on us as we walk but dare not look back. I sigh when I'm sure we are out of earshot and in the clear.

"That was different," I practically whisper as I turn to look back, finally able to calm my racing heart. "What was the deal with that guy?"

Victor just shakes his head.

"Come on, what happened?" I persist.

"He thought he recognized me."

"I heard that, but how?"

"He was the Red Cap who executed my father."

My mouth drops open. I remember when it happened, but I'd never seen his face. After my mother was killed, Victor's family took me in. His father was a kind man, just not a smart one. He had a mental disorder called idealism. He was stupid enough to try and share that with others. He spoke out against the Patriarch. He challenged their leadership, said humanity could do better. I don't disagree. No one outside the Temple Sector does. We all thought it, but we knew saying it would get us in trouble. Conflict makes cowards of most. I respected his courage.

It's not like he wanted to start a rebellion. He was just tired of seeing his family go hungry. He wanted to make the world a better place. The Patriarch didn't take kindly to it. He was arrested for disturbing the peace then executed in the center of Market Square for treason. They chose to make an example of him to prevent any further outbursts. So, they put him on a platform and broadcast live across every screen in the city so all would see. They knelt him down, humiliated him, made him give a false confession, and then cut off his head with an axe.

I was there in the crowd, but I never saw the executioner's face. Victor couldn't say the same. They made him stand on the edge of the platform to ensure he had the best view. Six months later his mother killed herself, and Vic became an orphan like me.

Sometimes his cool-headedness makes me forget he hates the Patriarch as much as I do. Maybe that's why we're so close. We've both lost loved ones to a hypocritical government that pretends to care for the people it controls. There's nothing to say in a moment like this. Words don't make it better. Usually, they just make it weird. I can sense Victor's unease; it's a hard feeling to shake, I know. Once the memories come, it's like reliving the event again and again. Only one thing to do.

"Daily trivia?" I ask, hoping to ease Victor's tension.

Victor's stern look softens, and a smile forms. "How many lives were lost in the Great War?"

I shrug. "Just over five billion."

"Tsk. Tsk. Tsk." Victor shakes his head. "Six point two billion. Come on, you remember that."

The Patriarch says that education is for valuable members of society. Expending resources on people they consider to be worthless is a waste of those resources. When Victor and I were growing up, there was a teacher, Mrs. Harbin, who left her window open every day. She said she liked the fresh air. Of course, if any Undesirable wanted to learn, they could sit outside in the grass. Every now and then, you could see Mrs. Harbin look outside and smile. We sat outside her class every day.

I nodded. "I remember, that was before we got too big. Then we had to learn on our own."

"Yet somehow, at the start of every year, there were two mysterious textbooks just left outside her window," Victor chuckled. "I wonder how she explained losing exactly two books every year."

"How many people were there on the planet before the Great War?" I countered.

"Two billion. The Great War killed everyone three times." Victor smirks playfully. Then his tone shifts. "How do we survive?"

"Be invisible. Don't draw attention. Don't get noticed. Don't stand up. Don't stand out."

He asks these questions every day. It's our little routine. "How do you be invisible?"

"Move with the crowd. Don't act suspicious. Don't react. Don't be clever. Don't take risks. Avoid eye contact." We added the last after a Levite threw me into a prison pit for three days for looking at him.

"Right. The last thing you want to do is give those Shinshew any reason to remember you." I nod in agreement. "So if, say, a Commander were to grab you and pin you to a wall. It might be a bad idea to, I don't know, comment on how bad his breath smells?"

I let out a nervous laugh. Certainly, he wasn't close enough to have heard that. How could he possibly know? I don't respond. I just stare at him dumbly.

"Well...?" Victor shakes his head. "What if I hadn't been there, Jett? If I hadn't shown up just then, you'd have gotten twenty lashes and your name in the Lottery."

I shrug. "I'm sorry."

"Sorry isn't going to save you. You have to be smart. You have to bite your tongue. Getting noticed gets you killed. Or worse, sent to the Outlands."

The Outlands are a sort of looming threat that hangs over everyone all the time like an approaching storm cloud. You can't do anything about it but just hope it doesn't affect you. Dios is one of the five remaining cities in the world. Everything outside those cities, we call the Outlands. The Outlands are the most dangerous place in the world. It's a barren wasteland so lifeless in places not even weeds grow. Everything in the Outlands is evolved, mutated, or determined to kill you. It is despair incarnate. No one has ever gone to the Outlands and returned. It is a long, slow, painful death sentence. It haunts the nightmares of almost everyone in Dios.

"Jett," Victor presses, though he doesn't need to. Victor is right. Again. It's his thing. I was wrong. I know. I knew it when it happened. Talking back is stupid. It puts you at risk. Dios is a well-organized machine designed to break any who don't fit the mold. The more I understand, the more it makes me mad.

"I get it—just sleepwalk through like everyone else. That way no one ever notices me."

"If it keeps you alive, then yes!" Victors voice rises. "I get it; it's hard pretending to be like everyone else. Anonymity is our shield and our safety blanket. It keeps us warm at night and safe during the day. Its protection comes at a cost."

"The low, low price of your soul. Tell me, how long do you think we can act like we don't exist before it stops being an act?" Victor just stares at me. Sometimes that's more effective. If he says something, I can argue with him. If he's silent I have to argue with myself. "I'm just—" I stop myself and reform my thoughts. "It's not like we chose this. What are we guilty of? Being born into the wrong class? They hate us because we are an inconvenience to their system. It's their system that rejects us in the first place. We didn't do anything wrong. To them, we are nothing more than waste to be discarded."

"Just because they say we are worthless, that doesn't make it so. Jett, who you are isn't about what anyone else says. Only you get to decide who you are."

"As long as it blends in. Doesn't draw attention. Conforms to the neat pattern of the Patriarch." I smirk. Victor shoves my shoulder.

The rest of the journey home is silent. We understand each other. He will let it go, and I will be more careful. There's nothing else to say.

We walk until the train station is no longer visible behind us. Just over the hill is a large forest that runs alongside the Education Wing, which is where we live. The familiar patch of trees leads up the street to our home; just a few more minutes and we'll be there.

"Hey, Vic," I break the silence. "What do you think would happen if the Undesirables banded together and revolted?"

Victor stops walking and looks up to the sky. "It depends on how they did it, I suppose."

"Really? We outnumber them like a thousand to one."

Victor nods. "If wars were won by numbers alone, that would mean something. We aren't trained. We don't have weapons. We aren't organized. We have no leader. Why do you think they don't bother policing us? They know we are not a threat."

"There has to be a way," I protest.

"There's always a way Jett. Sometimes the cost is far too high."

"If we would work together—"

"The challenge isn't uniting. It's uniting without the Patriarch realizing it. If we could catch them off guard, get a supply of weapons, regroup, train, strategize...sure, we'd have a small chance of success. Or if everyone rose up, all at once..." Victor shrugged. "That might work. With their surveillance drones, it'd be almost impossible for us to organize any effort without them finding out."

I sigh. That's not really the answer I was hoping for, but he has a point. Moving on, it was weird that a Commander was roaming around the Market, right?"

Victor nods. "One thing I know he wasn't doing was roaming around. Something must be going on. The Patriarch wouldn't have sent a Commander unless they were really worried about something."

"What do you think it is?"

Victor shakes his head, "I've heard some whispers but nothing concrete. You said his name was Stone?" I nod.

Our home is almost in view. We don't own it, of course; we aren't allowed to own property. Lucky for us, it was abandoned. Across the street from our neighborhood is the Advent School for New Beginnings. It's a rundown old school they were going to tear down and replace with several larger new schools. They built our little neighborhood of twenty or thirty homes for the teachers to reside. After the houses were built, they decided to put the schools someplace else. Our little partially-complete neighborhood was abandoned, giving us an unclaimed, unwanted community of homes secluded from the rest of the sector. Practically paradise for the hundred or so of us who live here.

The house itself is in decent shape. The roof leaks. The floor creaks. There is a weird breeze on windy days. But it has four walls and locks on the door. The real benefit is the forest. The Class C sector, being primarily common laborers, is filled with farmland, mines, lumber mills, and factories. Directly behind our house is a large forest that backs all the way up to the train tracks. If Red Caps ever show up looking for us, we have a lot of places to hide. When you don't have a place in the world, you'd better always have a plan.

The old parking lights from the school herald us home as we draw near. We walk alongside the road in an adjacent ditch. It reduces visibility and gives us a little more time to hide in the event we stumble past unfriendly onlookers. Even with some connections with the local Red Caps, we try not to push our luck. There's something about being close to home that makes me safe, or at least, safer than usual. My guard starts to drop.

Victor freezes. Instinctively, I do the same. The sound of the engine approaching was almost completely imperceptible as we walked. Now, I hear it plain as day. Whatever it was, it was moving in our direction. Victor's eyes go wide as I look over at him. As a Jeep clears the hill, I see a long, thin antenna holding a little white flag with a gold fist. Levites.

Like menacing eyes piercing the darkness, the headlights of the Jeep grow larger. I tell myself it's just a coincidence. I can't help feeling like a rabbit being stalked by a pack of wolves. My heart pounds in my chest. I freeze.

Suddenly, I'm not an eighteen-year-old standing in a ditch on the side of the road. I'm six. I'm hunched over on the kitchen floor holding my mother's lifeless body, rocking back and forth as I try to coax her back to life with my tears. I don't understand what's happened. I don't even understand she's dead. Her warm blood pools under her body and soaks my hands. I can't see clearly through the tears in my eyes, but I see them: four men in their white robes with fancy golden trim.

Two of them are running scans and inputting data into their distinctive golden bracers. I can't make out their faces, but their uniforms are clear enough. The fifth man is wearing black with a red sash. He's holding a knife that's coated in blood—my mother's blood. He's her killer. The Levites aren't arresting him. They are helping him. These "noble peacekeepers" who exist to protect truth and justice are helping the man who killed my mother.

A strong tug on my arm brings me back to the ditch on the side of the road. I shake off my deer-in-the-headlights impersonation. My knees bend and my body slumps to the ground, lying on the incline of the ditch closest to the road. The damp grass is cold, and it soaks the sleeves of my shirt and makes my pants feel sticky.

Victor is lying next to me. His face looks how I feel. He motions for me to follow him and starts crawling on his stomach away from the road.

I look back and see the reason for Victor's panic. The vehicle isn't just passing by. It's creeping along. Two men are standing in the back of the jeep with search lights moving them up and down the sides of the road. They are searching for something. For someone. I doubt they'd be looking for us. We hardly merit Levite attention. If they find us, it won't matter. They aren't the kind to let things go. I turn back to see Victor is already halfway to the tree line. I start crawling after him faster. Stupid. I got so lost in thought I left myself exposed. A sinking feeling hits me. I don't have time to make the woods.

If I stand up, I can get to the trees faster, but it's still light enough for them to see me get up to run. If I don't do something, their spotlight will reach me before I make it to cover. An urgent need drives me forward. I dig my elbows into the damp, wet grass, sliding and shooting my body as fast as I can, terror propelling me forward. My right elbow finds and digs into a rock. Shooting pain dances up my arm. I don't have time to adjust. I let the rock scrape my forearm as I pull myself forward and grit my teeth. My arm burns from rubbing my skin raw. The pain drives me forward even faster.

The throbbing gets worse as I try to push through it. I look up as I speed crawl. Victor is hunched down near the edge of the tree line coaxing me forward, reaching out his hand to pull me in when I get close enough. The expression on his face does not give me confidence. If I don't reach the woods before the light hits me, things are going to get really bad. I can feel the light getting closer. I push. I strain. I will my body to move. I see it. Out of the corner of my eye—the spotlight, moving closer to me, almost in view.

Four feet from the woods, the light almost on me, I do the worst thing I can think of: I freeze. I shove my face into the grass, close my eyes—

like that makes a difference— and hope that if I remain still enough, they won't see me.

CHAPTER THREE

My eyes open, expecting to see the light encasing my body. It's not. It has stopped inches away from where I am lying. As the vehicle comes to a stop, the shriek of the Jeep's brakes fills the air. Then still silence. At this point they can probably hear my heart pounding in my chest. The light is close but not close enough for them to see me. I tilt my head back just enough to see Victor. He motions for me to stay. I fight the compulsion to turn and look. My mind races through possibilities. Why are they stopped? What is going on? Have they somehow realized I'm here? It feels like my brain is telling my body it is better to risk getting caught and know than stay still and wonder. It takes all my will not to move.

"You there! Identify yourself!" comes the voice from the Jeep. This is it. I'm heaped. I exhale and start to shift onto my side when I see Victor once again signal for me to remain still. My heart bounces off my ribs like a ping-pong ball.

"Red Cap, sir. ID 42139." There's someone else there? What is he doing just walking down the road? I have so many questions.

"What are you doing out here?" comes the voice from the Jeep. I assume the Red Cap is walking toward them because their voices get softer. I can hear they are talking, but it's much harder to make out what they are saying. Slowly, carefully, I resume my crawl, moving out of the light's path and into the cover of the woods. I get up next to Victor and turn to see what's going on. It's a little easier to hear now that my heart isn't playing a drum solo.

"We patrol these streets every night. Got to make sure everything is quiet and orderly," the mystery Red Cap says. Even if I know him, he's too far away and it's too dark for me to recognize him. What I do know is that's a lie. We live off the main road. They are patrolled about once a month, not once a day.

"He shouldn't be out here," Victor whispers. "There's something strange going on."

"Have you seen any suspicious activity?" someone in the Jeep asks.

"You mean more suspicious than a Levite patrol in the middle of nowhere of the C-Block?" he asks. I smirk. "Block" makes the sectors sound more like prison cells; it's a great description. The Levites don't seem nearly as amused. "You guys here to take some night classes? The school down this road is shut down, but I can give you directions to the main buildings if you'd like." Education did little to benefit life in Class C, so most kids skip school and go to work with their parents.

"What have you heard of rebel gatherings in this area? We have reports of a person of interest being seen. We are here to—"

"Enough," comes another voice from the jeep, louder and more authoritative than the other. "What we are doing is not of your concern. You are to report anything out of the ordinary to the office of the Patriarch, understood?"

The Red Cap jumps to attention, dramatically saluting the Jeep. "It is a privilege to serve the great Patriarch! Praise Bealz!" The Levites in the Jeep repeat the benediction. "Oh," the Red Cap starts up, "word of caution, I'd stay close to the road. We've had some animal attacks in these parts. I'm sure you could handle it, but it would definitely draw attention to your presence here, which could spook your query."

I look over at Victor. "Animal attacks? When?" He shakes his head. The Levites exchange a few more words with the Red Cap too quietly for us to hear before driving off. The Red Cap remains. He doesn't move. He just stands there until the Jeep is well out of sight. Then he turns toward us. Could he see us? No. That's crazy. No way he knows we are here.

"You two need to be more careful. You're no good to anyone in a Levite cell," he says, his tone warm and friendly, the way an eager merchant greets prospective customers.

Victor and I just stare at each other, dumbfounded. Do we stay hidden? Do we respond? He knows we are here. This could be some kind of trap to lure us out. If it is, why did he help us avoid the Levities? I step forward out of the cover of the woods and look back to where the Red Cap was standing. He's not there. I scan the horizon. He's not anywhere. He seems to have disappeared completely. I rush to the road while Victor shouts my name, trying to get me to stop. When I reach the pavement, I look around, scanning the horizon for a glimpse, a sign. Nothing. It's like he's a ghost.

After giving up on the search, Victor and I return home. We are too busy processing what just happened to talk. Who was that guy? Had we met him before? Why did he help us? What did he mean we'd be no good to anyone? Did someone have plans for us? And what were Levites doing all the way out here late at night? What were they searching for? Questions barrage my brain relentlessly.

When we reach the house, Victor knocks. Three quick knocks, pause, two quick knocks, pause, one knock. It's easy to remember but unusual enough that a stranger wouldn't accidently do it. Our knock serves as a sort of all-clear. If we ever hear a different knock, we get ready to make a run for the woods behind the house. I hear a beeping sound followed by a turning mechanism sliding the deadbolt and releasing the seal on the door. It clicks open automatically, and we step inside. It is good to be home.

Before we can step inside, a tiny little head appears from around the corner of the house. The head belongs little Brelar, the boy from next door. Brelar is a sweet, happy kid, he's four-year-old with bright green eyes and sandy brown hair. He's always smiling as he runs around outside on some imaginary adventure. Unless of course, he sees a bird. Brelar loves birds. Everywhere he goes he carries around this half blanket, half stuffed animal. He's too old for it, but that doesn't stop him.

Brelar is the walking embodiment of joy. He's always laughing and giggling. No matter how bad my day was, seeing that little boy washes all the worries away. He is typically waiting when we get back, rushing to us and hugging our legs tight the moment we come into view of the house. Brelar is probably the best part of the neighborhood. He exists in the blissful ignorance we call childhood. I envy that. His hope hasn't yet been robbed by the reality of his future.

"Brelar, it's late, you should be at home in bed. You know how your parents worry," Victor scolds with such softness in his voice it doesn't even sound like an admonition. Brelar loves Victor. Whenever Victor is outside Brelar follows him around like a puppy.

The boy steps around the corner of the porch into the light. "I make this," he says in his little voice. He holds his head down as walks over and stops just in front of Victor. Shuffling his feet and turning his head down even further he extends his hand. In it is a bracelet made of braided red leather threads.

Victor takes it and examines it, "this is fine craftsmanship. You're quite talented." This invokes a bright smile but is not enough to gain eye contact.

"You like it, I make it for you."

Victor ruffles Brelar's sandy brown hair before tying the bracelet around his wrist. "It's wonderful, I'll keep it on me always." Victor kneels down and lifts Brelar's chin. "Do you think, if I got you more of this thread, you could make one for everyone?"

"Everyone?" Brelar repeats.

"Yes, for all of our friends," Victor stands back up, "otherwise they might be jealous that I have one and they don't."

Brelar smiles brightly, "Ok Mister Victor, I make more. I go-"

"Not tonight Brelar, go home. Go to bed." The boy nods and rushes off like an excited squirrel to bury a freshly discovered acorn.

"You do realize he's going to make like a thousand of those things now," I jest. Victor smirks and pushes the door to the house open.

Our dilapidated home in all its glory might as well be a palace for Undesirables like us. When you have had nothing, you learn to be content with anything. Our house is one of the smaller ones in the neighborhood. It is a small two-bedroom, one bath house with a single room upstairs that we use as a third bedroom. It's the largest room, but there's a big hole in the roof. We have a patch over it to keep rain from coming in, but there's no chance of sleeping when the sun is out. Our little home houses eight Undesirables: six boys and two girls. The girls have one room to themselves. Despite being outnumbered three to one, they still manage to spend more time in the bathroom than the rest of us combined. Girls are strange.

Victor is our unofficial leader—the man with the plan. He is able to calculate how long we can work a certain area before we start drawing unwanted attention from the Red Caps. It's an incredible gift. It's almost like he can sense changes in the crowd by instinct. We trust him to move us around and direct us so we can operate freely without garnering extra attention. His ability to read guard movements and predict changes in behavior makes our jobs a lot easier.

Every day we break into four teams of two. One team stays home to guard the house and keep an eye on what's happening in our neighborhood. It's like having a day off. One team goes to one of the wings in Sector B or Sector C. Victor says rotating where we go helps us stay under the scanner. One team goes to the Market Sector. Both these teams focus on gathering basics: food, clothing, blankets, small items of value we can sell if needed. The last team is in charge of specific tasks, whether that's selling loot from the previous day, getting medicine, picking up materials to repair the house or actually doing the repairs.

Each night we meet up at the house after dark to take inventory. We dump everything out into a pile in the center of the cozy living room to get an idea of what we need to focus on the next day. Most of the stuff is small knickknacks: a locket that opens up with a little mirror inside, some coins, a beaded necklace, a data-disc that holds electronic information, a couple of books, and some random kitchen supplies. After dinner we will come back and divvy up the loot. The rule is, everyone gets to keep one thing for themselves. The person who swiped it gets the first shot at it. Everything else goes to the collective. Collective goods, we divide, sell or use. Trial and error taught us that a little personal motivation plus caring for the good of the community creates the maximum effort.

While Victor gets dinner started, the rest of us work on our presentations. I don't remember when we started doing it, but for years during dinner, each person tells a story—the most exciting grab of the day. The story doesn't have to be true. As they tell their tale, the rest of us determine if we think the story is true or made up. The made-up stories are fun but ineligible to receive the coveted prize.

It was not meant to be a competition, but it sure turned into one. Whoever has the best story, that actually happened, wins the title— thief of the day—and gets to take an extra piece of loot for themselves. Sometimes it is actually tempting to take stupid risks just to win the title. It's strange how silly little things can bond you to other people.

I sit down at the table as Victor finishes preparing the food. Olivia and Becka, the two girls in our crew, are already sitting down laughing about something. Olivia has long blonde hair that looks as if it is made of silk, soft features, a warm smile, and bright green eyes that draw you in like a light shining through gemstones. Her body looks like it was deliberately sculpted for the perfect aesthetic. She looks like a Prime;

even her posture is eloquent and feminine. Living like we do takes its toll. Most of us look older than we are. Victor says the street has a way of aging you, street miles he calls them. Olivia is not affected by it. Her petite frame and sweet, almost childish innocence are disarming, and she knows how to use it to her advantage. She has a way of making men weak in the knees. The others pile in around the table.

"Who's ready for thief of the day?" Telmen asks, plopping down at the table. "I'm definitely going to win today." Telmen is about my size but lanky with long, thin arms and legs. He kinda looks like over-stretched clay. He has messy blonde hair and a long face. His most notable feature is his oversized mouth that never stops moving.

"That'd be a first," Becka shoots back. Her black hair is pulled into a tight ponytail, whipping around as she turns her head. Becka's dark features, from her deep brown eyes to her always tan skin, make her look exotic. Her skin is smooth and unblemished, her lips soft and ample, her teeth pearly white. Her smile is as genuine as any you'd ever see. Her glare, fierce and unnerving. "Olivia is first since she won yesterday."

Olivia smiles and sighs, batting her eyes playfully. "Okay, well today, I stole a jar of honey from a shopkeeper while he was staring right at me."

"Ugh, yea, bet it wasn't your eyes he was staring at," Jensen grumbles. Becka punches him in the shoulder. "What?" he protests. "It's true. That's what all the guys do when she's around."

"Don't be a Shinshew," Becka responds.

"Whatever, I'm just saying, she has a natural advantage. The rest of us need skill. Olivia just uses her body as a distraction. No one notices her taking things because they are too busy—" Becka hits him again, this time harder enough to make a loud thwacking sound. Jensen mutters something under his breath. I just ignore him.

Olivia may be the best thief in our group. Becka is by far the worst. A blind man could catch her in the act. She has no sense of timing, subtly, or distraction. She just walks up, grabs what she's after, and runs. She might as well announce it. "Hey, I'm stealing this from you now." Despite her incredible lack of skill, Becka is the only one of us who hasn't been caught. When we get caught, we bribe our way out. When Olivia gets caught, she charms her way out. What Becka lacks in craft, stealth, and skill, she makes up for with speed. Her legs move like a blur. You blink, and she's gone. Catching her is like trying to catch the wind.

Spike leans back in his chair. "Notto story from ye then, Becka?" he asks in his thick accent. He doesn't have anything to show today; he was on house watch with Jensen. Unfortunate company. Spike is tall, well-built. His salt and pepper hair is just long enough to run his fingers through. He is the oldest of us but not old, early or maybe mid-thirties or something like that. He has broad shoulders and a stout frame. His scruffy facial hair and strong jawline make him look fierce. His effortless smile is like a warm cup of coffee on a cold night. With one look he seems as soft as mashed potatoes. With another as hard as nails. Spike is one of my favorite people. He's always helping. He's handy. He's good with tech. He's good with repairs. He doesn't steal. Whenever he gets sent out, he usually finds a merchant and does odd jobs to earn a few coins. He always says a man should work for what he has. Even being a broke outcast isn't enough to make Spike abandon his principles.

"Nothing exciting," Becka says sweetly. "By the blessing of Bealz, I got some blankets and a couple of bags of spices. Nothing crazy happened. I just took them and ran." We all chuckle a little.

"Give me a break! Bealz didn't help you. You outran them, like you always do, because you are freakishly fast," Jensen scoffed.

Becka smiles her sweet smile, "and just how do you think I became freakishly fast?" She baits the trap.

Jensen rolls his eyes dramatically, "I thought you left all that Shinshew behind when you left the Temple Sector. Becka was born into a noble family. She did well in school and was a Potter in training before she committed some horrible heresy. What her infraction was, she's never told us.

"Um, I'll have you know," Becka bobs her head from side to side for dramatic effect, "I did not leave the Temple Sector. They revoked my class, my occupation, changed my identification number and branded me an Undesirable then kicked me out." She sticks out her tongue at him. No one else says a word, mostly to ensure Jensen feels as awkward as possible. It's Victor who breaks the silence:

"Did you finish the patch, Spike?"

"Aye, brotha. I wired the field into da power directly. Long as we got electricity, it should keep da place dry as a Levite's flask. Give da upstairs a nice purple night light as well." Victor nods approvingly.

Telmen twitches with nervous energy, rocking back and forth in his seat. "Okay, so you ready? I've got you all beat today. I got a roast!" he declares proudly, standing up as if accepting an award. "Just like I told you I would. I said it last night. None of you believed me." He waves his arms accusatively. "You all never believe me, but there it is, roast."

"Like when you swore you'd steal a Levite flag and bring it home to burn as kindling, right?" I said.

"What?" Telmen shook his head. "Never happened. You're making that up. I never said I'd do that."

Victor laughed. "That's why we never believe you, Telmen. Anytime you don't do it, you deny having ever promised it."

"I do not!" Telmen folds his arms over his chest in protest. Telmen can be a bit much. He's not a bad guy; he just makes a lot of bad decisions. One time he was convinced we needed some weapons to protect ourselves, so he tried to steal a knife from a Red Cap in the middle of Market Square. He got three days in the stocks and a broken rib for it. It would have been worse, but I convinced the Red Caps he forgot to take medicine for his brain disorder. The worst part about him is silence seems to cause him physical pain. He talks loudly. He talks often. He never stops. Maybe he's partially deaf. "Whatever, I told you I'd get a roast, and there it is, a roast! Boom, I win. I am the best!" Telmen boasts, bobbing his chin up and down proudly. His chin bob spirals into a full-on uncoordinated dance celebration. "I'm the Thief King, baby!" He claps his hands together while obnoxiously biting his bottom lip.

Hardly a day goes by where Telmen doesn't declare himself Thief King. Each night, we declare the winner of the thief of the day competition our Thief King. Olivia protests the name, but that just makes it more fun. Telmen never actually wins. Even if he deserves it, we all vote against him on principle. It's annoying enough he declares himself the winner every day. If we actually let him win, he'd be insufferable.

I reach into my pocket where I kept the Prime data-pad I'd swiped before Commander Stone grabbed me. I am waiting for the right moment to drop it into the pile. It'll definitely beat Telmen's roast.

Gibbs moves in front of me, cutting off my access to the table. Gibbs is the yin to Telmen's yang: quiet, calm, humble. He doesn't try; he just is. Gibbs is a mystery. He likes it that way. I don't even know his proper name. We just call him Gibbs. Gibbs has a full beard which contrasts with the complete lack of hair on his head. His head is round like an egg, his cheeks almost chubby.

The best thing about Gibbs is that he always steals something better than what Telmen gets—without fail. He's like a magician. He never tells the story, never embellishes. When he shows us what he stole, he places it down and says, "I got this." Never one to waste words. As Telmen continues his self-proclaimed victory dance, Gibbs places his loot on the table without saying a word.

Olivia and Spike cheer and nearly topple the table, reaching for it. Pie. Chocolate pie with a white fluffy cream on top. Still not saying a word, Gibbs pulls another pie from behind his back and slides it across the table. This one is still steaming. The crust is covered in a brown powder or spice I've not seen before. Under the lattice crust are delicious looking peaches, also flaked with the strange brown powder.

Gibbs steps back and smiles as everyone claps—everyone but Telmen who is no longer dancing.

Telmen's mouth drops open as he stares at the table in disbelief. "H-how...w-where...ugh, that's not fair. How did you get pie?"

Gibbs just smiles.

"Idle hands pave the road to disorder. Disorder is the speedway to collapse." Gibbs smirks. He's quoting Patriarch ads broadcast all the time to promote greater productivity. Who knew it was also a great way to make fun of Telmen?

"Thief King!" I shout, standing up and holding Gibbs' arm in the air triumphantly.

"Thief King!" everyone but Telmen echoes. Telmen becomes a stammering mess.

"Sorry, bud. Better luck tomorrow," I tease. I pocket the data-pad. It may be good enough to beat the pies, but this is enough to celebrate for one night.

"It's so unfair! I got an entire roast and still you guys pick Gibbs! This is ridiculous." Telmen folds his arms over his chest and pouts.

"Yeah, yeah, you lost. Again. Get over it," Olivia teases. "Gibbs, you sexy man, what is this?" She turns to look at Gibbs, holding a finger over her top lip to try and hide her smile.

Gibbs shrugs. "Peach cobbler." Desserts are hard to come by in Dios. The Patriarch controls the sugar supply and deliberately limits its availability outside of special occasions. Most Class B citizens couldn't even afford it regularly. What's more impressive is how Gibbs could steal it and hide it on his way back. An Undesirable walking around with a dessert might as well flash a giant neon light that says "thief" over their head. It's probably easier to steal a Red Cap's uniform while they are wearing it.

Gibbs is mysteriously good, the best I've ever seen. Or, rather, not seen. Even when I partner with him, I have no idea how he gets the stuff he does. I try to catch him, see if I can learn something, but I've never actually seen him steal anything. It's incredible.

The pies last about as long as an ice cube over an open flame in the heat of summer. I can't remember the last time I've had something sweet. I sit back in my chair and wipe a bit of crust off my lip. Victor puts our bread and potatoes into the pantry. It is a good haul, enough food to feed us for days, which is important. Winter is just around the corner, and food will be harder to come by. Even though our take is the most practical, it can't compete with pie. Once we are done eating, I head to the back room where we keep a set of lockers. We use the lockers to store our personal valuables and the items we keep from the daily loot. I slide the data-pad into my locker and seal it with my thumb print. I come back to help with dishes and hear Telmen running his mouth.

"So, there I was walking down this alley, free and clear. Roast in my pack. No one saw a thing. It was a clean getaway. I turn the corner and what should I stumble across?" Telmen pauses for dramatic effect. "A pack of dogs! Can you believe it? Just passing by. Well, of course the dogs smell the roast in my pack." I will give him this, Telmen tells a great story. "I take off. Pack of dogs chasing me. I crash into a Red Cap. He starts yelling." My mind drifts away as the warm water runs over my hands. I hand Victor a cleaned plate, completely blanking out. A burst of laughter snaps me back to attention. I look over my shoulder. Everyone is hunched over, laughing. Becka and Spike are in tears. "I knew I couldn't outrun these dogs forever. If I didn't act fast, they were going to get me. I took the bowl of melted cheese and I threw it behind me, thinking the dogs would stop to lick it up and that would give me time to get away. Noooo! Right as the dish hit the ground, a cat passed by, and the cheese splashed all over it. So, now the dogs are chasing this cat, which is hissing and running for its little life."

"What happened to the cat?" Becka's voice sounds, almost pleading between laughs. Telmen smiles, holding up his hands.

"There was a small hole in the half-wall. The cat darted through it. The dogs were chasing so close, they didn't even notice it. The first three slid headfirst into the wall. The others crashed into them. Dogs piling up everywhere. It was perfect." I picture it and can't help but laugh.

Telmen eventually gets tired of hearing his own voice and shuts up. The house falls quiet like the calm after a storm. There's nothing quite as relieving as the silence that follows Telmen talking about how great he is at everything. For the rest of the evening, we don't say much. We don't need to. We all just sit. Apart from Gibbs, we all grew up together. We've been doing this for nine years.

The sky is a clear grey canvas pierced by sporadic specs of white. The air is cool but not too cool. In the distance, crickets orchestrate their songs, giving the night a sense of perfect, relaxing calm. One by one we start heading to bed. Spike first. Then Becka. Jensen. Telmen. Gibbs. Victor. I take a deep breath, feeling a sudden burst of melancholy. I don't know why. We have it pretty good for societal pariahs. Food to eat. Clothes to wear. A roof over our heads. I'm surrounded by people who care about me. That's a luxury that many don't have, even in Class A. Inside, I feel a yearning—a slowly burning desire for something more. Something is missing.

Every day we go out, gather, steal, acquire what we need. We store up for winter, ride out the cold and repeat. It's like going around and around the same circle. All I feel is dizzy. We keep our heads down. We survive. We play by the rules. Blend in. What's the point? What's the point of living if we aren't doing anything with our lives?

"You don't look like someone who just enjoyed a fabulous pie." Olivia pushes my shoulder as she walks past me, before sitting across from me. "Who drained the broth out of your soup?"

"Do you ever feel like a ghost in a city of empty vessels?"

Olivia leans back in her chair. "Wow, straight for the deep end."

I shrug. "You asked."

"Tell me about it," she presses.

"Do you ever wonder why we do what we do?"

"What do you mean, like the stealing? You been talking to Spike again?"

"No, not just the stealing. It's everything. We work, we plan, we do all this stuff to get what we need so we can make it to the next day, so we can get more stuff to make it to the next day."

"Right, because that's how we survive."

"Exactly!" I point at her. "Exactly. We fight so hard to survive. Why? What does it mean? What have we really accomplished? We aren't really living. We are just waiting to die. If we all died today, what happens? The world moves on. Nobody notices. Nothing changes. There won't be weeping loved ones remembering all the things we meant to them. No ceremony. They will throw our bodies into an unmarked hole and pile dirt on top of us. 'Here lies Jett Lasting. He survived. Until he didn't.'"

Olivia just sat in silence, looking at me for a minute. "I get it." She nods. "You want purpose. You want your life to mean something. You want to tear down the Patriarch and build a better world. Right?"

I nod.

"Sometimes in life we can make a difference. Sometimes storms come. All you can do is hold on. In those times, that's enough. Surviving is enough. We aren't just waiting to die. We are refusing to die. They tell us we are worthless. They tell us our lives don't matter. Here we are, living them anyway. Sure, we play it safe. We follow the rules. We suppress the part of ourselves that makes us who we are because it doesn't fit with the world around us. We don't do it because we've given up. We do it because we haven't. In a world that says you don't matter, living is rebellion. I'd much rather rage against the machine. It's easier. It feels better. It just gives them the excuse; then they win. Every day I wake up, they lose. One day their grip will slip. One day they will be vulnerable. Then, because I didn't give up, I'll be here to bring them down."

Her words warm my spirit. The dark cloud hovering over my mood dissipates. "I thought pretty girls were supposed to be stupid," I tease. Olivia, as pretty as she is, cannot take a compliment to save her life. It's really the only weapon I have against her. Sure enough, she blushes and shakes her head, avoiding eye contact. "Seriously, thanks. I needed that." I smile at her and stand up. "I better get to bed. It's late." I make my way upstairs to the room I share with Gibbs and Telmen. I flop down on my lumpy mattress and close my eyes. Ugh. Telmen is snoring like a wild beast. He can't even be quiet in his sleep.

CHAPTER FOUR

I gasp for air, my hand clutching my side to try and calm the tight burning sensation cramping up my stomach. I lean over, bracing myself on a wall as I try to catch my breath. I hear my mother calling to me, desperation in her voice. I grit my teeth against the pain and force my body forward, running toward the sound of her voice. It feels like I'm trying to run in water. Everything moves in slow motion. Only my mind is operating in real time. My body aches. I ignore it. I have to get to her.

I hear her cry out again, desperately pleading for help. My heart races faster than my legs could ever go. Warm sweat beads on my forehead. I turn the corner to the Market Square. Standing just a few yards away is Lorth Drant, host of the To Keep the Peace show. He is wearing his silky black suit that glimmers and shines against the light. His black hair is greased back. His hands and the sleeves of his suit are dripping with blood. Behind him, with a satisfied and sinister expression stamped on his face, is Commander Stone. Stone's hand is wrapped around my mother's neck, holding her in place for Drant. The smile on his face is haunting.

I race toward my mother, crying out for her. I launch my body forward, arms stretched out. Just as I reach her, she disappears into dust. The dark ash where her body had been floats up around my arms as if she'd been vaporized right in front of me. Stone and Drant grab me and carry me to the city gate. I kick my feet, desperately pleading for them to let me go.

Stone chuckles, his eyes bright with delight as he looks down at me. "Don't worry. Your friends will be joining you soon enough," he says with a toothy grin. They throw me to the ground. I feel the warmth of the scorched earth through my shirt, burning my skin. It feels like dry clay that was just pulled from the furnace. I push myself to my feet and rush toward the opening, but the gates close before I can get through them.

I slam my hands against the gate, and an invisible field propels me backwards. I hit the ground with a painful thud. The air tastes sour in my mouth. I look around. The sky seems to have no color. I can feel the burning heat of the sun against my skin but see none of the light it usually provides. I stand up, swallowing hard, my heart pounding in my chest. I muster my courage and turn around. I am in the Outlands.

Sweat pours from my forehead as I open my eyes. I let out a relieved breath as I see the ceiling of my bedroom. I hate dreams. Same thing every time. Although, Commander Stone was a new addition to this one. At least that's something.

I nearly crash into Becka as I come down the stairs and make my way into the kitchen.

"Rough night?" she asks.

I rub my eyes with my thumb and forefinger. "Yeah." I nod. "Is there any other kind?"

Becka smiles and shrugs. "I sleep just fine." I start to walk past her toward the fridge.

"Oh hey, I wanted to ask you about the Middling Days. Do you have a plan for what you're going to do?" I ask.

"Ugh...I totally forgot about them. When are they?"

"I've heard they may start next week."

"Come on, Jett, you do this every year. Every time you say, next year I'm going to come up with a plan. Here we are. Still no plan."

"I'll come up with something," I grumble in defense as I grab a glass for water, my head still groggy from sleep. I blink, trying to focus my attention. "What a pain."

"Well, I'll like to avoid last year's debacle." Victor likes to be prepared. He thinks everything through. Pretty sure when he sleeps, his brain is running probability scenarios or something crazy like that. No better way to earn his ire than to get caught unprepared.

"That was a fluke. I didn't realize they could see me."

"I'm going to put some small pebbles in my shoes," Becka interjects proudly. Always the considerate one, Becka isn't a big fan of conflict. She's quite adept at distracting us from it.

Victor gestures at her with both hands. "See, it doesn't have to be something elaborate. Just something that keeps you from standing out. That's perfect, Becka!" It really is a good idea. Becka's most incredible quality is her speed. With pebbles in her shoes, even if she's tempted to run, she won't do it as quickly.

"Hey Vic," Becka says turning to face him. Victor raises an eyebrow. "If it's not too much trouble, could you pair me with Jett today?" It was my turn to raise an eyebrow.

Victor scratches his head, "Yea, that should be no problem. Say thank you, Jett."

"Thank you?"

"That's not bad but try it as a statement not a question," Victor smirks.

I roll my eyes, "Why am I thanking Becka?

"You were supposed to be paired with Jensen."

I cover my heart with both hands and turn to Becka grabbing hers, "Bealz above, thank you!"

After breakfast Victor pairs us up. Poor Spike gets stuck with Jensen. Nobody wants that. Jensen is the worst. Becka and I get to the Market and make our way towards the square.

"What's up Becka?"

"Why do you assume something is up? Maybe I just wanted to spend the day with my friend?"

I laugh, "You've never requested to partner with me before, so-"

"Well not that you know of," she protests.

"Ok, fine don't tell me," I give her a playful smirk. Ever since I met her, Becka has been like a big sister to me. Even though I never had a sister, the way she looks out for everyone, takes care of them, goes out of her way to keep everyone else happy, she's everything I imagine a good sister to be. She's also like our in-house therapist. Maybe that's part of her Potter training.

"Just come with me," she sighs dramatically. Becka leads me down Street Six to a small shop called 'Vessels'. She pushes the door open and motions for me to follow her. The front room is like a narrow lobby with a little glass desk in the middle and a door on either side covered by a decorative sheet. A set of little brown sticks sitting in a clear glass jar fill the room with a faint smoke that smells like flowers and fresh cut wood.

"What is this place?" I ask looking around at all the oddly colorful decorations.

"This shop belongs to an old friend. She was in Temple with me training to be a Potter."

"A Potter friend."

"No, she had to drop out. Her test scores were too low. Now she uses some of the tools we learned to help people."

"Help people how?"

"You'll see. You're going to spend the day here."

I chuckle, "Becka, we have a lot to do. I can't take-"

"You'll notice I didn't ask," Becka injects. "Jett, you've been through a lot. You aren't sleeping. You have nightmares every night. You're lagging in the middle of a job. Trust me, a little relaxation will help."

"Becka, I can't just take a day for my-"

"Oh no, you can, and you will," she holds up a hand to keep me from arguing, "ah, ah, ah, this is happening." Becka avoids confrontation the way Telmen avoids silence, but with one exception, when she's someone she cares about struggling, she is relentlessly stubborn. This is a fight I cannot win.

"Why?" I protest feebly.

"Do you know why I wanted to be a Potter?"

"I assumed you wanted take control of people's minds and make them dance around like puppets." That remark earns me a solid punch to the shoulder.

"A Potter's job is to mold people to the Paragon virtues of their class. They use medication to help clear the mind and let go of any individual quality that doesn't fit the mold."

"Oh, ok, so you want to brainwash me?" I grin.

Becka gives me a disapproving glare, "I never really understood how making everyone the same creates peace and harmony. Or how a caste system supports that. We were trained to help people let go of things. Why not use that to help people let go of pain, stress, and trauma?"

I open my mouth to make another joke but think better of it. I take a deep breath, "this is really nice, thank you. But, ummm...what do I do?"

Becka taps on her data-pad. A moment later a young woman appears from behind one of the blankets. She is thin with unnatural silver hair and thin rimmed glasses that sit precariously loose on her tiny nose.

"This is the one?" she asks.

"This is him," Becka answers before turning to me. "Jett, this is Silva. She's going to take care of you. Do what she says. I'll be back to get you before the last train."

"Wait, what about m-"

"Don't worry. I've got your portion down. It really doesn't take me long."

"Does anything?"

She shakes her head and then disappears from the shop. Silva walks from around the counter and puts her hand on my shoulder, "you come with me." She leads me into a dimly lit room and points to a large couch, "You sit."

The couch is surprisingly comfortable. It feels like sitting on a cloud if, clouds could support you just enough to make you feel weightless. "Shirt off," Silva commands and walks out of the room. She returns a moment later holding a steaming mug. She hands it to me, "You drink." I take the cup and sip it while she places what feels like a cool thick cream on my back, rubbing it all over my skin. The drink tastes like tea if tea were made from straight dirt and mint leaves. I suffer through the "earthy" flavor before she snatches the cup from my hand.

Music starts to play softly. No, not so much music, but an ambient noise, like a bubbling brook. I inhale and there is a strange scent in the air. Suddenly, my back feels warm and then cool, my skin pulsing as if being massaged all over at once with just the right amount of pressure. Everything relaxes all at once.

"Close your eyes," her voice sounds more soothing all of a sudden. "Picture a wall with many glowing lumelights." I try to visualize the picture she is painting. "Now picture on the floor in front of you, a giant chest with the lid open." I do, "One by one, I want you to visualize something you are stressed about, something that worries you, or something you fear inside a lumelight on the wall. Take that lumelight off the wall and place it in the chest."

I do as she says, not really sure why I'm bothering. "Do this again with another concern until you have placed all the lumelights in the box." As odd as it seems I start doing it, slowly placing all my lume-anxieties into the chest. I have no idea how long I'm doing this, but eventually she continues. "The chest is glowing with all the light of your worries, yes?" I nod. "Now, close the lid and seal all that light away. Then imagine you are on a cliff holding that locked chest of worries." My mind transports me to a tall cliff looking over the sea. "Throw it over the cliff." I do. As the chest falls, I feel lighter, freer. "Very good, now lay back, close your eyes, and picture an empty void. Hear the soothing sounds, smell the relaxing aromas, feel the massaging pulses, but picture nothing." I lay back and let my go blank. Time fades. Thought disappears.

"Hey, sleeping beauty, time to get up." I feel my body shaking. I open my eyes just in time to see my shirt flying at my head.

"What are you doing back?" I pull my shirt on as I stand up slowly.

Becka shakes her head, "It's time to head to the train."

"No way, you just left like-"

"Like eight hours ago. Come on."

We don't talk on the train ride home. Mostly because I'm too out of it to put a sentence together. When we get back home, I eat three meals worth of food and make my way up to bed early. I'm asleep before I hit the mattress. Best night's sleep I've had in years. I wake the next morning to a soft hum and a blueish-purple haze glazes over the windows of our home. Nothing like the morning broadcast to interrupt a perfectly good sleep. As much as I'd rather ignore it, being unaware of what is going on is dangerous for us.

"Good morning! Welcome to a special broadcast of To Keep the Peace. I am your host, Lorth Drant, with a special message from the Holy Father himself. It is my honor..." Drant bows to the camera in some faux attempt at humility, "to announce—" Just get on with it already. So much to do, so many things to steal. "It's time, dear citizens of the great city of Dios, for the Middling Days!" He pauses for applause from some invisible audience. "Each year, we take this joyous opportunity to protect the unity and the harmony of our great people." More like the take the opportunity to force everyone into the same mold. The whole idea makes me sick.

Lorth Drant continues, his booming voice dynamic and engaging. He speaks with such conviction it is hard not to agree even when you hate what he is saying. "Our great city endures because we protect it from those who would cause another Great Collapse—men and women who, by no fault of their own, simply do not fit into our great society." He points at the camera, giving it the appearance that he is pointing directly at us. "As the Sacred Text says: 'Behold, I say to you, be one. If you are not one, you are not mine. For where there are differences there too shall be divisions and war. Not so for you, my children. If you belong to me, you shall find your peace in oneness of mind, and oneness of heart." Drant places his hand over his heart in silent reverence. "Brothers, sisters, division is death. Oneness is life. We strive to be like one another that together we may have life. Expression is arrogance. Duty is devotion. Conformity is virtue." For a moment the picture zooms out to a great crowd all cheering and shouting with him, "Praise Bealz! Praise Bealz!"

Lorth Drant raises his hands above his head. A hush falls over the crowd. "Those who don't fit in, who don't devote themselves to our standards of behavior and belief, are like a little crack in a piece of glass. It may seem small at first. It may seem harmless. It is not! If it is not treated, it will grow and shatter the glass, breaking it forever. Citizens of Dios, we cannot allow these cracks in our society to destroy the unity we have built! Brothers…sisters…let the Middling Days begin!"

The picture zooms back out to show a crowd wild in celebration before the image fades away, and the bluish-purple haze over our windows dissipates.

"Guess they don't start next week," I grumble, shaking my head. "Well, what's the plan, Vic? How are we going to get enough stock to make it through winter with the Middling Days going on?"

Victor looks agitated. The Middling Days are sector-wide tests run by the Patriarch. Assessors come out from the Temple Sector and move throughout the city, usually staying in an area for about a week, searching for anyone who stands out. During the Middling Days there are two or even three times the number of Red Caps on patrol making stealing much more difficult. The easiest thing to do would just be to avoid them. They move between sectors randomly, adjust train schedules, and all around make themselves difficult to avoid. Even if we could, we do not have enough food and supplies stocked to make it through winter. We can't afford to lose a whole month of gathering.

Victor sighs. "Nothing we can do about it. Stealing may be too risky until the Middling Days are over. We may have to try selling off some personal inventory so we can buy goods. That should buy us the time we need. Then it's just a matter of making sure we don't draw any attention."

"I better go wake the others, let them know what's going on," Victor says.

"Go wake them, brother. For unity and harmony in our house." I wave my hands dramatically, imitating Drant's voice as best I can. "Sleep is the great danger to the safety of our Undesirable nation and must be eradicated from our lives."

Victor shakes his head and rolls his eyes. Becka giggles for a strangely long time. As she giggles, a distinct snorting sound escapes her. She covers her mouth, and her face shifts to a bright pink hue. Victor and I look at each other. We each try to force our lips closed. Looking at each other makes it worse. We break into laughter simultaneously. Victor shoves my shoulder as if trying to chastise me for laughing while he laughs harder than I do. I lean my head back, holding my stomach for support.

When I look down, Becka has her hands on her hips in protest. "It's not that funny!" she insists. That just makes the laughter start all over again.

"Better make sure you don't do that when the Assessors are around. They will tote you away for sure," I tease.

Becka slaps me on the shoulder. "Don't even joke about that. I had a friend who had to take growth suppressants because he was growing too quickly. He didn't want to be too tall and get selected."

Victor shrugged. "Before my dad died, he used to get me drunk every morning during the Middling Days, thinking it would keep me from standing out."

Becka gasped, her eyes wide in shock. "Your dad got you drunk?"

Victor nodded. "It didn't work though. Even drunk, I knew more than they did. All he needed to do was convince me to keep quiet. You don't stand out if you don't talk." Victor is one of those people with a naturally quick mind. If the Middling Days actually worked, they'd have taken Victor a long time ago.

The Middling Days couldn't catch everyone's gifts and abilities. What they did was create a fear around using them. Anyone who stands out gets banished to the Outlands. The best thing to do is to make sure you don't ever show any qualities that will set you apart from anyone else. Thus, they destroy our gifts by making us afraid to use them.

Victor gathers everyone together in the living room after giving them a little time to wake up, so they'll be able to focus.

"Bad news," he starts. "With the Middling Days, we are in a tough place. We can't afford to be cautious and avoid the Sectors until its done. We are going to focus on valuables. Find things you can sell. We can use the money to buy the supplies we need. We aren't going to keep anyone at home today. Even though they announced the start, it's not likely they will be fully prepared in the Market. It's a risk but one we have to take. I need everyone on this. Empty your packs, and get as much as you can. Be careful. Security may be building up. We will meet back here tonight. If we do well enough, Lazy Loafer is on me this evening." That lightened the mood and even earned a little cheer. The Lazy Loafer is our favorite late night hang out. It's like a bar and grill that is open all night; it's one of the few places in Sector C that is.

We partner up and make our way into the Market Sector. I get partnered with Jensen. He's the worst. The guy could make a sunny day seem like a Levite prison cell. Jensen is a weaselly-looking man with pale, very freckled skin. He is lean and muscular, wears his hair spikey, and is always sneering about something. We really don't get along, but I make do. He's not a bad thief, just a pain to spend time with. Thankfully, you don't have to talk much to steal together. Knowing that we need to bring in a good haul, we work quickly snagging as much as we can. We try to snag as many small but valuable items as we can—anything shiny and metal, any piece of tech. The shops that surrounded the Market Square itself are by far the nicest, carrying either higher end goods or more variety than their competitors. The risk is a little greater, but there it's the most efficient way to snag a bunch of stuff in a hurry. My pack is three-quarters full before the sun has reached its zenith. Nothing like the threat of Middling Days to motivate prolific thieving.

I move away from the Market Square to get a break from the hectic hustle and bustle and turn down a relatively abandoned alley for some peace and quiet. At the other end of the alley, I hear a crashing sound. Curious, I rush over. The alley opens up to Third Street. Lying on the ground is Telmen rubbing his head. Kneeling over him is a young woman—slim figure, dark hair, wearing a uniform with the yellow sash of a teacher. The air around her smells like a freshly picked flowers. I recognize her immediately. It's Lilly.

Lilly looks over her shoulder as I come around the corner. Her eyes shine like the sun and her gaze rivals its warmth. Lilly is Class B, an Artisan. Primes and Artisans tend to view us as an annoyance. To them, we are what is wrong with their otherwise great society. Not Lilly. She actually seems to prefer us.

She just showed up one day when I was about ten and declared that we were going to be friends. We would play games, go on adventures, and all the while she would boss me around. No, Jett you go there. I'm going to be the captain. You have to row the ship. I can still picture her scrunching her little face up with her arms crossed making demands as she led our little pirate crew across the imaginary seas. Then, her parents found out. A Red Cap caught her sneaking back into Sector B where she lived. Her parents were less than pleased to learn their good little Artisan girl was slumming it with some Undesirable children. We didn't see her for years. Until about six months ago, she started showing up again.

Ever since she came back, things have been different. Just looking at her makes my heart race like after a long run. It's like electricity surges through my body whenever she's around. Every time she flashes her perfect smile, it's like my brain crashes and needs to reboot. I talked to Becka about it and she says I have a crush and I need to tell Lilly how I feel. I'd love to do that, except whenever I try to say anything to her apart from generic pleasantries, my mind and my mouth disconnect, and I become a stammering buffoon. Not even Olivia, for all of her beauty, can shut my brain down like Lilly can.

I rush over to get a better idea of what happened. At first, I think she's crying. As I lean in, I see she's trying to stop herself from laughing. I'm not even sure why she's laughing but hearing her makes me start to chuckle.

"Are you okay?" She turns back to Telmen, shaking her head, her hands on her knees. Telmen just groans.

"What happened?" I ask.

"He…he…" she tries to explain between laughs. "He tripped walking down the street." Her free hand points to a shop on the far side of the street. "He reached out and put his hand on the glass. Then—" She breaks out into laughter again. I join her, knowing how the story ends.

"The forceshield sent him flying?"

Lilly nods, wiping her eyes with her fingers as she laughs. Two disgruntled merchants dust themselves off and scurry away. "He was like…wooooo!" Her eyes close as she moves one hand over the other in a rotating fashion. "Boosh." Her hands gesture like an explosion.

"Come on, it's not that funny," Telmen protests. "It could have happened to anyone."

"But it didn't," I laugh. "It happened to you. It always happens to you." It takes us a few minutes to get control of ourselves. Even Telmen joins in eventually.

"Are you going to be at the Lazy Loafer tonight?" Lilly asks, looking up into my eyes. My words catch in my chest as my heart races. I lick my lips, and I try to respond. My brain freezes.

"Uhhh," I manage to groan out like a championship idiot. Speak man. She's talking to you. She's looking at you. Just use some words. My mind goes blank. It's as if her eyes are melting my brain. All I can think about is how pretty they are, how good she looks. She smiles warmly waiting for my reply, but that just makes it worse. Eventually I manage to nod. Brilliant.

We help Telmen back to his feet. Lilly touches my shoulder. All thoughts leave my head. "I'll see you tonight then." She smiles showing her perfect white teeth and walks off. Her smile feels warmer than the sun. Telmen says something to me, but I don't listen.

The rest of the day is a blur. I move on autopilot, absent-mindedly swiping a band, a piece of jewelry, a few coins. I can't stop thinking about Lilly. Evening can't come soon enough. I make my way down an alley between Third Street and Fourth Street when I see someone out of the corner of my eye—a large man in a cloak with the hood pulled up over his head. Doesn't get more suspicious than that. I turn to head back the way I came. Suddenly, I feel a hand grab my arm. I tug my arm free, spinning around. I've dealt with enough beggar gangs to know how to defend myself. My free arm raises, hand clenched into a fist, ready to strike as I turn. The man releases my arm and holds his hands up defensively.

"Jett," he says. I freeze upon hearing him say my name. "We've been watching you." That's not creepy at all. "It's time for us to meet."

"Seems like we are meeting right now. What do you want?"

The hooded figure shakes his head. "Not me. Not here. Our leader wishes to speak with you." He hands me a clear plastic card with a single word written on it: Nightlings. Behind the word is an eagle swings spread forming a circle around itself. I recognize it immediately. They're a group of resistance fighters led by a guy named Grent Blackfur. His name is on every wanted bulletin in the city. The Patriarch call him the most dangerous man in Dios. They are offering a sizeable reward for any information that leads to his capture.

"Great, if he wants to meet me so bad, why did he send you instead?"

"He can't take the risk and expected you'd need time to think it over. He gave me a message for you: when you are ready to make a difference, to stop getting by and start doing something that really matters, tap the name on the card."

"Tap...the card?" I ask suspiciously.

"It will send a signal that lets us know you are ready. Click it, and we will reach out."

I glance down at the card. "You guys—" I start, but when I lift my head back up, the man is gone, as if he vanished into thin air. "Are really creepy," I finish out loud to myself. I flip the card over before sliding it into the holder on the bottom side of the data-pad on my wrist. Victor is going to be pissed. Not only did I get noticed, I got noticed by the most wanted man in the city, who somehow knows my name. This is not good.

As the sun begins its descent, I make my way to the train station. In all the excitement, I completely forget about Jensen. Luckily, I see him leaning against one of the shops at the end of the street.

"Where've you been," he asks with a sneer. "Glad I had you watching my back."

"Shut up." I shake my head, not bothering to stop as I walk past him.

"Right, what was I thinking? Middling Days, extra caution, maybe a partner that does what they are supposed to and stays close."

"I stayed between Third and Fourth street, where we were supposed to be. Where'd you go that was so far away?"

Jensen glares at me. "I'm sure you didn't notice the extra Red Caps arriving." He points to the station. There were more Red Caps than usual. A lot more. The whole train car was filled with them as they piled out. Their distinctive bright red hats and the red on their shoulders make it hard to focus on anything else.

We wait until the platform has cleared of the surplus of Red Caps before getting onto the train. I'm curious how much Jensen had collected, but I don't really care to deal with his patronizing attitude, so I just sit back and close my eyes.

When we reach the house Spike, Becka, Gibbs, and Telmen are already back. We put down our supplies. I head to the back room and open my locker. On the top shelf is a project hologram of my mother's face. I look at the trinkets and what amounts to all of my worldly possessions. Years of running, hiding, stealing, and this is what I have to show for it—a locker of junk. I pull out the data-pad I stole from the Prime and close the door, using my thumbprint to seal it. I walk back out to the living room to see Victor has arrived.

He smiles. "It looks like you guys did well. I'm feeling Loafer. What do you say we celebrate tonight and do thief of the day in the morning?" His suggestion garners instant support.

CHAPTER FIVE

The Lazy Loafer is a two-story log cabin made of rustic looking wood planks. The entry level is loud, but there is a large seating area around the bar where people can come and mingle. There's music but no dancing. Dancing is strictly forbidden. According to the Patriarch, not only is dancing lewd, but it leads to sexual immorality. If you are dancing and you fall over and your clothes fall off, you'd be having sex. Therefore, no dancing.

The second floor is filled with games and group activities. It's a little quieter, but is still pretty active. The real magic is the basement. It's quiet, almost private. The dim lights give the space a casual, more relaxed vibe. There are a bunch of couches and booths where you can gather with friends and actually enjoy each other's company without suffering hearing damage from the club upstairs.

When we walk in, there are a half dozen middle-aged men and a couple of women nursing glasses of amber-colored liquid and engaging in casual conversation at the bar. All eyes move to Olivia as we make our way into the room. They aren't even trying to hide it. They just stare right at her. Spike steps in front of her, blocking their view of her from the bar until most of the guys turn back to their drinks.

Downstairs the room is deserted with the exception of a table in the back corner. It's occupied by Seamus, one of the Red Caps who works the train station. He seems decent enough for a Red Cap. My biggest issue with him is that Jensen seems to like him. The only other person, outside of the basement bartender, is Lilly. She's sitting at the bar, laughing and joking with the bartender who is more focused on her than he is the glass he's been wiping dry for the last minute and a half.

Becka screams, "Lilly!" The two girls rush to each other and hug in an oddly energetic embrace. They giggle excitedly for a minute as we make our way to the bar.

"It's so good to see you. I asked Jett if you guys were coming tonight, but he didn't really give me much of an answer," Lilly teases giving me a playful look that makes my brain lock up again. She tucks her hair behind her ear, still looking at me, before turning her attention back to Becka. Victor nudges my arm. Jerk. Spike orders a drink and then takes Telmen, Gibbs, and Olivia upstairs to play a game of blast darts, leaving the rest of us to sit with Seamus at his open table.

Lilly smiles and asks, "So, what do you think about this year's Middling Days? Exciting right?" I cringe. If she weren't so cute, that statement would send me over the edge.

"We don't really like to talk about it," Becka nobly tries to change the subject.

"Because you're all salvage and don't understand the benefits," Jensen interjects plopping down next to us.

"Benefits?" I challenge.

"Oh, don't play dumb Jett, we all know your girlfriend here got promoted to Artisan status, how do you think that happened hmmm?" I look away to ensure I can't make eye contact with Lilly. I can't believe he just blurted that out. Jensen is the worst.

"Not with the Middling Days," sweet, wonderful Becka tries to divert attention from his comment.

Jensen leans back and rolls his eyes. Somehow his entire body seems condescending. "I'm sorry for my friends Lilly, these buffoons," he pauses to emphasize the word as if showing off that he can become more obnoxious at will. "They are convinced it's all part of a big government conspiracy to remove any potential threats to their power from society." How does he not get punched in the face more?

Seamus raises an eyebrow. "Interesting. Is that what you think?" He looks around. Great. That's just what we need, more suspicion from the Red Caps.

"They are just bitter they aren't good enough to get selected for Prime status," Jensen continues. He means it as an insult, but it actually calms the tension a bit. If only that was his intention. "This year is my year. I'm going to show those Assessors what I'm made of. Then it's goodbye trash heap, hello paradise."

"That's real nice, Jensen. You're such a sweetheart," Becka snaps. "Always so gracious to bless the rest of us lowlifes with your delightful presence." Jensen smiles. Did he not catch her sarcasm or is he just owning his role as the resident scrap sink? "You don't mind that they are taking people and throwing them out of the city just because they are below average?" Becka's voice sounds disgusted.

Jensen shakes his head, "No. I don't. You know what else I don't mind? When the cleaners come and take the trash away. It's a public service. You should be grateful." Being around Seamus makes Jensen express his views louder and more confidently than normal. I know he has dreams of escaping this life, but thinking the Patriarch is going to make those dreams come true is just crazy.

"Jensen, you're telling us, that you think it's right to cast entire families into the Outlands to die just because they are...different?" Victor asks.

Jensen squirms a little. "Outlands Officers are given the honor of helping retake the world that was lost, so one day we can live in it again. There is no more noble calling."

"Then do us all a favor and volunteer," Becka snaps. I couldn't agree more.

"Wastelands, toxic fumes, savage beasts, uncharted jungles, cannibals, marauders, and windstorms that could throw a bear around like a child's toy. But it's okay; we give them a survival kit. If it's such a noble calling, why don't you volunteer?" Victor shakes his head. Jensen just stares back dumbly.

"I think he has you, bud," Seamus interjects. Here we are, nervous to badmouth the Patriarch in front of a Red Cap, and he's joining in. "Seems to me they use exile as a form of punishment. Rather than risking causing a revolt for being unnecessarily punitive, they make it sound like an honor. Much easier to justify it that way. I think they use it to get rid of people they don't much care for. What about you?" Seamus turns to Victor. I'm shocked to hear a Red Cap speak so openly against the Patriarch. There are plenty of people who feel this way, but hearing it publicly makes me uncomfortable and suspicious.

It's the perfect trap. What better way to lure us into sharing our own grievances than to appear to agree with us? Victor smiles, and I see his mouth open. I want to warn him, caution him to be careful. I can't without drawing attention.

"The Patriarch began as an anti-government organization. It came into power after the Great Collapse when people lost faith in their governments. Now, they find themselves in the odd position of being the very thing they started out opposing. As leaders, they must weigh two warring issues with every decision: what is right and what is best. Sometimes, doing what is best for the masses doesn't seem right. Yet, that is the burden of leadership. The Middling Days are a way of ensuring the city's survival, making it a greater good. The sacrifice isn't easy, but nothing worth having comes without sacrifice."

I exhale in relief—clever as usual. Jensen remains quiet. Victor words each statement in a way that was unclear whether or not he was supporting or criticizing the Patriarch. Lilly listens intently, leaning forward with her elbows resting on the table and her chin resting on her palms. This is my chance to impress her. I've studied a lot on the World that Was. For some reason I can't bring any functional thoughts to mind. All I can do is sit and stare at her like a stupid puppy. I'm so lost in my hopeless stare that I jump in surprise when I hear Victor say my name. I look over at him, dumbfounded, and he smiles, slapping his hand on my shoulder and repeating for my benefit. "That's right, Jett was telling me about the power struggle after the Great Collapse just the other day. Why don't you share it with us?"

My throat is dry, my palms sweaty. My mind feels like a pinball is ricocheting around in it. I force myself to swallow. "Y-y-yea...so, after the Great Collapse the ummm...Patriarch was struggling for power with another group called the uhhhh Sandurans. The Sandurans had more power, more weapons, more supplies. The Patriarch won the hearts of the people, which allowed them to seize control of the city and banish the Sandurans and all their supporters to the Outlands."

Lilly's eyes light up with excitement. "That's amazing! How did you learn that?" I stare at her, mouth gaping open like a buffoon.

"I ummm..." Words are hard. At least, they are hard when she's around.

"It was in a book of histories, right?" Victor bails me out. Again. Bealz love him. I manage a somewhat dignified nod.

The conversation went on for a while, but my part in it is over. One of Lilly's friends joins us. I didn't catch her name. As the evening draws to a close, we say goodbye. Seamus follows us out. Spike and the others have already left. Victor, Becka, and I make our way home. They walk ahead of me as I chastise myself for not being able to say anything. Victor drops back, shaking his head.

"What happened, man? You still can't talk to her?"

Becka smiles and bumps into me, placing her arm inside of mine and playfully resting her head on my shoulder. "Jett, are you scared to talk to girls?" She bats her eyes and then giggles softly.

"W-what? No! I'm not. I'm not scared to talk to…all girls." I pause. "Just that one. She's different." I pull my arm free dramatically and pretend to pout as I try to walk away.

Becka catches up to me, "I get it. That's the thing the Order never really understood."

"What do you mean?"

"The Order of Bealz teaches that we should strive to be like one another. That's what Potters are supposed to do. The law requires everyone to dress a certain way and behave a certain way. Potters were created to make people think a certain way. To shape their minds to the Paragon Virtues of their class."

"I never understood that, Paragon Virtues," I protest.

Becka chuckles, "Here, I'll show you," she draws on her datapad for a minute and then turns on the projection.

PRIME

PARAGON VIRTUES
☆INTELLECT
☆WEALTH
☆ SUCCESS
☆ LEGACY
☆ INFLUENCE

"The Paragon Virtues are built around the three key groups who designed Dios. The first provided the idea and the resources to build it, the Primes. Primes represent less than one percent of the population but control over eighty percent of the resources in Dios." Her fingers slide across her datapad.

ARTISAN

PARAGON VIRTUES
☆ ORGANIZATION
☆ COMMUNICATION
☆ SKILL
☆ CRAFTSMANSHIP
☆ RESPONSIBILITY

"The second designed and worked out the logistics, the Artisans. They are gifted with a lot of the practical arts, like design, technology, architecture. They are meant to take the vision of the Prime's and develop a realistic plan from it." She swipes to the next display.

PLEBS

PARAGON VIRTUES
☆ HARDWORK
☆ SERVICE
☆ SACRIFICE
☆ HUMILITY
☆ PRODUCTIVITY

"The third, worked to build and maintain the city, the Plebs. They do the work to bring the plans and ideas of the other two classes to life. Plebs make up a vast majority of the population and yet live in the worst conditions of any of the official classes." Her projection screen disappears with a soft zsssph. "Potters get assigned a 'focus' and are sent to one of the classes to lead services and spend time molding the minds of the people of that class to its respective Paragon Virtue. It's like shaping the culture of that class."

"And anyone who doesn't fit into those groupings gets slapped with Undesirable status," I say half in humor half in anger.

Becka nods, "the system is pretty flawed."

"Becka?"

"Yea?"

"What does this have to do with anything?" I try to keep a soft playfulness to my voice.

"Sorry, got off track. The Order says peace and harmony are found when we are in perfect unison. When we are all the same, we are all one. But, I can't help but wonder, if Bealz wanted us to be the same, why did he make us all so different? It can't just be a test of our devotion and willingness to sacrifice, can it?" Becka shrugs, "What I'm trying to say Jett, is no matter how hard the Patriarch tries to suppress it, we are all different. There are people who make us feel something that no one else does. That bond is special not because it's the same, but because it's different."

"Thanks, Becka." I smile at her warmly, she really is like a big sister, "Of course, that really doesn't help me find the courage to talk to her does it?"

"I could teach you," she offers graciously. "I know what she likes."

"That may take longer than you think, Becka," Victor teases. "He's pretty hopeless." I turn and shoot him an evil look. His hands shoot up, and he smiles playfully.

"Not helping!" I grunt back.

"Come on now, you know I'm just playing. Give it time. It will get there." My face relaxes, and I nod. "Maybe a year or two from now you'll get past 'hi'." Becka and Victor chuckle at his joke.

"You know what?" I stop and turn around. "Head back without me. I'm going to go talk to her." I'll show him, scrap sink, I'll talk to her right now...

Victor laughs. "It's about time. Good luck. Try not to be too long."

When the doors of the Lazy Loafer open, I am assaulted by a wave of noise. I descend the stairs quickly, hoping Lilly will still be there. She is—looking as good as ever, laughing and talking with her friend.

"Jett! You're back?" She smiles standing up from her seat at the table. Ugh, this was a bad idea. My nerves are tingling, my heart racing, my breathing quick and unsteady. I can do this. I have to.

"Yea, I uhh...do umm...I have...I was...so...can we?"

She excuses herself and tells her friend she will be right back as we walk to one of the corners of the room. Still visible but at least out of everyone else's hearing. If I was going to make a fool of myself, I'd prefer to do it without an audience. This is the part where I should say something. Instead I stand there. I look at her and say nothing. I am a gargoyle. She smiles warmly. That doesn't help. Now all I can think about is how nice her smile looks. I open my mouth to talk. Just as I do, she reaches up and tucks a piece of her dark silky hair behind her ear. I stare, mesmerized. Why? She relocated one piece of hair to a slightly different position. That shouldn't make it impossible for me to think.

"How are you?" she asks.

How difficult can it be to answer the most common question one person asks another? It's the easiest question in the world. All you have to do is answer it. Any answer will do. Pick a descriptive word. Nothing. Just a really impressive impersonation of a mime. I'm so focused on what I want to tell her I can't even engage in normal conversation. Perfect, I'll just stare at her like a creepy guy in a trench coat with an unkempt beard and a bunch of pet snakes. She waits graciously.

She breaks the silence again, "I'm glad you came back. I wanted to ask you something."

"Oh?" Idiot. That's not even a word. At least I got a sound out. Hooray for progress.

"Are we ok? I feel like ever since I came back things have been weird between us. Are you mad at me?" She flashes me this puppy dog look that could melt an iceberg.

"Mad? Why would I be mad?" I manage to get out.

"You don't really talk to me. It's been six months. You talk to everyone else except me. Victor said I should just ask you directly. What do I need to do to get you to talk to me again, like we used to?"

Victor, you rotten trash licker. She smiles so sweetly my legs feel like overcooked pasta noodles. I want to explain. I want to tell her that— after months of sitting next to her, smiling at her, seeing who she is and how she treats the people around her—she is the most mesmerizing person I've ever met. Do I just say that? Blurt it all out? What if it's too much? Maybe I should just start with something simple, like a date or something. It's not like I haven't imagined myself having this very conversion a thousand times.

She nods slowly and looks away. "I'm sorry, I shouldn't have just ambushed you like that. I'll let you g—"

"No, no, no." I hold out my hands, practically grabbing her shoulders without realizing it. "It's not that." She turns and stares deep into my eyes as if trying to see my thoughts.

Her lips curve into a faint, almost imperceptible smile. "What is it then?"

"I don't—" You are in it now, Jett. "You make me nervous." I blurt out. Well, that's great. First thing you get out and sounds like an insult.

"Nervous, why, did I-" She's tenacious.

"No, you didn't do anything. There's just something about you that-" you're spiraling you salvage vomitous mass. "It's easy to talk in front of other people because, if they don't like what I'm saying, heap them. But you..." I pause trying to give my thoughts time to form, trying to

70

hear them over the drum beating beneath my ribs. "You are sweet and smart. You are beautiful and strong." Well words are coming out now. How do I turn this thing off? "It's just, like, everything about you, from the way you tuck your hair behind your ears to the little dimples that form on your cheeks when you smile. It's the sparkle in your eyes that lights up a room. It's intimidating."

"Ohhhhh," she says her eyes widening. "You didn't want to spread that out over a couple of days or anything?" She smiles and her eyes sparkle in their enchanting way.

"Look, I'm not good at this. I guess I've been trying to work up the courage to tell you-"

"Tell me what?" She slowly and deliberately tucks her hair behind her ears without breaking eye contact. That's just rude.

"W-wha-I ummm-"

My thoughts are interrupted by her chuckling. The sound of her laughter is so intoxicating I forget what I was going to say. "Victor was right. All I had to do was back you into a corner and force it out of you."

"Oh, I see. So, you were just playing with me?"

She shakes her head dismissively. "No. I was creatively encouraging you to figure out how to be a man and talk to me."

"To what now?"

She puts her hand on my shoulder, "You like me," she slides her hand down my arm and then pulls it back. "Is it that hard to say?"

At this point I'm pretty sure my jaw may unhinge. My face feels hot, as if a volcano is erupting under my skin, replacing my blood with liquid hot lava. She pushes my shoulder away playfully. I've always thought that was odd. Girls do it when they like someone. What's weirder is, it works. Her little shove makes me want to wrap my arms around her and pull her close. Girls are confusing. Her entire demeanor shifts: her shoulders sway from side to side, and she turns and bumps into my chest. "Oh, you silly salvage boy, you don't get it do you? Why do you think I used come over all the time? You think there weren't any Artisan kids to play with?" Her words are like honey to my ears.

"Really?" My mouth stretches into a wide smile.

"Yes, silly. Why you do you think I come here every night?" Yup, I'm an idiot. Should have picked up on that earlier.

"So, would you like to…"

"Hey Lilly," Candace's perfectly timed voice cuts me off. "Girl, it's time to go," Candace shouts from the table she was sitting at. I look over trying to hide my annoyance. Candace smiles, making her freckled cheeks puff up. Her bright red hair almost reminds me of a Red Cap.

"Jett, I'm so sorry. I have to go. But I'll see you here tomorrow night?" Lilly bites her bottom lip as she looks up at me. I don't know what it means, but it's cute.

"Yeah, that should work."

She thanks me again and kisses my cheek. Now I'm sure there's a volcano under my skin. The journey home feels more like floating than walking. I'd managed to, maybe not really talk to her, but we'd had a meaningful exchange.

When I reach the house, almost everyone is standing outside, which is weird this time of year. It doesn't take long to figure out why. Sometimes it is better to deal with the cold than it is to deal with Jensen. Even with the door to the house closed, I can hear him. I don't hear her voice, but I deduce his argument is with Olivia. She's the only one missing from the collective outside.

Brelar rushes over to me as I approach, bird blanket in one hand, accusatory finger pointing with the other, "They fighting, Mister Jett, they fighting," he announces.

"Oh, are they?" I ask playfully.

"Yea," he responds sounding genuinely concerned, "it's loud."

"I hear that," I resist the urge to chuckle and look up at the rest of the group giving them my best disappointed expression. "Look at you, leaving poor Olivia alone with Jensen."

"Oh, on the contrary." Victor grins. "We took a vote. The decision was unanimous. You get to go rescue her."

This is why I shouldn't sass Victor. It never goes well for me. The others wave me to the house. Stepping inside is like walking into a war zone. Olivia, who is normally so mild manner and sweet, is pacing back and forth in an uproar. Jensen appears to be, well, Jensen—a button-pushing Shinshew.

"Why are you so desperate to be a Prime anyway?" Olivia hisses.

Jensen folds his arms across his chest and closes his eyes, shaking his head just enough to look extra condescending. "Are you joking or just stupid? You've got to be stupid. I'm tired of being treated like garbage everywhere I go by everyone I meet. I'm tired of stealing and risking my life every day just so we can have enough to eat to get through winter. Maybe you're okay with being a garbage person, but I'm not. I'm better than this. I want more from this life."

"So, you think you are better than us?"

"Obviously. This life is fine for you people, but—"

"And you think getting discovered during the Middling Days will get you promoted to Prime? Then your life is going to just magically be better?"

"Yeah. Prime citizens have cars, big houses, fancy clothes. They never have to scrounge for food. They have pools. They don't have to put up with winter like we do just because the Patriarch thinks it's funny to freeze us out. They have everything they could ever want right at their fingertips. They throw more away than we have. Who wouldn't want that?"

Olivia nods. "You think the Patriarch controls them any less? You think because they have more stuff, they have more freedom?"

"She's right," Becka peeks around me as I stand in the doorway. "My family is well off but they still live in constant fear of losing what they have. Having more didn't change the pressure we felt to be like everyone else. It just made the cost of failure feel higher. Sure, they don't go hungry, but they don't have friends either. Everyone is just waiting for you mess up so they can win favor with the Patriarch by turning you in. My own family disowned me because-" she shakes her head. "Life isn't better as Prime. They have just as many problems as we do. They are just different problems."

"No one asked, Becka," Jensen snaps.

"Hey! Don't snap at her, she's just trying to help, it's not her fault you're too salvage to listen," Olivia counters.

Jensen stares at her in stunned silence. His face turns angry. "What the heap is your problem? You could make Pleb. Or Artisan with ease if you just applied yourself. Anything, any life is better than this one. You don't want to? Fine. Live on the fringe of society with your little group of rejects. I don't want to do it anymore. And why do you care anyway? What does it matter to you what I do?"

"It matters," I interject. They both turn to look at me, apparently just now realizing I'm in the room. Olivia looks away. Jensen stares at me with contempt. "It matters what you do because, for some reason none of the rest of us can understand, she actually cares about you."

"If she cares so much, she should be excited that I could get adopted into a class."

"Think, Jensen. When was the last time you talked to someone who got adopted into a class?" He opens his stupid mouth, but I hold up a finger to stop him. "They take plenty of people during the Middling Days, but have you ever seen any of them on the other side? Ever seen a Pleb who became an Artisan? In your entire life, do you know of any?" Jensen looks puzzled. "They keep farmers near farmers. Doctors near doctors. Everyone has a place. Right?" Jensen nods. "Do you know what makes this little group work?" He shrugs. "We are different. We have different strengths, different weaknesses. We think differently. That's how eight of us, with no place in society, survive. Our differences allow us to adapt to our situation. They make us strong when we use those differences to work together."

"What is your point?" Jensen asks aggressively.

"What do you think would happen if the entire city started intermingling—if everyone worked together? If we shared our knowledge, our abilities, our resources, we could do anything. We wouldn't need the Patriarch. They know it. Why do you think they work so hard to keep us separated?"

"So, you're saying the Patriarch keeps us in poverty and divides us from each other so they can maintain control?" His tone is surprising. It lacks the usual arrogance. I half expected him to launch into some angry rant criticizing everything I said. I'm not even sure how to respond. This is a Jensen I don't recognize.

"To conform us," Victor says now standing in the doorway. He steps inside. "They don't want to rule smart, capable people who think for themselves. The more we think for ourselves, the less power they wield over us. They can't take away our talents. They can't make us dumber. But they can make us afraid. They can make us hide who we are so completely that we become like sheep."

"But they unified us to protect us from another Great Collapse." He sounds less argumentative and more confused, like he's struggling to reconcile this idea with everything he's heard and believed.

"There is a difference between unity and uniformity," Victor explains. "Unity comes from a diverse people who work together for a common goal. Uniformity comes from everyone trying to be the same. Unity makes us strong. Uniformity makes us sheep—sheep who are docile, easy to control."

"Why have the Middling Days at all?"

"Human nature. When we know we are being controlled, we rebel," Victor explains calmly. "The only way to truly control us is indirectly: create rewards for fitting in, create punishments for standing out, matching uniforms, organized Sectors. Even the Order's mantra 'Expression is arrogance. Duty is devotion. Conformity is virtue.' From the visible, to the practical, to the spiritual everything drives toward one goal: conformity. That's the message of the Middling Days. Don't stand out. Don't be different. Don't draw attention."

I half expect to see Jensen's mind explode through the back of his head.

"That's why Olivia is so upset," I add. The issue may not need pressing, but this is the most receptive I've ever seen Jensen. "Wanting to get adopted into a class, to go through Processing, you'd be giving up the one thing that is truly yours in exchange for some petty comforts."

Jensen turns to Olivia who is wiping tears from under her eyes. "You mean, all of this is because you don't want me to stop being me?"

Olivia nods. "We are a family. If you get brainwashed by the Patriarch, who's going to call us stupid all the time?" She laughs, looking like she's barely able to hold in her tears. Jensen wraps his arms around her in a comforting hug. Now my mind is in jeopardy of blowing out the back of my head. I had no idea Jensen was capable of being sympathetic.

 The next morning, we meet up in the living room to go over our take from the day before. We all pour out our packs onto the living room table. It's impressive—three or four times more than our normal haul. I put everything on the table except the data-pad. I'm saving my coup-de-grace of our special edition of Thief of the Day for the end. Everyone debates what item is the best and who should win the prize. As they argue back and forth, I slowly pull out the data-pad and place it on the center of the table.

The room goes silent. They stare at the pad and then back up at me. I cross my arms over my chest proudly. "Did someone say Thief King?" I ask with confidence.

Victor picks up the data-pad, turning it over in his hand. "Jett, where did you get this?"

"I took it off some Prime guy who was too lazy to secure it to his wrist. The access information on that should be worth more than enough to get us through the winter."

"When did you get this?" Victor asks.

"Couple days back. I was just saving it for the right time."

"Jett." Victor's tone is serious. "What color was his sash?"

"What do you mean what color was his sash? I don't remember; it was light colored. He was definitely Prime." I start getting defensive. "Look, I get it. Data-pads are risky to steal. We can't do much with the Middling Days going on anyway. It was the perfect time to snag one. And now, we don't have to worry about having enough supplies. We can—"

"What color was it?" Victor repeats, this time louder.

"It was white," I answer. Victor sighs, looking weirdly relieved. "Or—" I start picturing the sash in my mind. "It may have been like a light grey."

Victor's eyes go wide. "Jett, this is very important. Was it white or light grey?"

"What does it matter? He didn't notice me. He didn't even notice I took it. We're stocked."

"Jett." The sternness in his voice is discomforting.

I picture the guy in my mind, focusing hard on what he was wearing. "It was light grey. Why does it matter?" Victor's shoulders slump forward. Everyone else just stares in silence. Spike stands up and puts one hand on my shoulder, rubbing it as if comforting me. "What is going on?" I pull away from him, my mind racing. "Why are you freaking out?"

"Because, brotha, grey is a Patriarch Official," Spike explains. "Ye stole a data-pad from a member of the ruling council. Things are going to get really dicey round here." He tried to keep his voice calm and soothing, but I could hear the subtle worry. In my excitement over the easy mark, I just went for it. I knew white uniforms were for the high society intellectuals: doctors, nurses, scientists. Stealing from the Patriarch, that was a whole other level. How was I supposed to know? I'd never seen a grey uniform before.

CHAPTER SIX

Victor rubs his face with his hands, ruffling up his hair the way he does when he is deep in thought or very frustrated. I'm guessing it's both. He snaps to attention. "Okay, we can't risk keeping this; it's too hot. I was hoping we'd be able to take the day off, but this changes things."

"Great. Thanks, Jett. You ruined our—" Jensen starts. Guess he's still a Shinshew.

"Shut yer wee mouth, Jensen, or I'll shut it fer ya," Spike interrupts, pointing at him aggressively. "It happened. Getting upset about tis not gonna change nothin'." I nod to him in appreciation. He winks back.

"Gibbs, I want you to reach out to your contacts—see if there is anyone who'd be willing to take this off our hands. Spike, I want you to scout good exchange locations. Someplace remote, but with lots of exit routes. Becka, you and Jensen are going to prepare a distraction. It needs to be big. It needs to be as far away from the exchange site as possible. Olivia, you're going to be lookout. As soon as Spike finds a location, I want you on the rooftops making sure we don't get any unwanted company. Jett, Telmen, you're going to fill your bags and go sell off as much as you can. Once you are done, head back to the train and come straight here. No detours. We do this, then we are staying out of the Market Sector for as long as possible."

Everyone bursts into action. Gibbs, starts dialing in contacts on his data-pad. Telmen and I scoop as much stuff as we can into our bags and head out the door.

The sky is bright and sunny. Birds are singing. The breeze is refreshing. What a waste of a beautiful day. Telmen starts talking as we make our way to the station. I try to find a mental frequency to tune him out. I'm certain getting partnered with Telmen is part of my punishment for grabbing the data-pad. Loud, obnoxious Telmen. Despite my attempt to shut him out, I hear him say, "You know, I could give you some pointers if you want. I've learned a lot of really cool skills. I'll show you sometime."

I roll my eyes and look away. I don't respond, hoping it will quiet him. It doesn't. I look over at him as he talks, relentlessly. All I can think is that if there was a way to turn his words into energy, we could power all of Dios for decades.

He keeps talking as we board the train. I did not know it was possible to use so many words and say absolutely nothing. It just goes on and on like a conscious stream of words projectile vomiting over anyone close enough to hear. I can't tell if he's speaking to me or just saying words because silence causes him physical pain.

I lean my head back and groan. He doesn't take the hint. I look over, and the guy sitting next to me is wearing headphones. Never have I been so envious in my life. I consider offering him my right arm in exchange. Or maybe a kidney. Anything to end this torturous babble.

Telmen's not a bad guy. I think I'd like him if he ever shut up, which he doesn't. I've never met someone who loves to talk so much. Maybe he has a medical condition where he can't breathe unless he's talking. It would explain some things. Normally, I just tune his jabbering out, but today the alternative is worse. I listen to him go on and on about how he is great at everything. I'm not sure he even knows or cares who is listening. If Telmen were the last person on the planet, I don't think it would change his word count.

When we finally arrive at the Market Sector after the longest train ride in history, I convince Telmen we will be more effective if we split up. We'll get our goods to more vendors faster that way. Which is true. It also gives me a reprieve from his verbal onslaught.

"Remember what I told you," he says as he makes his way to the door ahead of me. "The first one who names a price loses." I nod and force my mouth into a somewhat painful smile. I'm not sure how to respond to that little pearl of wisdom anyway.

I barely make it off the platform before the guy behind me plows me over as he pushes his way past. His shoulder catches me mid-step and knocks me off balance. I manage to catch myself on one of the nearby lampposts. Charming. I straighten my jacket and head into the Market.

All the shops start blurring together as I move from one to the next getting rid of our stolen merchandise. Several of the shop owners on Sixth Street buy a lot. We barter regularly. They always give me good prices and good stock, and they don't mind working with Undesirables. Good news for us. I zip my bag closed and sling it over my shoulder, stepping out of Gordon's Gifts. Outside the doors to the shops are lines of various vender stands with brightly colored canopies. Most of them are selling food, but a few have odd trinkets. I sigh. I can't stop thinking about how things are going with the data-pad I nicked. There's another vulture circling overhead. I wonder if it's the same one from before.

"Jett!" Hearing my name, I look up. "Hey! Jett!"

A young woman comes rushing over toward me. Her dark hair blows in the wind behind her as she moves. I feel my cheeks warm, and the palms of my hands get sweaty. Just looking at her makes my heart start pounding in my chest like a gorilla playing the congas. My mind turns into a black hole. I take a deep breath. Just talk to her.

She stops next to me, taking a minute to catch her breath. "Sorry," she pants, "I saw you from down the street. I wanted to come say hello, but you kept disappearing into stores. I didn't want to miss you." She irons out the yellow sash she wears with the palms of her hands. It's an unfortunate color for teachers, but she makes it look good.

"Did you hear about what happened?" She continues without waiting, "a Patriarch Official was here in the market on some secret assignment. Apparently, someone stole his data-pad."

"Huh," I manage.

She nods. "Yeah, they think the Nightlings are involved, and they are going to use it to launch some kind of rebellion."

"From a data-pad?" I blurt out.

She nods again. "It's bad. More Red Caps have already started arriving. They are talking about locking down the sectors and searching every home until they find it. Whatever that data-pad has on it has them on edge."

"How do you know all this?"

"One of the other teachers in my school—her brother works for Patriarch Intelligence. She was telling me all about it."

A loud crashing sound echoes all around us. I turn to see a Red Cap sprawled out on the ground. He's stumbled out of a pub and appears to have tripped over one of the outside dining tables. Plates, glasses, a couple of napkins, and silverware are sprinkled around his body. Silence follows. The Red Cap moans and slowly pushes himself up. From across the street comes the distinct sound of a child's laugh. I look over. His mother, wide-eyed, frantically puts her hand over the boy's mouth. It's too late. The Red Cap is on his feet. He crosses the road and grabs the boy. His mother tries to protest, but the Red Cap shoves her back, knocking her over. He lifts the boy off the ground, holding him by his shirt.

"You think that's funny, do you? Little brat, you need to learn your place." Disbelief bleeds into disgust at the thought. The boy is maybe ten years old. I look around. Everyone is watching, making the same weary face. No one moves or does anything. That's worse. A drunk Red Cap abusing his power is bad enough. A crowd of people sitting by, watching, doing nothing—no wonder this city is messed up. They haven't taken our power; we've surrendered it. We are to blame. The Red Cap sets the boy down, grabs his arm, and starts tugging him down the street. "Let's see how funny it is after twenty lashes at the Justice Block."

Justice. That's not the word I'd use. The boy's mother screams and pleads with the Red Cap, begging him for mercy, begging him not to take her son. "Don't like it?" The Red Cap says looking back at her. "File a Trespass." He laughs and keeps walking.

"A Trespass, seriously?" Lilly mutters. No one files Trespasses. Once they do, they get flagged for disrupting the peace and taken to the Justice Block for processing. A Red Cap's word is law. We can't question it, challenge it, or complain about it without consequences. This kid is going to get beaten horribly and have scars for the rest of his life because he laughed at a drunken Red Cap making a fool of himself.

I move without thinking. As the Red Cap passes, I side-step purposefully crashing my shoulder into his just hard enough to knock him back a step. He spins around, face red. He releases the boy and turns his attention to me. It's not like I knocked him over. I bumped into him. A simple "excuse me" should be all that's required. Not today. He's cursing my worthless, classless, pathetic excuse of an existence.

Everything in me wants to respond—just a little jab to point out how ridiculous his response is. I imagine punching him in the face, giving his mouth something more productive to do, like bleed. Out of the corner of my eye, I see the mother covering her son and rushing him out of sight.

The Red Cap shoves my shoulder hard. My hands clench into fists. Bad idea. I take a deep breath. Don't respond. Just be smart and keep your head down. Assaulting a Red Cap would result in getting sent to the Justice Block with an added bonus of a free lifetime membership to the Outlands Lottery Pool on Lorth Drant's show.

I tuck my head into my chest, keeping my eyes down and lifting my hands up. I apologize for my horrible misdeed. The yelling stops. My submissive posture seems to calm Captain Rage-a-Lot. He steps close, looming over me. It would be so easy to just—no. I push the thought from my head. Let him feel powerful. Play to his fragile little ego. It's hard. I hate bullies. I hate a system that cares more about the letter of the law than about the people who are crushed under it.

"You, worthless street scum. You know what the penalty is for assaulting a Red Cap?" I'm sure he's going to tell me. "I could have you flogged to within an inch of your life."

I shake my head. "You've got to be kidding; I didn't see you there. It was an accident, not an assault," I protest. Victor will not be pleased.

"It is what I say it is."

Bite your tongue, Jett. Don't respond.

"Now, get down on your knees and beg for my forgiveness."

"Forgiveness? For bumping into you? Seriously?"

My legs give out. My body curls in on itself. The air bursts from my lungs against my will. Heat raging in my chest as it burns. I clutch my stomach and drop to my knees, coughing. I can feel my pulse in my chest. His mother must not have held him enough. I wince, pushing myself to my feet. At least it takes my mind off Telmen's talking. I close my eyes bracing for another unseen blow.

"Excuse me, officer." I hear Lilly's voice. Her tone is forceful. There's a cracking sound followed by a muffled groan. Did he just hit her? I release my chest and shove the ground underneath me. The Red Cap is facing away from me as I lift my hand. I catch a glance from Lilly out of the corner of my eye. She shakes her head. I freeze for a moment. She doesn't appear hurt. Lilly leans in and whispers something in the Red Cap's ear. He steps back with his hand covering his face, blood dripping between his fingers.

Lilly looks as innocent as a dove before turning her gaze back to the Red Cap. "I believe it is against Patriarch regulations for officers of the law to drink while on duty." The Red Cap takes another half-step back, his eyes shifting from anger to fear. One question and she robbed him of his power. "What's the penalty for interfering with an official messenger of the Patriarch?" She lets the question linger. My brow furrows as I turn back to where the boy had been. What was she talking about? The Patriarch doesn't use children from Class C as messengers.

"W-what? The boy wasn't a—" the Red Cap began.

Lilly cut him off. "Are you saying you were too drunk to notice the Patriarch emblem on his jacket? Or did you see it and just ignore it?" His mouth gapes open, his eyes wide as saucers. The color flees his face. That's a clever bluff. Risky. If he calls her out, we are all seriously heaped. "Now, the way I see it, this young man crashing into you saved you. You should be thanking him."

I feel myself being lifted up. The Red Cap pats me on the shoulder, looking very solemn. "Umm...thank you," he manages.

"No, you thank him with credits." She is pressing this hard. Too hard. Without saying a word, the Red Cap clicks his data-pad and swipes it over mine. I glance down and see a hundred credits deposited into my account.

He looks at Lilly, almost pleadingly, like a puppy hoping to avoid punishment by looking miserable. Lilly waves her hand dismissively, and the Red Cap takes off, not looking back. The crowd erupts with wild cheering. They crowd in, circling around us. They push against us, swarm around us, smiling, laughing, expressing their amazement. I don't think they've ever seen a Red Cap back down. It feels like something is in the air, some invisible energy moving among the crowd like an electric current.

Finally, the crowd disperses, leaving us with a semblance of peace. Lilly looks at me, her face turning a bright pink before she breaks eye contact. She just faced down a Red Cap with nothing but a bluff, and she's nervous to look at me?

"So...um...what just happened?" I chuckle.

"What do you mean?" She asks flashing me some sweet, innocent glare to distract me. It almost works.

"It seems like you've done this before," I stare at her suspiciously.

She shakes her head dismissively, "it's just something my dad taught me."

"Your dad taught you to lie to Red Caps?"

"No, not that. He taught me how to deal with the guards should they ever behave in a manner that was no appropriate. Didn't want his daughter getting in trouble from some 'thug in a uniform,'" she imitates his voice as if his goal was absurd. I don't know why. It seems like a very wise thing to me. What do I know? I've distrusted the guard my whole life.

"I see."

Lilly diverts her gaze even more. "Are you mad?"

"Mad? Why would I be mad?"

Lilly turns her head up a little. "It's wrong to talk to a Red Cap like that."

"You did the right thing."

"How do you know?"

"You did something. A whole crowd of people saw what happened and didn't say a word. They were going to let it happen."

"But we are supposed to trust in—"

"In a system where the enforcers of the law wield it as a weapon but don't keep it themselves? In a system that lets innocent kids get beaten?"

She looks me in the eyes. She seems both surprised and relieved. A slight smile forms on her face. "Glad you finally remembered how to talk to me." She sticks out her tongue playfully.

I chuckle, feeling my face get warm. "It's wasn't my fault."

"Oh?" She raises an eyebrow dramatically, "So it was MY fault you couldn't talk to me?"

I nod, "Yea, obviously. Look at you. You're beautiful. You're brave. You stood up to a Red Cap and put him in his place. That's hot." She turns into me as I step closer to her, my hand moving toward her lower back.

We walk past a jewelry store and she stops, "Oh, look at that." She points to a window ad that projects a small, thin, silver chained necklace with a shining blue sapphire encased in a black titanium setting. "My mom used to have a necklace that looked just like that. I always thought it was so pretty."

"What happened to it?"

"She had to sell it years ago when my dad got into a little trouble. It's no big deal now but, I was sad she got rid of it."

"Well-"

A shrill squeak pierces my ears, interrupting me. The light purple hue of the display screens covers all the glass. The sky fills with a projected image of an attractive girl in a shiny dress. They never say her name. She just shows up and waves her arms around to get everyone's attention. The image turns to a man: dark silky suit, slick black hair, pearly white smile. My stomach turns as I look at Lorth Drant.

"Greetings, citizens of Dios! Welcome to a special edition of To Keep the Peace. I'm your host, Lorth Drant." He takes a far too rehearsed bow before holding his hand up next to head. A separate image appears in a little box as if floating in his hand. "Last time on our show we met Hunter Vollis: husband, father of two, disturber of the peace, endangerer of society. A man of chaos and disorder who used violence to try and steal from you, the good people of Dios. Thanks to the hard work of our Red Caps and Levite division, he was brought to swift justice. You cast your votes, and the results are in. Fourteen percent voted for imprisonment in the Justice Block. Fifteen percent voted for public flogging. Thirty-one percent voted for death by beheading. Forty percent voted for exile as an Outlands Officer. You, the people, have spoken. We have heard you."

The image shifts to a middle-aged man in a thick leather tunic, a bow and quiver draped awkwardly over his shoulders. An unkempt beard covers his face. He's standing before one of the massive gates on the outside wall. The gates creak and open. Hunter Vollis walks reluctantly out of the city. As the gates close behind him, the image moves back to Lorth Drant who is now holding a hand over his heart.

"It fills me with joy to be a part of such a merciful city that would see a sinful, violent man, deserving of death, offered a chance at redemption." Drant smiles warmly. "Now to today's Lottery..."

On the right of Drant's head, a group of square images appear. Each one displays a man's face with their criminal ID number underneath. At first there are so many images it's hard to make out any one specifically. To Drant's left, a girl in the shiny dress walks over and pushes an oversized button. Around her, a bunch of glowing, almost transparent, balls appear like little bubbles. She giggles and reaches up and pokes one. The bubble bursts, and a two-digit number appears on the screen.

"Our first number, thirty-eight." Drant smiles, and a large group of the pictures on his right blink and then disappear. The remaining images become slightly larger on the screen. The girl in her shiny dress pokes another bubble. Another number. More pictures disappear. She pops a third bubble. Then a fourth. Only a dozen or so pictures are left now. She pops a final bubble. One picture remains: Talm Jestdin. Under his picture is a bio: height, weight, hair color, occupation, listed as classless. No surprise there. His crime is listed as assault, which could mean anything from violent criminal to clumsily bumped into the wrong person. Lorth Drant starts sharing the man's profile before setting up the public voting for how to punish him.

Lilly whispers something, but I can't really hear what. My gaze is fixed on the screen projection in the sky. I feel sick. Watching To Keep the Peace is mandatory. The Patriarch says it helps promote lawful, orderly citizenship by giving the people ownership in the carrying out of justice. Funny thing, "not guilty" isn't a voting option. Most people love this show. It makes them feel safe. Every criminal punished makes them sleep a little easier at night. Nauseating. We don't just invite the wolves in; we give them power and thank them for preying on us. The show is bad enough, but it feels different today. It feels worse. It's not just how things are anymore. It feels wrong. My whole life I've focused on one thing—survival. That's not enough anymore. I'm sick of feeling claustrophobic in my own skin. Sick of always looking over my shoulder. Sick of fitting in. Sick of being invisible. Adrenaline can be dangerous.

Lilly takes my hand, and we walk down the street.

"I wanted to ask you something," she says almost bashfully.

"OK..." I respond, "should I be nervous?"

She shakes her head. "You risked a lot trying to help that boy."

"That was—" I start to object before she puts her hand on my chest to stop me.

"And the way you spoke. You aren't just afraid of the Patriarch. You hate them. I just wanted to know if there is a reason."

"A reason I hate the Patriarch?"

She nods.

I sigh. "I have this dream, a memory, that I keep seeing over and over again. When I close my eyes to try and block it out, the images barrage my thoughts with even greater clarity. My mother lying in a puddle of her own blood. My father lies next to her on his stomach, his eyes closed almost as if he is sleeping. Standing above them is a man, his face hidden by shadow. I try to remember, but the only thing I can't see clearly is the one piece I want to remember. I try to picture some identifying mark on the man who killed my parents. It's as if his face is covered by a dark cloud. I only remember two things about him. He was very young and his eyes...his eyes were wild like a savage beast."

I pause. Lilly's expression is sincere but also confused like she's processing but not really understanding. I continue, "My earliest memory is of the shadowed face of the man who killed my parents. He was wearing a Patriarch uniform."

Lilly's eyes widened in realization. I try to wave it off. Graciously, she lets me change the subject. We wander, roaming around chatting about anything and everything. Before long, I'm talking about how Victor and I became so close, how I met my little band of outcast friends, and even my terrifying encounter with Commander Stone. She listens so intently, seems so interested, I find myself wanting to tell her more. I practically blurt out that I'm the one who stole the data-pad. She tells me about herself, why she doesn't really care about what class someone belongs to, and about some of her friends. I could listen to her talk forever.

A silver lining cast by the setting sun rides the tops of the buildings as we walk. I realize I've lost all track of time. We've wandered away from the crowds and are on the far east side of the Market Sector. Panic sets in. This is not a safe place to be. During the day, the beggar gangs are relatively dormant, but there's a reason the Red Caps clear out before nightfall. A sense of urgency surges through me.

"We need to go." Her hand tightens around mine as she stops in place. She gives me a nervous look. Something feels off. My muscles tense up, and I feel uneasy like we are being watched. It's like we've accidentally wandered into the den of a sleeping lion. Now we need to tiptoe away quietly before the lion wakes.

Lilly is out of her element. She's an Artisan. She has a real house, a real job. She comes to the Market, but she doesn't have any idea how dangerous it can be here on the outskirts, nor should she. She'd have no reason to come out this far. The shops are run down. There's no one in sight. This is on me; I got distracted. Welcome to the lion's den, Lilly. I put my finger to my lips, encouraging her to remain quiet. I take her hand and pull her after me, all but sprinting down the alley toward the Market Square.

Her nails dig into my wrists. We keep going. Maybe I'm just being paranoid. Beggar gangs might look the other way for an Artisan, but an Undesirable roaming their territory is not something they'd let go. We pass one street, then another. Still no one in sight. The look on her face is masked terror. She is naïve enough not to know the Market can be dangerous but smart enough to realize I'm not messing around. No footsteps behind us. No lurking shadows. I slow down, starting to think I overreacted.

Stopping in a plaza around Street Twelve, the coast is still clear. I was worried about nothing. Lilly still looks shaken, and I turn to reassure her. Before I say a word, two men approach from the alley in front of us, both of them considerably larger than I am. Brown cloaks, white emblems. I don't have to see it to know what it will depict. My arm extends in front of Lilly as I put myself between her and the two men. At least big usually means slow. We can outrun them. A tightening grip on my arm and soft gasp tell me that plan isn't going to work. Two more men approach from behind us, cutting off our option to escape back the way we came. I circle around trying to use my body to shield her as both pairs of men descend on us. We can't run. We wouldn't put up much of a fight. Maybe I can talk them down. More likely, we are totally heaped.

My hands shake as I hold them up, palms out. "Lovely day, isn't it?" Weird opener, but it's the best I could come up with. The four men continue to move forward, boxing us in and closing the circle around us.

"You were warned what would happen if you didn't pay." The voice was raspy and unevenly pitched. A fifth man looms behind the other four. His hooded cloak is adorned with a patch of a white howling wolf head inside a circle of fire. He is a big man, even bigger than the thugs surrounding us. He pulls down his hood.

His head looks almost square. His jaw is covered by a thin blonde beard connected to a thick, long goatee. The sides and back of his head are shaved short, but his hair is long and straight, pulled to hang over one side. The smile on his face is sinister and cold. His head is cocked to the side slightly, the way a cat does when playing with its prey. No mistaking him. I'm moving up in the world after Bill Sonder's warning. It's not just any member of the Fire Wolves beggar gang hunting me. It's Heywin Varel, one of their captains. Such an honor.

Victor and I worked with Varel a few months back. They had a line on a transport of sugar and other valuable goods. They brought us on to help orchestrate a clean getaway. Turns out the take was much smaller than they were led to believe. Now they wanted our cut. Victor told them to heap off. When we didn't pay, they promised to hunt us down and kill us one at a time. I guess Heywin is here to make good on that promise.

Dropping my hands, I take a deep breath and reach into my pocket, careful not to move too quickly. I grip a small steel marble I keep with me to create distractions. My eyes dart back and forth between the two pairs of menacing thugs encroaching on us. One of them pulls an energy knife. The blue glowing blade shimmers and buzzes out. This is how a mouse must feel when a cat bats it around between its paws—trapped, powerless, just waiting for the end. Lucky for me, I have a marble and a plan.

"When I move, follow me. Run as fast as you can. Don't look back," I whisper to Lilly, my tone as firm as I can make it. The briefest moment passes before she nods. Why did she hesitate? What other option does she think we have? The thug with the energy knife is the biggest threat. He stumbles back as my marble crashes into his forehead. Before they have time to react, I charge into the man next to the one with the knife. I lunge forward with my shoulder, checking it into his chest and sending him toppling to the ground. There's the escape window. "Lilly, go!"

I notice her hands are balled into fists. I shake my head at her. It's cute that she wants to help but, she's not prepared for a street fight. I shake my head and point, which unfortunately feels like a shooing gesture. She glares at me as if frustrated.

She's faster than I would have thought. She charges past the two stumbling thugs and heads straight for the alley that leads to the Market Square and safety. Good girl. Now get out of here. Spinning back around, I put all four of the thugs and Heywin in front of me. She may be fast, but I can't risk them catching up to her. Four on one, I don't have a chance. I don't need to beat them, just slow them down enough and then escape.

The other two thugs are already charging right at me. No time to think. My senses are heightened, my reflexes ready. Turning sideways, I force the thugs to charge one at a time. The first lunges at me. Quick side-step and he slides past. The other swings his giant fist at my head. Ducking under it, I drive my fist into his chest, just under his rib cage. He coughs and gasps for air. Seizing the momentum, I turn my hips, driving my other fist hard across his face, sending him collapsing to the ground. This is going well. Victor's insistence we train for fights is paying off.

The first thug, the one I'd side-stepped, wraps his gorilla arms around me from behind, holding me in place. Heywin is yelling at the other two, angrily telling them to get me.

The thug with the energy knife is still rubbing his forehead as he approaches. "I'm going to take my time with you! You'll be begging for death before I'm done with you!"

The problem with weapons is they give a false sense of confidence. You don't think as much. Why would you? Weapons can make you dumb. The knife goes back slowly as the thug prepares to thrust it forward. Waiting until the last second, I stomp my heel down hard on the toes of the thug holding me. Then I pull my shoulder forward and rotate my hips as hard as I can. Off balance, the thug is easy to move.

The energy blade seers into his side, and he screams in pain, releasing me from his grip.

That only buys me a second. My elbow swings up and catches the head of the thug with the knife, sending him stumbling to the side. That's where my luck runs out. The fourth thug dives straight into me. No time to react, my body crumples under him. His massive weight keeps me pinned to the ground.

Pain surges through my back and limbs. I feel myself behind, hoisted up and slammed against the stone wall of the alley—one thug on each arm, Heywin standing in front of me. I wrench and turn my body, trying to pull free from their grip. They are too strong. Finesse gave me a chance, but this is a contest I have no hope of winning. Out of the corner of my eye, I see one of the thugs rolling on the ground, holding his lower back. At least one of them will remember me.

"I'm going to enjoy this," Heywin sneers holding his energy blade up to my neck. I shake my head. That really isn't really how I wanted it to end. I thought I might do more. Nothing to do about it now. Gritting my teeth, I brace myself.

CHAPTER SEVEN

"**S**top!" The voice from behind Heywin is commanding. It's the thug I punched in the chest and then face. He's rubbing his face, the skin already starting to bruise. Must have hit him harder than I thought. He moves past Heywin and steps directly in front of me, his eyes fierce like a burning flame. His dark hair is pulled into a knot behind his head, and a long scar runs from his forehead down his cheek to his jawline. He turns and spits, blood splashing on the ground. He seems to appraise me for a moment. A sinister-looking smile forms on his face. He points at me and turns to face Heywin. "I like him."

Heywin's face turns red. "He's mine. Don't—"

The fiery-eyed thug shakes his head. "He's not like the others. Most people would give up and beg for mercy at the sight of you. Look at him even now; he's a fighter. He's awake." He turns back to me. "Why didn't you beg, boy?"

"Would it have done any good?"

The thug laughs. "No, probably not. Sorry, Heywin, you can't have this one."

"What? We had a deal!" Heywin snarls, holding up his knife threateningly.

The thug nods but seems completely unconcerned with the knife. "That's true. We did. That was before I saw his eyes."

"His eyes? What are you talking about?" I've heard of people getting so hooked on doltine their brains become like scrambled eggs. Never thought I'd meet one though.

The thug uses two fingers and points to my eyes. "He looks at you. Even when you are threatening to kill him. He doesn't turn his head down in fear. He's not some insecure shell of a person trying to avoid conflict. They haven't broken this one yet." Red Caps view eye contact as a form aggression. They have no problem with clubbing that aggression out of us. Most people in Dios keep their heads down everywhere they go.

"I could give two—" Heywin starts.

"What's your name, boy?" The thug completely ignores Heywin. I try to tug my shoulders free, hoping to catch one of the thugs holding me off guard. No luck. They slam me harder against the wall. The fiery-eyed thug chuckles and waves them off. "I'm Kane. And you are?"

"Jett," I reply reluctantly. I'm not thrilled about telling street thug my name, but he could get it from Heywin anyway, so there's not much point in resisting it.

Kane reaches down and picks up a card from the ground in front of me. He turns it over in his hand before holding it up. It is the Nightling card that guy had given me. I'd completely forgotten about it. Kane smiles and lifts the card up for Heywin to see.

"This one belongs to Grent." Kane tucks the card back into my data-pad.

"No! No way! He owes the Fire Wolves a debt. Code says if he doesn't pay, I get to collect in blood." Heywin pushes past Kane, lifting his knife toward my throat. "He's mine—not yours, not Grent Blackfur's. No one can take what is mine."

96

In a flash, Kane's large muscular arm wraps around Heywin's neck, his other arm holding under his shoulder, forming a sort of arm bar. Heywin stumbles back, energy blade falling to the ground as he grasps Kane's arm, trying to pull it off. The soft humming of the blade fizzles out as the switch on the handle hits the ground. The glowing blue blade-shaped beam disappears. He should have kept the knife. He might have had a chance.

"Don't forget who you are dealing with. I'm not one of your lackeys." The vein in Heywin's forehead throbs wildly as he struggles to breathe. He taps on Kane's forearm quickly but softly. "If I let you go, you going to leave like a good boy?" Heywin manages to nod his head ever so slightly. Kane grins up at me, waiting a moment longer before releasing his hold. Heywin collapses to the ground, gasping for air. "But the next time you try something like that, you'll be rat food, understand?"

It takes him a minute to get to his feet. Leaving his knife on the ground he makes his way toward the back alley of the little plaza. "This isn't over," he growls out before running down the alley.

Kane nods, and the two thugs release me and follow after Heywin.

"Thanks, I think," I say with a squint.

Kane laughs a little too loudly. "You don't trust me, do you?"

"I don't know you."

"Not yet at least. You will. I think we will be great friends. We are more alike than you think."

"I doubt that."

"It's true." Kane scoops up Heywin's knife and slowly tucks it into his cloak. "We didn't meet by chance."

"Right, you tried to kill me."

Kane throws his head back and laughs, his amusement echoing like a wolf's howl. "That I did. Grent says you're ready. I wanted to see for myself, test your mettle as they say."

"And I passed."

"Like gas after a can of beans. We've had our eye on you for a while. Nicking a data-pad from a Patriarch Official takes a certain type of courage. Or stupidity." Suddenly my mind is a starless night. Panic sends my stomach into an awkward dance. How did they know about that? If they knew, who else did? The air becomes heavy. My thoughts become erratic and unproductive. "Either way, you have our attention. Grent believes we need people like you—people who are tired of fitting in to the status quo, people who are sick of living on scraps while being ruled by some nutters in an ivory tower."

"Yea, I've heard the sales pitch before. Join the Nightlings. Change the world."

Kane laughs showing his perfect white teeth, which somehow seem to contrast his rough, worn features. "Come on, you're smarter than this. You want the world to change, you have to do something to change it."

"Yea, except we can't. We don't have the power to stand up to the Patriarch."

"Don't we now?" Kane's eyebrow raises. "You'd be surprised. We may have more power than you think, especially with that data-pad."

"Not buying."

"Not selling. It's an invitation. Next week. Come and see."

"Cryptic." It's definitely the most thorough attempt at recruitment I've experienced. He's got me curious now. "What happens next week?"

"It begins."

"More cryptic."

"Tell you what, you show up next week, Grent Blackfur will show you himself."

"How am I supposed to—"

"You've got our card. Use it, and we'll find you." Kane gestures goodbye, pulls up his hood, and disappears into the alley.

The dim light of the alley feels strangely soothing. The buildings I'm walking between are tall enough to block out any direct sunlight. My knuckles throb.

"Jett!" I turn toward the sound of the voice. Her body crashes into me. The sudden weight makes me stumble back a step. Her arms wrap around my shoulders. I blush, hugging her back slowly. "You're okay!" She sounds equally surprised and relieved. I have to tap her shoulders to get her to loosen her grip enough for me to breathe.

Behind her are three Red Caps looking around. I point to the plaza, and two of them rush off. Not sure if the thug who got stabbed was still there. If not, at least there would be evidence of a struggle.

The remaining Red Cap glares at me in disgust. Lilly obviously didn't mention her friend in need was a classless Undesirable. Most Red Caps wouldn't lift a finger to help us. We ranked somewhere between pond scum and kidney failure.

"Well, aren't you going to take a report?" Lilly stomps her foot.

"I don't think that will be necessary," his glares over at me like I am some giant piece of litter he doesn't want to get stuck cleaning up.

"Do you know who my father is?" Lilly taps on her datapad and the guard glances at the screen. The Red Cap sighs, reluctantly opening a blank screen on his data-pad.

"Go ahead." The way he said them, it was clear the words were painful.

"No incident. Just a misunderstanding, officer."

He closes his data-pad screen and gives me a slight nod of appreciation. He turns to Lilly and tips his red beret. "Miss."

"Oh, before you go..." Curiosity overwhelmed my disdain for Red Caps. The guard said nothing, just stared. "Anything special or unusual happening in the Market next week that you're aware of?"

His eyebrows furrow. His eyes narrow, suspiciously. "Why do you ask?" Thanks for that confirmation.

"I, um, had some supplies I was going to bring in. But they are big and awkward, you know. I didn't want to tout them around if the Market was going to be extra busy."

He just kind of grunts and walks off. Rude.

"Why did you lie? Those guys were going to kill you!" Lilly places her hands on her hips. She deserves to know. They were threatening her life as well. She's also an Artisan. She may sympathize with us, she may enjoy our company, but I doubt she sees the Patriarch the way we do. I could tell her. If I do, I could be putting her in danger.

"Beggar gangs power struggles," I lie. "Whenever turf wars start getting intense, the gangs try really hard to recruit new members." That much is true, just not relevant to this situation, I don't think. Kane may have been trying to recruit me. I don't think so. The Nightlings aren't a beggar gang. They are freedom fighters or terrorists, depending on who you ask.

"They didn't look like they were trying to recruit you, Jett."

I shrug. "They tried asking nicely. It didn't work. I guess they shifted tactics a little. Thought they could motivate me to join by force."

"And then they just ran off when you said no?"

"I said no pretty convincingly."

She eyes me suspiciously. "Okay."

"I need you to do something for me."

"What's that?"

"Promise me you will stay out of the Market for the next week."

"Why? Because of beggar gangs? I'll just stay in the Square."

My stomach flips. I don't have a good reason to push the issue. If the Nightlings are up to something, even the Market Square could be dangerous. How do I tell her that without telling her a rebellion may be brewing?

"Just for a week or two. Please. It's probably nothing. If a gang war breaks out, I don't want to see you get hurt."

"Okay, fine. I'll stay away. I promise."

We walk back toward the Market Square together. I notice something painted on the wall of one of the shops. It's a yellow crescent moon with three straight lines coming out of it. Maybe it's some new way Beggar Gangs are marking their territory? I put it out of my mind and turn my thoughts back to Lilly as we walk. She holds my hand the whole time, swinging my arm with hers ever so slightly. As we cross each street, I look down them, surprised by how few people I see. Something is going on.

"You there! Halt!" A couple of Red Caps come rushing toward us. My instincts scream run. Lilly releases my hand and turns to face the guards. They don't stop. They run right past us. Turning around, I see more Red Caps further down the street, chasing someone. I can't be sure, but I think I see a tan girl with dark hair turn the corner and disappear just in front of the Red Caps.

My ear vibrates with a soft buzz. I push on it until I feel a little click under my skin. "Jett, the sale was a setup. They may be watching us, so act natural. Go into some shops. Be unpredictable. Don't go home. Meet us at the Lazy Loafer when you can get away unnoticed. We'll head home together from there." Victor hangs up the digi-call before I can say anything. Heap. What a day.

"Hey, sorry I have to get going. Got to finish a couple things up before I go home." I smile and keep my voice calm. If someone is following me, I don't want Lilly to become a target.

"Oh, everything ok?"

"Of course; just need to grab some stuff for Victor."

She nods, "Well, I'll see you tonight at the Lazy Loafer then, right?"

"I wouldn't miss it." Lilly says goodbye squeezing my hands in hers and then heads off. I watch her until she is well out of view.

I keep an eye out for any signs of a tail. I weave in and out of streets and alleys until I end up in front of the jewelry shop we saw the other day. I scan the display of the necklace Lilly liked with my data-pad before stepping inside. The door to the shop opens, and a bell chimes overhead. The storeowner, an elderly woman with long grey hair that she wears up and wrapped around itself like a funnel, moves toward the front counter. Her black uniform is accented by the merchant profession's standard purple sash.

Her eyes scan me with disdain. Undesirables rarely have credits. Pretty much any merchant in a shop before Street Seven treats us like vermin. It's enough to make me want to rob the place. I tap my data-pad, and the projected image of the necklace lights up from my arm.

"I'd like to look at this, please." Manners don't cost anything. Maybe they will help soften the grimace on her face. "It's for this girl I like," I add. Typically, a little personal connection and charm goes a long way.

The old merchant rolls her eyes, "I didn't ask. No offense, but don't see many of your kind who can afford it." Why is people think saying 'no offense' gives them permission to say offensive things? "My hip is hurting today and that piece is in the back. Show me you can pay, and we'll talk."

"How much is it?"

"It's 1200 credits," you'd think she was getting dental work done.

I rub my temple, and the projected image shifts to my account. I double tap my data-pad, and my account information opens: 1431 credits.

The shopkeeper grunts in response. The utter shock on the old lady's face brings me great joy. "Wait here," she says.

I'm a thief. When I need something, I steal it. Not much use for credits, so I just let them store up. Olivia spends all her credits on clothes. Becka burns through shoes pretty quick. Spike keeps a collection of trinkets from the World that Was. I save.

I could just steal the thing, but it feels wrong to give Lilly a gift that doesn't cost me anything. Here's my gift. Hope you don't get caught wearing it or you'll end up in the stockade. Super romantic.

It takes her like five minutes to get down from her seat behind the counter and walk to a display ten feet away. She returns with the necklace. It looks even better than the ad. I tap an access button, she scans my data-pad, and the credits transfer. Securing the necklace in a hidden pocket in my jacket, I make my way out of the store. Now it's just a matter of finding the right time to give it to Lilly.

I make my way towards the train station via alleys and back streets. The journey back to the train is perilous. With the Middling Days in full-swing there are Assessors everywhere. I turn to make my way through the Market Square and freeze. Soldiers, Levites, and other Red Caps are herding everyone into lines to be tested. The Square is full of Assessors. Assessors are easy to spot, they dress in white hooded robes with red stitching and a large red half circle meant to represent the holy symbol of the dome, the source of our salvation. Their faces are covered behind white, almost featureless masks with red trim around the holes for the eyes. Each Assessor is accompanied by two Red Caps to ensure their instructions are followed explicitly. Ducking behind a corner, I slip out of view. If I can't find a way around and fast, I'm heaped.

The entire Market Square is turned into a testing ground. The standard test consists of three parts: a speed test, a strength test, and a mind test. If nothing is flagged, a red stamp is placed on the person's hand, and they are sent on their way. These bulk tests are more for show. The real danger is the Assessors positioned around the city, looking for any indication of special talents. At the front of the lines, they are patting people down and checking their bags. They aren't just testing. They are looking for something—the stolen data-pad.

Crouching behind a pile of shipping boxes, I make myself as small as I can and remain still. Two Red Caps walk out of the alley and head up the street in the direction I'd just come from. Thank Bealz for small blessings. As quickly as I can, I move alongside buildings until I reach an opening. After checking it carefully, I dash across and wait on the other side to make sure no one sees me.

It takes longer than I'd like. Anything else is too risky. If only I could get to the rooftops; this would be so much easier. Careful to avoid passing guards and the line of sight of any nearby Assessors, I slowly make my way around the Market Square toward West Street and my train home. Hiding in a store won't solve anything. It just delays the inevitable. To get home, I have to get past those Assessors. I can try to sneak by, but I need to reach the other side of the Square. I see my window, a group of people are exiting the Square, having completed their test. If I can reach them, I'll have a clean shot the rest of the way.

A distinct, fizzling electric hum makes me jump. Even the wind falls silent. Peaking around the corner, I see the unmistakable glowing blue strands of energy dangling from the thrasher's black metal handle. It is uncommon, but not illegal, for someone to get flogged outside of the Justice Block.

The scream that follows is gut-wrenching. A man, maybe forty, with thin greying hair drops to his hands and knees. He clutches his face, and blood seeps through his fingers, a burn mark running over his temple. Flogging someone in the Square is harsh enough. Striking them in the face is just wrong. The man's body slides back as the guard grabs him by his ankle and starts dragging him away. Dragging him is a man in a black uniform. The tops of the shoulders are red, adorned with three black, shining bars. Across his back, I can see his red sash—Commander Stone. Stone drags the poor man away like he's little more than a sack of potatoes.

A crowd of thousands of bystanders all watch in terror and disgust. No one protests. No one objects. They turn their heads to face the person in front of them while they wait for their turn to run the Middling Day test. My stomach lurches and threatens to remove its contents. There's nothing I can do. Just like everyone else, I'm reluctantly giving my approval through silence.

Stone drags the man up the steps of a temporary platform set up in the Square before dropping his defenseless body onto the floor of the platform. All eyes are on Stone. A moment later, the screens and glass in the Market Square hum to life, and Stone's face is projected on them. Not in the sky—this is some type of limited broadcast.

"Citizens of Dios, a very important item has been taken from one of our officials. Stolen here in this very Market. Someone has it, knows about it, has seen it. Come forward, and you will be rewarded. Do nothing and—" Stone gestures to the man on the platform who is still groaning and holding his face. He lifts the thrasher above his head and brings all nine-tails down over the man's back. It takes a full minute for the screams to die down enough for him to speak again. "The Patriarch has been lenient. They have tried to give you a good life. To ensure you are safe, that you can enjoy peace and harmony. This is how you repay them? This is how you thank them for their tireless service on your behalf? Lenient no more. I am the fist of Bealz. You sinners will know my wrath." Now I really want to puke. Without thinking, I pull the card out from under my data-pad and push the word Nightling. I return the card to its place in case they use it for tracking or something.

Sliding in among a group of Plebs who finished their test makes boarding the train easy. My nerves are rattled. My adrenaline pumping. I don't even realize I'm heading back solo. The ride gives me time to settle down and catch my breath.

When I reach the Lazy Loafer, I head downstairs. Spike is sitting alone at a table in the back corner. The whole floor is empty. Spike greets me by lifting his tall glass of dark beer. I don't know how he drinks it. It's so thick light can't even pass through it.

"Welcome, brotha. Join me for a wee drink before the others get here?" Outside of Victor, Spike is my favorite person in our house. He's clever but playful, and he gives good advice. Sure, it's not as good as Victor's, but it's a lot more fun when he gives it.

Sitting across from him, I lean over the table and whisper, "What do you know about Grent Blackfur?"

"Oi, heap me. Ye mean the rabble rouser?" Spike raises an eyebrow as he looks at me. "Who've ye been talkin' to, brotha?"

No sense in hiding it now. I explain to him everything that's happened, from the cryptic card to the Fire Wolves attack to Kane and his invitation.

"Interesting. Ye really stepped in it, didn't ye?"

Frustration boils up in me. I don't know what to do. I need answers. Not more questions. I need Victor. He always knows what to do.

"Brotha, take a wee breath. Calm down." Calm down? I'm plenty calm. No, I'm perfectly calm. If he thinks this is me not being calm, maybe I should show him what that truly looks like. A thud from the stairs behind me makes me jump so hard I hit my knees on the bottom of the table. Gibbs walks down the stairs and over to the bar to get a drink. Spike gives me an I told you so sort of glance. "Jett, this is not something ye want to be impulsive about."

"What do you know, Spike?"

He hesitates for a moment as if deciding whether or not to say anything. "He's a dangerous heaper, ye be sure of that. Best if ye just avoid him all together."

"Not sure that's going to work."

Spike winces and nods. "Aye, data-pad. I shoulda thought of that. Definitely something he'd be wanting."

"You know what he's up to?"

Spike shakes his head. "Nah, I try to steer clear. He's sort of a trouble magnet, that one." Was this fear? Cowardice? I've seen Spike stand up to a Levite, take a flogging for someone else on two separate occasions. I didn't know he felt fear.

"How so?" I press, eager to get to the bottom of this little mystery.

"Grent's been around for a while. He's as dangerous as they come. Free thinker. He's got no love for the Patriarch, that's for sure. But he's never the one who gets caught. Tis always the people with him, the people who support him or even just associate with him. They are the ones who end up in the Justice Block or worse." Worse being the Patriarch's favorite punishment, the Outlands.

"If he's so dangerous, why don't they just kill him?"

"Kill him, he's a martyr. He may be the most dangerous man in Dios, but he's not a threat. So, they leave him be. Let him play hero to the people, and he actually draws out potential insurgents for ye."

"So, he's tried to start a rebellion before?"

"Oh aye, six times that I know of. As ye can tell, he's not made much difference." My heart sinks in my chest. Six failed attempts. Kane's words had given me hope, stirred something inside me that made me think maybe, one day, things might change. Six failed rebellions. Hope is an ant under the Patriarch's boot.

Gibbs walks over with two glasses, sliding one in front of me. I scoot in to give him space. Thankfully he's not Telmen, or the conversation would get side-tracked immediately.

"The data-pad!" I practically yell. Spike and Gibbs look at me wide eyed. "The heaping data-pad! Maybe they have failed because they haven't had the right tools. If Grent and the Nightlings had that, it could make all the difference."

Spike just shakes his head. "No, not Grent. Trust me, ye can't give him the data-pad."

"Have you just given up? Just accepted things the way they are? What are you so afraid of, Spike?"

Spike's shoulders sag. The warm expression fades from his face. "Why are ye so ready to throw in with a man ye dunna know?"

"At least he's trying. He's not just sleepwalking through this life. He's standing up to the Patriarch. Here we are living for nothing. At least he's fighting for something."

"Aye, he fights. Fighting is easy. Rage is easy. It's the aftermath ye never ready for." Spike points his finger at me, his frustration coming through. "Fighting for something ye believe in seems noble. Seems honorable. What do ye think happens to the people who fight alongside him? They get beaten. They get their minds reprogrammed. Or they get dead. As an added bonus their families get sent to the Outlands. It's not as noble a sight as what yer picturing."

"Yea, well at least it's something," I snap back. That was petty. All he is doing is trying to look out for me. I may not agree with him, but that's no excuse to be a Shinshew about it.

"Drink," Gibbs interjects. Spike and I obey without objection. Something about just taking a drink together calms the situation.

"Have you heard from any of the others?" I try changing the subject. Gibbs and Spike both shake their heads. "They should be here by now."

Spike looks toward the stairs. "Aye, yer right. This is not good. Gibbs, ye want to check outside, see if ye can spot anyone?" Gibbs nods and wordlessly slides out of the booth, making his way up the stairs and out of view. Spike turns back to me, a sudden look of confusion setting in on his face. "Oi, where is Telmen? Weren't ye two together?"

Air involuntarily evacuates my lungs. My body locks up in disbelief. I forgot about Telmen. I left him alone in the Market during the Middling Days.

CHAPTER EIGHT

Telmen can be annoying, but he doesn't deserve this—getting abandoned by his partner. I can't believe I did that. It's one thing to split up. Leaving him there without a word, that's not okay. My hands blanket my face in an effort to cover my shame. It doesn't help. When my hands drop, I can tell from the look on Spike's face he's figured it out. I sigh. Tapping on my data-pad, I hit Telmen's contact, and the phoni-plant rings in my ear. Come on, Telmen, pick up. It's a chance to talk. He never passes up a chance to talk. The digi-call goes dead. I try again. Spike looks at me, concern brewing on his face. I shake my head.

Spike slides out of the booth, his tall, stout body stretching out as he stands up. He motions for me to follow him. I do. We head up the stairs and bump into Olivia, who is yelling at Jensen for something. Hard to tell what in passing, but I'm sure he deserves it.

"What? I'm just saying he probably found some Market chick to hook up with," Jensen protested.

"You are such a scrap sink!" Olivia grips the air in front of her in a strangling motion, shaking her arms at Jensen as if wringing his neck. "Not all men are salvage wrappers like you!"

Two guys who were seated at the bar walk over. The taller one puts his hand on Olivia's shoulder. "Excuse me, miss. Is this guy bothering you?"

Olivia turns her head slightly before looking back at Jensen. "Not any more than usual." She shrugs pushing the guy's arm off her shoulder along with his hopes and dreams. She calls Jensen something unladylike and stomps down the stairs. The two men skulk back to their places at the bar, looking defeated. Jensen stands there looking indignant like he's the victim of some unfair verbal accosting. Nobody who's met Jensen buys that act.

Gibbs is standing at the open front door to the Lazy Loafer as we walk past.

"Tell Victor not to wait for us," Spike says to Gibbs. "We've got something to take care of. Won't be back until late."

He nods in response. "If he asks what?"

"Tell him we went to ask around, see if we can figure out where the Assessors are gonna be tomorrow." Gibbs nods and steps inside.

We make our way back to the train station. Evening has turned to dusk. The light of the artificially generated sun hides behind the horizon. The cool night air brushes over my skin, making my body shiver. A small crowd of people descend the train platform, scattering like dandelion seeds in a stiff breeze.

"What are we doing here?" I ask.

"I think ye know, brotha."

"It's almost last call, Spike. We take that train—"

"Aye, good chance we end up in the Market overnight."

"No, no, no, that's not happening. We just got out of the Market. Victor said to meet—"

"Do ye know why we partner up, Jett?" He pauses for a moment. I'm not sure if he wants me to answer or if it's rhetorical. "What we do is risky. We work with a partner so ye have someone to watch yer back. Ye are responsible for yer partner. Yer partner tis responsible for ye. That's how this whole thing works. Ye left yer partner."

"Come on, we split up. A lot happened. That's not—"

"I'm not blaming ye. Maybe it is not yer fault, but it is yer responsibility. Ye lost yer partner, and I'm going to help ye find him. We aren't coming back until we do." His words flow with such strength of conviction, I don't dare argue. Sometimes it's really annoying trying to argue with someone whose moral compass never points south. "Telmen would do the same for you." No, he wouldn't. Telmen wouldn't come back for me because he'd never have left me there in the first place. He's as reliable as he is chatty. Spike was right. Doesn't make the idea of going into the Market when we should be leaving any less daunting. I guess if doing the right thing was easy, everyone would do it.

I nod. Spike smacks me on the shoulder hard. I pretend it doesn't sting as we step onto the train. Well, here goes nothing. We are the only two people riding the train into the Market at this hour. That's a warning sign if ever there was one. Yet Spike sits calmly. Not sure how under the circumstances, but he does. I'm rocking back and forth like a doltine addict in need of a fix.

The best part about this journey is that it gives my mind all the time it needs to run every "what if" scenario imaginable. It works its way systematically, from the annoying what if Telmen got on the train as we are getting off and we miss him? or what if he went back to the house instead of Lazy Loafer? to the more upsetting what if he was grabbed by an Assessor? or what if he got caught by a Red Cap and was taken to the Justice Block? My whole body feels jittery. Deep breaths. Calm down; it'll be okay. At least I'm not making the trip alone.

We sit in silence until the train pulls in, and the seal on the doors pops open. I wish I had some kind of weapon. For the most part, weapons are illegal in Dios. The Red Caps, Levites, and Patriarch Defense soldiers have guns. The Levites also have thrashers, which look like the long metal handle of a flashlight. Thrashers project nine three-foot-long strands of controlled energy used for flogging. The beggar gangs have knives. We have...our charm. It doesn't hold up in a fight but it's better than nothing. Getting caught with a weapon is a surefire way to get sent to the Justice Block. Getting caught on the streets at night without a weapon is a good way to get dead.

"We move in a grid. West to east down and den east to west back. Ye take odd streets. I'll take even. Stay close. Make sure ye can hear me shouts. We get lucky, find Telmen, maybe catch da last train home."

"You're optimistic," I chuckle.

"Aye, no point in planning for disappointment. Let's go."

The thought of getting stuck overnight in the Market Sector is haunting. I've had enough encounters with beggar gangs during the day when most of them are sleeping or hiding. No one lives in the Market Sector, officially. The merchants and storeowners lock down their shops and secure them. The glowing force fields that cover the shop windows during the day are used to cover the whole building at night. Unless you have the right access card, the field is impenetrable. Merchants leave at seven. The Red Caps leave on the final train at eight. After that, the Market belongs to the beggar gangs. Each night the gangs fight for who will control the Market streets. Most of the Undesirables who live outside the Rim end up in one of these gangs.

We sprint down the street. Spike cuts up an alley and turns down Street Two. Most of the shops are closed or actively closing. All of the vendor stalls are packed up and vacant. A faint purple glow covers most of the buildings like a transparent film. The occasional Pleb or Artisan I pass are all heading to the train station.

Anxiety builds its mighty fortress in my mind. The Market is big. The Square alone is a huge open-front market, about five hundred yards wide and a thousand yards long. It's bordered by two- and three-story shops made of dark grey stone with muted red, green, or blue shutters.

Street vendors set up temporary displays in concentric squares starting in the middle of the Market Square and working out, leaving twenty to thirty feet walkways for crowds to move in and around.

Four main streets open into the Market Square, one from each direction. The main streets then open up to dozens of side streets which run like a square frame around the Market Square, each street longer than the one before it. Each of the dozen streets that frame the square are named by their number. The closest street is Street One then next is Street Two. It's very creative. It will a long time to search them all. I swear to Bealz, if he's just standing around somewhere talking, I'm going to kill him.

"Telmen!" Spike shouts from the street parallel to mine. "Telmen!" Having spent most my life conditioned not to draw attention to myself, the idea of running around the Market shouting feels wrong. If we are going to find Telmen before the final train leaves and we are stuck here, it's probably the smart play.

"Telmen!" I join in. No response. Scanning the alleys as I run, I search for any sign of him to no avail. The Assessors are already gone. Most of the Red Caps are gone as well. It's weird seeing the Market so empty. Weird and unnerving.

We run up and down the streets in an organized pattern, calling out Telmen's name. No luck. I try digi-calling him again. No answer. Spike and I make our way back toward the Market Square to start trying the streets to the south. At this point, if Telmen were someplace he could respond he would have. Time to start considering Telmen may have been grabbed by a beggar gang. Or worse.

We pass a lonely merchant as he locks his door and activates the forceshield around his shop. He turns to look at us. His face is covered in a full beard. Mostly white with a few patches of black too stubborn to surrender the fight. His skin is leathered, his wrinkles pronounced but not yet sagging. The merchant tucks his head down and scurries off like a rat caught in the open. That's odd.

Suddenly, Spike grabs my arm and pulls me into an alley off the main street. A trumpet sounds loudly, echoing through the Market. Boots crash down the street in rapid succession, creating a low, thundering rumble. Red Caps and Levites are speed marching toward the train station.

We follow their path on the street running parallel to theirs, stopping in view of the train station. A bright iridescent light sits in the middle of the platform, towering thirty feet in the air, illuminating the entire platform. The light on the tracks shines bright green as the Red Caps and Levites pile in, a few scattered merchants among them. The lights on the track turn yellow. Then red.

"Wait. What's going on?" I ask as the train doors close. "It's not time yet."

"Train's leaving early." Spike looks over at me.

"We've got to try to get on it. We didn't find Telmen by now, we aren't going to tonight. We can come back—"

"Tis too late for that, brotha. We're here for the night." A loud popping sound like the release of a seal comes from the track, and the train slowly slides away. Great. A night in the Market Sector; what could go wrong?

"We need to get off the streets before—"

"Well, look who it is. Back so soon? I knew we hit it off, but I didn't think you were this magnetized." That playfully unnerving voice is unmistakable.

Spike looks at me and shakes his head. "Come on," he shouts, taking off. He doesn't make it far before a huge, beastly man cuts him off. Spike stumbles back. The man in front of him is well over six-feet tall. He looks like a grizzly bear, or at least, like the pictures I've seen of grizzly bears, minus the fur. Well, minus some of the fur. His face is mostly a giant black beard. He's wearing a strange-looking shirt with no sleeves, though I doubt his tree trunk arms would fit inside sleeves anyway. I've never seen so much black hair on a person.

"Spike! My oldest friend!" The burly man's voice booms and echoes like he's speaking from a cave. Despite his size and rough exterior, his words feel surprisingly warm and heartfelt, even jovial. Something about it feels off.

"Grent," Spike sighs, unenthusiastically. This is Grent? Victor told me stories about him when I was little. Grent the Great, a champion of the people who stood up to the tyranny of the Patriarch. Grent is a far throw from what I pictured. He looks like a Viking from the World that Was. His body is covered in thick scars. If the legends are true, these scars came from beatings he suffered in his fight for freedom. The obvious hits me like a sack of bricks. Spike knows Grent? How is that possible? How could Spike know Grent and never mention it?

The lumbering bear of a rebel leader smiles from ear to ear. His teeth are remarkably white. Without warning he wraps his big bear arms around Spike, fully lifting him off the ground in a big bear hug. Spike's arms are trapped inside Grent's and remain at his side. It's unclear as to whether Spike is unwilling or is simply unable to return the friendly gesture.

"No love for your old friend? Agh, you're breaking my heart." Grent lowers Spike back to the ground and releases him. "Don't tell me you're still mad." He shakes his head, looking disappointed. "It was a long time ago."

Spike doesn't respond. Grent shrugs and turns his attention to me. He points at me and glances over to Kane. "This is the one you were telling me about?"

"It is. He's quite the scrapper. He took on four guys, one with a knife. Popped me in the jaw so hard I almost lost a tooth."

"And he—"

"Yea, he's the one who stole the data-pad. I'm telling you, this one's a keeper."

Grent grunts and nods. I think that's approval. "Well met. Kane doesn't like most people. He's taken quite the shining to you." It's hard being so popular.

"I'm stocked, really, but what do you want?"

Grent smirks. "Tsk. Touchy." He shakes his head. "You activated the card we gave you. We told you we'd reach out when you did." Spike looks at me in disbelief. I may have forgot to mention that when I told him what was going on. "But first," Grent grabs my arm and lifts it, sliding his data-pad over mine. His screen lights up, and several displays appear. He scrolls between them. "Very good. Just making sure."

"Sure of what?" My tone is a bit more hostile than intended.

"Can't be too safe. The Patriarch is not above using spies to try and infiltrate our group."

"Scanning my data-pad helps how?"

"Oh, well, there are certain access codes embedded in Patriarch-issued data-pads. You can build an entirely fake persona, but you can't hide those access codes. If you had the codes, we'd know you were a plant."

"And if I was?"

"Oh, well, I'd kill you and leave your body for the rats." Grent smiles. Weird time to smile. "So, you're ready to join the Nightlings, overthrow the Patriarch, change the world?"

Spike shoots me a look. Something about it unsettles me. It's like a warning. I try to brush it off, but I can't get the look out of my head. Something inside me yearns to say yes—to be part of something, to do something that makes a difference for once in my life. I can't shake the feeling that something isn't right about this.

"Actually, no. We have to find a friend of ours. He was here in the Market earlier. We haven't seen him since."

Grent walks over and whispers something to Kane.

"What's your friend look like?" Kane asks.

"He's about five foot ten with long arms and legs. Medium length blonde hair. Big mouth. Never stops talking." Kane and Grent whisper back and forth again.

"Is he wearing a greenish-grey jacket and a grey shirt?"

"Yeah!" I almost shout. "Have you seen him?" Hope builds up inside me.

Kane sighs. "Yeah, I've seen him."

"That's great!"

"No, it isn't. When I saw him, he was getting taken into the Levite outpost off the Main Street North."

Hope collapses around me like a top-heavy tower after being hit by a demo ball. Levites aren't as common as Red Caps, but dealing with them is far, far worse. Levites are what mothers tell their children about to get them to behave. "Be good little Johnny or the Levites will get you." The only real difference between Levites and the boogeyman is the stories about the Levites are usually true. Levites are the self-proclaimed voice of the Patriarch. They are brainwashed in the Temple Sector as children, taught to love the letter of the law so much they actually delight in torturing people who break it.

I think that's what makes them so dangerous. They are incredibly cruel. Cruelty is not what drives them. They are driven by conviction. The Levites genuinely believe what they are doing is right. Cruelty has limits. Conviction doesn't. Levites are a combination of a priest and a street thug. Give them a reason, and they will make you suffer. Sometimes they don't even need a reason—just an excuse. For a Prime or Artisan citizen, the Levities are almost amiable. They protect and serve the great peace of Dios. For the rest of us, they are dread incarnate.

If Telmen is in Levite custody, not only is he unreachable, but it's my fault he's there. At least if the beggar gangs had him, we could try to trade for him or something. With Levites, we'd have a better chance convincing water not to be wet. Only Telmen could get this heaped this quickly. Spike buries his face in his hands and sighs loudly.

"You're in luck," Grent interjects. "I think we can help you save your friend."

"How?" Spike challenges. "The building is locked down, forceshield around it. Ye'd need an actual Levite clearance card to get in."

Grent and Kane chuckle. "I wouldn't worry about that." Kane responds. "I've got an automatic code scan and clone generator."

"Is that supposed to mean something?" I ask.

"It's like a universal key," Kane explains. "Opens any door, well, any door with low or moderate security protocols. In the Market, it disarms any forceshield." Hope is a rollercoaster. "Good news is, the Levites left the outpost mostly unguarded. Too busy searching for this missing data-pad. There's probably two men guarding the entire building. The rest won't be back to check on your friend until morning."

"Great, let's go get him." I start down the road. No one else moves. Exhaling my frustration, I turn back around.

"You're getting ahead of yourself," Grent warns. "I said we could help, not that we would." He smiles, his perfect white teeth in blaring contrast with his massive black beard.

"What do you want?" I ask, making my tone as cold as possible.

"You," Grent says, like the tactless blunt instrument he is. "If you agree to join the Nightlings, we will help you rescue your friend."

A cloud of suspicion darkens my mind. Trading with merchants, I learned you can't show too much interest in something or they will jack up the price on you. He's been watching, gave me a card, sent thugs. Now, the leader of the rebellion is here in person trying to bring me in? He's a little too interested. The idea of joining the rebellion excites me. I've dreamed of seeing the Patriarch fall since I was a boy. Now, I have the opportunity to be a part of it, and I'm hesitating. Before I can answer, Spike grabs my arm and pulls me away, moving us out of earshot.

"Ye can't do this, brotha, I won't let ye."

"Telmen is in a Levite outpost. You said it yourself, it's my responsibility. I don't have a choice."

"Ye daft tosser, don't pick today to start listening to me. We can find another way."

"Another way? Another way to disarm a Levite forceshield, enter a Levite outpost, and rescue Telmen without getting caught? Who's being the tosser now?"

Spike sighs. "I'm telling ya, ye can't trust him. You agree to this, there's no going back." Spike and I don't always agree. He is one of the best judges of character I've ever known. He obviously has a past with Grent, and if he's this against it, there has to be a reason.

I pat Spike on the shoulder and walk past. He doesn't bother turning around.

"So, it's decided?" Grent asks.

"It is. You help us get Telmen out of the Levite outpost."

"And you join us?"

"No, you don't get me."

"Excuse me?"

"You get the data-pad. I know you can use it. We don't want to get caught with it. You help us, we help you."

Grent and Kane whisper back and forth for a few moments. Spike appears over my shoulder. "Well, that's an interesting solution."

Grent nods. "Okay." He extends his hand. "Give us the data-pad, and we will do it."

"I don't have it. But you have my word, I'll get it to you."

"Doesn't work that way, friend. You pay up-front."

"It does today. We have an open window to rescue him. Trains are stopped. I couldn't get you data-pad right now if I wanted to. I'll leave my tracker on; I assume that's in the card you gave me. That way if I don't come through, you know right where to find me."

Grent exhales loudly. "I see why you like him, Kane. All right. You've got a deal. One condition." He pauses. "Consider what we could do together. No commitment. Just promise to think it over."

"Deal. Now, let's go."

Grent and I shake hands. The four of us make our way to Main Street North. Kane seems oddly upbeat.

"We are going to have a good time, friend. Let's go get your boy." Aww. Kane may be the only friend I've ever made by punching them in face. Weird way to bond.

We reach the Levite outpost—a tall, white stone building with no windows. The building backs up to the North train station platform, providing easy access for Levites traveling to the Temple Sector. Levites have an outpost in every sector. How they get in and out is mysterious. We rarely see Levites just walking around or moving between places. Victor thinks they use underground tunnels. Who knows? When they show up, they are always on a mission.

Kane opens his data-pad, and the projected screen flashes to life. From his pocket, he pulls what looks like an access card. He swipes the card over the reader on the door. The soft hum of the electric current fizzles and disappears. It's like I didn't realize I was hearing it until the sound was gone. Kane grins as the door to the Levite outpost springs open.

"We'll take care of the guards. You find your friend," Kane says with a nod as we slip inside. The entryway is a small rectangular room with alternating white and gold tiles lining the floors and the walls. Midway up the walls are two separated golden stripes with evenly spaced plaques between them. A large, intricate chandelier hangs from the ceiling. Each side of the rectangular entryway hosts a single frosted glass door. Straight ahead is a hallway that comes to a 'T' about thirty yards down.

Kane and Grent take the left hall. Spike and I go right. We pass through a frosted glass door that slides open automatically as we approach. The hallway is decorated in similar fashion. At its end, it opens up to what looks like a herding pen for livestock. Rather than livestock, its evenly arranged, squared-off desks create a little personal space for two dozen people to work. The hallway is separated from the worker pen by a solid marble half-wall with mostly transparent projection screens running up the rest of the way. Spike grabs my arm and points to a digital sign on the wall that reads "Holding Cell" with an arrow.

We follow the arrow to another frosted glass door. Through it we can see a shadowed silhouette inside. Telmen—it has to be. To the right of the door is a circular button with a red ring around it. I push it. The ring turns green, and the door cracks open.

Telmen's face and neck are decorated with some sizable bruises of blue and purple. He has some minor cuts over his eye and lips as well as some dried blood on his nose. I assume his clothing is covering more of the same. We scoop him up, sliding our shoulders under his arms and help carry him out. For perhaps the first time in his entire life, Telmen doesn't talk.

For a scrawny guy, Telmen is surprisingly heavy. We drag him down the hall and back out the way we came. We reach the entryway when I hear a loud crashing sound. A moment later, Grent and Kane appear rushing down the hall.

"All good, let's go," Kane says, not waiting for us and pushing his way out the door. He holds the door open so we can drag Telmen out. It takes us half an hour to lug him across the Market Square and down Main Street West, far enough from the Levite outpost. We finally find a place to stop. Telmen keeps slumping to the ground as if his limbs are made of gooey pudding.

"Looks like his damage is mostly cosmetic. That's good," Kane says examining Telmen. "You have a place to stay tonight?"

Spike's head slumps. We are stuck in the Market for the rest of the night. Haven't encountered a beggar gang yet, but if we stay out on the streets that will change. It's not like we can just wander the streets with semi-conscious Telmen all night long. Staying with Kane is the best of our bad options. Kane leads us to a jewelry store on Street Three, "Shine for Shine" written on a sign above the door. The Patriarch is all about symmetry and order. The shops in the Market Square alternate between two and three stories. The two-story shops extend about four feet further out than the three-story ones. Shine for Shine is a three-story shop with a flat roof and nice, freshly painted green shutters bordering the windows. The forceshield disappears, and we step inside.

The storeroom is filled with jewelry. Shelves with glittering necklaces and earrings line the walls. Clear display cases separate the merchant area from the customer area. Kane leads us past the displays and through a door to the back of the store. Here, there are even more display cases, though these appear to be more for storage than actual use. Grent pushes one of the cases, sliding it out of the way effortlessly. I hear a click. A rectangular piece of the floor drops down about a foot and slides back, creating an open staircase into a secret basement.

Spike, still serving as a human crutch for Telmen, follows Kane's lead. We move down the stairs, descending into a large circular room with tunnels zig-zagging in every direction. Not the work of the Patriarch, it was far too chaotic for their taste.

"These lead all over the Market Sector," Kane explains, pointing to the tunnels. There are at least a dozen people moving around a table in the center of the room, discussing, examining charts, moving pieces around on what appears to be a digital diagram.

We follow Kane down a series of winding tunnels into a tunneled-out room that appears to be sleeping quarters. Hammocks hang from the walls four levels high with ladders placed sporadically. The open dirt of the earth is covered by gridded wooden beams. It makes our rundown home look like a king's palace. There are lanes between the hammocks, giving a semblance of order to the room.

We make our way deeper into the Nightling base and discover another room, this one lined with actual beds. Not nice beds—beds that seem to have survived a battle with a pack of wolves. Each beat-up mattress has a single blanket and pillow.

We lay Telmen down on one, and he lets out a slow, almost satisfied groan. A young girl, maybe late teens with golden blonde hair and ruby red lips, walks in with a tray of water and what appears to be soup. I sit down on the mattress next to Telmen; it's been a long day.

"What's your history with Grent?" Kane asks, squaring off with Spike.

"Not sure what ye mean, brotha,"

"Yes, you do. Don't play salvage with me."

Spike grins. "My history tis not any of yer business, now is it?"

Kane lifts a finger, holding it perilously close to Spike's face. "Fine. But if you get in the way of what we are doing, you will regret it."

"I've no interest in playing rebel in Grent's little game. Mind yer finger, brotha, or I may have to take it from ye."

Kane smiles, a glint of respect in his eye. He drops his finger. "You can stay here until your friend is able to leave. After that, you sign up or you get out."

Kane steps out of the room, leaving us alone to rest. I lie back on the bed.

"Soooo…"

"Yea?" Spike asks.

"We are in the middle of a Nightling secret underground base."

"Yup," Spike responds holding out the sound dramatically.

"That's ummm…different."

"Yup."

"Found Telmen though."

"Yup."

"I bet Victor's going to be nuked."

"Yup."

CHAPTER NINE

Thundering boots wake me. Chaos surrounds us as Nightlings in blue-grey hooded cloaks rush down the halls. Electricity surges through my body as panic combats weariness. My eyelids are weighted down by some invisible force too heavy to hold open for long. It feels like my brain is being blended into a smoothie of confusion as a I try to grasp what's happening.

Spike's words send an illuminating course of adrenaline through my veins, "Ambush." The sweet symphony of the skirmish above confirms his decree.

I'm on my feet. Everything moves in slow motion. Telmen stirs in the bed next to me. I shake the mattress under him, and he groans in protest. I shake the bed again. Finally, he sits up slowly, rubbing his eye with the palm of his hand. Spike and I help Telmen up and start guiding him down the winding passageway under the jewelry shop. He seems to be moving better, but his legs are still shaky. When we reach the main room, a group of Nightlings are rushing up the stairs toward the commotion above.

"Think this is the only way out?" I ask, glancing over at Spike.

"I doubt it, but it's the only one we know of."

I lean Telmen against the planning table in the middle of the room. Sitting on a shelf nearby, I find two energy blades. I toss one to Spike; I'm not about to give Telmen a weapon in his condition. I snap the sheath over my belt and slip the hilt inside it.

"Stay with him, I'll go check it out."

Spike nods. I make my way up the stairs into the back room of the jewelry shop. The clash is even louder here. I keep my body low, sliding into the main room behind a display case. I peek my head over the glass to get a view of the street outside. The jewelry store sits right next to a large streetlight which provides surprisingly good visibility. Disbelief sweeps over me. The street is lined with a least a dozen bodies. Blood runs down the grey stone street as if it had been raining from the sky. A metallic smell stings my nostrils, blown in through the open door of the shop.

At least two dozen men are fighting, some with fists, some with energy weapons of various kinds, knives mostly by the look of it. The grey-blue cloaks of the Nightlings seem to be outnumbered by the deep brown cloaks of the attackers. On the brown cloaks, I see a white wolf head inside a flaming circle. This is too far even for Heywin—attacking the Nightlings just to get at us. It's crazy.

Grent and Kane are standing back-to-back in the middle of the street, fighting off the overwhelming number of Fire Wolves. We need to get out of here. Crawling on my hands and knees, I return to the backroom. When we came in, I was more focused on our situation than our surroundings. The shop has a back door. I descend the stairs in a rush and motion for Spike to follow.

The back door opens with the grinding creak caused by irregular use. Outside, the street looks clear. I step out to confirm. Just as I do, the door slams closed behind me. Whirling around I see a man in a brown cloak, holding what appears to be an energy axe. He's a short, stout man with a large scar running across his neck.

"Well, look at who I found. Trying to sneak out the back like the rodent you are? Looks like I'll be getting the bonus."

"Give me a break. We aren't a part of this. Just let us go, and we'll be on our way."

Bill laughs. "Oh that's rich. Not a part of it? Why do you think we're here? Heywin's got it bad for you. Promised a reward to anyone who brought you to him. He wasn't really particular about the breathing part. I warned you. Now, you've insulted us for the last time."

"Insult you? How did I insult you?"

"You attacked our pack, refused to repay your debt. Now, you will pay with your blood."

My hand slides to the sheath on my belt as I step back from the Fire Wolf enforcer. "You got it backwards. Your guys tried to kill me. I just defended myself."

Bill swings his axe at my chest with an upward arc. Jumping back, I narrowly avoid the blade. I pull out the energy knife and click it on. A six-inch, blue, glowing beam in the shape of a double-edged knife shimmers to life. Victor had insisted we all learn how to handle ourselves in a fight, a skill that has come in handy on numerous occasions. Those fights were different; they lacked murderous intent. This one doesn't. Bill swings again. This time I duck under his attack. Lunging forward, I thrust my knife at his chest. He side-steps and turns. My knife finds only air. He grabs my extended arm with his free hand and brings his axe back right at my neck. I arch my back and drop my head as low as I can with his grip on my arm. The heat of the energy passes over me in a whirl. I manage to pull my arm free, but his axe is already hurling toward my face.

My knife collides with his axe, causing a bright flash of light and a loud cracking, popping sound. I stumble back from the force of his swing. I plant my feet, trying to recover. As I turn, Bill lifts his axe above his head, bringing it down toward me. My eyes close instinctively as I wait for the blow. Nothing. The scent of cooking meat wafts over me. Bill stands still, a glowing blue tip sticking through his chest, the heat from the blade charring the skin around it. The blade disappears, and

Bill crumbles to his knees where he rests for a moment before collapsing to the ground.

Standing behind him, Spike tucks his knife away. "Sorry it took me so long, brotha. Had to set Telmen down. The door was a wee bit stuck."

I prop my body up on my knees, shaking my head as I catch my breath. "Your timing was perfect. Had him right where I wanted him." Spike laughs and returns to the shop to retrieve Telmen.

"We need to get off the streets," I say as he comes back out, helping to hold Telmen up. Spike nods, looking around as best he can with Telmen hanging on him. The commotion starts moving our way. I rush over to the side of the building and peek around the corner. A handful of Fire Wolves are rushing down the alley toward us.

"Back inside!" I shout, moving around the door Spike propped open. The door slams closed just as we hear angry voices outside of it.

"The roof!" Spike commands as he adjusts under the weight of Telmen's mostly limp body as it starts to slump. "Tis a flat roof. Has to be stairs somewhere."

I make my way around the room. In the front right corner, I find it. The door was painted to blend into the wall, and the handle has been removed to camouflage it even further. I push on one side, and the door slides in. Behind it is a hidden set of stairs. We make our way up two flights to the third floor. The stairway gets narrow. We sandwich Telmen between us and help him up to the door leading to the roof.

The roof provides a short ledge, easy to look over, with a great view of the streets below. At least from here we can wait things out for a while, give Telmen a little more time to recover in the event we need to run. We slide him down so his back is pressed against the ledge of the roof.

Kane and Grent are still standing back-to-back in the middle of the street, a moat of dead Fire Wolves surrounding them. At least there was something behind the legend of Grent.

"The Fire Wolves could win. They have a lot more people than the Nightlings. What happens to the rebellion then?" I comment almost absently.

"This appears to be the majority of the Fire Wolves, but it's not even a portion of the Nightlings. The Nightlings operate all over the city. This is one base, probably not even their main one. I may not trust Grent, but there aren't many who can beat him in a fight."

We watch for a few minutes. Despite lacking in numbers, the Nightlings are much better fighters. Most of the bodies on the ground belong to Fire Wolves. Then I see him just at the edge of the fighting, Heywin Varel. He is screaming orders, trying to push his gang forward, but they are slowly withdrawing. The fighting moves further and further from the shop. With each passing moment, the number of Fire Wolves in the fray lessens. I should feel relieved. I don't. Something about this makes my blood boil. Why are we fighting each other when we have a greater enemy to deal with?

I slide down next to Telmen. I've seen enough. My data-pad reads four in the morning.

"It'll be over soon," Spike says with a peculiar confidence. "Takes about an hour for the clean-up crews to get rid of the bodies, which they will need to do before the Red Caps return."

"Get rid of the bodies?"

Spike sighs. "Aye, on the south side of the Market there is a butcher shop with an incinerator. One crew will take the bodies there while the other washes the blood from the streets. They take a final pass to collect any debris or weapons. By the time the Red Caps show up, ye'd never know there was a fight to begin with."

"How do you...?" I start, not even sure how to phrase the question. He was a little older than I am now when we first met almost ten years ago. Yet, he seems to know more than he should about beggar gang fights. It's almost like he had a whole life before I knew him.

"Not my first sleepover in the Market, brotha. Patriarch couldn't care less about Undesirables killing each other. We're doing them a favor, population control and all that. But if merchants start finding blood and bodies on the streets, then the Patriarch's farce of being all loving and protecting goes out the window. So, they don't care what we do at night, so long as we clean up our mess after."

"We?"

Spike chuckles. "Aye, ye didn't know that? I grew up here. Lived here until Vic found me. Even then spent a few years coming back at night when everyone else was asleep. Not easy just walking away from a beggar gang."

"But you'd have been like—"

"Aye, I was a boy. Beggar gangs don't care how old you are. I was born into it ye know. Parents were in. Nothing to be done about it."

"But—"

"That's enough story for tonight. We need to be getting back soon as da train's start running. Get some rest. I'll keep watch." I'm too tired to argue. My eyelids fall like anvils, and the world drifts away into black.

My body jerks, and my eyes open. I squint in surprise as it's already bright out. I must have slept through the morning trumpet that heralds the start of a new day. Telmen is back on his feet, talking with Spike. The streets below are in a flurry of commotion: Red Caps pacing, merchants in their purple sashes opening shops while other vendors set up the carts and stalls in their assigned spaces. It's like a coordinated dance of purple sashes turning empty streets into a lively market ready for business. Even from this distance, I can see the white rectangular frames on their shoulders. Inside the frame is each person's identification number, a less-than-subtle reminder that we aren't people. Just numbers. The Patriarch may be a bunch of controlling tyrants, but they get points for efficiency.

The sea of purple sashes flows down the streets. Colorful canopies, decorative carts, flags, fruits, flowers, and all sorts of goodies line the streets in place of the bodies that lined them the night before. The transformation is almost hypnotic to watch.

The first train arrives, and a wave of yellow sashes pours out of the train cars and moves into the Market. The educators have arrived.

"Train's here," I announce. "We should get going." I start moving toward the door to the stairs.

"Hold on, brotha," Spike stops. "Can't take the first train out without raising suspicion. Plus, need to get Telmen some food so he can walk on his own. Let's go down and get some breakfast. We can head out after we eat."

"Okay, you head down. I'll be down shortly." I returned to my vantage point on the roof, taking a long look out over the city. I'd never been up this high before. In all the chaos of the night before, I didn't appreciate the view. Something about being up above the calamity of the streets below felt freeing.

The next train unloads the farmers donning their green sashes. What was once a sea of purple slowly becomes a swirl of mixing colors. Craftsmen are in orange, miners in black, doctors and scientists in white, utility workers in blue, artists in pink, financial workers in silver, all brewing together in the organized pandemonium of the Market Square.

Downstairs, I find Telmen finishing up his second bowl of soup. It's good to see he's feeling better and, as if by magic, not talking. Kane, who is standing by the door to the showroom of the jewelry store, waves me over.

"You guys okay?" I ask.

Kane grins. "Course, was quite the night."

"You enjoyed that?"

"Nothing like almost dying to make you feel alive."

Kane is a crazy person. Good to know. "Do you know why they attacked?"

"Gang pride. Said you owed them a debt. They tried to strong-arm us. It didn't work out."

I shake my head. "Heywin?"

"He's a dead man. He just doesn't know it yet. The weasel stayed out of the fight as much as he could. Then he ran off like a coward when he saw they were losing." Kane shrugs.

"I feel like we should thank you," I start.

Kane shrugs again. "Nobody comes to our house dictating terms."

"Still, thanks."

Kane nods. Spike steps up behind me and puts his hand on my shoulder.

"Ye ready to go, brotha?"

We say goodbye to Kane and Grent, who again tries to get us to join the Nightlings, and we make our way to the train. When we reach the house, I see Brelar peek his head around the corner and then duck back out of sight chuckling to himself for evading detection.

"I see Mister Jett. I sneaky," I hear his little voice giggling from behind the wall followed by his excited quick stomping of feet. Little Brelar, so proud of himself.

Victor is sitting in the living room, waiting. He doesn't look like he slept at all last night. He stands up as we enter.

"How are you?" Victor asks, a tone of nervous agitation in his voice.

"We're stocked now. Don't worry." It takes the better part of an hour to explain the whole story, from Telmen's arrest to the deal with Grent to the street fight.

"Well." Victor pauses for a long time. "You did the right thing going back. Though I am concerned you brought back the wrong Telmen. This one is quiet." Victor smirks playfully.

Telmen grins and nods. "It's me. Still a little out of it."

"And Grent is active again?"

Spike nods. "Aye, and he's got a good network already up and running."

Victor shakes his head. "That's not good. Between the Assessors and the Nightlings, the Market is too hot. We can't risk sending in teams, but we need supplies."

"So, what do we do?" I ask.

"We'll have to make do with the Farmlands. At least it's something. You three better go get some rest. I'll take care of the others."

Spike helps Telmen up the stairs to his bed. I hang back.

"Not sleeping?" Victor asks in response to my lingering.

"Little wired from everything. Plus, I need to talk with you."

Victor motions with his head and walks over to the couch, sitting down and waiting. I walk over and join him.

"I just watched two groups of Undesirables killing each other."

Victor nods. "Yeah, I imagine that's hard. That's why we avoid the Market at night."

"That's not what's bothering me."

"Oh, well please, do tell."

I sigh and try to organize my thoughts in the cyclone of emotions the last day brought on. "So many people dead over nothing."

Victor nods. "It's the way things are, Jett. It's not pretty, but—"

"It's not how they should be. This is why no one has any hope. You can't win if you don't fight the right enemy. We should be rallying together, uniting the people. If we stop fighting each other, maybe we could actually put up a fight against the Patriarch."

Victor shakes his head. "One night in the Market with Grent and you're already talking like a Nightling. Jett, what you're suggesting..." Victor stops himself to take a breath.

"What I don't get is how you can sit back and do nothing. I don't mean that as an accusation. I mean, you are brilliant. Your ideas, your plans—don't tell me you couldn't devise a way to bring down the Patriarch. I know you've thought about it."

Victor shrugs. "Sure, I've thought about it. Who hasn't?"

"Are you saying there's no way to do it?" I challenge, a note of disbelief in my voice.

"I'm not saying that. I'm saying, the only way I can think of to do it would cost far more than I'm willing to pay."

"Really?" I sit up and lean in. "What price could possibly be too high? These are the people who killed our parents. They abuse their power and force us to live like animals. You've the seen the Rim. Freedom, real freedom, is worth any price."

"You say that. But if you can't live with yourself afterwards, what's the point of changing the world?"

"I just..."

"Jett, you have to understand. The Patriarch is like a turtle. Whatever vulnerabilities they have are protected by this great big, armored shell."

"Ok, so, it's not going to be easy, but, I'd rather fight. I'd rather do something than just take what they give me."

"I understand the desire. Blindly rushing into a fight you can't win, just because you're not happy with how things are, doesn't help anyone. It just leaves a hole in the lives of the people who care about you."

My mind rushes to his dad. He's gracious enough to not come out and say it, but he said enough to prove his point. Maybe it is better to not fight than to fight for a cause you can't win.

I shrug. "Maybe you're right. But maybe the most powerful weapon the Patriarch has is their ability to convince us we can't win. It just...it seems like dying for something...well it's a lot better than those people dying for nothing. If there was a chance, even a small chance, we could make the city better, wouldn't that be worth the risk?" I need to tell Victor about what happened with the guard and Lilly. Maybe if he knew how people responded, knew that someone actually stood up to the Patriarch, maybe he'd consider it. Or maybe he'd say something smart like, one is not a big sample size. Either way, my mind feels too sluggish to keep going. I wave my hand dismissively. "I don't know. Maybe I should get some sleep."

Every time I shut my eyes, I see bodies lining the streets of the Market. Blood flowing like the rapids of a river. Voices, ghastly and distant, cry out for help, begging me to save them.

It's already dark when I wake up. I look over to Telmen's bed, empty. Downstairs I hear Olivia yelling at Jensen. Again. Apparently, he'd stolen some make-up and given it to Becka, telling her if she used it boys might notice her. Somehow, whenever a guy says something stupid, girls always rally together. Or maybe it's just Jensen. Anytime there is conflict, we can always assume it is Jensen's fault.

Weirdly, their argument gives me a sense of peace. After everything that happened, it was good to know that somethings hadn't changed.

"What are you so upset about? I was trying to be helpful!" Jensen protests. He seems genuinely unaware of where his effort went wrong.

"Ugh! You are hopeless! Just apologize and shut up!"

"Okay, fine, sheesh. I thought eating more was supposed to make you less cranky," Jensen replies. Always shoveling deeper.

"You better watch yourse-" Olivia warns, her hands planted on her hips, shoulder cocked sideways.

"What? She's obviously been putting on some weight, she shoul—"

The slap echoes across the room as Olivia's hand bursts across Jensen's face. "You don't talk about her, or any girl like that," Olivia holds a finger up to Jensen's face.

"What are you so nuked about, I was trying to help," Jensen protests rubbing his face in his hand.

"No, what you were trying to do is make her look like you think she should, as if her value has to be tied to her appearance. If you can't appreciate her for who she is without pressuring her to look a certain way or act a certain way, then you are a pathetic excuse for a man." Olivia and Jensen go at it a lot, but, I've never heard her this aggressive. It's like he struck a nerve.

"But yo-"

"Brotha, ye got to learn when to just stop talking," Spike pats Jensen on the shoulder as Jensen continues to rub his cheek.

A silence falls over the room as I sit down at the table. Olivia walks around and sits next to me to get as far from Jensen as possible. Silence hovers still. I look around not sure if I am missing something or supposed to say something.

"They are waiting for you to tell them about Grent," Spike finally explains.

"Oh, I thought Telmen and his endless stream of words would have already done that," I joke. The response is a series of uncomfortable smiles. That should get at least a mild chuckle. What did I miss? "Wait, where is Telmen?"

"He's outside with Gibbs. Hasn't said much since he got up. Whatever the Levites did, certainly did a number on him," Victor said glancing out the window where Telmen could be seen sitting on a rocking chair. Without a word, I get up and make my way outside.

Telmen is rocking slowly, absently, back and forth in his chair. I kneel down in his line of sight and put my hand on his knee. "Hey, buddy. How you feeling?"

Telmen shakes his head at first. We sit in silence for a minute. "Some Commander grabbed me when I was on my way out of the Market. Dragged me out to a podium. Made a big show of turning me over to the Levites. Said I was going to be interrogated until he got what he wanted. Then they kept asking me questions. Questions I didn't know the answers to. When I told them I didn't know, they..." his voice trails off.

"I'm sorry. It's my fault. I left you behind. If I had been there—"

Telmen shakes his head. "No, it's not on you. You came back for me. Saved me. I don't know how."

"You only needed saving because I heaped up in the first place. Never leave your partner. That's rule one."

"If you'd been there, they just would have grabbed you too. That Commander, he's desperate. He's ruthless."

Almost a week passes. Victor sends everyone out to the Farmlands every day— everyone but me. On occasion Becka hangs back as well to keep me company. The rest of the time I am alone. I have to stay home, chop wood, twiddle my thumbs, combat epic boredom. Victor says it's too dangerous for me to go anywhere until we get a better understanding of what Grent is doing. My days consist of sleeping, eating, chopping wood, thinking of Lilly, watching Patriarch propaganda as it pops up on the screens.

My favorite is an advertisement encouraging enlistment. It's a cartoon of a young man walking down the street, wearing rags and looking depressed. He pulls his pockets inside out. Nothing but dust falls from them. Then he walks past a recruitment poster. He pushes the ad and is covered by a cloud of cartoon smoke. When the cloud disappears, his rags have been replaced by a black and red lined uniform. He strolls the streets with confidence. People take notice of him.

An unseen voice says, "Tired of the low life? Searching for a place in the world? Are you ready for a purpose? Ready to make a difference? Enlist now! Dios Military Training Program provides exciting opportunities, adventure, and a sense of value to your life. That's not all. At the end of your twenty-year contract, your family will be given Class B status! That's right, this special offer gives you meaning and advancement. Sign up today and change your future!"

The hypocrisy is so painfully obvious it's a wonder no one sees it. How does offering advancement fit with their forced conformity? I guess they realized that people will tolerate pretty much anything if you offer them the illusion of choice. What a load of shinshew. You can't beat us so join us. For the low, low price of your soul, after twenty years, your family status will be elevated to a higher class of sheep. You're welcome. Of course, the training program is just a nice way of indoctrination. It's clever, really. Condition people to comply, to fit in, to keep their heads down while offering a program for those who would resist it. Either way, they win.

The day drifts along like a cloud without wind. I sit outside, watching the sky darken as I wait for the others to return from the Farmlands. Brelar is running around swinging a stick with one hand, carrying his bird blanket in the other, yelling at invisible monsters before dropping the stick to chase after a blue jay that flies by.

"Mister Jett, there's a bird," he shouts out gleefully pointing at the branch where the winged rodent resides. I smile back. "Oh, he's blueee." I don't know how that kid maintains his sense of awe every time he sees a bird, but he does.

Becka sits down next to me as I stare up at the sky, mind wandering anyplace but here. She sets a drink down on the little table next to my chair and then sits on the other side of it with a dramatic sigh.

"Don't worry, you're not going to be stuck here forever," her voice is soft and comforting, but also confident.

"I can't just sit around anymore. I get it's dangerous to go out, but this may be worse." My complaint was interrupted by an official message from The Order.

"Citizens of Dios," comes the weak and weathered voice of High Father Ignatius. His sunken leathered face appears a moment later. "I was asked by the Ruling Counsel to share a word of encouragement with you. I know these have been trying times and rumors are spreading that may have caused fear and anxiety. In such times, I find comfort in the Sacred Text, which says: we are one when we are the same. When we are one, we are saved. Fear not my children, these rumors are baseless. All is under control. The Middling Days have proven to once again to be wonderfully successful. May the blessings of Bealz shine upon you! Good day." The light of the screens fades with a hiss.

I roll my eyes, "Why do people listen to him?"

"They believe," Becka leans in as she looks at me. "Hundreds of years ago, just before the building of the domed cities, Bealz had a servant. This servant followed him and honored him so faithfully that Bealz made a pact with him. Bealz promised that he would provide for and protect the human race through the bloodline of his servant. Through him and his heirs, Bealz would bless humanity. If the servant's bloodline was ever broken, Bealz would sever his ties to this world and leave humanity to destroy itself. The Order teaches that the High Father isn't just the prophet of Bealz, his bloodline is the only thing keeping Bealz from abandoning us to death and destruction."

"Why have I never heard that? They teach you this in Temple?"

Becka smiles, "yes, and they teach it to every student of every class, which means-"

I shake my head, "we got skipped over just like with everything else."

Becka and I spend the rest of the afternoon talking about her time as a Potter in training. She teaches me all sorts of things about the Order and how it uses the faith of the people to help mold them into what the High Father wants them to be. We chat until the sun starts to set and the rest of our friends return.

Finally, after days and a great deal of insistence, Victor promised we could go to the Lazy Loafer after dinner. If I spend one more day locked up in the house, I'm going to lose my mind. Everyone is excitedly getting ready and talking about the day. Victor is cooking dinner when I corner him.

"Hey, I was thinking, the Assessors should be moving out of the Market Sector. We can probably start going back there."

"I was thinking that as well."

"Good, I want to come."

"Jett." Victor puts down the pan he's stirring potatoes in.

"I can't stay cooped up in this house anymore. With the Assessors out, it's not as dangerous. Once I get that data-pad to Grent, that danger should be done too. So…"

Victor exhales loudly. "I'm not sure giving the data-pad to Grent is a smart play."

"We made a deal. I can't imagine going back on that deal will be good for us."

Victor nods. "Yeah, you're right about that. No choice, I guess. I just wish we had more time. I'd like to figure out what's on it."

"Let me take it to them tomorrow. I may be able to get something out of them."

"Fine, but I'm coming with you."

After dinner, we head to the Lazy Loafer. Finally, an escape from my prison home. The main level of the Lazy Loafer is perpetually raucous, which is one of the reasons we stay on the lower level. Over time, the upstairs uproar becomes like white noise. As the others head downstairs, I look around for Lilly, hoping she will be there. I can't find her. I check with the bartender to see if she's seen her. She tells me she hasn't been by in about a week. Suddenly, I feel uneasy. Has something happened to her? Was she caught by an Assessor? I try to convince myself everything is okay, but my stomach feels unsettled. I push the thoughts from my mind as best I can. I need to enjoy being out of the house for a bit.

"Clocks ticking, last chance to get your entries in! Want to win a date with the girl of your dreams? Put up your credits and you'll get your chance. All you have to do is fool her." Telmen shouts to a group of five men congregating around our table. "Give me your answer cards and line up. You know how the game works so don't get cute. Win and you get a date with Olivia, the beautiful lie detector. Lose, and you buy us all drinks. I have your answer cards so you can't cheat."

The five men huddle in front of our table forming a human wall. I'll have to wait for this to be over before I join the others. They play this game every night. The rules are always the same: the guys each make a statement or tell a story about themselves. Olivia has to guess if the story is true or if they made it up. If she gets the answer right, they have to buy us all drinks and leave her alone for the rest of the night. If she gets the answer wrong, she has to go on a date with them. She's been playing for over a year and has never had to go on a date. Plus, we never have to pay for drinks.

Each man tells her their story. Olivia listens and then waits for the next one. Once they are all finished Olivia leans back and points at them one at a time.

"True. Lie. Lie. True. Lie," she smiles sweetly. Each of the men grumbles and dramatically huffs off away from the table. A few minutes later the bartender arrives shaking her head laying down several trays of drinks.

"You're going to have to teach me how you do that," the bartender says.

"It's easy," Olivia smiles. "They are men. If they tell you a story that makes them look good, they are probably lying. If it makes them look silly, they are probably telling the truth."

The bartender laughs, "It's more complicated than that isn't it?"

Olivia winks in response and the bartender walks off.

We joke and laugh for a while relaxing in our favorite booth tucked in the corner of the lower level and enjoying the free drinks. It's nice to relax for a bit and not worry about everything. That's when we hear it. Silence. Complete, deafening silence. We all look at each other, and instinct hushes us all, even Telmen. Victor gestures with his head, and I follow him toward the stairs while the others remain at the table.

My heart is in my mouth as we climb the stairs. We move at a slow, agonizing pace to keep from disturbing the precariously noiseless room. We reach the stair's summit. Everyone is standing up, still as statues. A room full of people, and not even a breath can be heard between them. My heart plummets from my throat into the depths of my stomach. They are all staring at the door. My body turns slowly, as if being tugged by invisible arms. That's when I see them. Lined up in front of the door, blocking it completely, are two rows of Red Caps, a half dozen Levites, and a pair of Assessors.

My first instinct is to run, flee back down the stairs to the illusion of safety. Victor's grip on my arm steadies me. I force a breath from my lungs and assume the statuesque posture of the rest of the room.

The two Assessors are dressed in their identical white robes with their blank masks covering their faces. The one on the left is almost a half-foot taller and noticeably thinner than his counterpart. The short, round Assessor stands a little further into the room, looking down at the screen projected from the data-pad on his wrist. He starts talking.

"All citizens of Dios are to comply with random skill assessments to screen and better identify potential threats to the peace and safety of our city. Non-compliance will be viewed as an act of treason and is punishable by death or exile to the Outlands. Individuals found with exceptional quality may be selected for adoption into higher class. Any individual believed to be disunified from the standards of the community may be detained for further testing. Do you understand these rights as they have been read to you?" His tone is robotic. As he finishes, his masked face turns up and scans the room.

Silent nods confirm group compliance. The bulbous Assessor waves one arm, and the Red Caps swarm into the room, herding us into two organized lines. The Levites remain at the doors.

The Patriarch likes to keep things orderly. Anyone or anything that doesn't fit into their little box, they discard. It's the message of every Chapel service. 'The World that Was collapsed because people were different. Those differences led to war and would have destroyed mankind, had it not been for the founders of the Patriarch.' The Order teaches that differences lead to division. That division leads to disruption. Disruption leads to death. That's the real the purpose of the Middling Days. Identify people who are 'too different' and remove them. They sell it as an exciting opportunity. People buy it. Or at least, they pretend they do. The Middling Days are designed to weed out any outliers in the city. Those who are deemed considerably below average—either too slow, too weak, or too dumb—are gathered up and turned into Outlands Officers. Which is a nice way of saying, they are sentenced to death. They are given some primitive weapons and sent outside the city on a "sacred mission" to help reclaim the Outlands from the Depraved. This is done to help alleviate the burden they place on society.

On the other side, those who the assessors determine to be well above average are either made Outlands Officers or, if their talent is considered useful to the Patriarch, they are taken to the Temple Sector to be indoctrinated. I've never seen anyone return from that. They sell it as an opportunity for men and women of exceptional talent to better themselves. In reality, it is a brilliant tool to keep everyone in line. Can't start the fires of a rebellion if you take away everyone's matches.

"Once you have been screened, you will exit the premises and return home." The two Assessors walk to the front person in each line. A single Levite breaks from the group by the door and stands about ten feet from the first person in each line, as if preparing to receive them. The Assessors simultaneously walk around the front-most person, grabbing arms, poking chests, sizing up each person one at a time. They shout out a command seemingly at random.

The first guy in the fat Assessor's line is given a puzzle, a glowing projection of shapes with a timer at the bottom. He twists the shapes, trying to fit them together. What happens with the timer? If he finishes before time is out, does that make him exceptional? If he fails to complete it before the timer, does that mean he's below average? His survival depends not only on his ability to solve the puzzle but on not being too fast or too slow. My heart pounds. I can feel sweat starting to form on my brow. His best bet will be to finish as close to the timer as possible. He finishes with three seconds left. The Assessors glare at him for a moment. An eternal moment. The whole room exhales as one when the Assessor waves the guy through.

The next man up looks like an oak tree—strong, thickly built.

"Vitality," instructs the Assessor. Two Red Caps come over. They click their energy tools, and a glowing blue burst of current forms into the shape of a rod. The two guards start striking the man in the chest, back, and legs while the Assessor counts. When the oak of a man collapses to his knees, the Red Caps stop striking him and step back, putting away their energy weapons. "Twelve, acceptable." The man is forced to his feet and ushered out the door.

When the testing begins, the room feels tense but energetic. As the testing goes on, the energy fades, as if the collective will of the group is slowly breaking. Remind people of their powerlessness enough, and they will become docile sheep. Some of the tests are as simple as answering a series of multiple-choice questions, while others result in the person being rendered unconscious and dragged from the room. With each test, we step closer to the front of the line, my imagination running wild as I try and guess what test they will do.

Victor gets to the front of the line. The spherical Assessor circles him twice.

"Reflex."

That's not good. I've seen Victor catch a fly mid-air with his fingers. Before I can even process the command, the Levite in front of Victor swings his arm back. A single strand of electric whip from his thrasher zips to life. With a crackling snap, the blue strand of energy hurls toward Victor's face. Victor's hands come up just in time to stop the whip from hitting his face. If he catches the whip and holds on, it will look like a natural reflex, nothing out of the ordinary. Doing so will mean he willfully allows himself to get shocked by the current. If he knocks the whip away, he will spare himself the extreme pain of the current but demonstrate his reflexes are far above normal. His head turns a little, and his eyes meet mine. I see him exhale slowly, holding the strand of the whip. The current pulses through Victor's arms, and he grunts and lets out a scream. Falling to his knees, he grips the elbow of his shocked arm with his free hand. I clench my fists, holding them against my sides to keep myself from reacting. The Assessor waves his hand dismissively, and Victor is ushered out the door by two Red Caps, the shock making his legs too soft to hold his body up. I want to scream. I want to charge the Levite and pummel him into the ground. I take a breath, close my eyes, force myself to release the weights in my shoulders. This is not the time for resistance.

The lanky Assessor bends down to peer into my eyes, his faceless mask covering all but his beady, intrusive gaze. I wonder what he's going to see. What he will want to test? I wonder if he can hear the pounding of my heart in my chest. My anxiety builds to a crescendo as the tall Assessor circles around me.

"Compliance." The word slithers out of his mouth. Immediately, Red Caps grab five people out of line behind me and drag them off to the side. A silver orb is placed on each of their temples. One of them, a young woman maybe in her mid- or late-twenties with long black hair and a petite frame, is separated a few feet from the other four.

"When I command, you will press this button," the Assessor tells me, forcing a small remote into my hand. He pauses, placing a silver orb on each of my temples. His wicked eyes seem to illuminate behind his mask. I tilt my head as I look into his eyes, resisting the urge to question him. Nothing good can come from that.

The remote is a black metal cylinder with a red, glowing button on the top. What happens when I push it? What are these silver orbs supposed to do? Why is he making me push the button? What's the point?

"Press it!" he shouts in my face, his voice mildly distorted through his mask. I turn the remote over in my hand. I hate the idea of pushing this with no idea of what it will cause. I hate being told what to do. I look over at the five people separated from the line. Why did they pick five? Why did they separate the girl from the others? Is this going to do something to them? What would happen to them if I didn't? Better yet, what will happen to them if I do?

"Too slow!" he shouts angrily in my ear. He lifts his arm, revealing his own remote. He presses the glowing, red button. It clicks down. The four people grouped together scream out in pain as little flashes erupt between the silver-orbs and their temples. Each of them clutches the orbs on their head, desperately trying to pull them away as they fall to their knees, still screaming. He releases the button, and the sparks and subsequent screaming stops. The girl, separated from the others stands perfectly still, a look of terror on her face. For some reason, she was unaffected by the shocks.

A burst of pain erupts from my stomach forcing me to clutch my chest and cough. I gasp for breath, trying to replenish the air that was involuntarily released from my lungs. The Assessor catches my shoulder to keep me from falling too far forward, his tight fist pulling away from my stomach.

"If you want to avoid the Outlands, I would think you would obey the instructions of your superiors with a tad bit more haste." Don't punch him in his stupid mask. Don't punch him in his stupid mask. He grabs my hand holding the remote and lifts it up. "Now, let's try this again. Press the button."

Heart thumping in my chest, I look over at the four men being lifted to their feet by the Red Caps behind them. Two of them are older—one whose hair lost the battle of color and one whose hair just lost the battle and fell off. The third man is medium sized and middle-aged with an oversized belly. The last is young, barely a teenager by my guess. If I press the button, they will be electrocuted. If I don't, they will still be electrocuted, but I will risk getting sent to the Outlands. It's going to hurt them anyway, but the sooner I press it, the sooner the test is over. They may even be shocked more if I resist longer.

I turn my head and close my eyes, clicking the button on my remote. Screaming ensues. Not the screaming of four men, but this time of a single girl. My skin crawls. What have I done? I have given in. I just tortured a young girl simply to spare myself.

"Very good. Now, press it again." My head whirls around as I face the Assessor, defiance raging like a fire in my eyes. At this moment, I want to kill him. Anyone who takes pleasure from forcing someone to do this doesn't deserve to live. My teeth grind together, and I seethe. The Assessor wags his long finger in my face. "Either you press or I will. Shall four suffer or just one. Will you obey or will you defy?"

I glare into the lidless void of the man's mask. Why couldn't they just whip me like they did Victor? Why this? The four men look at me deliberately, their faces determined. I see it in their eyes, their wordless message. They aren't pleading. They aren't resisting. They are giving me permission. Permission to let them be shocked. My finger moves off the button.

The girl falls to her knees, screaming, her long black hair covering her face as she catches herself on the floor with her palms. I look at the remote in my hand. The button is still glowing red. As the girl's screams of pain dissipate, they are replaced by the muffled laughter of the Assessor behind the mask.

"So, you thought you'd figure it out. One verses four." The blank-masked face shakes back and forth. "It's not about which remote gets pushed. The results are random. That is twice you have failed to obey a direct command." The Assessor leans in and whispers in my ear, "The next time you fail to obey, it will be worse." A Red Cap pulls his sidearm and points it at the back of the head of the young boy in the group of four. He positions himself in such a way to ensure that I alone can see him. "You should be grateful I'm in such a gracious mood tonight. I will allow your previous indiscretions to go unnoticed. However, every time you fail to obey, I will execute one person at random." He stands back up and speaks loudly. "Now, press the button."

Sweat pours into my eyes, burning like a liquid fire. My palms clam up. I can't afford to wait. I push the button. This time, all five drop to their knees, screaming in pain. No sooner do the Red Caps hoist them back to their feet than I hear the Assessor demand again, "Press the button." I press it. Screaming. Again and again he commands. Again and again I press the button. The shocks aren't random any more. Each time I press, all five collapse in agony. After six rounds, his masked face nods, and a Red Cap pulls the remote from my hands.

"Next," he says as if he hadn't just forced me to torture five people. The Red Caps escort me from the Lazy Loafer, closing the door behind me.

CHAPTER TEN

Before we even get back to the house, I throw up. Victor rubs my back in a futile attempt to comfort me.

"There was nothing you could have done. You know that."

"What I know is I tortured five people tonight—people who didn't do me any harm. The only thing they did was be in the wrong place at the wrong time."

"You know that's not on you. You did what you had to do."

"Right, like always. We do what we must to survive." I can feel my voice rising. I try to calm it, but I'm too worked up. "What's the point of surviving if all we are going to do is keep on surviving? This isn't living. It's a cyclical pattern of not dying."

"You'd rather be dead?" Victor's tone is almost scolding.

"I'd rather risk everything than keep doing nothing. How can you go on like this, Vic? You are not average. You are not normal. We both know you had to force yourself to fail that reflex test. You're fast. You're smart, the smartest man I've ever met. You see things. You understand them. Yet, you hide it. You have to play dumb to fit the mold they forced on us. For what? Scraps? So, you can wake up the next day and play dumb again just to make the Patriarch happy? Crash this, I'm done."

"Jett, you need to take a breath. Calm down. Think." Victor tries to soothe my raging temper, a fruitless endeavor if ever there was one.

"I don't need to be calm. I need to do something. A rebellion is coming. I'm not sitting on the sidelines anymore."

Victor opens his mouth, but before he can speak, the sky lights up and the projection of Lorth Drant appears. He walks through his typical spiel about protecting law and order in Dios. This time the winner of the Outlands Lottery is a young mother. Her crime: assaulting a Levite for having her son flogged. Allegedly she struck the Levite repeatedly in an attempt to kill him. More likely she grabbed his hand in an effort to stop him. My stomach turns. How long can we really sit idly by while this happens? When justice is a corrupt instrument to serve the whims of the elite then peace is nothing more than a justification of cowards too scared to stand up for what is right.

When the sky-cast ends, Victor shakes his head. The rest of the group comes over to us as we stand facing each other in stubborn silence. Jensen decides he's not interested in our discussion and heads home. Becka chases after him, scolding him so loudly we can hear them long after the dark of night shrouds them from view.

Telmen starts in on us with, "What's going on? You guys having a staring contest? You mad? You debating? What are you debating? I like debating but it seems weird to do at a time like this. What were your tests? How do you pass them? Mine—"

"We can't keep going like this, and you know it," I declare, interrupting Telmen's torrent of endless words. "We have to fight."

"What are you guys talking about?" Olivia asks. "Fight who?"

"Jett wants to run off and join Grent's little rebellion," Victor grunts out.

"Why are ye so determined to join him, brotha?" Spike asks.

I whirl around to face Spike, pointing my finger at him. "Because he's not pretending this is all okay. He's not hiding and hoping that one day things will accidentally get better. Change doesn't happen like that. You want something to be different, you have to make it different."

"And ye think getting yerself killed on some daft fool's errand is going to make things different, do ye?"

"I think I'd rather die a fool than live as a coward." I don't mean it to come across as an accusation, but I know it does. "Spike, every day people are killing each other in the Market. Why? The Patriarch considers them to be lesser human beings. Based on what? Nothing. Why should the Patriarch live in luxury and excess while we struggle and starve? I don't understand how you can just keep pretending this is all okay. It's not right. The more we ignore it, the more we become part of the problem."

"Aye, yer right. This city is broken. Let's just say ye join this little rebellion. Let's say, by sheer dumb luck, ye actually win. Then what happens?"

I stare at him, confused. "We change things."

"Aye, and who makes those changes, brotha? How many lives will be lost to change the world and right all these wrongs, ye see? How many innocent people will have to die to make yer dream of a better world come true?" I blink, mouth gaping, too stunned to respond. "When you stand victorious over the tyranny of the Patriarch, are ye absolutely sure the leaders who take their place will be any better? If yer not, then yer just getting a lot of people killed for nothing, aren't ya?"

"You think we should just sit back and do nothing to oppose this governmental oppression? You don't think we need a revolution?"

"Aye, revolution is grand idea. It's nothing more than a spinning wheel. In the end, there will be rich and poor. There will be luxury and struggle. Bad things will happen. Innocent people will die. For all yer fighting, killing, dying, the world's going to have the same problems.

Brotha, revolution doesn't change the world. It just changes who runs it."

My mouth stings as my teeth grind against each other. "We can set the people free, remove the classes, stop the segregation, give everyone an equal chance. We can build a society that is free."

"Yer forgetting one thing, brotha," Spike says shaking his head.

"Yea, and what's that?"

"Grent."

"What about him?"

"Ye think he's doing all this to give power back to the people? He's not fighting to rescue the people. He's fighting to rule them."

"Well, something is better than the nothing we're doing, isn't it? What makes you think you know what Grent wants?" I snap.

"Well, he used to be Grent's right-hand man," Victor interjects. "During the last rebellion, Spike and his sister Talia fought alongside Grent. They raised an army, marched the Temple Sector, even got the Patriarch to parlay. The Holy Father offered better conditions for the Plebs. He promised citizenship to every man, woman, and child in Dios, forever ending the classless Undesirables."

"What? That would...so why didn't they?"

"In return, the Patriarch demanded that Grent disband his forces and that he and he alone would leave the city, never to return. They even offered safe passage to Marthon if he would just sign the peace agreement."

"He didn't sign it?"

Victor shook his head. "No, he did not. Instead, he demanded they surrender the city to him, promising that if they did not, he would bring down the wrath of Bealz on them. When they refused, he led a poorly conceived attack on the Temple Sector. When the battle was over, more than twelve thousand rebels were killed, the worst of which was Talia, who was part of Grent's assault team. When he realized he couldn't win, he fled, abandoning her, which ultimately resulted in her death."

My limbs become heavy as the blanket of regret and guilt settles around me. I try to open my mouth, try to express my sorrow, try to say something. Words have forsaken me.

Spike looks at me and the regret plastered on my face.

"I'm—"

"Ye didn't know, brotha." Spike waves his hand dismissively. "Water under the bridge." Spike's attempt at assuaging my guilt is ineffective. It feels like my body is made of bricks. Everything I said in my zeal to do something—my words wounded a friend. Boldness plus ignorance is a dangerous kind of foolishness.

"Jett," Victor looks at me a sternness in his eyes, "We are at the crossroad. Are you sure this is what you want to do? Are you willing to sacrifice whatever it takes for this?"

I nod, "If it means we can change this city, I'll pay whatever the price."

Victor sighs, "That's the thing about tough choices. The one who makes them isn't always the one who pays for them."

"I certainly hope I'm not ruining a moment," came a deep, gruff voice from behind us. It is familiar. It is none other than Grent himself.

"Speak of the devil," Spike hisses, glaring at him with his fists balled.

Grent ignores the slight. "We had a deal. Rescue your friend, you give us the data-pad." He shrugs his giant bear shoulders, looking both calm and menacing at the same time. "Time to deliver on your end."

"Sorry, I don't have it on me," I reply.

"Ahh, what a shame. See, I'm starting to feel like the girl who got stood up for the ball. I waited. Patiently. But my patience has run out. I'll be collecting on the debt you owe, one way or another."

"What does that mean?" Victor asks.

"It means I've decided to conscript your little friend here." Grent points to me. "And I'll be having that data-pad as well."

"The heap ye will," Spike yells, storming toward Grent. Kane steps between them, slowing Spike's charge. Spike squares off against Kane, staring him down. The air itself seems to change from the rage emanating off Spike. His shoulders rise and fall with every deep grunting breath he takes. It's hard to imagine Spike holding his own against an ogre like Grent. Victor grabs Spike from behind, struggling to pull him back.

"This is not the place," he whispers to Spike. Spike's resistance drops a little, and he takes a step back, allowing Victor to move between him and Kane.

"You know this isn't going to work, right?" I say looking at Kane. Grent grumbles behind him. "Forcing people to fight for you; that's going to cause more problems than it solves."

Kane nods. "You know that's not what I want. We have a chance, a real chance at victory here. We need help. We need people like you. I need you to hear him out. Give him a chance. If you don't like what you hear, we'll take the data-pad and go in peace."

"You mean, give him a chance to explain why he turned down a peace agreement the last time? Refused to do what was best for everyone because he wanted power for himself? Or give him a chance to explain how he abandoned his own people leaving them to die," I blurt out without thinking. Kane pauses, stunned by my words. He looks over his shoulder to Grent as if seeking verification.

Grent turns to Spike. "That's not how it happened." Grent's voice booms like thunder. "You have to understand, things are—"

Grent is interrupted by the sound of rushing feet moving toward us. A young boy charges into view—Brelar. He runs straight to Victor. In the light from the lumepost, I can see blood oozing down the side of his face. His head is discolored by a large welt. Someone hit him, hard. His neck and arms are covered in minor scrapes and abrasions, and his black uniform is covered in little cuts and tears. Who would do this to a child?

Brelar fondles his tattered bird blanket nervously, rubbing his fingers over the now black fabric. It takes the boy a few moments to catch his breath and even longer to try and speak. Victor kneels down, putting his ear near the boy's mouth. He nods in response to words I can't make out. Victor relays the message as he hears it. Levites came to the area, searching for something. The next words I hear, Becka and Jensen. I don't need to hear the rest to know what's happened. Victor curses.

"We have to save them!" I blurt out. Now I sound like Telmen, stating the blatantly obvious.

"You realize what happens if we get caught?" Victor asks.

"Slums?" I chuckle trying to lighten the mood.

Victor smiles softly. "Right, that's a pleasant fantasy. Maybe they will stick us in a room with Commander Stone and force us to smell his breath."

I groan. "Aww, come on. I think I'd prefer the Outlands."

A beeping sound comes from the data-pad on Grent's wrist. He taps a blinking light, and a screen appears. A Nightling's face appears on the screen. "Grent, they're here! Levites!" There's a booming explosion behind him, and a burst of light floods the back of the screen. The Nightling seems to be knocked forward by it. A moment later, he steadies the camera on his face. Behind him, we can see the walls of a shop, though which shop is unclear. "They are—" a quick searing sound cuts off his words, and the video falls from his face to a shot of the street.

"Heap!" Grent growls.

"We can help," Victor says looking to Grent. Grent looks as surprised by Victor's words as he was by the video. "You have an underground infrastructure and the man-power we need to rescue our friends. Help us, and we will help you fight off the Levites." Spike runs his hands through his hair, pacing back and forth. Grent stares at Victor without saying a word. "Right now, our interests align. We work together. Then we go our separate ways."

"We've done this dance before. I held up my end. But you—"

Without saying a word, Victor pulls a data-pad from an inner pocket in his jacket and tosses it to Grent.

Grent looks at it and shakes his head with a smile. "And when were you going to—"

"When the Assessors moved on. It was too hot to get it to you sooner. Now we have a deal?" Victor's voice is firm and commanding.

"Vic, wait a min—" Spike starts.

"There is no other way," Victor shuts him down. "We have to get to them before they go through processing."

"So, we help you rescue your friends and—" Grent begins.

"And we give you the Market. Two people for an entire sector. What else do you need to think about?" Victor's face is stern and uncompromising.

"Why should I believe you can deliver on that?" Grent folds his hairy bear arms across his chest, leaning back.

"I know why you want him, why you need him," Victor states plainly. Who does he mean? Spike? Me? What's he talking about? "You've been watching us long enough to know what we can do. So, help us or get out of my way," he snaps.

"If you fail?" Grent presses.

Victor hands Brelar off to Gibbs, completely ignoring Grent's question. "Get him to Santio." Santio is the closest thing our neighborhood has to a doctor. "If it's safe, go home. When we rescue the others, I'll send them to you." Gibbs nods and escorts the boy down the road toward our home.

"Time to go," Kane says motioning for us to follow him. He leads us down a few hundred yards off the road to a patch of overgrown bushes, out of view of the lumelights.

Telmen starts in. "We aren't taking the train? The train would be faster wouldn't it? I like the train. Where is this going?" Olivia nudges him in the ribs. "Ouch, what'd you do that for?" he grumbles. He's the worst. Kane slides a stone out of the way, revealing a rectangular metal door in the ground. A keypad appears. Kane punches in a six-digit code then puts his thumb print on the pad. A soft beeping sound is followed by what sounds like the release of steam. The door dips down a few inches and slides out of view. Behind it, a metal staircase leads into a tunnel. We descend into darkness, and I hear the door slide closed behind us. A moment later, Grent's data-pad lights up. He types something on it, and a thick rope of bluish light flashes, expelling the darkness. The rope runs along the top and bottom of the tunnel walls like a trim against the floor and ceiling. Its soft blue glow makes it feel like we are underwater. It's oddly peaceful.

When we reach the bottom of the stairs, I see what resembles the rails for the magnetic track of the train. Hovering over them is a single silver train car. Well, it looks similar to a train car. It's sleeker and smaller. There is a front door with a single seat behind a series of controls and a wider second door that opens behind it. The train car boasts twenty or twenty-five seats. A slight breeze flows through the tunnel, making me shiver.

"What is this?" I ask in amazement.

"This is part of our operation—an underground transit system that allows us to move without the Patriarch's eyes on us," Kane explains.

"You have tunnels like this all over the city?"

"Well, not like this. These tunnels are for the speed cars. They are much taller and wider. They run around the city in a grid. They will get you to the general area you want to be in. From there, we have walking tunnels. They are much smaller than these but allow you to get a little closer to where you're trying to go."

"Amazing," Victor breathes out.

"Glad you like it. Now hop aboard, and let's go kill some Red Caps," Kane says with a chuckle.

Kane gets into the front of the speed car. The rest of us pile into the back. The doors close, and a moment later our underground train car is hurdling forward at an alarming speed. Something about its design makes the ride feel smoother than the commuter train while also clearly moving much faster. Resting even for a moment feels painful. Our friends have been taken. The Levites would have to take the train to the Market and then walk through the Market to the Northern Station if they were going to take Becka and Jensen to the Temple Sector. That would give us time. Even knowing that doesn't stop my heart from pounding so hard it hurts.

Pacing back and forth isn't going to help them, it just helps me feel a little less powerless. Sometimes illusions can be quite comforting. I check my pack, trying to feel productive. I've got some rope, a bottle, and my energy knife. I snap the knife back onto my belt. I have a feeling I'm going to need it before the night is done.

The underground train car stops as suddenly as it started. Kane hops out and opens our door. The train car sits next to a cement platform that runs like a sidewalk up and down the tunnel. Further back along the tunnel walls is another set of stairs like the ones we came down. Next to them, under a lumelight, is a sign that reads: Market Sector: Street Twelve.

"Street Twelve?" Telmen asks. "Why did we stop here? Aren't we trying to catch them on the train? Don't we need to go to the train station?"

"They're guarding the train station," Victor responds. "If they are trying to quell a rebellion, the first thing they will look to do is contain it. Once they cut off any route for escape, they will tighten the noose until they have all the rebels cornered in one place. The stations will be heavily guarded. Our only shot is when they're between stations."

We ascend the staircase. At the top right of the cement roof is a keypad, identical to the one Kane used to open the passage to the underground tunnel. Six digits and a press of his thumb and the door swings open. We emerge from the velvety darkness of the tunnels into the crisp darkness of the Market. We are in an alley tucked behind a store. This particular alley is completely sealed off from other streets. A single door in the wall in front of us provides our exit.

The streets are empty, the sky dark. Not even the wind dares disturb this unnatural calm. Our footsteps on the stone street are the only sound as we make our way through the Market to intercept a convoy of Levites and rescue our friends. Grent sends several messages on his data-pad to coordinate with the Nightlings, occasionally barking out directions to guide our group toward an intercept point.

Suddenly, screens light up all around us. A light purple filter covers the sky-screen. An automated voice echoes, "Alert! Alert! Citizens of Dios, your attention please. Attention please for this special announcement."

Barbra Boone's face projects onto the sky itself and graces every screen on every piece of glass. She's a pretty girl with dark hair done up with a fancy bow. Make-up covers any blemishes or imperfections, making her look better than any person could naturally. Her eyes are as bright and beautiful as they are unnatural, shining with an enticing purple color. Her lips curl into a warm smile, the rest of her face inert.

"Citizens of Dios, this is Barbra Boone from P1 News. Terror has taken the Market Sector!" She turns her shoulders to the side, and the angle of her projection shifts to another view. "Your diligent keepers of the peace have discovered something unbelievable! There has been an attack in the Market! Rebels! Heretics! Criminals who seek to destroy the peace we enjoy. Our noble city guardsmen are rallying to contain these vicious, savage beasts. The Patriarch has deployed soldiers to reinforce them. Hold on a moment." She pauses and presses one finger against her ear. "I'm being told that soldiers attempted to approach these rebels to negotiate a peaceful surrender when the rebels fired on them without provocation. For your safety, the Patriarch has ordered all transit to and from the Market Sector shut down. The brave men and women of the Patriarch Defense Force will not rest until every last terrorist has been eliminated and your safety secured. I'm being told the rebels are led by this man—"

The screens shift from Barbra Boone to a full three-dimensional scan of Grent, beard and all. "Grent Blackfur. Grent Blackfur is a known terrorist and radical. He is wanted for theft, murder, destruction of property, vandalism, terrorism, assault, and treason and is considered a threat, not just to public safety but to all life in Dios. Citizens of Dios, if you have any information on the whereabouts of this monster or know anything that could assist the Patriarch in his capture, hit 3-1-2 on your data-pad. Expression is arrogance. Duty is devotion. Conformity is virtue." She signs off with her token propaganda, and the screens and sky return to normal.

"Well, that's not great," I mutter under my breath. "Looks like we lost the element of surprise. They'll be ready for us now."

"Nothing wrong with that," Victor counters. "If they know we're coming, we can use that to our advantage." A sinister grin forms on his face. I've seen that grin before. I know it all too well. Victor has a plan.

"What is wrong with you?" Grent roars. "Without the element of surprise, we don't have a chance."

"Come on, we can take a squad of Levites," I chime in trying to boost morale.

"Not just Levites," Victor interrupts. "If we are going to do this, we need to understand what we are up against. The Patriarch, which is the whole system of governance, is ruled by High Father Ignatius. He may play the role of the meek and humble spiritual leader but, as the 'great prophet of Bealz' he is head of everything. The Patriarch itself is divided into two parts. The Control which serves as his right hand and the Order which serves as his left." Victor looks up and sighs, "Let me just show you." He pulls up his screen and starts drawing on it.

"Each branch uses different forces to maintain order and control," Victor explains drawing out another chart. "We've all dealt with Red Caps and the Levites. While Levites are much more troublesome on a regular basis, the Red Caps will be a greater problem in open combat due to their numbers and special training." Victor swipes the image onto his data-pad projection screen.

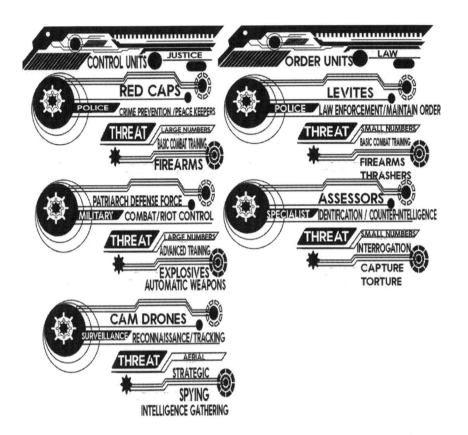

"Cam Drones may be a problem for our coordination and communication, but I'll worry about that. The real challenge is going to be the Patriarch Defense Force. In an open conflict they will get deployed. If they send a corps, they will outnumber us almost five-to-one. If they send a field army, they will outnumber us thirty-to-one. Every one of them will be better trained, better armed, and more experienced in combat than our men."

"Seriously?" I ask, "They have that many soldiers?"

Victor nods, "Equipped with the most advanced weapons and trained in counter insurgency."

"You see," Grent barks out, "we can't hope to win against that. Not when they know we are coming."

"Sure, we can. We just need to make a quick stop first." Victor and Spike exchange a look. Spike grins and nods.

Victor leads us quickly down to a shop a few blocks down. The forceshield is already up. Victor holds his data-pad up and types something into it. The shield dissipates, and an audible click pops the front door open. We slip inside quickly and close the door behind us.

The showroom is filled with elaborately carved and decorated furniture—chairs, tables, shelves, cabinets, all stacked and placed in nice even rows. The wood glistens and is smooth to the touch. I stare down at a table so glossy I can actually see my reflection. I run my hand along the edge, slowly feeling the perfectly shaped, perfectly smooth surface.

"Get your paws off my table or I'll hack them off," a voice shouts from my left. I turn to see its owner—a very old, very short man who is barely taller than the counter he's standing behind. His frame looks frail, his shoulders slouching forward. There is nothing intimidating about his stature, but something about his voice makes me obey with a sense of urgency and confusion.

Leaning on his cane, the old man waddles around the counter toward us. "I just finished polishing that wood, so keep your bratty hands off it." Bratty hands? Is that a thing? Can hands even be bratty? My sense of shock when I first heard his voice is replaced with amusement. I don't know what it is about him, but something in me likes him.

"You mean me?" I ask with a grin, playfully pointing to myself.

The curmudgeonly man looks up at me, his nose wrinkling as his eyes stare through his glasses.

"Oh, how original. A young brat who thinks he's clever." He lifts his cane without moving his arm and, with a flick of his wrist, smacks it over the back of my hand. I wince and pull back, rubbing the back of my hand softly.

"Ow, that's rude," I mutter.

"Rude is breaking into my shop late at night and scuffing up my work with your grubby little brat hands." I can't tell if he's messing around or legitimately annoyed. "Ugly mug like yours, you could have given me a heart attack." Victor and Spike start laughing. A faint smile forms on the old man's face.

"Wait, so ... you made this table?" I ask.

"Of course, I did. What of it?"

"Oh, well, I was just wondering how you did it. Did you have someone hold you up the whole time? Or do you have a bunch of ladders?"

The old man doesn't say a word. He just pulls a cloth out of his back pocket and starts buffing my fingerprints off his table.

"Ernest, still as cranky as ever, I see. How are ye?" Spike inquires.

The old man grumbles, "I'd be doing a lot better if you taught these kids some manners." I don't spend a lot of time with the elderly community, but if they are anything like Ernest, I plan to make it a higher priority. Ernest grouses under his breath and slowly totters his way to his office. The small room looks like a toolbox threw up in it. Gadgets and doohickeys cover every surface with no semblance of order. The floor is hard to find under miscellaneous boxes and objects, many of which look like they belong in a museum, not a shop.

Ernest does his three-legged waddle around his desk and reaches underneath. A clicking sound echoes around the room. With a slow, deep rumbling, his desk slides to the side, revealing a hidden stairway. Does every shop in the Market have a hidden basement? I'm starting to think Dios may have a larger undercity than an actual city.

"Well, you going to stand there like a bunch of idiots, gawking all day? Or do you want to rescue those friends of yours?" Wait, how

165

does he know about our friends? It isn't public knowledge. Rumors haven't had time to spread. I look to Spike and Victor suspiciously. They definitely know Ernest. Apparently, they trust him. Our friend's lives are at stake. What we are doing with this old man?

CHAPTER ELEVEN

Down the stairs we go, into another secret room. The contrast is alarming. The office and showroom above are classic, traditional, even old-fashioned. This secret room under the shop looks like a hacker's den. Screens running multiple programs line the walls. Access pads are mounted on each wall, providing easy access to the screens. Tech devices, the likes of which I've never seen, are carefully placed around the room on showcase columns.

"Jett, Ernest here is one of the greatest tech developers outside of the Temple Sector. He's like a wizard of technology," Victor says. The old man smiles, and the deep valley wrinkles of his face curl as he does. Kane and Grent look as surprised as I feel being down here. It's a clever cover, I have to admit. The last place I would look for a tech dealer would be in the shop of an old, frail craftsman.

"Enough flattery; it won't change my price."

Victor nods and retrieves a package of fresh, individually wrapped candies from his pocket. "I wouldn't dream of it." The old man reaches eagerly for the bag. Victor pulls it back, holding it above Ernest's reach. "Ah, ah, ah, show me first."

"You're a heapin' shinshew if ever there was one."

"You kiss your mother with that mouth?" Victor grins as he snaps back.

"My mother?" Ernest raises an eyebrow. "She died off with the dinosaurs long before you brats were even born."

"Focus, Ernest," Victor encourages. The old man retrieves a set of thin, black, glossy circles that look like coasters, stacked neatly in a clear plastic casing. The bottom of the casing opens up like a mouth, allowing a single coaster to be pulled from the pile with ease. Victor takes it and examines it. "Ernest, you've outdone yourself, you tiny little genius."

"Stick a sock in it." Ernest shakes his head. He lifts his data-pad up, and a blue array of lights scan over Grent's body. Grent steps back, his hand moving toward the handle of his weapon snapped to his belt. "Stand still, you giant troll. Don't tell me a Viking like you is skittish of an old man with a cane." That calms Grent down effectively. Ernest walks around, running the blue stream of lights all over Grent. "There, didn't hurt you one bit, did it? You giant baby."

Grent cocks his head sideways. I imagine most people don't talk to him this way.

"They are ready then?" Victor inquires.

"Course they are ready; I didn't come down here for my health. You know how to work them?" Ernest asks, his voice unnecessarily loud. Victor nods. "Good, saves me the time of teaching you." Ernest slides a black cylinder off a separate display column and tosses it to Victor who catches it with his free hand. The cylinder has four rings around the middle, which seem to slide, and a button on the top. Victor slides the cylinder into his inner jacket pocket and nods. He tosses the bag of candies to Ernest.

"Pleasure doing business with you."

Ernest nods. "Yeah, yeah. Now get out of my shop before I lose my patience with you."

"You mind explaining what's going on here?" Grent's voice thunders and echoes throughout the room.

Victor turns to face him. "You don't need to worry about it. You just do as I say and you'll get everything you want, got it?"

Grent steps forward aggressively, "You better—"

"You want to take the Market Sector?" Victor asks coolly. Grent stops his approach. "You want to win this fight Grent?" Grent nods. "You want to overthrow the Patriarch?" Again, Grent nods. "Then stop arguing with me. We have a lot of preparation to do and not a lot of time to do it in. Assemble your men. Have them do what I say when I say it, and I promise you, the Patriarch will not have a chance."

Grent grits his teeth audibly. Kane whispers something in his ear. "Fine, we'll do this your way. If you don't deliver, your missing friends will be the least of your problems."

Victor glares. "Let me know when they are ready for assignment."

Grent and Kane disappear up the stairs to make preparations.

Spike puts his hand on Victor's shoulder. "Are ye sure it's wise to rock that boat, brotha? They'd be dangerous enemies to have, ye know?"

Victor nods. "Yeah, but I needed him to storm off for a bit. Gives us a minute."

Ernest slowly ascends the stairs. "I'll let you know if they are heading back in."

"Listen." Victor's voice is urgent and serious. "There are two ways we can handle this. One, we use the Nightlings to get Becka and Jensen back. Then we bail first chance we get, let the chips fall where they may."

"You mean break our deal?" I ask.

Victor nods. "On their own, the Nightlings have next to no chance of victory. But, if somehow Grent were to survive, he'd come after us. It seems like the safer play, at least for now. We'd have to look over our shoulders for a while. Or, the other option is to go all in, honor our deal, and join the fight. It's risky. It would likely put us on the Patriarch's radar."

"But—"

"Either way we risk being hunted down either by the Nightlings or the Levites. It's a question of risk and reward. If we help the Nightlings, they could win. At least, they could win this fight. What happens after that is anyone's guess. If we run, the rebellion will fall tonight. The safer play is to run. But—"

"If we fight, we may actually make a difference," I interrupt, excitement coursing through my veins.

"Different may not be better, but yes."

"Yer that confident, brotha?"

Victor simply nods.

"All right, let's do it then. If we are going to risk dying anyway, might as well make it count."

Telmen's jaw drops. "Wait, wait, wait, you want us to fight the Levites? That's crazy. We aren't fighters. We can't stop them. We need to run. We can hide. We can just go. This is crazy, right?" he rattles.

"Just abandon Becka and Jensen?" I challenge. Telmen stares back in response.

"Well, could we just save Becka?" Telmen asks, a slight smirk appearing on his face.

"Olivia?" Victor asks. All eyes turn to her.

"What's there to talk about? They have our friends. We need to go get them back. After that, I'm with you, whatever you think is best."

Victor smiles. "I've got a plan." Victor starts sliding out the little black coasters. "Telmen, Olivia, Spike, I need you to take these holo-discs. Move carefully through the Market and place these on windows or walls as discretely as you can. Start with Street Four, and work your way in toward the Market Square. When you get to the Market Square, try to space them out facing the Square itself. Got it?" Victor slides the coasters out, handing a stack to each of them until the canister they were housed in is empty. "Once you are finished—this is very important—I want you to meet us on the roof of the Southwest building right of the Main Street West. If the Levites arrive at the Market before you are finished, I want you to walk away. Make your way back here, and wait until it's safe to head home. Go now."

Spike leads Telmen and Olivia up the stairs and out of sight. Victor turns to me. "We are going to meet up with Grent and Kane. Whatever happens, don't get in a situation where you have to depend on Grent. Our interests may align presently, but he is not on our side." I nod in agreement. After what he did to Spike's sister, I have no intentions of putting my fate in his hands.

The streets are strangely quiet. Apparently, the rebellion in the Market was not as intense as Barbra Boone would have us believe. We meet up with Grent and Kane and make our way to the Market Square. Victor insists we use the roof of a corner shop as our vantage point for the coming conflict.

Victor's data-pad projects a three-dimensional map of the Market Square and its adjacent streets. Victor presses his finger over various areas on the map, leaving green dots behind.

"Have your men set up here, here, here. Bring the largest group you have in from here and here." Victor draws up the plan. Grent and Kane send coordinates from their own respective data-pads. "The Levite force will come from here." Victor draws a line up from Train

Station West, winding between streets until they enter the Market Square. "They will rest here and fortify their positions."

"No," Kane objects. "This is the most vulnerable place for them to be. Why would they choose to stop here?"

"Because it's the most vulnerable place. The Levites will come alone. The Red Caps will remain in their positions at the train stations, blocking any escape. The Patriarch Defense Force, which is currently reinforcing the Red Caps, will wait to ambush us. They want to draw the rebels out. Appearing weak and vulnerable is the best way to draw the Nightlings into an all-out assault."

"Wait, so they want us to attack them here in the Market Square?"

"Yes."

"So, why are we doing that?" Kane asks. "Are you mad?"

Victor smiles. "Their plan is to catch us in a pincer attack. As soon as we engage, the Patriarch Defense Force will move in behind us, cut off our escape, and pin us in a fight from two sides. The Levites, who are likely waiting in their outpost on Main Street North, will charge in as well, giving them both greater numbers and greater position."

"Again, why are we doing this?"

"They want to take us out in one fell swoop. That is their mistake. The trains are shut down. That means it will take time before any additional reinforcements can arrive. Our only chance to take the Market is to take them all. From there, it's just a matter of guarding the stations." Victor shrugs. "At that point it's on you. We will give you the Market. Keeping it, that's up to you."

"But how are you going to keep us from getting trapped between the two forces?" Kane persists.

"By giving them the one thing they need to restore confidence in their power," Victor points to the giant bear Grent. "You."

Grent shifts his position. "Wait a minute, you never said anything about sacrificing me to them."

"No, I didn't. That's why you have to trust me for this to work."

Kane and Grent exchange a long look before finally nodding. Victor smiles. "Good, now we are going to need weapons."

"We have weapons," Grent objects.

"You have knives, close quarter weapons. They have guns. We can't take down an army of soldiers with a bunch of knives. Jett, this is where you come in." I look at him nervously. What could he want me to do? I don't know where any weapons are. "Spike will be back here momentarily. When he returns, I need you to get me an access card from a soldier. That will get us what we need." He might as well ask for an invitation to the Patriarch Festival of Bealz in the Temple Sector. It's equally impossible to steal.

"Right—"

"Listen, not far from here there is a secret Patriarch Armory. It's filled with rifles, explosives, everything we need. But, we need an access card to get in."

"Explosives? I thought those were all destroyed after the Disarmament Pact between the Five Cities."

Victor shakes his head, "Only explosives that cause massive destruction. Any weapon that could destroy something larger than a few buildings was considered too dangerous. Can't blow up the world if you don't have the tools to do it. The Patriarch Defense force stockpiles small, localized explosives in their armories."

"Yeah, I get that. How am I supposed to get an access card? It's not like they just hand them out, is it?"

"Jett, you're a thief. Steal it." A knot forms in my stomach. We spend our whole lives avoiding soldiers for a reason. Trying to steal an access card from one, that's just crazy.

"Yeah, but—"

"Listen to me." Victor grabs the shoulders of my shirt and pulls me in. "If we don't get those weapons, we can't win this fight. Becka and Jensen will die. The Nightlings will die. Any hope of change will die. All those times you said you wanted to do something, wanted to make a difference...I told you it wasn't the time, it wasn't the place. This is the time. This is the place. This is our chance to make a difference. We need those weapons."

Acceptance overcomes trepidation. "Why did you wait until now?" I complain defiantly.

"They didn't shut the trains down until now." Victor shrugs. "Without them isolating the troops, we'd have no chance. They could crush us with numbers alone."

"They shut down the trains every night. Why not take it then?"

"Seizing the Market is not enough. The Patriarch would just take it back and look like heroes. If you want a rebellion, you have to show the people the all-powerful force they fear isn't as invincible as they believe. The Patriarch just announced to all of Dios their troops are here, ready to squash the rebellion. They put themselves on the line. We take the Market now, we bloody their noses and show everyone they can be beaten. Once the people see the Patriarch is vulnerable, beatable, the flames of rebellion will ignite, and the city will rise up. Maybe, just maybe, the Patriarch will fall."

Well, if that's not enough motivation, I don't know what is. My body feels warm and electric. My blood rushes through my veins as if driven by newfound purpose. As if in response, Spike appears behind us. He nods to Victor and then turns to me.

"Ye ready, brotha?"

We descend from the rooftop to the street below. Time is of the essence. When the Levites leave the train station, our ticking clock begins. We race against it, darting up and down the streets, moving through alleys as fast as our legs can carry us. Train Station West is in view. Soldiers are everywhere—so many soldiers. The entire platform is covered with them. It's a truly terrifying sight. The Patriarch Defense Force are trained soldiers. Over their plain black uniforms, they wear thick black body armor that covers their shoulders, chest, and the tops of their legs and arms. Their faces are covered by a black visor that attaches to the helmets on their heads, making it impossible to distinguish one soldier from another.

"We need a way to draw them out," I whisper.

"Aye, but also something that doesn't alert them to us."

"Any ideas?"

"Aye, brotha, have ye learned nothing? Time for a little classic misdirection." Spike's eyes light up, and a wicked smile forms on his face. "Ye have to make a clean swipe. This will be the most important grab of yer entire life. If he senses it, even notices his card is missing, we are proper heaped." Spike gives me a stern look. "So dun go messing about." He grins, disarming the tension. I nod in agreement and punch his shoulder softly.

"Go then. Do your little misdirection. Leave the rest to me." Spike rushes off, disappearing into the shadows. Boots clapping against the stone street echo around me. We may not need a distraction after all. The soldiers are coming to us. I slip into the shadows of the alley behind me, watching as the soldiers go by. Red Caps, not helpful. We need a soldier. I move up and down the alleys slowly, looking for signs of any Patriarch Defense Forces.

Thieving taught me to move silently. Living in Dios taught me to be invisible. I'm going to use both skills against the very people who forced me to learn them. Blocking off an alley, I see two PDF soldiers. Even in the low light, I can see they are young, fit, and standing at attention with perfect posture. This is probably their first combat situation. They likely have enough adrenaline coursing through their veins to hear a mouse sneeze from three blocks out. Too risky.

The next street offers a more appealing target but another insurmountable problem: his access card is attached to a lanyard around his neck. No way to swipe it without him noticing. Two more streets, still no good option. My nerves start jittering. If I don't find a good target soon, we are heaped.

Ding, ding. We have a winner. The guard is either overworked or under rested. He's slouching forward, and his head tilts to the side as if trying to rest on his shoulder. He seems bored or sleepy or both. The real jackpot, his access card is sticking out of his back pocket, just begging to be swiped. It's like something out of a dream. I send a message to Spike with my data-pad. Two PDF soldiers are positioned at each street coming off the Main Street on the way to the Market Square. They are facing the Main Street with their backs to the alley, which makes lifting the card relatively easy. The challenge: the streets are built so symmetrically the guards on the other side of the Main Street can see anyone attempting to sneak up behind their counterparts. It's a problem but one that is easily solved. All I need is a distraction.

I see movement out of the corner of my eye, a shadow above me. I turn and look up to see a shadowed silhouette leaping from one roof to another. I hope that's Spike. If it's not, I'm heaped. The pounding of my heart is louder than my steps as I carefully move up the alley toward the PDF soldier, careful to shift my weight completely off each foot before moving them to avoid making a sound. Whatever Spike is planning, I need to be as close as possible. The window will be small, the cost for missing it dire.

An unusual fizzling, popping sound bursts from the roof. Light pierces the darkness as a glowing ball projects from the roof with a thump. The ball of light leaves a sparkling, glowing trail of little sparks as it whistles loudly by. A moment later, the glowing ball bursts with a popping sound. Colors and beams of light spray wildly in every direction, lighting up the streets below. Something about it is mesmerizing, the colors and the quick burst of light that disappears as suddenly as it appeared. Then another thump and another ball of light flies out.

The guards are all staring at the explosions of light, muttering to themselves, still too surprised to react—the perfect window. I lunge forward out of the shadows, in view of the soldiers on the other side of the street. My only hope is their attention remains on the exploding bursts of light in the sky. I pinch the edge of the access card in the soldier's back pocket. The guard shuffles, and I freeze. The sudden commotion is snapping him out of his sleepy stupor. My breath halts in my chest. My body arrests in place. If he or my hand moves the wrong way, even a fraction of an inch, it's game over.

My lungs burn, but I can't take a breath. My hand slides up slowly, carefully pulling the access card with it. Just a little more and it will be free. The resistance on the card shrinks bit by bit until I feel the edge of the plastic card pull free. I cover my mouth with my free hand, exhaling deeply into it as I slowly back away. The exploding balls of light seem to have stopped. The soldiers have begun to collect in the street, looking around and searching for the source.

Breathing heavily, I move further into the alley to ensure I remain undetected. The real question now is, will the soldier notice his card is missing? I wait, watching closely to make sure. He steps out into the street where several other soldiers are congregating. What they are saying, I can't be sure, but he seems unaware. Relief sweeps over me like a cool breeze on a hot summer day. I did it. I got the card.

Upon our return to Victor, he greets us with a proud smile and a firm slap on the shoulder. Spike covers his mouth to keep from shouting with excitement and giving away our position. I give the card to Victor.

"Grent, I need as many of your men who are not already positioned to meet us here," Victor commands. He pushes a shop just a few streets away on the digital display of the Market, and a green light covers it. "They will start by distributing weapons to the units in specified positions and then to the main groups we have here." Victor circles one of the areas on the map where Nightling troops were instructed to gather. "And here." He circles the other area. "This is it. Grent, Kane, come with me. Spike, Jett, stay here. If the Levites arrive before we

177

get back, message me." I nod, and the three men disappear from the roof.

My body feels heavy as the bursts of adrenaline and excitement take their heavy toll. The night is far from over. My heart races. My body pulses. My mind has never felt this alert. The air has never tasted this fresh. For the first time, I feel free. I look out over the Market Square. Shadows dart up and down, flurrying in and out of view. Preparations seem to be going well.

"Ye sure yer ready for this, brotha?"

"Too late to turn back now."

"On the contrary, this is yer last chance to walk away."

"You saying you don't want to do this?"

"Not at all. I'm just making sure ye prepared yerself. The reality of what's about to happen is a whole shinshew messier than how we picture in our heads. Ye better reinforce yer mental firewalls before it goes down."

I nod, exhaling. "Listen, Spike, about what I said before—"

"Laddie, save yer breath for coolin' yer pies."

That's an odd thing to say. I open my mouth to press the issue when Victor and Kane appear on the roof, hunching over as they rush toward us. They set down a couple of long grey tote bags. Inside I see a few high-tech looking rifles and some other miscellaneous weapons.

"We're in business," Victor says, a dash of excitement in his voice. All around the Market I see shadows of men climbing onto rooftops. "They may have planned for an attack; they definitely didn't plan for this." Victor smiles.

"Brace yourself, boys. This party is about to start," Kane says, almost giddy.

The thunder of synchronized marching rumbles our way. The pace is faster than I expected. I peer over the edge of the tall wall built around the perimeter of the roof. Levites in their white robes march their way into the Market Square. Accompanying them is a small detachment of Red Caps, all armed with rifles as well as the handguns they wore on their sides. The Red Caps break formation as they reach the Market Square, forming a thin perimeter as the Levites pour in.

Amidst the flood of white robes are a series of people in uniforms as well as a few dozen Undesirables. They are all huddling together faces down. Hostages. The Levites brought hostages. The citizens and Undesirables are led into the middle of the Square, Levites forcing them to their knees. I tap Spike's shoulder.

"You bring your zoomers?"

Spike nods, reaching into his bag and pulling out two thin, connected cylinders. He hands them to me. Zoomers use a series of lenses to make things appear much closer than they are. I hold them up to my eyes and start scanning the crowd, looking for signs of Becka or Jensen. Most of the people in the crowd are Undesirables. There are a few uniforms sprinkled throughout. Most likely they are Plebs who were caught siding with the Nightlings. I move the zoomers slowly over the crowd. Undesirable. Undesirable. Yellow sash, dark black hair. Undesira—

I pull my view back. My heart lurches in my chest. I don't believe it. I won't believe it. I pull the zoomers away and look at them as if they are showing something that isn't really there. Denial is the enemy of reason. Forcing myself to look again, my heart sinks. On her knees, hair disheveled, is Lilly. The pieces of the puzzle start fitting in my mind. The bartender told me she'd been gone for weeks. This must be why. What did the Patriarch want with her? Surely, they didn't care that an Artisan snuck into a Class C bar. What reason could they possibly have to detain her? My eyes widen—the drunk Red Cap she chased off. Maybe he reported her?

"Vic, we got a problem."

Victor takes the zoomers from me and looks out. "Heap, is that Lilly?" I nod, not like he can see me when he's looking through the zoomers. He turns his head more. "I don't see Becka or Jensen."

"Maybe they are lost in the crowd?" Spike suggests. Suddenly I feel very nervous. We are here for them, not Lilly. Finding Lilly here is a terrible surprise. If they don't see Jensen or Becka, will they still be willing to go through with the plan? It's one thing to risk it all for our little Undesirable unit. Lilly isn't a part of that unit. Grent stirs, seeming to share my concern.

"Possible, but it seems like they aren't here?"

"So, what does that...?" I begin to ask, afraid of the answer.

"Nothing changes. We can't leave Lilly down there. Not after you just worked up the nerve to talk to her." Victor grins.

I nod, the reassurance helping calm my nerves a bit. All we have to do is cheat death, rescue our friends, defeat the Levites, and take control of the Market from a small army of highly trained soldiers. What could go wrong?

"It's all good. We knew they'd have at least two with them. This doesn't change anything."

"Hostages change things. How can we be sure we don't hit them? No way any of these guys have fired a gun before."

"Doesn't matter," Victor responds coldly.

"Our friends are down there, Vic. It really does matter."

"No. Listen, these guns use auto-targeting. They don't require skill. You look through the scope, click the button here above the trigger when you've got your target. Gun does the rest."

"All right, boys. You're good to go here. I'm going back down. See you on the other side," Kane says with a grin.

"Wait, why aren't you staying here?" I ask.

Kane grins. "I've been waiting for this moment for a long time. I'm not going to waste it looking through the scope of some rifle." He pulls out his energy knife. When he activates the blade, it forms the shape of a long, single-edged sword. "You're going to need someone to create chaos on the streets. That just so happens to be my specialty." He laughs and rushes down and out of sight. He has to be the maddest man I've ever met.

I reach into the bag to pull out a rifle.

"No," Victor responds. "I've a more important job for you."

"What?"

"The battle will start with a series of explosions, one at each train station. That will send the reinforcements into disarray and prevent them from organizing their attack. The explosions will signal the shooters. They will focus on the Levites in the Market Square."

"Won't they be expecting that?" I ask.

"Aye, they will, brotha, but they dunna know we have guns," Spike interjects excitedly.

"Right, and they are expecting a brute force ground assault, not a coordinated strike from the rooftops. By the time they figure out what's going on, it will be too late. A few stragglers may make a run for it. That's why we have Grent and his men on the ground, waiting. Here's where you come in: Jett, I need you to get the hostages out of the Square. They may be scared. They may freeze up. You have to get them moving. If you don't clear the Square before the PDF re-groups, you..." He doesn't have to tell me what happens. I know the stakes. "The explosions will buy you time but not much, so be fast."

Great, no pressure there. I dust my hands off on the tops of my pants because nothing helps you run faster than dust-free hands. What am I doing? Take a breath. Think. It's going to be fine. You can do this. Spike grabs my hand and slaps a metal puck-looking thing into it. After examining it, I look up at him.

"Ye throw it, it creates a large cloud of smoke. It will buy ye a few extra seconds if ye run out of time," Spike says. Someone that's both comforting and discomforting at the same time. My hands shake a little. "Ye wanted to make a difference, brotha."

"Yea, next time remind me to want something less terrifying."

"Ye will be just fine. I've got a good feeling." Spike's demeanor shifts. The playful, easy smile fades from his face. His eyes turn stern and serious. "Now hear me, be careful. Dunna be a hero. If ye run out of time, run. Get to safety. Save as many as ye can, but get the heap out of there."

I open the door to descend the stairs when I hear an odd buzzing, almost soft humming sound like the blades of a fan swirling the air. The sound is familiar, but I can't place why. Realization hits me like a train car splattering hope across its windshield. Panic overwhelms me. I turn in time to see that same panic in Victor's eyes.

CHAPTER TWELVE

"**J**ett, go! Now!" Victor shouts with a sense of urgency. I leap through the door and descend the stairs two and three at a time. Multiple explosions resound around me. The building itself shakes from the force. The explosions must be massive to create this kind of effect. I catch myself on the railing to keep from falling. My knees throb from the force of each jumping leap I take. I have to reach the bottom as quickly as possible. Victor's plan centers on timing and surprise. All I can do now is hope that the surprise still works with Cam Drones.

Cam Drones are flying recording devices piloted automatically from a distance. They record video in every direction and broadcast it live back to a control center. They typically only use them for Sunday Services to ensure everyone can get a good view of the Holy Father as he goes through his long-winded liturgy. Every now and then, the Patriarch uses them for monitoring purposes. How long were they there before we heard them? Guess I'll find out soon enough.

The door swings open, and I burst out onto the streets, full stride. A sweet gunfire symphony greets my ears. Flashes of light from the rooftops break up the dark of night. Moving toward the Market Square, I see Levites dropping, their white robes sprayed with red. Red Caps shout and scramble around, desperately firing their side-arms into the air.

183

I rush to the edge of the street leading up to the Market Square. Two Red Caps have their backs to me, guns out, firing at the rooftops. I pull my knife free and activate the blade. The screams and chaos of the Market hide the sound of my approach. One of the Red Caps turns to fire at the roof of the building right next to him. No way he can hit anything that far away. Casting caution aside, I charge forward, throwing my shoulder into the unsuspecting Red Cap. I hit him in the back, just above the shoulder blade, and knock him sprawling sideways. His head hits the stone wall of the shop, and he falls to the ground. Planting my foot, I turn and bring the energy blade of my knife up into the other Red Cap's head before he has time to turn on me. Warm, wet blood soaks my hand. I pull the blade free, and his body stiffens and falls to the ground.

A high-pitched whistle shoots past me, and my shoulder burns with a sudden intense fire. I clutch it with my hand, wincing into the pain. No blood, but my jacket is torn and a streak of skin seared in an even line under it. I look up, and across the Market Square, in a perfect line from where I'm standing, I see a muzzle flash. One of the Nightlings must have fired at the Red Cap I killed right as I killed him.

Red Caps and Levites scatter toward the streets, trying to escape the Market Square. This part of the plan, at least, is going well. A roar sounds to my left. Grent, the battle-ready grizzly, charges at a pair of Red Caps. He is wielding an actual battle-axe. Where did he get that? Why is it so intimidating? Focus. Time seems to slow as I drive my body forward into the Market Square toward Lilly and the other hostages. My mind races as my body feels like it's running through a swamp. All around me, I see Red Caps and Levites, bodies contorting and falling to the ground as blood sprays from their wounds.

One of the Levites still near the hostages manages to pull his thrasher free. Typically, the thrasher generates a nine-stranded whip or a longer, thicker single whip of energy. I've seen them adjust to other, more lethal things as well. His hand moves to the activation switch on the shaft of his thrasher. Without stopping, I pull my shoulder back and hurl my knife, my only weapon, at the Levite. Amazingly, the energy beam buries inside his back. The thrasher falls from his hand just before his body collapses to the ground.

Two Levites remain around the hostages. I charge toward them, but someone else gets their first and tackles one of the captors. I hear the sickening crack of a breaking bone as the assailant snaps the second Levite's knee with an impressively well aimed kick. He collapses to the ground holding his leg and screaming. A moment later the assailant is up, holding a Levite thrasher in each hand. The attacker snaps the activated beams down on the Levite's backs. The Levites scream and spasm before passing out.

I stare in disbelief despite at the expert disabling of the two Levites. The attacker turns and I see the yellow sash.

"Lilly?!" I exclaim. I can't tell if I'm more surprised or amazed or confused.

I see her face. For a moment, I forget about the danger around us, a bright smile forming across my lips as I get lost in her eyes. She returns my smile, but her excitement quickly turns to confusion.

"Jett? What are you doing here?"

"I was coming to rescue you," I blurt out.

"Rescue me?" She puts one hand on her hip and cocks her head to the side, "Jett Lasting, why do you assume I need rescuing?" Her tone is both accusatory and playful.

I'm not really sure how to answer that, "uhh, I-I...you were with a group of hostages surrounded by Levites."

"You didn't even consider that maybe I was here to rescue them, did you?"

Once again, I find myself not knowing what to say. "Wh-what?"

She rolls her eyes, "Men."

"What are you doing here?"

"I tutor classless student's afterhours. A few them went missing about two weeks ago. The Red Caps couldn't be bothered to do their jobs, which, seemed suspicious." We have lived very different lives. She just described every Red Cap I've ever interacted with. "So, I followed them. I was trying to figure out a way to break them out when the Levites showed up and started taking everyone away. So, I followed them. Infiltrated them. They brought me here. I was-"

A loud burst of rapid gunfire booms from down Main Street West. The PDF soldiers must be charging, not long now. "We can continue this later. We need to get out of here. Are you familiar with Shine for Shine Jewelry on Street Three?" Lilly nods. "Good, can you get the hostages there?"

"What about you?" she protests.

"Don't worry. Victor has a plan." She smiles. I'm relieved that she doesn't appear hurt.

Some of the hostages are reluctant to go, frozen in place. "Listen up," I shout. "The Square is about to be overrun with PDF soldiers. I know you're afraid. I know you don't want to die. If you stay here, I promise you, you will. Get on your feet."

No one moves, they just awkwardly exchange glances. Lilly puts her hand on my shoulder and smiles. "Everybody ready? I'm going to take us someplace safe. Follow me." As a collective unit they stand up and nod in agreement. Lilly lets go of my shoulder and winks.

"Now run! Run like your lives depend on it!" I shout, hoping my intensity will get them moving. Nothing. I might as well be yelling at statues.

Lilly points, "Street Three, go, I'm right behind you." Immediately the group starts rushing off in the direction she pointed. Lilly hangs back helping people up. Somehow, in the midst of all this, she still looks amazing. The gunfire from the rooftops has stopped. The Nightlings are repositioning in preparation for the PDF soldiers closing in. The momentary relief and confusion I felt from seeing her dissipate. The tension of what's coming slams into me. The easy part of the fight is over. Now comes the real battle.

PDF soldiers are closing in on the Market Square from the streets in each direction. I'm still in the middle of the Square, helping former hostages get up and go. I hear Spike's voice in my head: Don't be a hero. If you run out of time, run. He's right. That's what I should do. But I can't. There are too many people here, and too many will be caught in the crossfire. Lilly is helping the final stragglers.

A Red Cap lies a few feet from me. Next to his body, I spot a rifle. I scoop it up. What are you doing, Jett? This is stupid, Jett. The soldiers approaching from Main Street West have a shot at the hostages, at Lilly and our friends. All they have to do is turn and fire, unless something else demands their attention.

Activating the smoke disc, I hurl it at the approaching cluster of soldiers. The smoke cloud that erupts from the disc prevents me from seeing any of the soldiers clearly. But I don't need to see them. The goal is distraction, not destruction. I fire blindly into the opaque cloud, pulling the trigger as fast as I can. Quick bursts of green light fire from the rifle and disappear into the cloud of smoke. Spike told me I'd have a few seconds. Those few seconds were almost up.

"Fire into the smoke!" I hear Victor shout from the rooftop. A series of gunshots follow. I fire four more shots before the thick cloud of smoke evaporates into a barely distorting mist. I turn back. The Square seems clear, the hostages funneling out of sight from the approaching soldiers. Time to run. A whimper catches my ear. Turning around, I see a small girl, maybe seven years old. She is curled up in a ball, clutching her knees with her little hands and rocking back and forth. I sling the rifle over my shoulder, holding it in place by the strap. The girl screams when I touch her. I don't have time to console her. I lift her off the ground into my arms.

His shoulder hits me in the chest before I even see him. My body topples back, and I land with a hard thump on the ground, the little girl bouncing off my chest and knocking the wind out of me. I gasp for breath and start to pick myself up. A firm hand pushes my shoulder, holding me down. It's Kane. What is he doing? Why did he attack me?

"Kane, what the—"

"Are you trying to get yourself killed, boy?" His tone is light, playful, and totally off-putting in our current situation. A sinister grin is plastered on his face.

"What are you doing, Kane?"

"Oh, just my good deed for the day—saving your life. And the world. Two good deeds in one, I suppose." He laughs. Several beams of green light fly over us, low enough that they would have hit us if we'd been standing. Suddenly, I understand. He really was saving our lives. Kane lifts three fingers. I don't know what that means. Then he puts one down. Then a second.

We stand up at the same time. I wince, still holding the girl in my arms, my legs wobbling beneath me.

"Grent!" "There is he is!" "Get him!" A series of cries burst from the crowd of soldiers. The focus of the assault shifts from the Market Square to the pursuit of Grent. I stumble forward, slowly limping out of the Market Square. Behind us, I hear other soldiers shouting they've spotted Grent. Weird. No time to think about it now. Just keep going. My legs finally stabilize, and I run as fast as I can. When we reach the edge of the Market Square, I kneel down to put the girl on her feet. She latches on so tightly that Kane has to pry her from around my neck. Shouts heralding Grent's presence sporadically ring out. Whatever Grent is doing, he is driving the PDF into chaos.

"Come on, let's get you out of here," Kane says slapping me on the shoulder so hard he almost knocks me over.

"Jett!" Lilly crashes into me, jumping and wrapping her arms around my neck before I have time to process it. I catch my footing, and my arms wrap around her, more for balance than intention initially.

"Popular with the ladies, are we?" Kane jests. Lilly gives him a stern glare, and Kane puts his hands up defensively. "Only kidding."

"You were supposed to—"

"They made it just fine. Don't worry. They are all safe. I had to come back for you."

"It's not safe here!" My tone is harsh. Too much adrenaline.

"Look around, Jett. It's not safe anywhere."

"Some places are safer than others."

"Just let me know when you're ready to stop objecting and accept the fact that I'm not going anywhere." Lilly folds her arms across her chest defiantly as if daring me to test her. I remember that from when we were kids, it's the 'do not mess with me or you will regret it' pose.

Kane stops me from saying anything. "Best to surrender when you have no chance of victory," he advises with a grin.

My shoulders slouch forward with reluctant acceptance. It would take longer to convince her to go back than it would to get her to the rooftops where we should be. This calm before the storm won't last much longer.

"Hold—"

Before I can finish the word, her lips are pressing against mine. They feel soft and warm. My heart feels like its stopping and racing at the same time. Body tingling, lips sparking with delight, I feel her arms wrap around my neck and pull my head closer to hers. My breath hitches as she kisses me before my mind can process to kiss her back. The Square, the city, the whole world is gone. In this moment, there is nothing but her. Here we are standing in the middle of a battlefield, kissing.

"Well, this is a fun time for that," Kane remarks. Lilly releases my neck and my lips, adjusting the sides of her uniform with her hands. She looks down bashfully, her cheeks a soft pink. Behind Lilly, I see Spike rushing over to us, a rifle strapped over his back.

The buzzing hum of fan blades descends toward us. Shinshew. Just what we need, Cam Drones.

"Well, if it isn't the little street rat. You've come a long way since last we met." That voice is oddly familiar. It seems to come from everywhere. A moment later, all the screens in the Market light up and project a close-up image of a man's face: square jaw; wild, savage, hateful eyes; sinister grin. It's a face I can never forget. "I'll admit, you were more trouble than I expected. Your bombs and guns slowed my men down. You had to know you couldn't defeat us. It was a dream. I am the light of the sun come to wake you from that dream. Your rebel leader has been surrounded by my men. At my order, he will be executed. Then your little Nightlings will scatter like the vermin they are. Only this time, we will not let them go. We will hunt them—their families, their supporters, anyone who even sympathized with their position. All will be brought low before the power of the Patriarch."

The screen closest to me shatters as a beam of energy blasts through where Commander Stone's head was. I grin. Shooting him in the face, even a projection of his face, felt really good. The buzz of the Cam Drone gets closer.

"Nothing to say?" Commander Stone laughs. "Don't worry, it will be over quickly but not painlessly. Fire!" He grins triumphantly. A series of gunshots erupt all over the Market. Just like that, with a single command, everything we had fought for is crashing down. Without the face of the rebellion, without Grent to lead them, the Nightlings will fall apart. The Patriarch will win. Retaking the Market is just a question of time. Could we still escape? Probably not. Even if we did, how long could we hide? Sorrow sweeps over me. This is the risk of taking sides. Sometimes you lose. I don't understand where we went wrong. I've never seen one of Victor's plans fail this magnificently. Commander Stone's evil laugh fills the Market.

Spike and I stare at each other, neither of us saying a word. Victor steps out of the building and walks over to us. Behind him, the great ogre of a man, Grent. Wait. How is this...? How can Grent be...? My mind starts melting as it attempts to process what is happening. Victor smiles confidently. He walks up to the Cam Drone and waves.

"You must be Commander Stone, rising star of the Patriarch Defense Force, youngest Commander in the history of Dios. Very impressive to be sure. The real question is, did your position come from merit or nepotism?" What is he talking about? Is he trying to make Stone angry? Who cares how he got to be a Commander? He beat us. We should be running not taunting.

"You're a brave rodent, to speak to me in this manner. I wonder—"

"You should. You should be wondering how your men could have executed Grent and, yet, here he is standing beside me." Grent steps into the view of the Cam Drone. Victor shrugs, speaking directly to the Cam Drone. He lifts a small remote in his hand and presses the button on it. A series of simultaneous explosions erupt all around the Market, screams echoing in their wake. Victor holds up remote. "Friend of mine made these, calls them holodisks. Basically, you scan someone and the discs project a perfect replica of them. I had these placed all over the Market. Here's the best part—we rigged the holodisks to explode. All I needed was for you to get your men in close like they would to confirm Grent was dead. Then, well...you get it. Goodbye men. Hope they were replaceable." Victor smiles. Spike looks just as surprised as I feel. How long has Victor been planning this?

Commander Stone's face is cherry red. I wouldn't be surprised if steam burst from his nose and ears. "You are dead! You hear me? Dead. Every last one of you."

"Good, enough with the games. Let's get down to business. We are in the Square. If you are the Commander you claim to be, come face me. We will settle this in the old way. You and your men versus me and mine. Just remember, I don't work for your father. I'm not going to take it easy on you."

I spin around, aim, and fire my rifle. The Cam Drone crashes to the ground splattering into a thousand pieces.

"Well ye nuked him off, brotha. What now?"

"Grent, Kane, move all your men. Position them exactly how I tell you. Spike, take Jett and Lilly. Wait for us in the corner building." Victor points. "There. Make sure you stay out of view. We will join you soon."

"What? No, we should stay together," I protest.

"Jett, we don't have time to argue. Go."

"I'm not just leaving you here. We go together!" I object.

"Have some faith, Jett. Everything is going just as it should."

Spike pulls me away before I can waste more time grumbling. We slip inside the shop as Victor instructed. I try to make Lilly wait in a back room to keep her further from the conflict to come. She hits me on the arm hard enough to leave a bruise.

"What is Vic doing?" I ask looking at Spike. "He can't seriously expect to take on Commander Stone out in the open. They'll be slaughtered!"

"Aye, makes ye wonder why he'd pick the most vulnerable stop to take his last stand, doesn't it?"

I nod. "And why did he try so hard to nuke Stone off? He never shows off like that."

"Well, if ye ask me, he's up to something. Never known Vic to pick a fight he wasn't sure he could win."

For some reason that comforts me. Despite the absurdly large challenge ahead, Victor is not a gambler. He doesn't take chances. He plots. He makes tactical moves. He finds weaknesses, gaps, opportunities to exploit. What sort of plan involves surrounding yourself with your enemies, positioning yourself in a vulnerable place, and waiting to be killed?

The Market Square begins to fill with Nightlings. They scurry about setting up tables, carts, and other barriers to form a wall around their ranks. Kneeling behind their defenses, they position themselves, rifles facing the streets leading into the Square. At least they look ready to put up a fight. Victor, Grent, and Kane stand in front of the cart and table fortress, making themselves visible.

The rumble of boots thunders down the streets as PDF soldiers march into the Market Square in perfect formation. They spread in even lines in front of the shops that form the perimeter of the Square. The lines of soldiers run five deep. A pit forms in my stomach. I've never seen so many soldiers in one place. It's a horrifying sight. The Nightlings are completely swallowed up by a sea of soldiers. From our hiding place inside the shop, all we can see is the back of several lines of soldiers.

Commander Stone emerges from the crowd and approaches Victor with a swagger. "Clever fortification, but you chose the ground for your final stand poorly." He pauses. "You should have kept your men on the roof. At least then you'd have had a chance."

"Maybe. Or maybe you'd have just had your men lob blast bombs onto the roof before moving into the field of fire," Victor answers.

"You are clever, whatever your name is. Doesn't matter; you'll be a distant memory soon enough. You should have known you'd be no match for my army."

"Hiding behind an army? Just like you hid behind your father? Tell me, Commander Stone, have you accomplished anything in your life that wasn't built on the shoulders of others?" Victor retorts. Is this a bluff to nuke him off or does Victor know something? How would he know about Commander Stone's family? Why does he keep bringing it up?

"Prepare to fire!" Commander Stone orders. "Goodbye, whoever you are." The soldiers raise their rifles in unison, aiming them away from us at the center of the Market Square. The table fortifications won't last long against those guns. Why did Victor choose this spot? Then it hits me. All the soldiers have piled into the Square. They lined up in rows just to fit. If the Nightlings can fire quickly and accurately enough, the numbers won't matter. The PDF soldiers in the back rows don't have a clear line of sight. This must have been his plan all along.

Before a single gun goes off, an explosion erupts in the center of the Market. I turn my head the light from the flames hurts my eyes. A cloud of smoke fills the air as the blast sends debris from the table and cart fortress raining against the shops and regiment of soldiers. There's just no way Victor was gone. This is some kind of trick. Laughter fills the air. Horror and rage clash together battling for control of me.

"Sorry, what was that? I can't hear you," Commander Stone jeers. "When will you rats learn?" I don't want to believe it. Stone's smug self-satisfaction gives me pause. Tears well up in the corners of my eyes. I fight them back. No. Not like this. There's no way Victor goes out like this. I refuse to accept it, but I can't deny what I saw. The explosion was right where Victor was standing. No one could have escaped that. No one could have survived. Then I see it, sitting on the ground a few feet from me. The little red bracelet Brelar made for Victor.

This can't be. Victor never takes that off. My closest friend—who's been by my side, watching out for me since the death of my parents—is gone. I feel sick. I don't want to believe it. I want to close my eyes and make it all go away.

Everything feels heavy. Everything feels dark. Spike walks to the bracelet in near slow motion. He bends down and picks it up. Holding it in front of his face he covers his mouth and slumps down to the floor, back to the window. Why didn't we just run? I pushed for this. I wanted to do something. Now, because of me, because of my selfishness, Victor is dead. I stare into the smoking chasm of despair as if continuing to look will change what I just saw.

Shadows of soldiers push in as Stone orders them forward, demanding someone bring him the corpse of the insolent rodent. The coward kills my friend and then has the gall to demand a trophy? If I accomplish nothing else in this life, I am going to kill Commander Stone.

CHAPTER THIRTEEN

Shouts back and forth through the smoke pierce the depressing silence. Soldiers try to stumble their way through the Nightling bodies. The smoke slowly clears away.

"What in the name of Bealz—" one soldier shouts.

"This doesn't make any sense," I hear another say.

"What is it?!" Stone demands, "What do you see?"

"N-nothing sir," shouts a soldier. "There's nothing here."

"What do you mean there's nothing there?"

"Just that, sir. There's nothing. No bodies, no weapons. The Square is empty." That doesn't make any sense. How could the Square be empty?

Rapid gunfire bursts forth from all around the Market. Muzzle flashes fill the air as beams of green light rain into the Square. Soldiers cry out. Screams of surprise and pain fill the Market Square. I watch, not sure what it is I'm seeing—seeing but not quite believing what I'm seeing. It takes seconds for the PDF soldiers to recognize what's going on. With each passing second, their numbers dwindle.

"Impossible! How is this happening?" Stone shouts in frustration, a note of fear in his voice. "Reform the lines. Aim for the buildings!" Stone shouts, recomposing himself. "Nice trick, vermin, but you've only delayed your demise." He's right. There are still too many soldiers.

In a flash, everything goes dark. Too dark. Unnaturally dark. The kind of dark that can only come from every light, both in the Market and from the dome itself, going out at once. Voices shout back and forth. I look at my hands, pulling them in front of my face. Even as I touch my forehead with my fingers, I can't see them. What could cause this?

A trumpet sounds from the east side of the Square. A series of rifle blasts pierce the stunning darkness. A trumpet from the north is answered again by a series of gunshots.

"What kind of game are you playing? Enough tricks!" Stone shouts.

A trumpet sounds from the north, then the east, then the west, as if at random. Each blast of sound results in gunfire and the shuffling of feet. Even sitting with my hand pressing against the wall, it's disorienting.

"Behind us—they are behind us! Shoot! Shoot!" comes a voice from the Square. The Market Square erupts with gunfire. The blasts are so fast and so frequent that, for a brief moment, I can see through the darkness. I hear the screams of those being hit by energy blasts.

"No, the other way! Fire! Fire!" Again, a series of gunshots.

"They are moving in; use your blades!"

I cover my mouth to keep from laughing. Victor, only Victor could think of something like this. He's disorienting them, working them into a frenzy, and getting them to kill each other. The Market lights up with blue energy blades as the soldiers prepare to defend themselves. They have no way of knowing who they are defending themselves from. The energy blades create enough light to see outlines but not people. The kindling is set. All they need is a spark to ignite it.

A man screams in pain. The Market erupts, blades swinging, stabbing, slicing as the soldiers start frantically cutting each other down.

"What? No! Defense Force, stop!" Hearing the voice of their Commander, the soldiers stop.

The sun is put to shame by the overwhelming burst of light that floods the Market. I cover my eyes, wincing from the shock of it. Before my eyes can adjust, gunfire erupts once again. The soldiers that traded their guns for knives are once again caught off guard. The blinding light is keeping them from focusing as those who are still alive, and they, bobble and stumble, trying to switch weapons.

Each step has been perfectly timed and orchestrated to keep the soldiers in constant disorientation. The Market looks like a mass grave site. Bodies are strewn everywhere. The stone streets are painted with blood. What started as the largest armed force I have ever seen has been reduced to a small band of surviving soldiers.

Kane and a few dozen Nightlings charge into the Square. The once organized lines of the PDF collapse. Soldiers scatter and run as the Nightlings charge after them. Wait, did we just win? Is it possible?

"I dunna believe it," Spike says shaking his head. "That did just happen, didn't it? This isn't some weird sort of dream?"

"How...?"

"Aye, I'm gonna ask him. Pulled a proper rabbit out of that hat he did."

The streets outside are a concert of celebration with Nightlings roaring and cheering. Not just Nightlings—several beggar gangs, the Emerald Eye, Red Dragons, and the Watchers, are cheering alongside them. The jubilation is deafening. We make our way to the Market Square. I check my data-pad, no messages from Victor. None of the ones I sent him seem to be going through.

Grent makes his way to the center of the Square. Standing on a makeshift platform, he begins his celebration speech.

"Today will be remembered in history as the day Dios was delivered from its oppressors! Where the heroes of the Market stood against all odds and defeated the Patriarch in the first of many victories!" The listening crowds cheer louder. "Brothers, sisters, today we struck a blow against the Patriarch! Tomorrow we bring them to their knees!" More cheering.

Victor is standing at the edge of Main Street West when Spike, Lilly, and I approach. He smiles. Spike grabs him around the waist and lifts him in the air, spinning him around again and again.

"Ye beautiful tosser, ye! Had us all proper fooled ye did." Spike sets Victor down before repeatedly slapping him on the shoulder. "How did ye manage all that? Tell us the whole thing!"

Victor smirks slightly, the way he does when he's proud of himself. "The key to victory when fighting a stronger, better-armed force is disorientation. If your enemy can't coordinate, then the strength of their numbers means nothing. We'd never match their firepower, even with the armory weapons. The bombs at the stations and the holodisks you placed helped trim them down, but it was still going to be an uphill battle. It's a little sad they fell for the same trick twice. Just used a large holodisk. We placed it while setting up the fortifications in the Square. I had Kane scanning as many Nightlings as he could to generate the projections."

"Aye, smoke, draw them in, blast them like crazy, but how did ye get it so dark?"

Victor's smirk grows, and he pulls out the black cylinder Ernest had given him. "This is a black hat device. It uses a single code to temporarily seize control of all electronics in an area, including the dome itself. Cut out the lights, get them spun around and nervous, let them kill each other for a bit. Then turn the lights back on."

"Bloody brilliant is what it is! Brotha." Spike shakes his head. Holding out the bracelet, "but why'd you have to use this?" His voice is almost accusatory.

Victor holds up his wrist, Brelar's red bracelet is still there. "That is not mine."

Spike holds the bracelet next to the one on Victor's wrist. They are almost identical. "How would this end up out here?"

Victor shakes his head, "this is troubling."

"Forget the bracelet, you're ok?" I press.

Victor's face warms as he looks over at me. "I told you, Jett, you just got to have a little faith. Our victory was never in doubt. Are you ok? I imagine that was a bit traumatic."

"Oh, not as traumatic as what I'm going to do to you will be." I grin. It is an idle threat, and he knows it. Not once have I pulled one over on Victor. I've given up trying.

"Lilly, I'm glad you're okay." Victor takes her hand and cups it between his. "Jett was worried about you." Victor looks over to me. "Did you see any sign of Jensen or Becka?"

I shake my head. "No. There's a chance they were in the group of hostages, but I doubt it. Can't imagine them not saying something even with all that's going on. Have you tried messaging them?"

"I have, but for some reason they aren't going through," Victor responds.

"What now?" Lilly asks.

"For us or for them?" Victor responds.

"Both." Lilly shrugs. "I need to know where to go if I don't want a bunch of soldiers shooting at me." She laughs.

"For us, we try to find our friends. We'll head home first. Maybe Gibbs has heard something. I can't get a message to him either."

"And what happens here?" I ask.

Victor shrugs. "That's up to the Nightlings. We played our part. We got the Market. Now it's time to get out of Dodge."

"We're just going to leave after everything we've accomplished?"

"It's one battle, Jett. One battle they weren't ready for. You can be sure we won't catch them unaware like that again. Look, I'm tired. We can have this debate again tomorrow. For now, let's go to jewelry shop, make sure Jensen and Becka aren't there. Then straight home." The promise of rest drives me to agree.

The door to Shine for Shine is propped open when we arrive. Nightlings are rushing in and out with various supplies, likely preparing to fortify their positions at the train stations before the Patriarch can send more troops. We step inside the shop, and a booming voice comes from behind us.

"We did it! We beat them!" Grent blares out.

"Yup," Victor says simply.

"Where are the hostages? They fled here during the battle," I ask.

"Downstairs getting some rest. They had a trying day. But your friends are not among them." How can he be sure? Has he met them before? I wrack my brain trying to recall.

"Where are they?" Victor presses.

The bear man shrugs. "No clue. Thought they were with the Levite group same as you. Guess not."

"We need to borrow some of your men to help look for them."

"Sorry, can't do that. I need all my men to keep the Patriarch from retaking the platform."

"Oi, ye really going to go back on yer word like that? We had a deal," Spike interjects, his voice loud and aggressive.

"Did we? I seem to recall our deal being we'd help you rescue your friends from the Levites, which we did. You'd give us the Market, which you did. By my count, we are square."

"We're a long way from it," Victor snaps.

Grent holds up his hands defensively. "My men risked their lives, followed your orders as you gave them to rescue the group of people downstairs, including the pretty little girl with you. We said we'd help you rescue your friends. She's a friend, isn't she? Where's the problem?"

"Don't play daft. Ye know full well who we were trying to get to. Ye know they aren't here."

Grent nods, his smile revealing his perfect, surprisingly white teeth. "Well, here's the thing, I can't spare men to help some random Undesirables. But if I were sparing those men to help new and promising recruits..." He lets his thought sit for a moment. "That's totally different. I've never seen someone pull one over on the Patriarch like that." He turns his attention to Victor. "We could use someone like you in the battles to come. Why don't you join us? Together we could—"

"Hard pass," Victor interrupts. "We are not tools to be used. We're people. Until you see the difference, you're no better than the Patriarch."

Grent growls and steps into the shop. "Watch your tongue, boy. You may be clever, but talk to me like that again and I'll bury my axe in your skull."

Spike steps forward, and Kane cuts him off. "Ah, ah, ah, can't let you do that friend." Spike glares over Kane's shoulder.

"I don't want to fight with you," Grent says with a sigh. "I want you to join us. I'll make you my tactical advisor, place my men at your disposal. Just say yes. Help us bring down the Patriarch once and for all."

"Won't do it," Victor retorts without missing a beat. "You want to fight a hopeless battle, be my guest. Taking the Market is one thing. Holding it, that's something entirely different."

"Don't give me that. The Patriarch can be beaten, and you know it. We've proved as much in a single night. Now, we have the Market, the center for distribution of resources. We control the most strategic position in the city. Still, you think we have no chance?"

The Patriarch uses the Market to wield control over the people. There are no shops outside of the Market. No privately owned businesses. Each class has its own sector where they are required to live and work. Each sector has schools, medical complexes, labs, distribution centers, work sites, and miscellaneous other facilities depending on the occupations of that class. Everyone works for the Patriarch. Farmers bring in crops that are taken directly to Patriarch warehouses. Goods from miners and craftsmen, anything produced in Dios goes directly to the Patriarch. The people are then paid a small sum of credits and given a portion of the resources they need to live on based on which class they are in.

Everyone is given an extra portion of supplies based on their occupation. Farmers are given a little more food. Miners are given more coal but less food. In order to prevent the people from establishing mutually beneficial exchanges, the Patriarch requires all trading to be done in the Market. The farmer with a little extra food can trade his excess to get other supplies he may need. Of course, those trades are taxed, and the merchants get a cut of the profits as well. The system prevents anyone from being able to get ahead. The centerpiece of the system is the Market Sector.

"Bring her in," Grent barks. A Nightling vanishes down the steps in the back room, returning a few minutes later with a middle-aged woman followed by a teenage boy. He's fit and tall with sandy brown hair. His face is covered in dirt and debris. The woman walks right up to Victor and takes his hand in hers, staring into his eyes.

"Sir." Her tone is respectful and gracious. For what? Does Victor know her? He doesn't look like he knows her. "My name is Maggie Sinder. This—this is my son, Naddler." The teenage boy is wearing a muddy red cloak with soft yellow-gold stitching. Running down the center of the cloak is an ornate pattern of interconnected shapes forming a slightly hypnotizing design. The sleeves are long and drooping like something a wizard of old might wear. Naddler is a Red Dragon. He nods to Victor, avoiding eye contact as he holds his head down. This is the standard timid posture of anyone living in Dios. Act like a sheep, look submissive, or else. "Sir, my son is alive because of you."

Her words rob the room of its air. No one speaks or even shifts. The moment is frozen in time. I can see from Victor's demeanor that her words hit him. Victor can handle strategy, planning, even the most intense of circumstances with a calm and calculating cool. Emotions, being forced to feel the impact of what he does—that is the crack in Victor's armor.

"I just wanted to thank you." She lifts his hand and kisses it, holding her head down as if bowing to Victor. "Thank you for saving my son. It means the world to me."

"Well, we're in it now. Aren't we, brotha?" Spike whispers over my shoulder.

"Why do you say that?" Lilly asks. Apparently, she has good hearing.

"Vic may act like a nothing gets to him, but could ye really walk away after hearing something like that?"

"What do you mean? He knows he saved lives," I counter.

"Aye, but it's not a strategic argument anymore, is it? Grent made it personal, emotional. The mind is a powerful tool. Yet no matter how well it works, it always plays second fiddle to the heart."

"That seems like a stretch, doesn't it? You really think he brought her in just to manipulate us?"

Spike shrugs. "What I know is, that woman, intentionally or not, just placed a lot on Vic's shoulders. By thanking him for saving one life, she'll make him feel like he's responsible for all the lives here. Pretty sure that's what Grent has in mind."

"No way he's that manipulative," Lilly objects. "That would be—"

"Maybe not, but something doesn't add up," Spike says, his tone hushed.

"What do you mean?"

"Seems a wee bit strange, doesn't it? Right as the Patriarch is preparing an all-out assault on the Nightlings, we are told our friends have been captured and brought to the Market. Yet, we have time to get here, get in position, and set up an ambush before the Levites, who had already taken our friends and already boarded the train, managed to arrive."

The events start replaying in my mind. Brelar warned us about the Levites, said they were searching for something. They took our friends. The announcement of the rebellion came later, once we'd reached the Market. If the Patriarch was cracking down on a rebellion, why would they have Levites out in Sector C? What could they be looking for that was more important than stopping a brewing rebellion? Why would they bother to take two random Undesirables into custody in the first place? Spike's suspicions were making a little too much sense.

"Right." I nod, starting to see the picture Spike is painting. "Levites capture Becka and Jensen. We find the Levites but no Becka or Jensen. Instead, they have completely different hostages."

"Aye, brotha. Now yer getting it. Someone has been lying to us. If Becka and Jensen weren't with the Levites, where are they? Were they really captured at all? Seems Grent got everything he wanted: data-disc, Market, our help. Now, he's leveraging what he already has to try and get more."

"We need to talk to Victor. We can't let him—"

"It was my pleasure, ma'am," Victor responds. "If you'll excuse us, we have some things to discuss."

"You say it's a battle that can't be won," Grent urges. "Don't you see, Victor, it's a battle worth fighting. This isn't about power. This is about doing what is right, bringing down the oppressors, creating a new world. Your plans, your strategies—you could save a lot of lives. People, like Naddler." Grent's sales pitch is hard.

"I'm not doing anything until I find our friends. After that, we'll see."

Grent seems disturbed. I get the feeling he's not used to being told no. "Think of your other friends, Victor." Grent's voice feels desperate, almost pleading. Is he afraid of something? "What happens to your cozy little neighborhood, to all those innocent people if you walk away now?" Something about his tone is off-putting. Is that a threat? If we don't join him, he's going to kill our friends? Is he trying to warn us? The Patriarch certainly has video of us now. Maybe he's just trying to say they are coming for us. It doesn't feel like a friendly warning of coming retaliation. His words feel menacing.

With the trains still down, the journey home is a long one. We've been up for a long time. I'm tired, my muscles are burning, my bones ache. I need rest. Instead of rest, we have a long march to the other side of Dios. We make our way into the tunnels, expecting to walk our way home. It's going to take forever. When we reach the bottom of the stairs, we see the tunnels are already lit. The underground train car is floating just off the tracks. Sitting in the front seat is Kane.

"What are you doing here?" Victor asks.

"Don't worry, I'm not here to try and talk you into joining. Truth is, we wouldn't have had a chance if it weren't for you. Grent may think we are square, but I don't see it that way. I can't do much about your missing friends. At least I can give you a ride home." Sweet relaxation. For a brute who loves violence, Kane has an oddly kind way at times.

The underground train car stops. "One last thing. If you ever need to access the tunnels, remember this code: 1030405."

"What about the thumbprint?" I ask.

"That code doesn't require a thumbprint. It will, however, alert us to your presence in the tunnels."

After saying goodbye to Kane, we make our way up the secret steps and exit near the Lazy Loafer. Seeing our home on the horizon feels good. Food, a warm bed, and sleep. Everything in me longs for sleep. Instead, Gibbs bursts through the front door and rushes toward us. This is just great. What now?

"Gibbs?" Victor asks.

"You're not going to like it," Gibbs responds. Victor glares over Gibbs' shoulder. "Jensen and Becka were at the house when I returned. I checked with the neighbors. There were no Levites in the area."

"That rotten vomitus mass," Victor curses under his breath as we reach the steps leading up to the house. Grent deceived us, used us, and now he knows full well the value Victor brings. It's going to be hard to stay out of the conflict now.

We walk inside the house. Everyone else looks up at us, somber expressions on their faces. Gibbs pulls up a video on his data-pad. It's a report being broadcast of the terrorists taking over the Market. The segment shows various aspects of the fight, but each segment ends with me looking particularly fierce, firing my rifle into the Cam Drone. They use the actual footage from the drone I shot, making it look like I'm aiming directly at the person viewing the clip.

"This is a real shinshew show, isn't it?" Jensen asks. I don't have the patience for him tonight. "Listen." His tone shifts. "We are here for you, whatever you need." The words leave his mouth reluctantly, as if saying them causes him physical pain. I turn and face him. He avoids my gaze. "I know I'm a pain. You risked your lives trying to save me. No one has ever done anything like that for me. So, thank you." He pauses again. "Just maybe try to avoid the cameras next time?"

"Aww, so sweet. I knew you cared," I respond.

"I don't! It's just a real pain finding idiots that are somewhat tolerable. It'd be a real inconvenience to replace you." Jensen shakes my hand. That's as close to nice as he may be capable of being.

The windows hum to life and the blueish-purple haze lights up. We all stop. Special broadcasts are rare, this one is certainly going to be about us. The screen flashes and the High Father's face appears. He is wearing his normal overly elaborate clothing, but his face lacks its typical composure. "Before the Great Collapse, the world was divided into many nations, each working against the others for its own agenda. They were disunified by language, by culture, by understanding. They built great weapons, then turned those weapons against each other. They killed each other by the millions with devices that poisoned the air itself. What little life survived was corrupted, was changed." He pauses. For a moment, he looks as if he is trying to settle his stomach. "The world outside our walls is home to chaos, death, and the Depraved. My forefathers built this great city- the dome that surrounds us keeps the fumes away. The great walls that encircle us keep the monsters at bay. Dios was a shield and a haven for the chosen people of Bealz. My Forefathers founded the Patriarch." Where is he going with this history lesson?

"My children, it is with a heavy heart that I confess to you. I have failed you. I have failed the legacy of my bloodline. I have allowed division to rear its ugly head in our great city." He hangs his head. Is this anguish or an attempt to hide his rage? "I thought we had reached a place of peace and unity. I let my guard down. I wanted to be gracious and loving to you, as you are all my children. In the process I allowed our enforcement of the law to become lax. I must take responsibility. Today, a group of divisive terrorists attacked and seized control of the Market Sector."

"Guys," Olivia shouts over the volume of the Broadcast, which we cannot turn down or mute. "You're going to want at the alerts post on your datapads. Olivia brings up an image on her data-pad. She holds her arm up projecting the screen for us to see. It's report about the attack. At the top of the page are pictures of Grent, Kane, Victor, Spike, Lilly, and me. My heart sinks into the depths of my chest. Why is Lilly on here? "They've declared you all to be enemies of the peace, given you criminal ID numbers, put out alerts. The have file for each of you with a link to report on sight, and a reward for any information given."

She sighs as if apologizing. "Domes-up, everyone in Dios is going to be looking for you now."

"Why is Lilly on the list? She's not a part of this," I challenge, my frustration bubbling over.

"Oh, am I not?" Lilly protests, folding her arms over her chest and leaning back, glaring at me.

"The videos they are showing, with you giving her instructions and her leading the hostages out of the Square, make her look involved," Olivia explains. Great, now my attempt to rescue her has put her in even more danger.

"We have to—"

"We aren't going to do anything tonight but rest," Victor cuts me off. "Lilly, you are more than welcome to stay here tonight. You can room with Becka and Olivia."

"Thank you, but I need to get home. My place is registered, so if they are looking for me, it won't take them long to find me. I've got some things I need to get. I can come back in the morning."

"You're not walking alone. I'll take you," I declare.

Gibbs puts his hand on my shoulder. "You need to rest. I'll take your lady home- make sure she gets there safely, okay?"

I'm too tired to argue. "Ok, but give me a minute." Gibbs nods and I guide Lilly away from the others.

"You need to be really careful, ok?"

She smiles, "Are you worried about me Jett Lasting?"

I nod. "Of course, I am," my fingers caress the necklace in my pocket.

Her smile brightens and she puts a hand on my cheek, "It's really cute that you are so protective, but, you know I can take care of myself?"

"Of course, youuu---" her lips press to mine muffling my words. For the briefest of moments, nothing else exists but this moment-her lips and mine locked together.

"Until I see you next," she licks her lip and steps back.

"I got you something," I pull the necklace from my pocket. Her eyes light up as she lifts it from my hand.

"Jett Lasting!" She exclaims grinning ear to ear, "When did you? How did you? Wh-" she shakes her head. "It's perfect. I love it. Do you mind?" She turns around and pulls her long, dark hair off her neck. My hands shake as I slip the delicate chain around her neck. The clasp is impossible to close with fumbling, trembling fingers, but eventually I get it. She thanks me again and gives me another kiss before Gibbs escorts her home.

Victor forces us to stay awake long enough to eat. Then I hit my bed like a sack of potatoes. I'm asleep the moment my head hits the pillow. When I open my eyes, my whole body feels toasty. The room is lit up with beautiful red-orange hues dancing over the walls around me. The warmth is relaxing. It feels soothing to my aching body. The heat grows. The warmth becomes uncomfortable. Something is wrong. Something is burning. I'm on my feet. My room is encased in fire. Leaping through the doorway, I burst down the stairs, looking back in time to see my bed engulfed in flames.

Stumbling through the front door, I cover my mouth with my elbow, coughing up smoke. The clean air soothes the burning pain in my chest. I look up and see the houses all over our neighborhood are on fire. Dark figures rush into the streets as men, women, and children flee the horror of their burning homes. Jeeps block the intersections. Around them, soldiers—not helping, not even moving, just watching. Perhaps this is the retaliation Grent was trying to warn us about?

The unmistakable sound of gunfire rings out. The first shot is followed by another and another. The soldiers are shooting families as they flee their burning homes. Mart and Canty Borden, who live in the house next to ours, rush down the street past me, begging for help. Six gunshots and their bodies collapse to the ground, sliding from their momentum. What sort of monster shoots innocent civilians like this? Around me are the bodies of several neighbors: Wes and Talli Grop and their daughter Victoria. They are Undesirables just trying to stay alive. They are not rebels. They pose no threat. The Patriarch has no reason to kill them.

Brelar, the bruised and beaten boy, hobbles down the street, crying. His arm is in a sling, and his right leg drags behind him as he slowly presses forward. His hand clutching a few strands of partially braided red leather. I want to run to him, to scoop him up, and to flee to safety. A gunshot behind me freezes my legs underneath me.

I see a single soldier walking toward Brelar. He's far enough away that I can't see him clearly. He's a bigger man, his uniform unique, memorable. Disbelief courses through my veins. It's Commander Stone. Brelar sees him and increases his speed, trying desperately to pull his useless leg faster, straining against his own injuries.

"They hurt me. I scared," he calls out.

Drawing attention to myself is the worst idea. The smoke and flames have kept me out of the crosshairs so far, but that won't last much longer. Standing here and watching isn't an option. I have to do something. Brelar doesn't deserve this. He's a boy. His whole life is ahead of him.

"Brelar!" I cry out, rushing toward him as fast as I can. I see recognition in his eyes, determination on his face.

"Mister Jett, help me?" His voice is desperate. His arm reaches towards me begging me to pick him up and take him away. He pulls with his one good leg, grunting and wincing. I reach for him. Something warm and wet splatters over my face and chest. My eyes close for a moment. When I open them, I see blood on my hands. Shock. Denial. Disbelief. They all swarm over me as Brelar's lifeless body falls into my arms.

I sit there holding him, looking at his motionless body. His arm hangs limp, hand clutching his ruined bird blanket until the very end. This isn't happening. Soldiers don't shoot children. Not defenseless, harmless children. This is a dream, a nightmare like the one I've so often had about my mother. I just need to wake up. I can't. I can't wake from this nightmare because it's not a dream. It's worse; it's real.

A cry of rage erupts from my mouth as I gently set Brelar's body down. Before I can charge headlong toward Commander Stone, I feel myself being pulled back. I try to wrestle free from the grip, but it's too strong. I look over my shoulder. It's Spike.

"Let me go, Spike!" I grunt between my teeth.

"No, brotha, I can't do that."

"I have to stop him," I plead.

"He's gone, Jett. You can't help him, not like this. We have to run."

Spike pulls me behind the house toward the woods. Giving in, I stop resisting and go with him. Victor is waiting at the edge of the woods.

"We have to get out of here now. The soldiers won't be far behind you," Victor shouts.

"What about the others?" I ask.

"They've already gone. Split up into teams of two. Making their way to the tunnels. We will meet them there."

"Why are they doing this?" I ask.

"Retaliation, brotha. We made them look weak, vulnerable. They are showcasing the depth of their power."

"But, how did they know where we live?" We are squatters. We don't own the house. We don't have a registered address. My question goes unanswered. Spike and Victor look at each other for a moment. Maybe one of the Red Caps we bribe when returning from the Market reported us? That would explain why they hit every house. They didn't know which one we live in.

"That's a question for a different time. Let's go!" Victor's command is urgent.

We rush through the woods, weaving between trees, using them as cover to hide our escape. The forest will give us plenty of space to get away as it runs almost the entire distance to the Lazy Loafer. I just hope they don't have other blockades set up. If we can't get to the tunnel entrance, escaping Sector C is going to be really challenging.

The woods end about three hundred yards from the secret tunnel entrance. It's all open. As soon as we step out, there will be no hiding. If there are any soldiers in the area, we are totally heaped. We scan every direction. When we are confident there are no soldiers around, we dash as fast as we can toward the tunnel entrance. I have no idea where the others are. We could be the first or the last to arrive.

Headlights approaching from a nearby street send my body into overdrive.

"Get down!" I shout, pointing to a small mound that should be big enough for the three of us to hide behind until the vehicle passes. Victor arrives first. I slide down next to him. Spike dives last, his body landing next to us just as the headlights slide over the mound.

"We can't stay here long; soldiers will be coming through the woods after us," Victor says. We're pinned down behind the hill. Move too soon and we risk being exposed to the vehicle that just passed us.

Move too late and we risk being seen by the soldiers pursuing us. No pressure.

"Look," Spike whispers. I follow his finger and see Telmen, Becka, and Jensen opening the secret access to the tunnels. Olivia follows. At least they are safe. We crawl on hands and knees until we are sure the vehicle is out of view. Pushing myself up, I sprint for the tunnel entrance, ignoring the pain in my gut as I do. My legs feel heavier with every step. My lungs are an open flame.

I don't dare stop until I reach the bottom of the stairs.

"Where's Gibbs?" Olivia asks.

"He's not here yet?" Victor's face appears concerned. Olivia shakes her head.

"We can't just wait here," Telmen says. "They will find us. We need to close the door, right? Before they see it."

"No, we wait for Gibbs," I scold. Spike is at the top of the stairs, peering out.

"No sign of him anywhere, brotha. What ye want me to do?" Spike looks down at Victor.

"We have to close it," Jensen interjects. "If the Red Caps find us, we are all dead."

"He's our friend," I insist again. "We can't just leave him here." My hands ball into fists as I square off against Jensen.

"You think I want to leave him?" Jensen retorts. "I know what it feels like to get left behind. I hate it. What good is it if the rest of us get caught waiting? Think about it for one second. You don't even know he'll make it. If we wait, you can be sure we won't. You want to risk all our lives in the hopes that maybe he shows up?" I feel my arm moving on its own as I draw it back. Victor stops me.

"He's right. We can't take the risk. Gibbs is smart. He can take care of himself. Waiting here is a risk he wouldn't want us to take," Victor explains.

"But, we can't just...we don't—"

"Jett, think, if he's been captured, we can't help him. If he's late, holed up some place waiting for the heat to die down, we can't wait for him. The best thing we can do for Gibbs is to make sure we don't get caught." Victor is right, as always. One day I'll be smart enough to stop arguing with him. The door to the tunnel entrance seals behind us, closing off the world we once knew.

CHAPTER FOURTEEN

On the far side of the tunnel, across the magnetic track that allows the train car to hover, is an automated sidewalk. We cross over, and the track starts propelling us toward the Market. It's much slower than the train car, but it gives us time to rest. I lie down, close my eyes, and try sleep. When I open my eyes again, the darkness of the tunnel makes me disoriented. I don't know if I slept for minutes or hours. In the low light, I see most of my friends still sleeping.

Victor and Spike are standing a few yards off, leaning against the railing of the moving sidewalk.

"I don't like it either, but do you see a better option?" Victor's words are hushed, probably trying not to wake or worry anyone. Slowly, my body still groaning from exhaustion, I make my way over to them.

Spike sighs. "I dunna see any other options. That's the problem. We're stuck between a lion and a serpent."

"What are you guys talking about?" I ask leaning next to Victor.

"The path forward, fate of the world, odds of our surviving the conflict to come. You know, light relaxing stuff," Victor answers with a smile.

"How long you think before we get there?"

Victor shakes his head. "Saw a sign for Sector A not long ago. Shouldn't be too much longer."

Spike smiles and shifts his position, leaning back to look up at the ceiling. "Ye know, brotha, there's something else that's been bothering me about last night."

"What?" Victor asks.

"We went into battle because that boyo, Brelar, told us our friends were taken by Levites, right?"

"Right."

"But it wasn't Levites that took them. Levites weren't even there. So, what would have given wee Brelar the idea they had?"

"You mean, why did he lie to us?" Victor asks.

"Aye, tis exactly what I mean."

"I've been wondering the same thing. And...did you notice our data-pads?"

"Aye, we tried getting ahold of ye after the battle. Signal wouldn't go through. Thought maybe the Patriarch had jammed communication signals or something."

Victor nods. "That was my first assumption as well, but I intentionally had Grent reposition several of his men right before battle. Made sure it was urgent. He sent them messages with his data-pad. They moved."

"Shinshew, ye can't be serious."

"Could be he has some way around their jammers. It is suspicious though. If the Patriarch had used jammers, the signal should have come back as soon as we got out of range. There shouldn't be—" Victor holds onto the word, reaching under his data-pad and pulling free a thin chip. "When would the Patriarch have planted localized signal jammers on us? It doesn't make sense."

"Ye think it was—"

"Think of it this way: Why would the Patriarch beat a child and have him deceive us into joining forces with the Nightlings? Why would they even think of it? It's not like we were known to them. If it wasn't them, who stands to gain the most from our involvement in this little uprising?"

"Heap! I'll kill him meself. That daft—"

"No, Spike," I interrupt. "You can't kill him. We need him, at least for the time being."

"You're learning." Victor smiles proudly and smacks me on the shoulder. "He's right. Grent must live. I've use for him."

"Oh aye, he beat a child, used our friends to trick us into risking our lives to win his battle, and ye just want to let it slide? Ye are a daft pair, the both of ye."

"Not let it slide, Spike. Delay punishment. When the time is right, Grent will die. Only after we get what we need from him, agreed?"

Spike grumbles, "Aye, but I get to be the one who does it."

Victor nods. "We should all get some rest. I've a feeling the days ahead are going to be long and challenging."

I take the remaining time to rest, lying back down and watching the ceiling of the tunnel slowly drift by as we move. The adrenaline of the night before has taken a toll. My whole body feels achy. My mind is clear from rest. My thoughts move from daydreaming of what the future could hold, to Lilly. Lilly. In the chaos of the moment, I forgot about Lilly. I am a fool. She is in danger. I type on my data-pad, shooting her a message. No response. I try again. Still nothing. My eyes grow heavy watching the screen of my data-pad.

When I wake, everyone else is up and waiting. We make our way into the Market. Nightlings and several other beggar gangs are patrolling around, moving supplies from one place to another. It looks similar to a normal day in the Market, only, instead of merchants frantically preparing goods, there are rebels frantically preparing weapons.

Victor grabs a passing Nightling and forces him to take us to Grent. He leads us to the Market Square. Grent has set up a command center there. Subtle. As we enter the square, Kane cuts us off.

"Look at this, Grent owes me 50 credits." Kane walks over and hugs me, leaning back to show his strange sinister grin. "I just heard the Patriarch attacked a neighborhood in Sector C. They showed your faces on the report. I was gathering some men to come find you. Here you are, saving me the trouble." I can't tell if he's serious or playing with me. His words sound so sincere, but he's kind of a crazy person. "Are you stocked?"

I nod. "For the most part. One of our friends didn't make it. Don't know if he was captured or worse. And Lilly." Why am I saying this to the crazy rebel leader?

"Lilly's your girl, right? The one that—"

"Yes, that's the one. Did you hear anything about her? Did they attack Sector B as well?"

Kane shakes his head. "Not that I've heard. I'll take some men and look for them. You have a scan of your other friend?" Victor swipes his data-pad over Kane's. "Very good. Don't worry. I'll find them."

"Grent said you couldn't spare the men," Victor challenges. "What's changed?"

"A lot, actually. The beggar gangs have all rallied behind us. We've had Undesirables, Plebs, even some Artisans showing up ready to join the fight. Since the PDF soldiers we killed last night were gracious enough to leave their weapons when they died, we are well positioned to hold the Market. I'm sending out teams to find more recruits so we can take the fight to the Temple Sector."

"Where is Grent now? Seems we can't get away from each other," Victor states.

"Just there, set up shop in the warehouse. This mean you're joining us?" Kane asks as he smiles.

"Not by choice, but since we are stuck in this fight now, I'm going to make sure we have a chance to win it."

Kane shrugs. "Win, lose. Just point me in the Patriarch's direction, and let me do some killing."

Grent has transformed the warehouse into a rebel headquarters. Plans are being drawn up, maps display unit locations, and motion sensors are being monitored in places rebels haven't been positioned.

"Well, look who's back! Kane was right." Grent scowls. "Now I have to pay him." Grent sets down the pad he was making notes on and walks around his little war table. Why is reality never how we imagine it? My whole life I've dreamed of being a part of something, fighting against the Patriarch. Here I am, in the midst of it, not just fighting but actually playing a role. I should feel excited. This should have all the allure of a dream come true. Instead, I feel like a rat being guided through a maze by some unseen hand for some unknown purpose.

I always thought taking sides was about doing what is right over doing what is wrong. In this moment, life seems much greyer. The Patriarch rules this city as tyrants. They have done unspeakable things. The only way to oppose the Patriarch is to join a rebellion led by a manipulative coward who would beat a child and force him to lie to trick us into joining forces with him. Do I choose the devil I know? Or could it be that the devil I don't know is a far greater evil? What do you choose when both options are bad?

Interrupting my thought process comes another report. The screens flash to life, and the sky projects the pretty young girl, Barbra Boone. It's a story about us, the violent terrorists who massacred the brave soldiers of the PDF and many city guards who were just trying to protect

220

innocent lives. It's sad that people will believe what these screens say, as if the messages come from the mouth of Bealz himself.

The camera pans out to the unmistakable figure of Lorth Drant. My jaw drops as I stare at the screen. My arms fall to my sides. Standing next to Lorth Drant, wrists shackled together, bright yellow sash covered in dirt and soot, is Lilly. The camera zooms in on her face so I can see a thick application of makeup, probably to cover up bruises. My stomach threatens to expel its contents. Her dark hair covers her face until Drant pushes it back behind her ears, giving the entire city a good look at her. The wood of the table in front of me creaks as my hands grip it.

"Good citizens of Dios, this woman, if you can call her that, is Lilly Moonslight. She is a Class B educator. She teaches at Paternal Blessing Secondary School. Despite her father's loyal service as a member of the Patriarch Defense Force, she has dishonored his legacy. This woman is a traitor, a rebel, a vile disrupter of the holy peace of our great city. As hard as it may be to believe, this foul woman was instrumental in the terrorist assault on the Market Sector last night."

Instrumental? She was a hostage, or sort of a hostage. She was trying to help her students. Yea, I guess that's more than enough reason for the Patriarch. We never should have let her go home. We should have made her stay with us. At least then, she'd be here.

Blind rage takes over. I slam my fist down on the table. Pain surges through my hand climbing up my wrist and into my forearm. "We have to get her back!"

Victor holds up his hands, "Jett, you-"

"If you tell me to calm down, I'm going to-"

Spike steps between us, "Take a breath, brotha."

"We shouldn't have let her go. It was too dangerous. Why didn't I stop her?"

"He offered brotha, Vic asked her to stay. Couldn't rightly force her now could we?"

"Maybe we should have. At least then she'd be here."

"Lilly's a big girl. She knew the risks. She left on her own accord."

"Vic! Why didn't we try harder?" I can see the hurt in Victor's eyes as he stares at me. He doesn't deserve this. I know he doesn't. I can't stop myself. I can't keep this rage inside, and he's the closest target. Rage boils over into pain and fear. I slump to the ground; my legs no longer willing to hold my body up.

I feel a hand resting gently on my shoulder. I glance up to see Becka standing over me, softly rubbing my back, "It's ok Jett. You're allowed to be upset. We will figure something out. We always do." She looks up at the others, "This broadcast wasn't an accident. They are trying to drive a wedge between us."

"And what would a girl like you know of tactics?" Grent snaps.

Spike turns to face him, "Talk to her like that again." I can see his hands curl into fists.

"Spike Joseph Raynor," Becka snaps. Spike spins around looking like a puppy who got caught peeing on the rug. "I don't need you to fight my battles for me." Spike shrinks down looking more docile than I've ever seen him. Becka turns her ire to Grent, "You want to know why you never win? You don't listen. You don't learn. You just truck ahead like the mindless buffoon you are. If you'd asked, if you'd learned, then you'd know I grew up in the Temple Sector. I was a Potter in training. I've seen firsthand how the Patriarch breaks people down. I was trained to do it." Becka's eyes flash with an intensity I've not seen before. "You want to rage like a child, go someplace else. Adults are talking." Grent's jaw dropped so wide a small jeep could fit inside it.

"The greatest victory is breaking the enemy's resistance without fighting," Victor says under his breath.

"What are ye talking about?"

"Becka's right. The broadcast is too perfect, too well timed. They are attacking our resistance." Victor explains.

"Oh no." Olivia's voice is soft and sympathetic. Her expression haunting. Her words might as well be a spear through my heart. I lift myself up using the table. Lilly is not alone. Next to her are her two brothers and her parents. My heart races. Why are they all there?

"Treason is one of the highest crimes a person can commit. Treason doesn't happen in a vacuum. This young girl's radical behavior is the result of a toxic family—a family that would have trained her better if they were good and fair people. Therefore, we find the entire family guilty of treason." It's not just Lilly. Her whole family is being branded as traitors by association? How can anyone think this is justice?

Lorth Drant continues, "But dear citizens, the Holy Father is as merciful as he is righteous. He has declared this treacherous family should receive a modicum of mercy. Rather than execution in the Market Square, they will be given the honor of becoming champions of our city. As Outlands Officers, they have a chance to redeem themselves, to restore their honor, and to defend the city they worked to destroy." Yea, more like they have the opportunity to get torn apart by the Depraved.

I bury my face in my hands. They took an innocent girl and her family, sentenced them to death, and are trying to make themselves look merciful and benevolent in the process? They know she didn't do anything and yet they're using her to help a quell the rebellious fire growing in their city. This cannot happen. This will not happen.

I slam my fist down onto the wood table and look up at Grent. "We get her back."

Grent looks at me as if assessing my request. "Now you want to fight when there's something in it for you?" He folds his arms in front of his chest.

"We get her back!" I shout, louder and with more determination.

Victor steps between us and pushes me away. Looking over his shoulder to Grent, he murmurs, "Give us a minute. We'll be back." Following Victor's lead, our group circles up outside the warehouse, out of earshot of any potentially curious Nightlings.

"You know what's at stake," Victor prompts. "This is not a decision I can make for us. What do you all think?"

Surprisingly, Jensen is the first to speak up. "All these years I believed the system was in place for a reason and I was just unlucky. After my parents…" Jensen shakes his head, "I thought I just needed to prove myself. Then, I'd be elevated to the class and life I deserved. After seeing what they did to our home, to Brelar, I don't believe any more. I put too much trust in them, and they betrayed that trust. I want them to pay! I say we fight. Besides, the Patriarch already wants us dead. At least with the Nightlings it'll be harder."

There's a moment of surprised silence that passes as we all just look at each other. I never thought I'd hear something like this from Jensen.

"Aye, maybe that's true," Spike offers. "But maybe Grent gets us all killed on some fool's errand. We got dangers on all sides."

"We don't trust him," Olivia responds. "We trust Victor. We stick together, and we can through this too. I'm with Jensen. Our best chance is with the Nightlings."

"We have to get Lilly back. Jett just figured out how to talk to her." Becka winks at me. "If rescuing Lilly means joining the Nightlings, I say we do it."

"Have you all lost your minds?" Telman asks, throwing his arms into the air. "You realize we are talking about the Patriarch? They have armies, weapons. We can't fight them. We definitely can't beat them. This is crazy. We have to run, hide. We're good at that. Sure, the Patriarch is looking for us, but we know how to hide. That's what we do. We are thieves, not warriors."

"Jett?" Victor asks, giving me a nod. "What do you think?"

"All our lives the Patriarch has told us we are worthless, meaningless. We are undesirable, unfit, unworthy because we are orphans, or we were born to the wrong families. They sit in their comfortable homes, enjoying their lives of excess while we struggle just to survive. For years, we thought surviving was the best we could do. Like drawing breath was enough. It's not enough. We are people, just like them. We may be different. Different does not mean lesser. I want more than survival. I want freedom. I want to be who I want to be, not who some government bureaucrat tells me to be. I want to see the world change. Maybe that change won't be better, and maybe the price of that change will be my life. But if I have to choose between accepting the world that is and dying for a world that could be, I choose the latter."

Victor smiles and gives me an approving nod. "Well, that's all I needed to hear. I'm in as well. We are in danger either way. Might as well try to do something with it. Anyone who wants to fight, stay here. If you don't, this is where we part ways. We won't hold it against you. This is your life, your future we're talking about. Make sure you make your decision for the right reasons. If you want to go, I've got some contacts who can help you hide out for a while."

"Well, let's get to it then, brotha," Spike says.

"You're going to stay?" I ask, looking at Spike with a confused expression.

"Aye, course I'm gonna stay. If I go, who's going to watch your back? Olivia? Pfff. Unless yer getting attack by a bunch of cute purses, she's not gonna do much, is she?"

"Hey!" Olivia objects. Spike chuckles.

"But Spike, you and Grent—"

"Well, I'm not fighting for Grent, am I brotha? I'm fighting for you. Let's go get yer girl back."

That leaves Telmen standing by himself across from the rest of the group. He paces back and forth looking at us.

"Are you serious? All of you? Really? You all want to fight? You're crazy. This is totally insane. Have you lost your minds? You must have lost your minds. This isn't real. You are playing a joke on me. Ha ha. Everybody laugh at Telmen. Guys, this is a rebellion against the Patriarch. You get that, right? Like we run from the Patriarch. We hide. We do anything but fight.

"It's okay, Telmen," I assure him. "You don't have to fight. You can—"

"Be the only one who runs away?" Telmen interrupts me. "You guys rescued me from the Levites. Now you think I'm just going to abandon you? I'm in. I just want you to know how crazy you are."

Victor smirks. "Good, now let's go join a rebellion."

"Give us a minute?" I ask more than say. Vic nods.

I grab Jensen by the arm and pull him around the corner away from the others.

"What?" Jensen already sounds annoyed.

"We don't talk much about the past, or personal things. At least, you and I don't. Ealier, you mentioned being left behind earlier, now your parents. Can I ask what happened," I say trying not to sound forceful or aggressive.

"What do you care?" Jensen snaps.

I sigh, "I know we don't always get along. But, for better or worse, we're family."

Jensen rolls his eyes, "Fine, if it'll shut you up, I'll tell you. My dad was a dreamer. He was never content with what he had. He convinced my mother that if they worked hard enough, they could prove themselves to the Assessors and we'd get assigned to a Class where we could have a proper life. They trained every day in preparation for the Middling

226

Days. One year, they got noticed. The Assessors came to our home and told them they had been selected to work with a special team on the Filia Lucem project. It was a high honor for only the most qualified and dedicated citizens. They got so excited. We started packing immediately. When we showed up at the train station to meet them, the Assessor's said children were not allowed. If they wanted this honor, they'd have to leave me behind. They did. Right there at the train station, with my bag packed and ready, they left. They promised of course that once they were settled, they'd come back to get me. Told me they were doing all of this for me. They left and they never came back. I waited at the station for days not knowing what else to do. That's where Victor found me."

I stare at him for a moment as I let what he shared sink in. "I am sorry to hear that. I had no idea. Why didn't you say something before?"

"What's the point? You wouldn't understand," Jensen's tone loses some of its edge.

"Are you serious? You think I wouldn't understand? Of course, I know exactly what it feels like to lose your parents," I try not to hold back my frustration, but I can feel it seeping through.

"That's not the same thing," Jensen snaps.

"How is that not the same?" I press still failing to get a lid on my frustration.

"Because your parents didn't leave you by choice!" Jensen snaps his teeth grinding together. "Your parents were killed. That's horrible I'm sure, but it's not the same as watching the people who are supposed to care for, leave you behind like a piece of garbage."

The wind rushes from my lungs as I exhale. He's right. I didn't even think of how it would feel to watch my parents leave. No wonder Jensen always seems so angry.

Finally, after what feels like an eternal quiet, I nod, "Your right. I don't know what that's like." I put my hand on Jensen's shoulder and look at him, "We aren't going anywhere. Like it or not, you're one of us."

Jensen offers a slight smile, "Can we go now?"

I nod and we make our way back to where the rest of the group is waiting. We follow Victor inside to the war table in the center of the warehouse where Grent is reviewing some scans on his data-pad. He spins around to face us.

"So, what did your little band of merry men decide?" he asks, grinning at his own joke.

"We're in. Under one condition," Victor replies.

"You're not really in a position to negotiate. The Patriarch is hunting you. Don't go busting my—"

"Brelar." Victor's word cuts Grent off.

"That supposed to mean something to me?"

"It should. He's the boy you had deceive us into thinking our friends were captured by the Levites."

"Careful, that sounds a lot like an accusation."

"It doesn't sound like an accusation. It is one." Victor pulls out the chip he'd shown Spike earlier. "So is this—you placed jamming chips in our data-pads so we couldn't communicate with each other during the battle. That way, we wouldn't be able to discover your deception until after the battle was over."

"Good luck proving it." Grent crosses his arms over his chest.

"Don't need proof. The rumor alone will make people question you. The more they question you, the less likely they are to join you."

Grent scowls angrily. "What do you want?"

"Do you know why your previous rebellions failed?"

Grent leans back as if trying to get away from the question. "We didn't have the resources and manpower to win."

"No. Your previous rebellions all failed because of one thing."

"What's that?"

"You." Grent's jaw drops at Victor's accusation. His shoulders slump forward. Victor knows how to find a person's soft spot, and he just found Grent's. "When I was a boy, my father told me stories of Grent the Great. I followed your rebellions, studied them intently. Every time you fight, you rely on brute strength. There's no strategy, just raw force. The Patriarch defeats you because you are brute, and they are smarter than you are." The expression on Grent's face makes him look more like a wounded puppy than a bear.

"Ex-excuse me?" Grent's hand moves back toward the handle of the giant axe he wears behind his back.

"I don't have time to repeat myself. You have all the tools you need to win. I can make it happen. The question you have to ask yourself is simple: do you want to win, or do you want to be in charge?"

Grent appears stunned. He offers no response but silence. His scowl softens, his face turning from forceful and aggressive to what seems almost submissive.

"What do you suggest?" he asks, his voice soft.

"You have a lot of people ready to fight. They are disorganized. They are here because they are angry. That anger gives them courage. When the battle comes and the fear takes over, what happens?" Victor pauses. "They scatter. They scatter because when the fear overcomes the anger, they lose their nerve. What they need is not an emotion. What they need is a reason, a vision, a belief that this fight can make the world a better place. Give them something worth living for, and they will willingly die in pursuit of it."

Grent shakes his head. "If you think you can just walk in here and steal my—"

"I have no intention of stealing your men. I'm not the leader the rebellion needs." That's not true. Victor is brilliant. He's led us for years. He's the reason we haven't been turned into Outland Officers already. "I don't have any interest in position."

"Good." Grent seems to relax. "I'm not about to—"

"You're not the leader we need either." Grent looks as if he took a blow to the head. He blinks, and his eyes seem out of focus. "An effective army requires three key components. Do you know what they are?"

"Men, weapons, and resources," Grent blurts out, looking proud of himself.

"No, those are important, but plenty of armies have those things yet remain ineffective. An effective army needs a leader, a commander, and a strategist. With the right people in these positions, an army of a hundred can defeat an army of several thousand."

"You would be the strategist then?" Grent sounds like he's asking.

"Yes, the strategist's job is to devise the schemes and tactics, position troops, and implement the right attacks in the right places at the right times. The commander must be able to make decisions in the heat of battle. That's where you come in. Your strength is your decisiveness. You make clear calls in the heat of the moment with the confidence needed to mobilize units. That's a very important trait in a commander. A leader must be more. If you want to win this rebellion, you are going to need the right people in the right places. Jett, come here." Victor extends his hand toward me. Why does he want me? What do I have to do with this discussion? Timidly, I walk over to Victor.

"Who will lead? Certainly not this boy?" Grent scoffs.

"This is why you are not a leader. You see only what's in front of you. A leader sees not just what is but what could be. A leader inspires people, drives them. He doesn't just command them, he makes them better. A leader can unite enemies and motivate people to do things they'd never have thought to do on their own. That is why all your other rebellions have failed. You didn't have a leader." Victor points to the courtyard outside the warehouse.

"Vic, what are you talking about?" I ask. What he's describing sounds impressive, but I don't know what it has to do with me. "I'm not any of those things."

Victor shakes his head. "You are, and you don't even know it. You don't understand the power your words wield. Why do you think our little group has worked so well all these years?"

"You. You, show us what to do. You lead us, Vic, not me."

"No, Jett, I've never led. I've only guided. It was your passion, your energy, your way of seeing the world that held our group together. All Telmen wanted to do was run away. In less than a minute you inspired him to join the greatest and most dangerous war Dios has ever seen. You motivated Spike to overcome his hatred and distrust of the rebels. Even Jensen, he sees the world differently because of you."

"I can't do this, Vic. It's too much." I am Atlas; the weight of the world comes crashing down on my shoulders. My feeble legs cannot hold up this vast sky. Victor asks too much of me, thinks too much of me. I'm not a leader. I'm not a hero. I'm just me.

"You have to, Jett. You're the only one who can. But you don't have to do it alone."

"You think this will help us win?" Grent protests. "Hmm? Trusting our fate to some untested boy who is too afraid to lead? What if you're right? What happens after we win?"

"Still concerned with the prize before ye even finish the race, Grent?" Spike interjects. "I see ye haven't changed a wee bit. Why dunna we worry about winning first and then take care of the after?"

"Fine, I'll go along for now. After this is done, things are going to change," Grent states.

"Great, agreed," Victor says with a nod. "Now, Grent, I need you to bring all the beggar gangs together, especially their leaders. Have them all assemble in the Market Square."

"Shouldn't we be focusing on guarding the train stations?" Grent challenges.

"Leave a small force of your most loyal Nightlings at each station. Instruct them to warn us if the rails go active. It's time to turn this ragtag group into a proper army."

By the time we reach the Market Square, there are thousands of beggar gang members grouped together in various clusters. We walk in, accompanied by a few Nightlings to guard us from any potential threats. All eyes are on us. A hush rumbles over the Square. My palms sweat, and my breathing is quick and labored. I struggle to focus, to think, to even move. My body resists every step. A thief lives in the shadows, a thief avoids attention. A thief doesn't walk out onto a platform with thousands of people watching him. Maybe today is the day I stop being a thief.

I lean over and whisper in Victor's ear, "What am I supposed to do?"

"You need to inspire these people to overcome their differences and work together against the Patriarch. I thought that was obvious."

"Oh sure, yeah. That's all. How am I supposed to do that?"

"With words, I'd imagine."

"You are super helpful. What I am supposed to say?"

"Jett, if I knew that, I would be the leader. Wouldn't I?"

"Right, so you want me to walk up onto that platform and speak to a crowd that doesn't know me, motivate them to overcome years—if not generations—of animosity, and inspire them to follow me—someone who has never led anything before—so they will fight for me against a force no one has ever defeated."

"Exactly, I knew you'd get it. Oh yeah, and if you fail, Lilly and her whole family will be sent to the Outlands, all your friends will die, and the people who murdered your parents will get away with it. You know, no pressure." Victor flashes a warm smile. I want to scream and then throw up.

Hordes of beggar gangs and Nightlings pile in closer. Spike activates a vocal projector to ensure everyone can hear me. Now, it's just the small task of having something worth saying. I walk up the makeshift platform looking out over the massive crowd. The gangs are arrayed, each in their unique style. Some gangs are wearing their own version of uniforms, matching cloaks and tunics. Others are identifiable solely by the patches their wear on their clothes. Beggar gang badges are a symbol of honor, of brotherhood between members. Any identifying feature for a gang is brandished with great pride by all its members.

"My parents are dead." That's not the start I was hoping for. I take a deep breath. "Murdered by the Patriarch. Murdered right in front of me. For my parents' crimes, the Patriarch branded me Undesirable, cast me off like trash." This motivational speech is becoming an awkward sharing time really quickly.

"My name is 2413985-U, or that's what the Patriarch would have you believe. That I'm nothing more than a number, a line in their code. To them, I'm not a person. I'm a tool for their self-glorification. You are here because, like me, the Patriarch branded you worthless. Undesirable. Garbage. We have all struggled. We have all fought to survive, to make it in this hostile world they created for us. We have fought. We have stolen. Killed. Why? We want to live. We are not worthless. We are not what they say we are, and it's time we showed them that. For too long, we have fought amongst ourselves. Fought for the scraps that fell from their feasts. You may look around and see enemies. Do you know what I see? Not Watchers, Red Dragons, Nightlings, not beggars, not Undesirables. I see an army. An army of men and women ready to say, 'we've had enough.' I see an army of people like me—people who are sick of oppression, who are tired of being treated like sewage because the Patriarch didn't deem us worthy. I see a people united in their pursuit of freedom. The truth is, we are all brothers. We are all sisters. The Patriarch has wronged us all. It's time we made it right."

The expressions on their faces shift. Defiant hostility fades into soft intrigue, which turns suddenly into wild agreement. Several voices shout out in agreement. This is going better than I thought it would.

"After all your fighting, what do you have to show for it? Has it improved your lot in life? Changed your status? No. We've been fighting the wrong enemy. We've been doing the Patriarch's job for them. Every time we fight amongst ourselves, we reduce the ranks of their enemies. Why do you think they make no effort to stop it? They want us to kill each other. Whenever we fight each other, their power grows. I've said enough. I'll say no more. I say it's time we show the Patriarch who we are. It's time we show them our worth. You are not a number. I am not a number. My name is Jett Lasting, and I'm done being cast aside." I extend my hands to the crowd as if reaching for them, inviting them in. "Comply. Keep your heads down. Don't stand up. Don't stand out. That's what they demand. But no more. No more submission. No more being herded." I cross my arms in front of my chest to make an X tapping them twice. "Today, the Patriarch will learn our names. Today, we rise up. Today we take back our lives!"

Silence fills the Square. My heartbeat sounds like an explosion in my ears. Time moves agonizingly slowly. The seconds creep along for what feels like an eternity. This may be the longest moment of my life.

"Yeeeeeaaaahhh!" shouts a single voice from the back of the crowd. Then another. And another. The cheer gets louder as more and more add their voices to the choir. One by one the crowd crosses their arms in front of their chests making the same X shape that I had. "Rise up! Rise up! Rise up!" They begin to chant. The cheering turns to celebration and into jubilee. The clusters of gangs collapse as the people meld together, embracing each other, laughing, slapping each other on the back. I look over at Victor. Spike claps and runs up onto the platform, wrapping his arms around my stomach and lifting me into the air, laughing as he does.

"Aye, brotha, that was the best speech I've ever heard in me whole life." Just like that, I am a thief no longer. I am the voice of a revolution.

CHAPTER FIFTEEN

Walking off the stage, I find myself in a sea of strangers, slapping me on the back, hugging me from the side, shaking me vigorously. This is a big moment. Why can't I enjoy it? Last week I was a nobody, hiding from most of these people. Today, I'm somehow leading a revolution? I have no idea what that means. All I know is a lot of people are going to die. If I make a mistake, I'm going to be responsible for those deaths. An emotional raincloud follows me as I make my way to the warehouse headquarters. I feel a hand slide into my jacket. I smack my hand against my chest to stop it. Nothing is missing. Rather, something has been added. I look around, but there are too many people crowding in on me to see who is responsible. Whatever it is, it's meant to be viewed in secret.

Victor meets me at the entrance to the warehouse. He's leaning against the door, slow clapping as I approach. "Very well done." He bows his head. "Mr. Leader."

"Shut up," I bark out. "What happens now?"

Victor grins. "Now we meet with all the former beggar gang leaders. We need to lay out a clear leadership structure and then start planning our next move."

"What about Lilly and Gibbs?"

"I haven't forgotten. Kane is out looking for Gibbs. I'll have each gang send their best scouts to join them."

"And Lilly?" I press desperation in my voice.

Victor looks away. "That's a much bigger challenge. Warfare is about deception. We know the Patriarch can manipulate footage. If they are smart, which we know they are, they will use that. Disinformation is one of the greatest weapons in warfare.

"Wait, are you saying Lilly might not have been captured?" Hope practically lifts me off my feet into the sky above.

Victor closes his eyes and takes a long breath, "I'm saying we don't know. If she's is with Lorth Drant, she's in the Temple Sector. That's what we know they want us to think. In reality, she could be anywhere."

"We can't just—"

"I'm not saying that. Give me some time to get some intel. It's not like we can just sneak in and find her. I'm working on it." I nod. That's the best I'm going to get for now.

"I need a little break. Is it okay if I step out for a bit?"

Victor nods. "Just don't wander too far. You're kind of important."

Far from the warehouse and the crowds in the Square, I sit down under the canopy of a shop. Leaning against the wall, I pull something out of my pocket—something I didn't put there. It's a folded-up piece of paper. Paper is not rare, but most people just transfer messages via their data-pads. It's odd to see someone using paper. I unfold it slowly. The message is simple: MEET ME AT THE TRINKET SHOP ON STREET ELEVEN TONIGHT. COME ALONE. Signed, A FRIEND. Great, that's not cryptic.

The day drags on as Victor organizes information and tries to transform the riffraff into a formidable fighting force. Something about the note nags at the back of my mind. Who put it there? Why? The only way to find out was to show up. Do I go alone? The smart move would be to tell Victor, but he'll just worry and forbid me from going. I could tell Spike, but he'll insist on coming with me. Even if he follows from a distance, there's a chance it could spook the guy. Then I'd never know. Curiosity is a cruel monster.

I wander around, wrestling with what to do. It's probably a trap. Like something in a story. If it is a trap, it's a terrible one. I sigh, mulling it over before crashing into Spike. I show him the note.

"Brotha, ye can't seriously be thinking of going," he says, folding up the paper and handing it back to me.

"Wouldn't you?"

"Oh aye, course I would. Imma curious wanker after all. But I didn't just become the leader of the first rebellion in Dios with an actual chance to stop the Patriarch." Spike grins playfully.

"I need to know who gave me this. We can't afford to turn away potential allies, even if it is a stupid risk."

Spike just nods. "Then whatever ye do, dunna tell Vic."

I laugh. "Yeah, he'd lock me up to keep me safe."

"Oh, aye and lock me up just to be certain. Not worth the risk, he'd say." Spike looks at me for a moment and then smiles. "I've got an idea. Let me see your data-pad."

I lift my arm, and Spike starts typing away and sliding his fingers over the pad, moving faster than I can process. "What are you doing?"

"Since we both know yer gonna go no matter what I say, I'm installing a tracking mod on yer pad. It sends a signal directly to mine. If something happens, I can bring the cavalry." Spike taps me on the shoulder and lets go of my wrist. "All done, brotha. Best of luck to ye."

I nod in appreciation before parting ways with Spike. I make my way back to check in with Victor. If he didn't confirm I returned, he'd be

238

sending soldiers out to find me and probably spook my contact. I'll have to get settled in and then sneak out later if I want this to work.

Sneaking out after dark proves to be no small feat. Victor has me in the innermost room of the underground tunnel base. He posts guards outside my door. If I didn't know better, I might feel like a prisoner. Beggar gangs make poor guards, and I'm used to avoiding real ones. It takes some caution to pull off, but after some time, I'm able to slip past my jailers while they're occupied with an arm-wrestling match, and I dash up the stairs to the streets above.

The cool night air chills my skin. It's an oddly refreshing feeling when the crisp of the air makes everything tingle. I make my way alone to Street Eleven, moving slowly toward the trinket shop and keeping to the shadows. It's starting to feel more and more like a trap. I shouldn't have come alone. This is stupid. I shouldn't do this. I turn to head back.

"Leaving so soon?" comes a voice from behind me. My hand drops immediately to the energy knife at my side. I turn to face him. He is wearing a brown cloak with a white trim patch of a howling wolf head inside a flaming circle. I slip the energy blade into my hand, finger on the switch as I size up my alleged friend. He is older, late forties, maybe early fifties. He appears to be in good shape. Something about him feels familiar. I don't recognize him. Something inside me says this is not the first time we've met.

"Who are you?" I ask.

"You don't remember? I guess I was a long way off." Long way off...his voice. That's it. I do know him. He wasn't wearing a fire wolf uniform the last time we met. He was dressed as a Red Cap. Realization collides with even greater confusion. This is the man who distracted the Levites when Victor and I were on our way home. The man smiles, catching the recognition in my eye. "Call me the ghost of Christmas past," he says.

"The what?"

He waves his hand dismissively. "Perhaps a better question is, why did I help you avoid the Levites in the Jeep while you were hiding in that ditch?"

"Yeah, okay. Why?"

He smiles. His teeth are perfect. When his cheeks turn, I can see a subtle scar next to his right eye. "You may find this hard to believe, but I'm a friend. I want to help you."

"Okay, friend. Who are you and why do you want to help me?"

"That is complicated." He looks over one shoulder then the other.

"Well, why did you want to meet if you don't have anything to say?"

"I do have something—a warning."

"Oh, here I was worried you were going to be vague and cryptic."

He smirks, "The key to the future, is found in the past. Be careful who you trust Jett Lasting. Betrayal always comes from those closest to you. It could even come from the person you trust the most."

"Well, my daddy used to say, never trust strangers who put notes in your jacket pocket to lure you alone into a dark alley and then speak in riddles while claiming to be your friend."

"Wise. In your position, you shouldn't trust anyone. Not Grent or his wild dog. Not your friends. Trust no one"

"Oh, why is that?"

"The most effective way to end a rebellion isn't with force. It's by dividing your opponent and letting them destroy themselves. You are aligned with Grent-"

"Don't trust Grent, the manipulative rebel with an agenda he's never really clear about. Thank you for that deep and surprising insight, Mr. Stranger Man."

"Jett you can't rely on Victor to do all your thinking for you. "Are you familiar with an old adage: a snake in the grass?" I am, in fact. I've read it in several old books. It was used to refer to an untrustworthy person with malicious intentions. No one uses that phrase anymore. No one knows it. How does he? I nod. "Grent may be a snake in the grass, but he's not the snake you need to worry about. Betrayal rarely comes from the most obvious place, trust me."

"Certainly, you see the irony in telling me not to trust someone else when you won't even tell me your name."

He sighs. "My name is Keagen. I'm-" he glances over my shoulder and shakes his head. "I see you didn't come alone." He sighs and starts to turn, and his voice becomes more urgent, "You don't have to trust me, just heed my warning. Caution costs you nothing. I'll reach out again when it's safe." Safe? What is he talking about? Something about the way he continued looking over his shoulder has me creeped out.

Becka peeks her head out from behind a pile of crates stacked against a wall, "Sorry, did he notice me?"

"Yea he noticed you; you're a terrible thief. What makes you think you'd be a good spy?" I shake my head.

"I'm really fast," she says with a soft smile.

"How does that help when you are standing still?"

She punches me in the shoulder, "Look if you think I'm just going to let you take some secret meeting with no one to watch your back, you've got another thing coming."

"How did you find out about this anyway?"

She shrugs, "Maybe I'm a better spy than you think."

We make our way back to Shine for Shine Jewelry before parting ways. I settle into my room, lay my head down on the small bed, and fall asleep.

I wake close to midday. I never sleep this late; I must have still been fatigued. Stepping outside, the warm sun heats my skin. The Market is no longer a market. It has been transformed into a staging area. What was once a bunch of shops and stalls for the trading of goods has become supply stations, training areas, briefing rooms, and a few other things I don't recognize. They've been busy.

Market Square is even more shocking. The entire open space is now a mess hall of tables and chairs for the rebels to gather and eat. One of the shops has been retrofitted to serve as a kitchen.

"You're finally up," I hear Becka's voice as she walks up behind me.

"Yea, guess I was pretty zeroed."

She smiles, "I'm glad you got some sleep. You definitely earned it. I meant to tell you, your speech. It was really inspiring."

"Thanks, Becka. Hopefully it worked."

"Look around Jett. Things are happening. I don't know what will happen. Bealz will guide us. I've never been more certain."

"You're not upset that I got you caught up in all this?"

Becka shakes her head, "Why would I be? I never really told you why I got branded a heretic and disowned did I?"

"No."

"I asked a question," she pauses to let that sink in. The instructor was explaining to us how to mold people to the image of their class paragon. That's the whole point of a potter, to help people conform. 'If we are all the same, we are all one.'" She mocks. "I wasn't even trying to challenge the teacher. I just didn't understand. If it is the will of Bealz that we would all be the same, why did he make us all so different?"

"They branded you a heretic for that?"

She shrugs slightly, "I don't know what will happen but, I feel like we are fighting to make a world where people can ask questions without fear of losing everything. That, that is worth fighting for."

"Thank you, Becka."

"You're a leader now Jett. Like it or not, people are looking to you. Don't add worry or guilt to your burden. You're not the High Father. Everyone who is here, is here for their own reasons. They made their own choices. You're already carrying their hope, don't try to carry their reasons with it," she puts her hand on my shoulder and stares into my eyes, "And, don't you dare try to carry it alone."

Her words lift an invisible weight from my shoulders.

A rumbling grumble in my stomach threatens to cause pain if not dealt with soon. I thank her again and make my way over to the kitchen shop to see what is available. A tall, skinny man with a large white hat and dirty apron leans over the counter and says something to me. I'm too preoccupied with my hunger to hear it. He disappears out of sight and returns a minute later with a plate stacked with eggs, rice, and strange looking diced potatoes. There are also two strange, thin strips of crunchy, chewy meat covered in grease. Delicious.

Appetite sated, I make my way to the headquarters. Spike and Victor are looking over several maps of the city while Grent paces back and forth looking frustrated. Screens have been set up all around the room, each displaying different types of information and data. There are at least a dozen rebels monitoring screens and reviewing data.

"We can't do anything without better intelligence," Victor says, pushing away from the table.

"We've got plenty of information; we need to do something," Grent growls. "All these men ready to fight and you've got them running drills and analyzing data. This is not—"

"Patience. It's been two days since we took the Market. The Patriarch hasn't attacked. They haven't even turned the tracks back on. Wonder why?"

"I'm sure you're going to tell me."

"They are waiting patiently for us to do something stupid, like mount an assault without the information. Acting without knowing our enemy's positions would certain bring an end to our rebellion."

"All this waiting around is making me crazy."

"Then go do something productive. Train. Teach some of our new soldiers how to fight." Despite Victor's efforts to remain calm, his voice flares with frustration. Grent grumbles and stomps out.

"Soooo, how are things going?" I ask with a grin.

"Not as well as I'd like but better than they could be. Grent's really the only problem right now."

"Sweet victory, I've got something, brotha." Spike smiles and without saying another word, runs out of the headquarters. Victor and I look at each other, waiting in silence. Is he coming back? Were we supposed to follow him? What did he find?

A full minute later, Spike rushes back in. He drops a black and red uniform onto the table in front of us. He looks down at it proudly like a dog presenting a bone to its master. He looks up at us and back down at the uniform as if the reason for his excitement should be readily apparent.

"Red Cap uniforms, brotha. We're swimmin' in them," Spike says.

"Right, from when we killed them while taking the Market," I respond.

"Aye, but now we can use them."

"Use them for what?" I ask.

"To infiltrate the Temple Sector. We put our men in these uniforms, they sneak into the Temple Sector using the tunnels, Bob's yer uncle, and we've got eyes and ears on the inside."

"Spike, these uniforms have holes in them and blood on them," I point out. "That might be hard to explain."

"No, he's right. We patch the shirts, wash them, and we're set. Good thinking, Spike," Victor says.

"We can rescue Lilly?" I ask, my voice sounding desperate even to me.

"Not we," Victor shakes his head. "The Patriarch knows your face. Even in a Red Cap uniform they'd catch you the second you stepped foot in the Temple Sector."

"Look, I'm not just going to stand around-"

"Jett, you can play hero and get yourself caught or we can have a team of agents sneak in and rescue Lilly. You can't have both. You want to save the day, or do you want her safe?"

I sigh, "Fine."

"First day as a leader and you already want to put your men's lives at risk to save your girlfriend?" Grent gibes. "Somehow you're more fit to lead than I am?" He turns accusatorily to Victor. My hands clench into fists. There's nothing wrong with wanting to save people you care about. It's natural. Why is he making it sound like I'm abusing my power? I stop myself from driving my fist into his face. I'm certain it would hurt me a lot more than it would hurt him anyway.

"Better than leaving your people to die while you save yourself, you scrap sink," I snap back. It's unwise, but it feels good.

"You don't know the first thing about leading because you've never had to do it. Being a leader is about making the hard calls. It's not fun. It's not cool. You are responsible for the hard decisions. Everyone blames you for whatever goes wrong."

"I'm not leaving Lilly behind. She didn't deserve this. Saving her is the right thing to do."

"Right for who? You want to risk lives to go save your girl. What about them? What about their friends, their families? Did you think about that? No, because all you care about is getting in-"

"Watch it," Spike interrupts.

Grent grumbles, "you don't have the slightest clue what it means to lead. You can't let sentimental attachments get in the way of the mission."

"Actually, that may be exactly what we need," Victor interrupts. "The Patriarch has never lost ground like this before. They don't know what they are dealing with. Our assault on the Market was a surprise. I think they took Lilly and her family to test us."

"What are you talking about?" Grent grumbles.

"They've seen Jett and Lilly together. Certainly, that's the reason they put her on Drant's show. They want to see if we are clever and tactical or if we are driven by emotion. They want to lure us into a fight. We give it to them."

"You mean, walk into a trap for some girl?" Grent growls.

"A trap works both ways," Victor grins his mischievous grin. "We won't be the ones walking into it, but we make it look like we are. We send a small detachment with Jett, here." Victor gestures to a place on the map near the Temple Sector. "We use some explosives and various other tools to make it look like a massive assault. The Patriarch will re-deploy their forces, leaving them vulnerable, here." Victor circles a second point on the screen. "With their units distracted, our main force will strike here, breaking through their defenses. Jett's force will retreat and, with any luck, draw the Patriarch Defense Forces out, allowing our main force to sweep behind them and catch them off guard."

Grent looks like a kid on Bealz day. "Yes, finally! We rain destruction down on the Patriarch!"

"Our goal is not destruction, Grent," Victor corrects.

"Excuse me? Maybe you've missed the point of what we are doing here. We can't win a war if we don't kill our enemies. We are going to kill every last one of them."

"Great, so we wipe out the entire PDF," Victor starts. Grent grunts happily, a smile on his face. "Naturally, we take some losses in the process." Grent nods reluctantly. "Now, the Patriarch is defeated. We control the city. Our defenses are reduced to a small army. What do you think happens when the other four cities hear about our little rebellion? They have no interest in protecting the Patriarch, but imagine how tempting it would be for them to come and take the city. They have the full strength of their armies, and we would be weak, still unorganized. How would we repel such an assault?" Grent's jaw drops. I imagine he's never thought this far ahead in his life. "What good is winning the battle if we lose the war?"

"You want to let the soldiers live who have tortured us, abused us, and killed us?" Grent responds.

"The soldiers are not our enemy. The Patriarch is a cancer. You don't fight cancer by destroying the body. You go in with a scalpel and cut the cancer out. We need to be surgical, remove the toxic influences while doing as little damage as possible. Once the battle is over, we have to live with what's left."

"If we let them live, what's to stop them from working against us the first chance they get? Starting their own rebellion? No, we kill them."

My temper gets the better of me. "You really are savage, aren't you?" I bark. It's hard enough being in a room with Grent, knowing what he did. Listening to him argue just makes me want to hit him. What I can't do with my fists, I can do with my words.

"The little pup speaks. You haven't earned the right to speak yet, boy. I was fighting in rebellions when you were still in diapers."

"Maybe if you'd won any of them—"

Grent curses and stomps toward me. Victor steps between us. "That's enough. You two need to calm down. We can't do anything until we have a better understanding of what we are up against," Victor says, calming our growing conflict.

Grent turns around and starts pacing back and forth. "How do we not have enough information? We have the data-pad from the Patriarch official. We have all the access codes we need. We have them on the defensive. Why are waiting? We need to strike now before they have time to organize." Even speaking calmly, Grent's voice is intimidating and loud. He is not speaking calmly. His words roar out of his throat. I feel them in my bones.

"That's exactly what they want us to do—charge ahead blindly. If you think they aren't prepared for that, you're a fool." Victor's tone is calm, unemotional, a perfect contrast to Grent's flaming temper.

"Gahhh, so what do we need then?" Grent begins pacing again. He has all the self -control of a rabid beast.

"The Patriarch divides their intel into two parts, which is smart. That way, if someone, like us, were to obtain a key piece of intel, like the official's data-pad, we have some information but not all of it. Officials have access codes for entry and logistics. Only a military officer's data-pad has access to the size, location, and structures of their forces. We have the codes we need but no idea where their soldiers are placed. It's a perfect trap. It gives us the illusion of sight while leaving us blind."

"We need a soldier's data-pad?" I ask.

"Not just any soldier. It has to be a high-ranking soldier."

"What's the problem? I'm sure we killed plenty of them," Grent declares proudly.

"Actually, we didn't. I looked. None of the soldier we killed have a high enough access."

"So, we're heaped? How we do get a data-pad like that?" Grent asks.

"I have a plan." Victor smirks.

"Fine, run your schemes. Let me know when it's time to fight." Grent storms off again.

"No wonder his rebellions always failed. That man has the patience of squirrel." Victor shakes his head.

"I don't know how I ever looked up to him."

"My dad used to say, 'Never meet your heroes. They will always be a disappointment.'"

"He's not wrong," I agree. "So, tell me this plan of yours."

"Jett, you're not going to like it."

"That's not foreboding. Your plan gives us a chance to save Lilly, right?"

"A chance, yes. Not a great one, but there is a chance. There's also—"

"Ugh, just say it."

"What we need is the data-pad of a commander in the PDF." I already don't like where this is going. "I only know of one you can get to." Victor pauses. There's no point; I know what he's going to say. "Commander Stone." Even hearing his name makes my blood run hot. How am I supposed to sneak up on a Commander who hates me and will definitely see me coming? After what he did to Brelar, maybe I can just kill him. That won't be easy either. My normal bag of tricks isn't going to work here. I can't imagine a worse situation to be in. My only hope of saving Lilly means facing the man I hate more than anyone else.

"Okay, what do I need to do?"

Spike slaps his hand down on my shoulder. "Brotha, if ye think I'm going to let ye face him alone, ye've got another thing coming."

"Wait, no I have to—"

"It's not just Spike," Victor interrupts. "Telmen, Olivia, and Kane are going with you as well."

"Kane? Kane is back? I thought he was out looking for Gibbs."

"My men are still out searching," Kane says, stepping into the room. "I thought you could use the help. Plus, all that searching got me itching for a fight."

"You think taking him is a good idea?" I ask Victor.

"Ouch, I'm right here. Words can hurt, you know," Kane says. I can't tell if he's making fun of me or sincerely wounded by my question.

"What I mean is, we are trying to avoid a fight."

"Just because you try to avoid a fight, doesn't mean it won't find you," Kane responds.

"He's right. Ideally, you will find a way to steal the data-pad from Commander Stone. If force is necessary, you're going to want someone like Kane there," Victor says.

"Someone like me? What's that supposed to mean?"

"A brawler." Victor smiles.

Kane laughs and nods. "Perfect." Kane grabs my shoulders with his hands and squeezes several times. "We're going to have a great time! Let me go get my stuff." Kane walks out of the room briskly.

"Vic, I don't trust him. He's with Grent. We don't—"

"We don't have to trust him. Right now, we need him. That's got to be enough."

Kane comes sauntering in, holding a pile of what appears to be clothing in his hands. He drops them down on the table. "If we are going to get close to a Commander, we're going to need a disguise, right?" I look at what he brought. Black uniforms and body armor. It is the perfect disguise. The helmets will cover our faces, allowing us to get close to Stone without him recognizing us or drawing suspicion. Kane glances over at Olivia. "Don't be shy."

Spike steps in front of him. "Mind yer eyes, brotha."

"Haha, relax. I'm teasing. Look at her—if I didn't say something, she might think I'm crazy." Kane grins.

"Say less," Spike warns.

"You're no fun at all, are you?" Kane sighs dramatically, "get changed then. We've no time to waste."

We strip down awkwardly in the middle of the headquarters and slip into our lightly used PDF uniforms. I try to keep my eyes down, feeling wildly uncomfortable. The others appear to do the same with the exception of Kane. Kane is very proud of how he looks. Sliding out of his clothes without a moment of hesitation, I see why. Kane is in surprisingly good shape. The tattered jacket he wears makes him appear bulky. In truth, he looks like he's been carved out of stone. He could compete in the City Wars.

City Wars is a once-a-year sporting competition. Each of the five cities sends their best athletes to compete for the Great Golden Trophy. The other cities provide a bounty of special resources, like sugar and various sorts of fruits, to the winner as a reward.

Once we are all dressed and ready, Victor walks us through his idea. Using a digital map of the city, he shows us where we are and where

Commander Stone is likely stationed. Spike hands each of us a rifle. I sling mine over my shoulder, so it drapes across my back. Now we look the part. No one will question us unless we do something to raise their suspicion.

"Jett, when we get there, I need ye to stay away from Stone," Spike says. "I'll get the data-pad."

"What? No!" This is my mess. I'm the reason Lilly got caught. I'm the reason her family is about to be banished to the Outlands. I need to be the one to fix it. I know what Spike is trying to do, but I can't let him take that risk. He's not a thief. Olivia isn't a good one, and in the PDF uniform, her natural ability to distract her target is worthless. Telmen's not bad, but Spike is the worst. He doesn't steal. He's too honorable to take that which he did not earn. I have no idea how good Kane is at stealing, but anyone would be better than Spike. "No way!" I press.

"Brotha, I'm not asking. Yer too close to this. I don't blame ye for that. Not after what he did to Brelar, but this is too important. We got one shot at this. If we blow it, Lilly ends up in the Outlands. Ye really willing to bet her life on yer ability to control yerself?"

CHAPTER SIXTEEN

Kane drives us on the underground train car to the stop nearest to where Commander Stone is stationed. The group sits quietly as we ride. With Telmen around, a single moment of unpolluted silence is unusual. I appreciate the silence. It gives me time to process everything that's happened. I think of Lilly and her family. Then of Gibbs. I wonder if he is okay and worry that he may be captured as well. I fear the worst. If Gibbs did get away, why has he made no efforts to contact us?

"I have to ask," Kane says looking over at Olivia. "What's a girl like you doing caught up in all this?"

"A girl like me?" Olivia's arms cross and brow furrows in response.

"You could charm your way into a cushy life with some foolish Prime boy if you wanted. So why slum it with this lot?"

"Watch it," Spike warns.

Kane chuckles, "Don't get me wrong, I like the slums. I'm curious."

"Does it matter?" Olivia replies.

"Does to me. I meet a lot of people. I tend to get a pretty good sense of them. Something about you doesn't add up. I don't like it when things don't add up," Kane says.

"Ye better just get used to not liking it," Spike suggest.

"It's ok Spike," Olivia says calmly. "You want to know why I'm here, fighting?"

Kane smiles and nods, "Everybody who stands up against the Patriarch has a reason. What did the Patriarch do to you?"

"Nothing."

Kane turns his head and thinks for a moment, "Then what are you doing here?"

"My friends are here," Olivia says plainly.

"You're fighting with a group of unorganized rebels who you just met and don't fully trust against one of the strongest forces on earth that will almost certainly end with your death, or worse, because your friends are?" Kane sounds amused.

"They aren't just my friends Kane. I wouldn't expect you to understand this, but they are my family. Where they go, I go. When they hurt, I hurt. Their enemies are my enemies. When they fight, I fight. That is what family does."

Kane chuckles.

"You have a problem with that?" Olivia growls.

Kane shakes his head, "No, not even a little."

The underground train car comes to a stop, and the doors slide open with a gusty hiss. Spike leads us through the winding tunnels of the secret underground. Strategically placed lumelights provide just enough light to maneuver the tunnels without crashing into anything. The strips on the floor and ceiling glow a soft blue. The dampness of the tunnels and the cool breeze that rushes over us as we walk creates the illusion of being underwater.

Kane walks next to me. I don't know how I feel about him. He's crazy but quick to help, and he seems to like me for some reason. I know he hates the Patriarch. If it weren't for Grent, I think I'd like Kane. His loyalty to the ogre man makes me question his intentions. Perhaps he is as ignorant as I was, seeing Grent only as the noble and courageous rebel. Or maybe he's just better at luring us into his confidence. The one thing I know, Kane is much cleverer than he lets on. Victor is right; we definitely need him. The question I keep asking is, can we trust him?

We reach the stairs to exit the tunnels. Spike motions for us to wait. He slowly creeps up the steps and disappears. I hear a door creak open and then slowly slide closed.

"What's he doing? Why's he going alone? Shouldn't we all be going together?" Telmen whispers, breaking the longest streak of consecutive non-sleeping silence in his life.

"Making sure the coast is clear," I whisper back, "so we can slip in under the radar."

"What's radar?" Olivia asks. I forget most people don't spend as much time reading about the World that Was as I do. Back in the old days when I was just a thief, I would spend several hours in a shop on Street Eleven that was filled with antique books. The shop owner let me sit in the back and read in exchange for little trinkets or goods I'd stolen.

"It's an old expression. It means to avoid detection," I explain. Olivia nods and smiles her bright smile. It's not hard to see why all the guys are crazy about her. She is genuinely kind, she's gorgeous, and her eyes sparkle when she listens, making her seem sincerely interested in whatever you are saying.

The door above us creaks, and Spike appears at the top of the steps. He waves for us to follow him up, holding a finger to his lips to keep us quiet. The secret stairs open up into what appears to be some kind of storage building. The room is lined with rows of shelves towering ten feet into the air, creating little streets between them. The shelves are stuffed full of uniform grey storage bins, each one with a unique label code glowing on the small screen on the front of it. The only windows in the room run along the top of the far side wall, allowing light in but too high up for any passersby to see in. Spike points to a grey-green door along the cement stone wall behind us as we emerge.

The door leads to another set of stairs. We climb up two flights to a single door at the top of the building. Pushing it open, I am blinded by the sudden bright burst of light as daylight pours into the dark stairwell. My head throbs for a moment as my eyes adjust. Shapes come into focus. Then colors.

The sun has already begun its descent, slowly hiding itself behind the horizon. The journey through the tunnels took longer than I anticipated. This must be the industrial sector of Section B. I've never been here before. Not much worth stealing that can be put into a bag and carried around. The buildings and factories are aligned much like the shops in the Market Sector, creating perfectly straight streets that form an isolated square. The main difference here is the variety of buildings. In the Market, buildings alternate between two-and three-stories. Some shops are wider than others, but they all share a matching design.

Here some buildings have rounded roofs, others flat, and others pitched. Some buildings are made with red brick, some with stone, others with poured cement. Each building has its own unique personality and feel. Why did they save this for factories?

Soldiers wearing armor similar to ours patrol the streets below in triple-file lines, boots thumping the ground in perfect unison.

"Pay attention to how they move," I say. "The more we can blend in, the better our chances." We watch the soldiers, studying their movements while we wait. The light dwindles. The lumelights' sensors respond and click on, pouring artificially blue light down onto the streets. Not much more we can observe tonight.

The second floor of the storage building has a closed-off room in the back with no windows. We set up shop there. Everyone huddles in a circle around a table, sorting through some of the food Spike brought. Kane is sitting next to Olivia, telling her all kinds of crazy stories, much to Spike's dismay. His eyes light up as he looks at her. She smiles warmly, laughing and giggling at each story he tells. It takes me a second to realize we are down one. Telmen isn't here. I turn to Spike, panic seizing me.

"Dunna worry. I sent him out. He's spreading rumors," Spike says with a smile before chuckling. "Have you ever heard of a more perfect assignment for Telmen than that?"

I laugh. There never has been a more perfect person to spread rumors. Plus, if Telmen is able to create some confusion, that will make our presence much less noticeable. Who'd have thought Telmen's unique ability to never stop talking could actually give us a chance? I sit down next to Spike, and he hands me a half-unwrapped sandwich.

"Have you given any thought to how you are going to swipe Stone's data-pad?" I ask. There's a fine art to stealing. Stealing something without the person noticing it's missing, especially when that thing is something as important and frequently utilized as a data-pad, is next to impossible. Sprinkle a little inexperience on the top and you've got a recipe for failure.

Spike chuckles. "Oh aye, but I'm not gunna swipe it." I inhale loudly at the statement. Kane and Olivia stop talking and look over as well.

"Come again?" I ask in disbelief.

"Aye, how would I even go about it? Excuse me, sir. Ye have the time? Mind if slide that data-pad off yer wrist fer a minute and then walk off with it?"

I stammer, not knowing how to respond to that.

"Hold on, I thought stealing that data-pad was the reason we are here." Kane asks the question I'm too dumbfounded to parse out.

"Aye, it is." Spike just smiles and goes back to his sandwich. The three of us exchange a long, confused look. "Dunna worry. I've got a plan."

Kane tries again. "A plan to not steal the thing we came here to steal. The thing that, if we don't get, we are heaped."

"Aye, exactly."

Kane laughs. "He's a crazy one. I like him." He points to Spike and reverts his attention back to Olivia.

"All right," I sigh. "What's your plan?"

"Better to show then to tell ya, dontcha think, brotha? Olivia, why don't ya show these lads how it's done with them special skills of yers."

"Special skills?" Kane asks looking between Olivia and Spike, a mischievous grin on his face.

"Go on, lass. Show him," Spike says.

Olivia puts her hand on Kane's knee and looks up into his eyes. She tosses her hair back and, as if possessed by some magic, it falls perfectly to one side. Her mouth forms into an alluring and seductive smile. Kane is frozen in place. He's not moving, not even blinking as he stares into the Olivia's eyes. Olivia blinks, and Kane—as if coming out of a trance—shakes his head from side to side.

"That's her thing, brotha." Spike grins.

"All she has to do is make eye contact with him, and he'll be done. She's your shade?" Kane asks. Spike nods. "That'll work," Kane admits.

Kane continues his flirting with Olivia on into the night. Spike and I discuss the future, and he listens to my concerns and guilt about Lilly. He tries telling me it's not my fault, but I don't believe him. I know it is. He tells me by the time we get back, Victor will have a plan to rescue her. That, I do believe. It is some comfort. Relying on others is a necessity that never gets easier. Sometimes it's just hard to know how completely not in control you are, even though Spike has never let me down before and hasn't given me reason to doubt him now. It's hard to rest knowing I'm not in control.

After stirring and turning for too long I get up. Maybe walking around will clear my head a bit. The dark sky is sprinkled with little shimmering gems making the rooftops feel peaceful and serene. I move to the back of the roof to get away from where the rest of the group is sleeping. When I turn the corner, I see Olivia reclining against the wall, staring at the floor of the flat roof with her head between her legs.

"You ok?" I slide next to her leaning against the wall.

She exhales and shrugs.

"What's wrong," I press.

"Have you ever felt like, no one can see you?" She asks.

"We're thieves, isn't that kind of the point," I tease, hoping to lift her spirits. It does not help.

"Forget it."

"No, sorry I was just-what's going on?"

"I'm just, tired of being invisible."

"Invisible?" I chuckle, "Olivia when you walk in a room everyone stops to look. All eyes are on you. You are as far from invisible as it gets."

"Jett, when you look the way I look, people treat you a certain way. It's nice, it's flattering. You become more like an object than a person. Everybody looks at you, but nobody sees you. When I accomplish something, everyone just assumes it's because of how I look. When people are nice to me, it's because of how I look. Everything about me comes back to my appearance. It's like, that's all I am to people. I'm a walking, talking decoration. It's like nothing else matters. Do you know what it's like to have your entire identity boiled down to one thing? Then to have that one thing be something as shallow and insignificant as your appearance?" She shakes her head, "Sorry, with everything going on, I guess I just needed to get that off my chest."

I put my hand on her shoulder, "I'm glad you told me. I had no idea. I can't imagine how lonely that must feel, like no one really knows you at all."

A subtle smile adorns her face, "Thank you."

"If it helps, I don't see you as attractive in the slightest," I nudge her shoulder with mine.

"Thanks," her smile grows as she fights back a chuckle.

"No, I mean it. Like, looking at you is like looking at a garbage heap...if a garbage heap were a person with blonde hair."

"Ok, that's enough," she rolls her eyes. "I'm not trying to complain about how I look, it's just-"

"You're more than that. You're more than how you look," I sigh. "I'm realizing through all of this, that I've been looking at you, at all our little friends, and just focusing on your most obvious trait. Telmen talks a lot. Jensen is a shinshew."

"I'm not blaming you," Olivia starts to protest.

"No but, the last place you should feel unseen is around your family and your friends. It was pointed out to me recently; I let Victor do my thinking for me. Maybe that's true. I've been so consumed with my anger over what happened to my parents, about what happens all around us, that I got lost in it. I'm sorry, truly. You all deserve better. My eyes have been closed for too long. I want to fix that. Starting now, I want to start seeing you all not for your utility, but for who you really are.

"Wow," Olivia chuckles, "Where's all that been?"

I nod, "That's what we are fighting for isn't it: to create a world where no one tells you who you are or what you are worth? What good is it if we free ourselves from the tyranny of the Patriarch only to end up treating people the same way in the process?"

Olivia sighs, "Just like that the boy becomes a man." She laughs, "Maybe you really are the leader Victor says you are. Thank you, Jett, I needed that." She slowly stands, dusting herself off as she does. "We better turn in. It's pretty late."

"For what it's worth, I think you are one of the most loyal and trusting people I've ever met. You've been through so much. Yet you never stop believing in the people you care about. That's truly an amazing quality."

Olivia smiles, "Goodnight Jett."

Falling asleep proves harder than expected. My body is fatigued, but my mind won't stop racing. Every possible scenario plays out in my head from fantasies far too good to be true to nightmares too terrifying to dwell on. I toss and turn through the night, sleep eluding me except for a short burst of exhaustion as the night draws to a close.

At some point during the night, Telmen must have returned. He's talking with Spike. Olivia seems to be gone, and Kane is putting his body armor on and grabbing his rifle. We share a meager breakfast, and Telmen talks the whole time. Somehow, he is able to talk while eating. Like he has two mouths.

We make our way outside. Thankfully, the dark glass of our visors also dulls the brightness of the morning sun. We step out into the street. The buildings are so much larger than those of the Market. These are towering structures, some of them as many as ten or fifteen stories tall. They are cloud breakers, like the housing units and business units in Sector A that can be seen for miles, but they are monstrously large in their own right. Down the streets, there are pairs of soldiers positioned in front of various buildings while others patrol up and down. Under normal circumstances, this seems a bit like overkill in a place like this. Commander Stone appears to have turned the industrial sector into a mobile deployment area for his remaining PDF troops.

We line up in as similar a fashion to the soldiers we've seen as possible and hope to move without drawing too much attention. Our first mission is to find Commander Stone. My skin crawls as we move through the streets. I take quick, shallow breaths as if breathing too loudly might give us away. It's one thing to blend into a crowd as a thief. It's another thing to intentionally be behind enemy lines.

My instincts and years of training as a thief urge me to run. Doing so would condemn many people, including Lilly, to death. This is a do or die mission. We move up and down the streets, deeper into the belly of the beast. Certainly, Commander Stone has created some kind of headquarters for himself. We just need to find it. This would be so much easier if we split up, but moving alone would seem even more suspicious.

"We meet back up in the room of the storage building when it's done. If we get separated, make sure yer not followed and get back there and wait," Spike whispers.

A pair of soldiers run up to us. "Where is the rest of your unit?" one of them asks. My hand drifts back to my knife. If we can dispatch them quickly and quietly, maybe we will be okay.

"Our unit? What do you mean?" Telmen says before anyone else can react. "We were told to patrol the street and keep an eye out for deserters. What are you doing?" He reaches for his rifle. "Sir, they may be the ones we were warned about." It's a good thing this visor covers my face, or the two soldiers would see my jaw drop. This has to be the single most brilliant moment of Telmen's life. Did he really just turn the tables on soldiers who were suspicious of us?

Both of them take a step back and hold their hands up defensively. "No, no, we are not deserting. We were responding to reports that a group of rebels is trying to sneak in through the southern gate."

"Better go check it out. If rebels are coming, we can't be too careful," Kane says boldly. The two guards nod and rush past us toward the wall.

"What just happened?" I ask in a low voice, still stunned.

Telmen pats himself on the chest. "Spike sent me to spread rumors, so I spread rumors."

"Aye, ye did fine work. We stocked now. Let's go. We can celebrate Telmen's rumor skills after we've finished."

We continue our march around and then deeper into the converted military base. Soldiers rush back and forth. The careful, neat order of their movements from the night before is gone, replaced with chaos and confusion. Telmen's rumors are far more effective than I could have imagined. I wonder what other things he can do with his non-stop talking.

We turn the corner of one of the larger factories and enter an open area, similar to the Market Square. Against the far wall of a red brick factory, there are several large tents set up. The two on the sides are closed off with flaps making it difficult to see inside them. The center one is open, and I can see a large table in the middle. Standing on the other side of the table is a man I'd recognize anywhere. Even his posture looks cruel and angry. Once again, I find myself staring at Commander Stone.

The mission disappears from my mind as images of Brelar's dead body flash in front of me. I close my eyes to try and block them out, but it only makes the memory clearer. The fire of our home burns around me, roasting my skin. The cries of our neighbors pleading for mercy echo in my ears. I see Brelar, dragging his injured leg, pulling it as fast as he could, only to collapse in my arms again and again. I am going to kill this man. If it costs me everything, he will die. Something in me snaps. I watch outside myself as I break formation and reach for my rifle. I'll never have a clearer shot than this. One quick motion and so much justice will be served.

"Jett, don't. I need ye to turn around right now and run. Run like ye just received an order to report to somewhere else. Go back to the room." Spike grabs my shoulder, trying to stop me. I tug my shoulder free and sling my rifle from it. I will not be deterred. "Jett, if you do this then Lilly dies."

"Lilly," I repeat dumbfounded.

"Yes, Lilly. Think of Lilly, brotha,"

"No, Lilly." I point in the direction of Commander Stone.

Standing just behind Commander Stone, face down toward the ground, hands shackled together, is Lilly.

CHAPTER SEVENTEEN

The world around me becomes a blur. Seeing her makes me hopeful and fearful at the same time. How can she be here? She was on Lorth Drant's show. She should be in the Temple Sector—not here, not with him. Brelar's face pops into my head again. What if Commander Stone does to Lilly what he did to Brelar? Panic seizes me.

Lilly is not wearing her normal uniform with the yellow sash. She is in a brown, hooded cloak that covers most of her body like a blanket. Her dark hair drifts down past her face. I can't see her clearly from this far away, but she doesn't appear hurt, at least not physically. Is her family here too or just her? What is going on? This can't be a coincidence.

"Kane, I need ye on a roof keeping an eye out," Spike orders.

"If things get messy, you're going to—"

"If things get messy, it's not going to make a difference. You've a fighter sense about ye. If ye see anything, create a distraction and give us a chance to run."

Reluctantly, Kane rushes off and disappears around the corner of the building behind us.

"Olivia, make yer way back to the tunnels. I need ye to get to Victor as fast as ye can. Tell him, and only him, what's going on."

Olivia looks over at me and gives me a reassuring smile. Her hand runs over my shoulder and down my arm. She squeezes my hand with hers and rushes off. There's no way she will get to Victor in time to save us. Even if she messaged him, he couldn't get anyone here in time. Spike is getting her out of harm's way. Old fashioned to the end.

"Jett, I need ye to stand guard here, brotha. Make sure no one traps our escape route. Telmen, yer with me," Spike says.

"What about Lilly?" I ask.

"One thing at a time, brotha. Dunna worry. We won't leave her behind. There are a lot of lives depending on us getting that data. What do ye say we worry about that first?"

Spike and Telmen rush over to Commander Stone. My heart pounds like a drum in my chest. Lilly is right there, within reach. All I'd have to do is rush over to her, grab her arm and guide her to safety. Too many guards, I get that. At least I could let her know we are coming for her. She looks so scared. I step closer, keeping an eye out for any sign of trouble while listening closely. I look over my shoulder to see Spike walk around to the table to stand next to Commander Stone. Stone looks up at him with a scowl. Telmen, standing across the table, provides the distraction.

"Commander," he starts, stopping himself from going into his usual slew of connected thoughts.

"I thought I said I was not to be disturbed," Stone growls.

"Yes, sir. Sorry, sir. It's just, there seems to be a lot of confusion in the ranks, sir."

Stone exhales loudly and looks up at Telmen. "Well, out with it then." Time stands still. Telmen often acts without thinking. With each passing moment, my anxiety rises. Can Telmen, overly chatty Telmen, really pull this off?

"Sir," Telmen pauses. His words usually flow like the rapid-fire burst of an automatic weapon. Here he speaks slowly, pausing as long as he can between thoughts. Smart. The less he says, the less likely he is to give himself away. Perhaps I have underestimated Telmen. "The men are responding to numerous reports of rebel attacks, deserters, fires— it's creating a bit of chaos."

"That's what the officers are for, soldier. Why are you bothering me with this?"

"Sorry, sir. It's just, all the reports seem to be false. The officers are responding to each report. My concern was the men are being pulled from their posts to chase down ghosts and rumors. Perhaps it would be best to order all units to remain in position and assign a few to investigate these claims specifically?" Telmen's performance is masterful. Spike, however, is just standing there. Telmen has given him multiple windows to move. He can't buy time forever. Spike is wasting this opportunity. The air in my lungs feels like it's made of iron, weighing down each breath I take. If Spike doesn't do something soon, I'm going to take it. Heap what he said.

Stone's brow furrows as he looks at Telmen. "You think to instruct me on-" Stone stops himself, his jaw clenching. Telmen may have overplayed his hand. "Who do you think you-" Stone stops again his eyes narrowing. "Something is off, why are you violating protocol?" That's not good. "Identification, soldier." That's really not good. Spike still hasn't moved. What is wrong with him? He wasted his chance. He's giving up? Spike moves away from Stone. That data-pad has the information we need. It is the hope of our rebellion. Spike talked me out of rescuing Lilly to get it. He didn't even try. He just stood there like a frozen lump of ice. This is why an inexperienced thief shouldn't be in charge of stealing something so important.

Before Telmen can answer another soldier rushes up to Commander Stone. "Sir," he barks out loudly before bending over. His hands brace on his knees and his back arches as he pants for breath. He must have run a considerable distance.

"Out with it, soldier," Commander Stone demands without sympathy for the clearly exhausted soldier. "You're interrupting."

"S-sir," the soldier pants, forcing himself to stand. Spike moves around the table, and Telmen slowly backs away, trying to use this. They both move toward an alley, trying to duck out of sight as quickly as possible. Spike motions for me to follow. I do. I move slowly, wanting to hear this report, lingering longer than I should. "We received a report from our contact in the Market." The soldier is compensating for his lack of breath by projecting loudly. That's good; I can slip further away and still hear him. I duck behind the flap of the tent next to the one Commander Stone is in, moving myself out of sight. "A group of rebels have acquired PDF uniforms and are headed this way. They may be here already." He pants loudly, "Sir, there are spies among us." How could he know that? There are only a handful of people who know what we are doing. Shinshew. We have been betrayed. Someone in the Market who knows what we are doing is selling us out to the Patriarch.

"Rumors spreading wildly, you say," Commander Stone says and then stops. "Where did he—" Stone scowls. "Soldier, sound the alarm. Bring two units here. Captain!" Stone barks out.

A soldier rushes over, "Sir?"

"Have your men escort this traitor back to her cell. Put her under heavy guard. Scan everyone's data-pad, even if they are dressed as one of us, understood? It seems we may have company." There goes my chance of rescuing Lilly. It's almost painful to be so close yet so powerless to do anything.

"Yes, sir." The boots click, and I can hear movement. Time to go. I slip away and head down the alley Spike and Telmen went down.

"What are doing, Jett? Ye need to pull yerself together." Spike grabs me and pushes me against the wall.

"Me?" I scowl. "Just when where you planning to take his data-pad? Hmm? The whole reason we are here." I grab Spike's hands and pull them off me, pushing him away. "Telmen gave you more than enough time. You did nothing!" I accuse.

"Nothing? Oh aye, I did nothing." Spike pulls a thin clear card out from under his data-pad. He swipes it over the screen, and a series of military access pages appear.

"What is this?" I ask confused.

"This is an exact copy of Stone's data-pad, brotha. That's why I needed a distraction—not to steal it but to give the device time to synchronize and clone all of the data. I told ye I wasn't gonna lift it, not that I wasn't gonna get it. Ye can't steal something like that without getting noticed. As soon as he noticed, he'd assume the information was compromised and reposition the men, making it all for naught. So, I had this little copying device made up."

"We got it?" I ask, hope filling my body.

"Aye, we got it. Access to all the codes, positions, and military data in the Patriarch network. Since it's a clone, we will see all changes in real-time. Vic's gonna lose his bloody mind."

I nod. "Sorry, it's just a really intense—"

Spike sighs. "I get that, brotha, I do."

"We have another problem," I say.

"Did we get it?" Kane comes charging down the alley.

Spike nods to him and then turns back to me. "What is it?"

"I heard the soldier tell Stone a group of us were coming here in PDF uniforms." Spike, Telmen, and Kane exchange a long silent glance. We all know what that means. "Someone has betrayed us, someone who knew we were using uniforms. That means someone close to us, someone we trust."

"We have to get back," Telmen says. "We've got the data. Let's get it to Victor. He'll know what to do."

"I can't leave her here," I say firmly.

"Jett, brotha, we can't rescue her. Not here."

"I have to try," I counter. This may be the only shot I have. If I don't save her now, I may never get another chance.

"I'm not about to leave ye here. If yer staying, I'm staying. We will rescue her together."

"No," I protest. "That information is too important to risk you getting caught. Saving Lilly, that's about me. That data is about the whole city. All the families who have suffered, all those who have lost loved ones to the Patriarch's tyranny. That data is for them. That is the hope of our rebellion, the tool we need to bring them to their knees. Spike, I know you. You'd never leave someone behind. You're not leaving me, you're helping save our city. There's no one I trust more than you to do what needs to be done. Not just for your friends but for everyone."

"Ye can't ask this of me, brotha. Ye can't ask me to let ye do this alone."

"Not alone," Kane says confidently. "The rebellion needs that data. We can't risk losing it. Spike, you take it. Get it to Victor. At least then we will know we accomplished something. I'll keep an eye on Jett, see if we can't find a way to rescue his girl. Everybody wins."

"I'm not leaving him in the hands of someone I hardly know. I dunna exactly trust ye."

"If he's going to rescue her, there's going to be a fight. We both know I'm a lot better in a fight. Trust me or don't, I could care less. It changes nothing. The data you have is important to everyone. This girl is important to Jett. I swear to you, on my honor as a warrior, I will do everything I can to protect your friend."

"I'll stay too," Telmen says. "You trust me, right?" Spike nods. "The three of us then will rescue Lilly and be back before you know it."

"I dunna like it," Spike objects.

"This is war, not what to have to dinner. The stakes are higher. The choices are harder. You don't have to like it. You just have to do it. Sometimes, there is no choice. We both know the only way you're getting this one out of here is if you knock him out and carry him over your shoulder. Something tells me none of us make it out like that. This isn't our best option. It's also our only option."

Spike nods reluctantly and hugs Telmen then me. Holding his arms tightly around me, he whispers in my ear, "Be careful, brotha. If ye see a way to save her, take it, but remember, ye can't help her if ye get caught. Be smart."

I nod in agreement. "Get out of here," I say.

Spike turns to Kane. "If anything happens to them, I'll hold ye responsible. Ye better make sure they get out of here, or I will find you and I will kill you slowly."

"I knew I liked you. Don't worry, I've got this. I haven't killed anyone in like a day. I'm overdue." Kane smiles his wicked smile. Spike disappears down the alley.

"Well, how are we doing this?" Kane asks holding his arms behind his back and stretching. It's a good question. How do we get Lilly away from a heavily armed group of soldiers who are on high alert? What would Victor do in this situation? I rack my brain, pacing back and forth for a moment, trying to channel Victor's brain. How would he lure their attention? When would he make the move? Victor always finds a way to put his target off balance. We don't have Victor's brain. We don't have many resources. All we have are the three of us, our rifles, and a couple of smoke discs.

"Okay, I've got it. First, we need to get eyes on Lilly. The soldiers are moving her. Victor always says transit is when things are at their most vulnerable. Telmen, you will find a spot in the rear behind the soldiers. At my signal you'll start firing. One shot then wait. Kane, you will get in front of them. After Telmen shoots, count to twenty. The soldiers will close ranks and adjust for the shooter behind them. At twenty you shoot. When the soldiers start to reposition, Telmen, you will fire five or six shots then get out of the building. Kane, after Telmen's shots, you do the same. That should create enough chaos to let me make my move." They both nod in agreement.

We race down the alleys between factories until we catch sight of a unit of PDF soldiers marching a prisoner down one of the larger streets. It's perfect—a long wide street with a few alleys to either side between buildings. At the front and back of the street there are two tall buildings where Telmen and Kane can set up their positions. All we need now is something to keep the soldiers from moving before Telmen and Kane can reach their posts.

Sprinting ahead, I get in front of the soldiers on the street parallel to them. I slide up the alley, careful not to make a sound. Keeping to the shadows, I creep closer to their location. A well-placed dumpster sits at the end of the alley just before it opens up to the street. I duck behind it and wait. I hear the sound of the boots clapping against the ground as they march past. Two rows pass, then another two, and another. At nine I slip out from behind the dumpster, careful not to draw attention. The tenth row is the last in this triple-wide procession of soldiers. I quickly slide behind the last, keeping my steps silent.

On their belts, the soldiers each have a few utility devices. One of them is a smoke disc. Slowly, I reach out as I walk behind the last solider closest to the buildings. Holding my breath, I click the button on his smoke disc. I stop, turn, and dive back into the alley, hiding myself in the shadows. I wait. Peeking out of the alley, I see the smoke disc starting to fume. Perfect.

"Halt! Smoke!" the soldier in the back row, middle column shouts, turning to the man next to him. The squad freezes and turns as they are engulfed in the grey vapor. I can see the shadows of the back row, and the man in the middle moves to try and remove the disc from his comrade. The squad breaks formation. Several soldiers move outside of the smoke, rifles ready, kneeling and looking through their scopes they scan the area. I duck my head back into the alley to keep out of sight. This should buy more than enough time. Hopefully, Telmen will recognize the smoke as a signal and fire when he's in position.

I hear boots stomping and dare to look around the corner. The smoke fades. The soldier with the disc I activated is holding his hands in the air defensively.

"I swear, sergeant. I didn't touch it. It must have gone off on its own."

"Sure, happens all the time. My smoke disc always turns itself on."

"Sarge, I'm telling you—"

"Save it for the report."

"You're writing me up?"

"Of course. Your lack of discipline put the unit at risk. Commander Stone will want to know about that." Come on, Telmen. Get in position. It's time.

"Please, no. You know what he's like. He'll—"

The last words to leave his mouth before the faint crack of a gunshot in the distance are a plea for mercy. At least he won't have to worry about Commander Stone anymore. The soldier's body collapses to the ground, red blood splattering the street. The sergeant turns, scanning the buildings, too stunned to make a noise as he searches for the source of the shot. The timer in my head starts ticking. Twenty, nineteen…five, four. I take a breath, my heart pounding in my chest. How does Victor remain so calm in these situations? The soldiers have formed a defensive line, rifles aimed toward the direction Telmen fired from.

Crack. Another gunshot rings out. Another soldier falls. The group repositions again, their formation looser, less organized. Five shots ring out in succession, three of them finding their marks. The soldiers fire rapidly in Telmen's direction. Then six shots, this time from Kane's position. The soldiers spin and fire, falling into disarray. This is the moment I was waiting for. Pulling my rifle free, I rush out of the alley and take aim. In full run, I fire three shots toward the building Kane is in.

I reach the soldiers, stepping in amongst them. I move toward Lilly.

"Rebels!" I shout, hoping to create more chaos. "They have us surrounded. Get the prisoner out of here," I yell. Answering my own instructions, I grab Lilly's wrist and pull her away from the group. This is it. Time to see if my plan worked.

"Reform positions, cover fire!" One of the soldiers' shouts. They fire rapidly down the street. Their shots seem very close to where Telmen and Kane were. Hopefully they got out in time.

Lilly tugs against my hand. "Let me go! I haven't done anything."

I tighten my grip on her wrist and pull harder. I want to stop, to tell her it's me, but we are still too close.

"Shhh," I whisper forcefully.

We need to clear the area. The more she fights, the slower we go. Something hits my leg and I feel my body falling backward. I hit the ground with a loud thud. My body freezes in shock more than pain as a stare up at the sky.

I feel her weight on my chest as she pins me to the ground fist pulling back.

"Lilly, wait!" I shout.

She pauses before hitting me and a confused expression covers her face. She pushes off me freeing my arms.

"Jett?"

"Yes, it's me," I pull the helmet off my head. Lilly looks at me in wide-eyed disbelief.

"What are you? How are you? Wha—"

"I'm rescuing you...or I was," I respond with a hint of amusement as I rub my shoulder.

"Rescuing me? How did you even know I'd be here?" she asks.

"Long story. I'll tell you later. Right now, we need to get out of here before the rest of the soldiers come looking."

Lilly nods in agreement. We make our way out of the area, keeping to alleys as much as possible. When we come to openings, I check to make sure the area is clear and then we sprint to the other side. It works smoothly. Lilly is naturally very good at this. Now I just have to hope Kane and Telmen remember our rendezvous location.

The storage building is in sight. My heart races faster than the hover train. We are so close. If I can get her to safety, on top of Spike having the data, this will have been an amazing day.

"Okay, when I say go, we are going to run for that building there." I point to the storage building. "As fast as we can. Got it?"

"Jett." Lilly pauses looking at me. "My family. Where is my family?"

"I don't know. We didn't see them here. They are probably still in the Temple Sector."

"I can't just leave them. They were arrested because of me. If they go to the Outlands—"

I grab her shoulders and turn her toward me. "I won't let that happen. Victor knows what to do. We will save them." Lilly nods and seems to relax.

Her face suddenly changes; her brow furrows. "Why did they take my family, Jett?" How do I tell her this is not the time or the place for this discussion? I look over her shoulder as a group of soldiers rush by. Thankfully they don't notice us. "First they arrest me. But then my family. They did nothing wrong. How can they do that? Why would they?"

"To get to me," I say plainly, hoping a little information will get us moving faster.

"What do you mean to get to you? Why would the Patriarch care about getting to you?"

"Well, I sort of ended up becoming a kind of...leader in the rebellion."

"You what?" Her tone sounds angry.

I hold up my hands to defend against her tone. "It just kind of happened."

"You just...happened to become the leader of a rebellion?"

I shrug. "Well, yeah." I nod with a smile. That will help. Nothing disarms frustration like an oddly timed smile. "It's not like I was trying to. Vic just sort of made it happen."

"So, when you rescued me and the other people in the Market?" Lilly asks.

"That's how we got involved. We only came because we were told the Levites had our friends. Then I saw you there and, well, you know the rest."

"Jett, this is crazy."

"You're telling me. Look, we have to get out of here. I promise I'll explain everything when we get back to the Market. Vic will devise some crazy scheme, and we will rescue your family. I'll make it all right. I promise."

I take Lilly's hand, check the street, and we run. We run as fast as we can. One final street and we are home free. We're so close I can taste it. I can get her to safety. Victor can handle the rest. We can put an end to this conflict once and for all. Things are about to change forever. My boots grind against the stone ground as I slide to a stop, catching my momentum against the wall with my hand. I pull the door open. We've done it. Made it to safety. Just wait for Telmen and Kane to arrive. Down the secret tunnel and back to safety. Two big wins for the rebellion. Maybe we really can pull this off.

"Just follow me," I instruct, stepping inside the storage building. Lilly follows, and the door closes behind us. Success, accomplishment, victory; they sweep over me, filling me with a sense of pride.

In an instant, my glorious feeling of confidence comes crashing down into terror. Standing in the middle of the room, arms folded behind his back, is Commander Stone. I feel Lilly clutching my arm. My hand reaches for the rifle behind my back. Stone smiles, the scar on his face prominent as he sneers at me. He glares at me with emotionless, compassionless, soulless eyes. He's surrounded by dozens of soldiers, rifles pointed directly at us.

"It's a shame how predictable vermin can be," he says with a chuckle.

I sense motion beside me, see movement out of the corner my eye. I turn. I hear it before I feel it, a loud cracking sound. Pain shoots through the back of my head. Everything goes blurry, and I fall to my knees. My vision gets cloudy, then dark, then black. I try to hold on to consciousness, but it is slipping away. I didn't rescue Lilly—I led her into the belly of the beast.

CHAPTER EIGHTEEN

Throbbing, mind numbing pain jolts me awake. My body is tense. I try to relax my muscles and move. I can't. My hands are bound tightly behind my back. I'm lying on a cold stone floor; my body is bound to the wall with a heavy iron chain, allowing me only a short range of movement. I look around trying to make sense of where I am. It's a poorly lit, damp room with mold and grime all over the walls. The room has the look of a long-abandoned prison cell. There are dim lumebulbs in each corner of the room, and a hole in the ceiling allows a small beam of natural light in.

Lilly is gone. I didn't see what happened to her before I was knocked in the head, but there's no way she escaped. That must have been the shortest rescue in history. I tell myself she's fine. The Patriarch already announced she would be sent to the Outlands. They couldn't hurt her. Their exile ceremony would be broadcast in the morning. For years, they've preached being an Outlands Officer is an honor. They don't want to do anything to diminish that now. It may not be true, but it's comforting. Comforting enough to let me focus on the problem at hand—my capture.

Since I've been branded as a face of the rebellion, the Patriarch has an opportunity. They can publicly torture me to demonstrate their power and discourage others from rebelling, though that might tarnish their public image a little. Could backfire on them too. That's probably just wishful thinking. If I don't get out of this cell, things are going to get really bad for me. It doesn't help that I don't even know how long I've been here, or even where here is. I could be in some old warehouse held prisoner by Commander Stone or I could be in the Temple Sector. No, they would need the trains. Victor has them on lockdown.

The data-pad! Hope blossoms its sweet fragrance. If Spike got the data-pad to Victor, then Victor has all the information he needs to launch his attack. If they put my arrest into their system, Victor may know exactly where I am. Maybe the best thing to do is hold tight and wait for rescue. I curl my body, my shoulders stretching, my arms reaching. I slide my hands over my feet. They are still bound, but at least now they are in front of me.

I spend most of the day pacing back and forth, working off my pent-up energy. They must think I'm important, locking me in a cell and chaining me to the wall. It's both flattering and annoying—more annoying. I tug on the chain periodically, testing its limits, trying to memorize exactly how far I can reach. Knowing could come in handy. Plus, it gives me something to do. Sitting all day doing nothing will certainly drive me mad.

My cell has no source of natural light by which to gauge the passing of time. My pacing turns to leaning, to sitting, to sleep. Meals slide through a small hatch at the bottom of the door twice a day, at least I think it's twice a day. After a while it gets hard to tell.

I'm sitting on the floor the sound of a keycard swiping at my door interrupts my thoughts. Light floods into the room, forcing me to look away. When I look back, I see a tall, well-built man. Black uniform, scar on his face. Commander Stone. His face is twisted into an evil looking smile. The chains rattle as they catch my body, tugging me back against the wall as I lunge at him. This seems to amuse Stone even more.

"Jett Lasting, this is a good look for you, caged and chained like an animal," Stone says, stepping further into the room. He paces slowly, flaunting his power over me. "You have proven to be quite the nuisance for an Undesirable." He paces in a half circle, staying close enough to taunt me but just out of reach.

"Making your life more difficult almost makes it all worth it."

Stone glares at me. "You don't understand what you have done at all do you?" He scoffs at me. "No, there are always those who feel entitled to more and who don't care what they risk to get it. I suppose you believe that I hate you, that I take pleasure in capturing and torturing children? I do not relish this. I am a man of principle from a noble family. In my education, I learned all about the World that Was: the freedoms, the individuality, the selfishness. The world was run by whim. Everyone did what they wanted. No one cared about the greater good, or about order, or what is right.

Man's inhumanity is his pursuit of himself. When left to our own devices, that is what we do. Until society is run by mass hysteria and the chaos that inevitably ensues leads to destruction. It's a tale as old as Rome. I will not let it happen here. Man is broken. We are sick. We need to be restrained. We need order and control. The Patriarch didn't just save the world. They made a better one. A world of peace and harmony for all. Unfortunately for you, you're a cog that doesn't fit into the machine. Thus, I am honor-bound to snuff you out like the destructive vermin you are."

I resist the urge to lunge for him again. My inability to reach him would gratify his ego more than my desire to resist. Every fiber in my being longs to reach out and choke the life out of him.

He smiles his evil smile. "You really do hate me, don't you? It's only natural that you would hate those who are better than you. After all, I am everything you are not. I have value, significance, class, power, freedom. What have you got? Hmm? Some rags and a whole load of attitude. You are little more than a savage beast that's shed its fur. What gives you the right to resist me?"

I glare silently at him, picturing his head exploding. Just thinking about it makes me smile. His words make me hate him more. He is not just a man conditioned and taught to hate Undesirables. He has chosen to hate us. He understands we are human beings, like him, but chooses to treat us as inferior simply because society has deemed us such. The great pride he holds in his worth is shallow. The only way he can feel important is by degrading those around him. He is the ultimate bully, not acting out of ignorance but out of intentional, deliberate hate.

I force myself to laugh. Louder and louder. This drives him crazy. He stops his power pacing and glares at me, his brow furrowed, face red.

"Something funny, street trash?"

I keep laughing. "You. Think you have power?"

He leans back as if wounded. "I don't think I have power. I am a Commander in the Patriarch Defense Force. I am one of the most powerful men in this city. You will—"

I interrupt him with more raucous laughter.

"Stop laughing!" Stone sneers.

"You shot an injured child in the back. It takes a special kind of weakness to do that."

"Weakness? You still don't get it do you. Power is the ability to do whatever you want without anyone stopping you. Besides, you say it was a child. I say it was a rabid animal. By killing that diseased beast, I did the community a favor."

I feel like throwing up. There is no reasoning with a man like this, no talking to him. All I can hope to do is get under his skin. "The weak are always justifying their weakness by pretending it's a strength. The only power you have comes from diminishing others. You have to make them lesser because you know deep down, for all your titles and position, they are far more than you could ever be. Keep pretending. Keep lying to yourself. All you have is an illusion propped on fear." If I could just free my hands, I could hit him. It wouldn't get me out of this room, but if my last act in this world is putting a mark on his sadistic face, it'd be worth it.

"Tell me, since you have the moral high-ground, how are you different? How many soldiers did you kill in the Market? Hmm? How many children are waiting for parents who will never come home because of you? Wives, husbands who are now widowed? How many parents lost their child because they happened to be in your way. Don't pretend you're better than me. You are responsible for far more deaths than I am."

"It's not the same," I say, my voice wavering. My conviction is waning. He has a point; we've killed a lot of people. It's not like we enjoyed it. We didn't want to kill them. Does that matter? Does intention justify action? Our mission is good and just. Does that make our actions okay? Now he's in my head.

"Oh?" Stone raises an eyebrow. "Please, enlighten me."

"There's a difference between killing because you have to and choosing to kill. Killing is not our goal. It's a price we regret we have to pay to accomplish our goal. For you, killing is a pleasure. You delight in it. That's what makes you a monster."

"A monster? Fascinating. You run around this city like savage beasts, taking what you want, ignoring the rules upon which our society is built. You endanger public safety by threatening the balance of order in the city. It was this selfishness, this individualism that led to the Great Collapse. Yet you call me monster. I am no monster. I am the guardian of this city. I am a protector of its law-abiding citizens. Without people like me, Dios would be no better than the Outlands—"

"Without people like you, Dios would be a city worth living in," I interrupt. Stone smiles and steps forward. Perfect. Engaging in an ethics debate with a monster like Stone means nothing to me. I just needed to get him worked up so he'd let his guard down. I leap forward, arms extended, hoping to catch him before the chains tug me back. Success. My chained hands grab behind Stone's head just as the tension on the chains snag and pull me down and back toward the wall. I'm prepared for this, but Stone is not. I pull hard on his head as I fall, using the momentum of the chains to turn him so he lands under me. My shoulder slams against his chest. I can feel the air deflating from his lungs as my full body weight crashes onto his chest. I pull my hands free from behind his head and plant them on his neck, squeezing as hard as I can. His hands come up, gripping my wrists, trying to pull them away. The chains that bind my wrists together make pulling them apart impossible. His face turns red as he chokes and gasps for air. Fear rages behind his sinister eyes. He looks as if he's begging, begging for mercy. I'll show him the same mercy he gave Brelar.

The same joyous feeling I had when Lilly and I made it to the storage building sweeps over me again. I may die in this cell or in some horrible torture the Patriarch is preparing for me, but I can find peace in knowing I took Stone with me. Captured, chained, locked away, I took him with me.

One of the things I've read over and over in the stories about the World that Was is that history has a way of repeating itself. Stone's knee drives hard into my side. Pain shoots up my body. I grunt and push harder trying to hold my grip on his neck. His knee drives up again, and my body shifts just a little. That little bit is just enough. Stone rolls, gaining the leverage he needs to push my hands free of his neck. Still bound together, my hands push off the ground just in time to keep my face from smashing into it.

Blood sprays from my nose as Stone's fist smashes into my face. He doesn't miss a beat. He drives his fist into my chest. I cough forcefully, winded from the strike. His boot smashes against my ribs as he starts kicking me repeatedly. I curl up, my back pressed against the wall. My whole-body throbs with pain.

Stone rubs his neck, grinning down at me. "You can't help yourself. Beasts will always be beasts." He gives me a self-satisfied glare and walks to the door. He stops and looks back at me over his shoulder. "Let me leave you with this parting gift. A question really. How did I know where you were going to be? Doesn't it seem odd that of all the buildings in the industrial sector, I just so happened to be waiting in the one you ran to?"

"Why don't you just kill me and get it over with?" I groan.

"Kill you? Tsk. Tsk. Tsk. Death is easy. We have something far better in store for you. First, we are going to break you. Then, the Assessors are going to reprogram your mind. Finally, we will prop you up as a puppet of the Patriarch. If we kill you, they will just replace you. If we turn you, you will bring an end to the very rebellion you lead. It's almost poetic, isn't it?" He laughs his sinister laugh and walks out.

The door locks behind him with a click. I find myself alone in a dark cell once again. I try to put the question out of my head. The last thing I want is Stone poisoning my mind. But the more I try to ignore it, the more prominent the question becomes. No one else knew we would be there. The tunnels are still a secret, or he'd be boasting about how they are marching on the rebellion now. If he'd captured Telmen or Kane, even with torture they wouldn't have given up our position in time for him to be waiting for us. The answer I'm trying to avoid quickly becomes the only reasonable conclusion. The only way Stone could have known where we were going to be is if someone told him.

Then I remember the soldier's report. He does have a spy inside the rebellion, someone who is very well informed about what we are doing. Someone has betrayed us. But who? Olivia was the first to leave. There's no way it's her. She's the most loyal person I've ever met. Telmen either. They both chose to stay and risk their lives to help me save Lilly. Maybe that's why they stayed, so they could make sure we failed?

My mind piles scenario after scenario, accusing and imagining each of my friends to be guilty of betraying us. Stone's words are poison, corrupting my thoughts about my closest friends. No matter how hard I try, I can't shake it. Someone gave Stone that information. Someone is working for the Patriarch. But who and why?

Kane. Of course. Kane is the most likely culprit. He's not part of our group. He didn't grow up with us. In the industrial sector, he was out of sight when Stone was informed of our presence in PDF uniform. He could have told Stone where we'd be before shooting at the soldiers to help free Lilly. Someone forced Brelar to lie to us which dragged us into this conflict in the first place. Someone knew where we lived, told Stone how to find us. The more I think about it, the more it makes sense. Everything starts to make sense. He saves me from Heywin to earn my trust, pretends to be bonded to me, and stays close, always ready to help ensuring he knows what's going on. Kane is the traitor. Even with all the evidence piling up against him, he genuinely seems to hate the Patriarch though. I don't want to believe it. Who else could it be? It has to be him.

My mind turns on me again. If Kane is a traitor, why would Stone let that slip? He's an invaluable resource, the perfect inside man. Stone has to know there's a chance, even if it's a small one, that the rebels will try to rescue me. Why tell me? Is he that confident I'll be dead before a rescue can arrive? Is he lying just to torture me with doubt in my final hours? Maybe he is counting on a rescue and he's telling me this to divide us, to sow the seeds of distrust. Maybe this is all a lie just to torture me—a sick, sadistic question to drive me mad.

No, someone told Stone we were coming. Someone told him where I would be. There is a traitor. The only reason he'd be so bold as to lead me to it is that he knows I'll be dead. I need to stop. Every moment I think about it drives Stone's toxin deeper into my mind. It's another moment Stone is stealing from me. I don't know how many more I have left to give. I wish Victor were here. He always knows what to do.

Under the door to my room, a thin beam of light shines through. I lay my head on the ground, too worn out, staring at the little crack of light. My attention is drawn to a sudden clicking sound. The top of the wall slides down revealing panels of bright lumelights. They click on and it feels like I'm staring directly at the sun. The lumelights emit heat, making me sweat. Then, the lights click off. Loud sounds start barraging my cell, echoing and shaking the room. The sounds are as deafening as they are unpleasant. I curl up in a ball to protect myself from the light and sound which rotate on and off every few minutes just as I start to adjusting to them.

Days pass slowly and the nights sleeplessly. I close my eyes and try to focus my mind. All I can do is agonize on Stone's question and wonder how the rebellion is going. Are my friends okay? Are they safe? Guards slide what resembles food but tastes like soggy cardboard into my cell three times a day, giving me a short respite from the blaring lights and sounds.

Despair rears its ugly head as I sprawl out on the ground. The isolation and loneliness begin to work on my mind. I lose all track of time. I concoct numerous ideas, fantasies for escape. All of them involve tools I don't have. I wonder if Victor is trying to rescue me. As my thoughts darken, I worry that the reason he hasn't come is that the rebellion has failed and he is dead. Each day erodes my sanity like waves crashing against the beach. If I don't do something, my mind may never leave this cell.

One day the blinding lights and sounds cease. I'm left lying in the deafening silence of my cell. I lay on the floor watching the light from under the door go from bright to dim to dark and then back to bright again. Thrilling. I attempt pacing back and forth and even exercise to break up the infinite void of time.

The silence is broken by the sound of rushing footsteps. A door swings closed with a click down the hall. Even further away, I can hear guards yelling. Everything for my entire stay has been painstakingly scheduled. This is new. This is exciting. I'm on my feet in an instant, body tense and ready. The rush of excitement crashes over me.

Feet slide across the floor as someone crashes into the door to my cell. The little beam of light is broken up by shadow. Who could this be? Is this a rescue? I wait, hoping to see the door swing open. It doesn't. There is a short pause. Something comes sliding into the room under the door. The beam of light comes back as my mystery guest rushes off in the opposite direction. A few moments later, I hear guards rushing by, shouting for the intruder to stop. Does that ever work?

The gift my mystery guest slid under the door is just out of reach. My chains pull taut. I need another foot of slack. I wiggle and tug on the chains, stretching out with my leg. No use. The gift is wrapped in a greyish blue cloth, probably to keep it from making noise as it slid across the floor. It's also likely the reason it didn't slide far enough for me to reach. Excitement and anxiety collide. It won't be long before the guards bring more food. They will certainly notice the care package on the floor, which would mean my mystery friend will have risked his life for nothing. I can't have that.

I lie my body down on the floor, hands pulling as hard as I can, trying to wiggle and force every inch of slack out of the chains. My legs stretch out further into the middle of the room. I feel like my shoulders are going to pop out of their sockets. In this position, I can't see. I use the heel of my foot to try and pin the cloth to the floor so I can drag it closer. With no idea how far I am from the cloth, I blindly stomp my heel, hoping to feel the fabric. Thwack. Thwack. Thump. There it is. My heart skips three beats. I push my heel down hard and slowly bend my leg, trying to maintain tension on the cloth. I feel it pull. Slowly, sliding the cloth toward me. I scoot my body closer to the wall, then repeat, tugging the cloth inch by inch until I'm confident I can reach it.

My imagination explodes with possibilities as I pick the cloth up. I move to the back wall where there is more light and carefully unwrap my treasure. The cloth gives way. In my hand is a small black handle. It's perfect. This is exactly what I need.

CHAPTER NINETEEN

A soft, near silent hum of energy activates with the blade. A soft blue beam of light in the shape of a six-inch, double-edged knife springs forth. This is better than a key. I hold the energy over the iron binding my wrists, and a loud crackling, hissing sound erupts. The metal changes from cool grey-black to a bright yellow. It feels hot against my skin. I grit my teeth and endure it as the energy blade serves as a blowtorch. The unyielding grip of metal on my skin begins to loosen, and I pull as hard as I can. Iron rattles against the ground as I break free of my chains. I repeat the process on the chains that bind me to the wall. They fall away, and I find myself one step closer to freedom.

It occurs to me that I have no idea where I am, how many guards are around me, or how to get to safety. I can picture Victor saying, we need more information. If my mystery rescuer was sent by Victor, he wouldn't have left me with a blind hope of escaping. I pick up the cloth. In my haste to rid myself of my chains, I hadn't bothered to inspect the cloth further. Maybe there is another reason the blade was wrapped up.

The cloth opens. I shake it to free any contents that may have been caught in its folds. Nothing. That's disappointing. I examine the cloth itself just to be sure. One side is nothing but fuzzy, greyish blue fabric. I turn it over, and my eyes light up. Etched on the cloth in dark blue letters is a message: Wait for my sign. That's disappointing. What am

I supposed to do with that? What sign? How will I know it? Why not tell me something more useful? Ambiguity is the worst. I turn the blade over in my hands, desperate to be free of this room. I can do it. I am holding the means of my escape, wielding the tool of my freedom. But whoever gave me this tool says wait.

Wait. What torture is this? All it would take is sliding the energy knife into the locking mechanism of the door until it burned away, and then freedom. I should just go, face whatever is on the other side of that door. I have a weapon; that's something they won't expect. But whoever risked their life to help me may know something I don't. Perhaps there is a reason they need me to wait. I decide to trust them.

I slump back down on the floor. My heart thuds louder and faster. My body twitches with nervous energy. Every passing moment feels like an eternity. What if I miss the sign? I wish they had taken the time to write out a real message and not just a few cryptic words. Breathe in slowly. Breathe out. If I can control my breathing, I can control my feelings.

I hold the cloth under the beam of light from the ceiling hole, reading it again and again as if doing so will give me a new insight into its meaning. The light goes out. Then comes back. I turn the fabric over idly. The light goes out again. That's weird. A bird sometimes blocks the view for a moment but two so quickly? The light goes out a third time. I look up. Light. No light. Light. No light. This isn't an accident. Someone is covering the hole intentionally over and over. This is it, my signal! I drop the cloth and rush to the door. My energy knife sings to life, and I thrust it into the handle. The thick metal softens and slowly gives way. I feel the blade slide loosely through the hole—no more distance. I pull, and the door slides open. Freedom. Light rushes in. I cover my eyes with my arm, giving myself a moment to adjust.

In front of me is a hallway that terminates with a set of stairs leading up. To my right is a solid wall, no doors, no windows, no means for escape. To my left is a long hallway, maybe several hundred yards long, lined with thick iron doors just like the one I came out of. Next to the door is a small screen projecting a name and image of that cell's occupant. I turn to my cell, and sure enough it's a picture of me underneath: Jett Lasting.

Lilly could be in one of these cells. Telmen or Kane could be as well. I don't know what happened to them, but if they were caught, maybe they are here. I move down the hall quickly, checking each screen. Most of them are blank. The few occupants are people I don't know. Perhaps they are enemies of the Patriarch like me. Could be useful to let them out. I don't know them though, and I can't risk the time it would take. They could be criminals. It's just too risky.

I make my way down the hallway, past each of the rooms. Maybe I should go back to the stairs leading up. For some reason, up feels wrong. I wander down the hallway with no clue as to where I am. At the end of the long hallway is another hallway that runs perpendicular to the one I'm in. I look down the path to the left and then to the right. Both sides are clear. How do I know which one to take? Out of the corner of my eye, I notice something: a small white arrow pointing right on the floor. I kneel down and touch it. White chalk sticks to my finger and smears on the floor. This must be a direction from my unknown rescuer.

The hallway leads to another turn. I find another white arrow, this one pointing left. I kneel down and rub my hand over the arrow, erasing it. I don't know why I bother. Something in me says to hide my tracks. As I walk down the hall, stepping as quietly as I can, I realize this could all be a trap—another mind game from the sadistic Commander Stone. What choice do I have? Trust the guidance of a stranger or take matters into my own hands and hope for the best. At least it's better than being stuck in my cell.

The next arrow points right, then left, then right again. Apparently, I am imprisoned in the center of a maze. Each hallway is lined with cell after cell. No Lilly, no Telmen, no Kane, just miscellaneous names. If I get out of here, I can come back and rescue them all.

I hear a commotion behind me. The voices are too far away to hear what they are saying, but I can guess. The guards must have discovered my empty cell. I need to move faster. I'm sure an alarm will be sounding very soon. Things are about to get difficult. I should have gone faster. I start to run, pausing to check each screen I pass. No matter how crazy it gets, I can't risk leaving Lilly behind if she's here. Right turn, left turn, left turn, right. So many hallways, so many rooms. Ahead, I see a burst of light coming from my left. It's a window.

I sprint toward it. On the floor in front of the window is a white arrow pointing at it. Good! This is my escape point. Red lights start flashing. Sirens blare around me. The alarm has been triggered. The sound is deafening. Each burst of the alarm is like a sonic blast crashing into my organs. My ears cry out in pain, but it doesn't matter. It will be over soon. I hear guards rushing down the halls behind me, calling out. They're getting closer. I drive my feet into the ground, pushing off with every step, propelling my body as fast as it will go.

The white arrow is gone. Not gone, covered by the boots of a Red Cap. The man has a large frame and a mean, rock-like face. His scowl and size make him look a bit like a troll. I look back down the hallway where I came from. Several guards have reached it, cutting off my route back. I don't have time; they've got me boxed in. There's no going back now, so I charge at the troll-faced Red Cap. He lowers his shoulders and charges back at me. Troll-face extends his arms, trying to grab me and pull me to the ground. No time to think—I just react.

The hallways themselves are tall but narrow, too narrow to sidestep Troll-face. I jump, sliding my hips to the side, then I plant my feet on the wall, one then the other, kicking off with as much upward momentum as I can. I use the sides of my feet to slide along the wall, angling myself away from it and just out of Troll-face's reach. In his zeal to catch me, he had overextended himself. His momentum carries him past me, and as he tries to turn, he stumbles forward, catching himself on the wall—a mistake that will cost him valuable seconds and give me all the time I need to make my escape.

Troll-face looks over his shoulder at me, his angry expression now garnished with a note of confusion. All those years of having to run through alleys and dodge Red Caps has really paid off. I smile at him and wave; it's only polite. The window slides open and I look out. My knees nearly collapse under me as the breeze hits me. I lean out the window, looking around. This prison is built onto the side of a cliff, and I'm in a tower hundreds of yards in the air. Why would the arrow point to this window? This isn't an escape route, it's a death jump.

Even if I land in water, from this height, the impact alone will kill me. My heart sinks. I am doomed. Troll-face recovers and is lunging toward me. No time. I just have to choose: leap from the window to what is certain death or allow myself to be caught and returned to my cell, which is also certain death. For whatever reason, my mystery rescuer is guiding me to this window. Maybe there's a reason. Maybe I just misread the signs. I face the window and there it is. Written in small letters on the windowsill is a single word in white powder. Jump. Sure, that's all I need to hurl my body into the abyss. A single word. Thanks, mystery savior. Either way, going back means giving Commander Stone the satisfaction of making my death slow and painful. Or just using it to further the Patriarch's agenda. At least this is on my terms. If I'm going to go, I'm going to go on my terms.

Everything in me screams no. I ignore it. Push forward. Throw my body from the window. Nothing. Just empty space as my body plummets toward the ground below. Troll-face slips past the window again, clearly not expecting me to leap to my death. My last minor victory.

The air whizzes by me faster and faster as my descent toward death hastens. My body twists in the air. Sky, then ground, then sky again flash in front of my eyes. It will be over soon. At least there won't be much pain. Not from this height.

My rapid descent slows and is suddenly halted. The ground is softer than I imagined. It's disorienting. My body suddenly feels like it's moving up against gravity. For the briefest of moments, I am suspended in place. Then my body comes crashing back down. Impact. Again, soft like landing on a mattress. I look down. Underneath me is a glowing purple-hued half-circle that is opened like a bowl. It feels familiar. A low humming sound surrounds me. It reminds me of the time Telmen bounced off the forceshield around the window in the Market.

Forceshield, of course! My bouncing gets smaller and smaller each time I hit the shield. Suddenly, the purple hue disappears. My body drops to the ground below with a loud and painful thud.

I groan and roll over onto my back. This is not a great feeling. At least I'm alive, somehow. It feels very surreal. I just jumped from a tower at the edge of a cliff and survived. I start laughing loudly, rolling around on the ground like a crazy person. I try to take a breath. My body worn. I look around to try and discover the identity of my rescuer. All I see are a pair of black silhouettes. I can't make out faces. My vision fades to black.

When I come to, I am in a dark room with a shaky floor. It's an odd feeling. I rub the back of my head. My shoulder and arm feel sore, but nothing appears broken. That's nice. I sit up and look around. This isn't a room. I'm in the bed of a covered truck of some kind. Brakes squeal as we come to a sudden stop, not a gentle stop. My body slips forward on the bed of the truck. I use my hands to brace myself against the metal wall next to me, the wall that separates the bed of the truck from the driver's cab.

I hear voices yelling, but I can't make out what they're saying. Gunshots ring out. I reach for my energy blade. I don't know what's going on, but anyone trying to take me back to prison is going to pay for the privilege. Two more gunshots, then silence. For a moment there is nothing, the calm before the storm. I ready my blade, crouching down, preparing to dive forward as soon as the doors open.

 Light floods the truck, and I start charging forward blindly. Surprise will be my greatest weapon. I dive out of the door into the large man who opened it. I hit him hard. He stumbles back and falls to the ground. I land on top of him, clicking my energy blade to life. I bring it up, preparing to drive it into his chest.

"Jett, wait!" The deep booming voice is unmistakable. My eyes focus. Underneath me is the giant bear of a man, Grent. I freeze, holding the blade in place.

"Grent? What are you doing—"

"You have a funny way of saying thank you after I risked my life to rescue you," Grent says.

"Y-you..." Of all the people I might have expected to rescue me, Grent was at the bottom of that list. I shake my head. No, something is wrong here. Grent wouldn't be the one. He may not hate me, but no way he risks his life to rescue me. I look around. Maybe some of my friends are with him. "I don't believe you. What's going on?"

Grent sighs. "It was my fault you got caught. Kane was my man. I trusted him, I brought him in, and he betrayed us."

"Kane?" So, it is true? Commander Stone wasn't just playing games with my head. He was boasting in his victory.

"Yeah, Kane. He's a traitor. Now do you mind getting off me? I scared him off for now, but if he comes back, he will kill us both."

I slide off Grent and put my knife away. "What happened?"

Grent shakes his head. "We found information on Kane's data-pad. When the Fire Wolves attacked our base trying to get to you, that was him. The information Brelar gave about your friends, the attack on your neighborhood, all of it was organized by Kane. He's been in communication with the Patriarch for over a year. He's the one who told the soldiers you were coming. He told Stone where to find you." Grent looks away from me. If I didn't know better, I'd think he looks ashamed. "I'm sorry. Kane had me convinced you were an enemy. I was wrong."

My list of people to kill just got a little longer. Kane betrayed us. He's the reason Lilly got captured. He's the reason Brelar is dead.

"Wait, what about the others? What happened to everyone else? What about the Market?"

"The Market?"

"Kane knows the tunnels. If he's in communication with the Patriarch, couldn't they use the tunnels to sneak in and attack us?" I ask. Grent's face turns sour. Panic sets into his eyes.

"We have to go now." He rushes to the driver's side of the truck. I step over the bodies of two men in beggar gang uniforms and climb in beside him. He puts the truck in gear, and the engine roars as we speed down the road.

"Can you message Vic with your data-pad?" I look at my wrist where my data-pad used to be. It was confiscated when I was imprisoned. Grent nods. Putting his knees on the wheel, he types a message into his pad and sends it. "How far are we?"

"Twenty minutes, maybe less." Determination blankets Grent's face. We may not see eye to eye, but he is committed to bringing down the Patriarch. Perhaps I was wrong to doubt him.

"Why did you come for me? Why isn't Victor here?"

"I would have left you behind. Nothing personal. I don't think you're worth the hassle. But Victor insisted you be rescued, and he is hard to argue with." That's true. Never met anyone who could tell Victor no when he set his mind to something. "He was going to come himself, but we needed him to finish preparing our assault. The data-pad Spike brought back has all the information we need: formations, deployment, positions. It has everything. His planning is at a crucial stage, so I came in his stead. At least it's something to do. If I had to sit in that tent for another minute analyzing data, I might have gone crazy."

Spike made it back safely then. That's a relief. Victor has the data-pad. Our mission was successful. By now, he must be close to finalizing his strategy to bring down the Patriarch. We've never been this close. What seemed impossible months ago is now right in front of us. "There is going to be an attack?"

Grent nods. "Very soon."

"What about Olivia? Did she get out okay?"

"Who do you think brought you that gift?"

"That was Olivia?"

"She helped. Provided the distraction mostly. Becka's the one that got it to you. I certainly wasn't going to charge through those prison halls myself. Seems your friends are willing to risk a lot for you."

"What about Telmen? Where's he?"

Grent shakes his head. "He never came back after your mission. We have no idea where he is. Maybe he escaped. Maybe Stone caught him. Maybe he's dead." Grent shrugs. Loud mouthed, frustrating Telmen. For all the times I did anything I could to avoid his incessant talking, now I'd give just about anything to listen to him ramble. Guilt is a heavy burden to bear. He annoyed me, drove me crazy. I was terrible to him. When I needed him, he was there. Now he may be dead.

"Lilly. Is there any news on her or her family?" My barrage of questions continues. I'm sure Grent would prefer to drive in silence, but after weeks in a cell assuming the worst, I have to know. Grent takes a deep breath, turning his head from me even further. "What? What happened? Tell me!" I demand more loudly than I intended.

"Her family was exiled," Grent says, a note of sympathy in his voice. His words hit me like a bat to the chest. I promised her I would help. Promised her I'd make this right. Now her family is in the Outlands because of me.

"When?" I manage to blurt out, not really wanting to know the answer but unable to stop myself from asking.

"Two weeks ago," he says. This is a bad dream. It's not real, just a nightmare. Soon I will wake up in my bed. No rebellion, no exile, no friends missing. Just me and our little crew of outcasts in our house in the education sector. Life will be normal. My biggest worry will be finding my place in the world.

"And Lilly?" My stomach knots up as I wait for his answer. "Was she exiled as well?"

Grent shakes his head. "She's still in the city as far as we know. The Patriarch held her for trying to escape." Silence. We sit in silence as the truck speeds toward the Market. I don't know what else to say, if there is anything to say. "There is some good news though," Grent offers. I fake a smile and pretend to be interested. I'm not sure how any news could be good enough to make me feel better. "Victor located your friend Gibbs. He was captured trying to escape and is being held in the Temple Sector."

"How is that good news?" I scowl angrily.

"Well, he's alive. That's something. He's also in the same place as your girl. So maybe Victor can come up with a way to rescue them both." Well, it's not great news, but it's better than it could be.

The truck screeches to a halt just before the outer wall of the Market. Grent had pulled so close I thought he might just crash through it. He shuts off the engine.

"Do not move!" a voice shouts from the top of the wall next to us. Instinctively, I freeze before looking up. Almost a dozen rebels are positioned with rifles aimed directly at us. I hold my hands up and smile.

"Grent, what is this?" I ask under my breath.

He steps out of the truck. "Stand down. He's not a threat. Don't you recognize him?" Grent points to me. "This is the leader of the rebellion, fools. Let us in."

A minute later, a small service door camouflaged into the wall opens, and several rebels step out, looking around before gesturing for us to come inside.

"Wow, they are really prepared," I say.

297

"Victor has soldiers all along the outer walls. I told him it's not necessary, that we should focus our defenses on the train stations, but he wouldn't listen."

"Yeah, Vic is like that sometimes. But, thing is, he's usually right."

We make our way toward the rebel command center on foot. I can't help but wonder why we didn't just drive the truck in. Would have been so much faster than walking. Rebels patrol the streets, moving in organized formations much like the Patriarch soldiers did. On every corner, I see an armed rebel pacing back and forth on the roof. Victor has been busy. Supplies stock the streets. Defensive barricades create strategic fallback positions. The rebels seem prepared for just about anything.

By the time we reach the old warehouse, Grent is panting for breath. It takes a lot of energy to propel his massive body forward. I don't have time to wait for him. I keep going. I don't stop until I reach the doors to the rebel headquarters. Victor is looking intently at some data on a screen. Spike and Olivia are sitting on a couch, scanning various reports. Jensen is asleep in the corner.

"Vic," I burst out.

"Jett! You're back!" Victor rushes over to me, hugging me firmly. I pat his back a couple of times and release the grip. Something about it feels off, but I'm not sure what. I'm probably just paranoid after everything that happened.

"Yeah, Grent really came through." Spike and Olivia rush over hugging me as well. "How long was I gone? I couldn't keep track of the time."

"Almost a month," Victor answers. "We would have gotten to you sooner, but it took us over a week to break into the sealed files on the data-pad Spike copied. Then several more days to figure out where they had you. That's when we discovered Kane's treachery."

"Where is he?" I growl, "I'm gonna—"

"He escaped, brotha. Nearly took Grent's head off in the process," Spike says.

"Vic, he knows about the tunnels, our positions, plans, all of it. If he gets to the Patriarch—"

"We've adjusted accordingly. The tunnels on the way in are lined with trip wires. I've got guards watching all their exits. Honestly, they'd be stupid to try it. The tunnels force troops to bottleneck. We could hold them off with a few guards. Of course, I'll have to abandon anything that was in place while he was here. That's annoying," Victor says confidently. "How did you find out?"

"Stone all but told me when I was imprisoned. He taunted me with it, asked me how he could have known which building I'd come back to. It makes sense it was Kane and Grent confirmed it."

"I don't think so," Olivia says.

"What do you mean?"

Olivia shakes her head, "I talked with Kane, he's odd but, I didn't get the sense he was lying to us."

"Stone told me he was," I respond.

"Hmmm," Victor ponders.

"What is it?" I ask.

"Something doesn't feel right about this. I can't put my finger on it."

"What do you mean? I thought you found information on his data-pad that proved it."

"We did. That's what troubles me. It's too neat. All the evidence points to him like he was gift wrapped for us. Why would Stone tell you about a traitor and then leave you alive? He had to know there was a chance you'd escape. If you did, he'd have burned his most valuable weapon."

"I thought about that. I figured he was just overconfident."

"No, that's not it," Victor says dismissively. "Stone is arrogant, not stupid. Telling you there's a spy in our camp is a stupid risk. That's not like him. Unless..."

"Unless what?"

"Unless he wanted you to escape."

"Why would he want me to escape? That doesn't make any-"

"It does," Victor interrupts. "You are the leader of the rebellion, but you are still just one person. The rebellion could survive the loss of one person, even if it was its newly appointed leader. I need to check some things. We may have a problem."

"You think Kane isn't a traitor because there is too much evidence that says he is?"

Victor nods. "No. I don't think it's Kane because all of the evidence points to him. There's not even room for a shred of doubt."

"Sure, so of course he must be innocent."

"Reality is never that neat, Jett. Never. If I were Stone, and I was worried you might start getting suspicious about my spy in your camp, I would tell you there was a spy to make you even more suspicious. Only I'd make sure all the evidence points to the wrong person. You would alienate or maybe even kill an ally while the real enemy could bury themselves deeper into your ranks. Two birds, one stone."

Sometimes I think Victor overthinks things. Sometimes when all the evidence points to someone, it's because they are guilty. I want it to be Kane. It's just easier to think Kane is the traitor than it is to believe one of our friends would sell us out.

Suddenly, an explosion erupts from one of the outer walls of the Market. The blast is so big I can see the flames above the three-story buildings.

"Sound the alarm!" Victor yells, rushing over to a nearby computer.

The Market Square turns into a flurry of activity as men and women dash back and forth, grabbing weapons, setting up defenses, getting into positions. Their movements are wild and chaotic, and yet efficient as if rehearsed. The sound of gunfire resounds. Short, scattered bursts from inside the walls are answered by massive, overwhelming gunfire. How could this be happening? I just got away, and moments later the Patriarch attacks?

"We should have seen this coming," Victor says under his breath.

"Ye can't predict everything, brotha. We knew a fight was coming."

"I know, but how did they hit the wall? I have guards all around it. There should be no way they could get explosives that close to the wall without our noticing."

"That seems like a problem for future Vic to figure out, if ye ask me. Why dunna we deal with the trouble at our first?"

Victor nods and pulls up the video from the wall that was attacked. PDF soldiers file into the smoldering hole. Victor types instructions into his data-pad before turning to face us.

"They've reactivated the trains. I've ordered all units to reposition and defend the outer wall." Victor's face looks grey as if all the color has been sapped from it.

"Vic? Is it that bad?" I ask. He doesn't say a word, just walks over to a locker and slides the door open. Victor returns with an armful of rifles. He sets them on the table. "Vic?" I press.

"If we can't fend off this assault, the rebellion is over." His matter of fact tone makes his words even more haunting.

CHAPTER TWENTY

The gunfire gets louder and closer, now accompanied by the screams of wounded soldiers. I grab a rifle off the table and rush up the stairs to the roof. The warehouse is a three-story building giving it the best possible view of the Market Square.

The rifle almost falls from my hands as I stare dumbfounded at the scene before me. Flowing down the streets like a black flood are rivers of PDF soldiers. The rebels are doing their best to hold their ground, but they are being overrun. For all the defenses, all the positions, they've not even been able to slow down the PDF march. It won't be long before they reach the Square. When one soldier falls, another soldier steps into his place.

Rebels line the rooftops, firing rapidly into the endless wave of soldiers. The marching stops. The soldiers turn their rifles up and fire back. Most of the rebels are able to move back into cover. Several fall from the rooftops. The black sea keeps marching.

Hope is crushed under the relentless stomping of the soldiers' boots. I can see PDF soldiers climbing out on the rooftops of some of the farther buildings and engaging the rebels on the rooftops. They are going to overwhelm us. No question.

"We need to get out of here," I yell down the open stairs.

"I need a minute. Buy me some time?" Victor shouts back. Spike, Jensen, Becka, and Olivia join me on the roof. We line up and start firing as quickly as we can. The beams of light fired from the rifles crash into black uniforms, cutting through their armor. A soldier drops, but the line keeps moving. With no end in sight, we shoot and we shoot, but it seems pointless. How can their army be so large?

"Oi, this isn't gonna get the job done." Spike sets down his rifle and moves away from the roof's ledge. "Keep going. I've got an idea."

"Spike," I shout back at him, but he's already gone, making his way down the stairs.

"We are so heaped," Jensen says as his rifle recoils faster and faster.

"Fear not," Becka says, "All who stand against you will fall. I will stomp them into dust." Becka fires three rounds in rapid succession. She even shoots fast.

"Sacred Texts?" Jensen asks, glancing over at her.

"Mhmm. They told us that's what would happen to all who challenge them." She laughs.

"Seriously? What a bunch of-"

"You don't know the half of it. Expression is arrogance! Compliance is virtue! Duty is Devotion!" She mocks. Jensen laughs with her. We are fighting the tide. For a moment Becka manages to distract us from the hopelessness of our situation. Three blasts hit the wall just below us. We stop firing and drop down for cover.

"Vic will come up with something. We just need to buy him some time."

A moment later we stand back up and continue firing. Jensen laughs, his face pressed against the side of his rifle as he peers through the scope. "Time is expensive today." He's right. The way the soldiers keep pouring down the streets is disheartening. We aren't making a dent. We aren't slowing them down. What else can we do? Surrender? That's not an option.

The PDF troops reach the Market Square. The fighting intensifies. Crashing into the open Square, the black uniformed soldiers begin fanning out, lining the perimeter and continuing their march forward. This is bad. They are suffering heavy losses without hesitation. There's only one reason to willingly sacrifice so many troops: annihilation. They haven't just come to reclaim the Market. They are here to wipe us out.

Spike rushes from a building on the streets below into the Square, closer to the wave of soldiers. What is he doing? He's going to get himself killed. Barricades are falling. Rebel positions collapsing. It seems like moments ago the PDF just reached the Market Square. Now they have filled over a quarter of it. Spike is running right at them. I aim my rifle at him, watching him through the zooming feature of my scope. He has a black bag in one hand. He keeps reaching into it and pulling out what appear to be large, silver-black marbles. He rolls them down the street toward the approaching tide of PDF soldiers. He runs across the Market, continuing to throw his silver marbles like a farmer scattering seed.

The little orbs bounce and roll as Spike scatters them. Some roll almost to where the PDF lines have reached, others to the center of the Market. Spike reaches the buildings on the southern perimeter and turns, running back toward us. The PDF reaches the center of the Square by the time Spike makes it out. What was he doing? I try to zoom my lens in closer to the little silver orbs more clearly. Now I recognize them.

A burst of red and orange forces me to pull back from my scope. I blink to readjust my eyes as another set of little explosions goes off. Then another. Boom. Boom. Boom. The rate of explosions gets faster and faster as the Market Square fills with dust and debris making it hard to see.

Instant chaos. The nicely formed ranks of soldiers break up. For the first time there are gaps. Screams fill the air as PDF officers try to reform their lines. Spike, you little genius. The explosions accomplish what no amount of rifle fire could—a brief pause in the advancement of the armies. We fire into the smoke, not sure if our shots will land but hoping they will keep the soldiers pinned down longer.

Spike's plan seems to have inspired others. A series of small explosions erupt up and down the streets. Each explosion halts the soldiers. Maybe we aren't doomed. Maybe, with enough explosives, we can push the PDF back. The smoke clears away. The soldiers aren't shrinking back. Their lines are reformed, and they are marching again.

"Becka, check on Vic," I shout. "See if he's ready."

Becka looks up from her rifle. "Why? Because I'm a girl?"

"No, because you're a terrible shot. You aren't hitting anything." I wink at her and she scowls back, setting down her rifle. She turns around and starts toward the stairs.

"Jett, we got company," she shouts rushing toward the side of the rooftop. I spin around and see PDF soldiers bursting onto the roof from the stairway. Shinshew. Even with our positioning, the endless sea of soldiers is too much to contain. As a group, we turn and fire rapidly managing to cut down the soldiers before they could fan out.

"Heap this. We got to go," I shout to the others. The wave of soldiers charging up the stairs slows a bit. The bodies pile up around the door.

"We've got to create a hole-make our way to Vic," I shout.

"Easier said than done," Jensen responds firing into the doorway.

"I'll take lead. Olivia, you stay a step back on the other side of the stairs; help me clear out the soldiers as we sweep down. Becka, you follow Olivia and don't shoot. I don't want to get blasted in the back. Jensen, you post at the top and fire down at any soldiers you can hit. Should keep them from trying to swarm us."

We move well, almost like a trained unit. I guess working together for years allows you to handle new situations pretty smoothly. Thankfully, the stairway was relatively clear, allowing us to make it to the floor below without too much struggle.

We work our way to the warehouse where there are enough rebel barricades and soldiers to give us a little respite. "Time's up, Vic," I shout. A green burst of energy crashes into the wall next to me, charring it and leaving a black film over the grey stone. That was too close. "Vic," I repeat.

Victor sighs, "Not much we can do. I've got one card left to play but it's risky."

"What is it?"

"They are converging here. They are going to take our headquarters. We can't stop them. We can make them pay for the privilege." He shakes his head, "I really didn't want it to come to this," he laments.

"What do we need to do?"

Victor draws a circle around our location, "We need to pull everyone back, get them on the rooftops here. They won't engage until my signal. Then we throw everything we have at them. It's a long shot but-"

"We don't have enough firepower to drive them back."

"No, we don't. I'm going to use a bomb."

"A bomb? Where did you get-"

"Our friend Ernest designed it. It's not an explosive. It sends out a wave of electrical energy strong enough to stop the heart from beating. Anything within this space," Victor draws a circle across the image of the Market right around where we are, "will die."

"We're all in that range."

"The blast doesn't go up. Only out. Those on rooftops or even the second floor would be unharmed, but..."

"But what?"

"We have to set up rods for the signal. Four points," Victor taps specific spots on the map, "Four rods."

"Vic, getting to those points will be-"

"Hence, the longshot."

"We don't have time for this. Vic says this is our best shot, let's do it." Olivia states, picking up a rod out of the container sitting on the table next to him. "What do we do with it?"

"You need to place it chest level as close to the point on the map as possible. Once placed, push the button on the bottom to activate it. A little ring will turn green and you'll know it's on. Once placed, get onto a roof and message me on my data-pad so I know you're clear. Once you're clear, we can draw the PDF in and, well, boom."

Olivia nods, "I got this one," she states tapping the west point and rushing off.

Becka smiles and grabs the second rod. "Last one back buys drinks." She rushes to the south. Jensen grabs the third rod nodding and heads north without a word.

"Jett, if this doesn't work-" Victor shakes his head.

I put my hand on his shoulder scoop up the last rod, "When has one your plans ever not worked?"

"Be careful," he urges, his face grim.

I smile, "Just another day in the life of an Undesirable."

I move as fast as I can, every moment counts. I keep my gun at the ready but, try to avoid conflict as it will only slow me down and draw attention. Thanks to their overwhelming numbers the soldiers are marching down the larger, wider streets, leaving many of the alleys completely open. I duck behind a dumpster as a large group of soldiers marches past my location. They were moving with a single-minded focus, but I don't want to tempt fate. Keeping my back pressed against the stone wall of the building, I slide deeper out of view. I glance up to see the rebels on the rooftops moving in towards Victor. There don't seem to be many left.

I pull up my position on my datapad, three blocks over, one block up and I'm in position. I peek my head around the wall to make sure the path is clear. I exhale and race across the open street, slamming my back against the wall and freezing long enough to confirm I wasn't spotted. Two blocks over, one block up.

"Jett," Victor's voice in my ear makes me jump. "Becka is clear. Her piece is activated." With a click the digi-call channel closes. Of course, Becka already had hers in place and made it to safety. How is she so fast? I slide along the wall to the opening of the next alley. It should give me an open lane to get closer to my target location. I swing around the corner and crash into someone.

Stumbling back, I raise my rifle. The solider turns around slowly. There are several standing there assessing information in a little group. The soldier's eyes go wide. The others reach for their weapons. I fire, aim, fire. I turn my hips lining up each shot as fast as I can and squeezing the trigger. The surprise gave me just enough time before the last solider could raise his weapon.

"Rebel, over here!"

A zzrrrp sound echoes in my ear as I feel the heat from an energy blast whizzing by me. Shinshew. I take off running down the alley, leaping over the bodies of the soldiers I just killed. I'm halfway down the alley when the soldiers start firing again. Energy bursts crashing into objects behind me, hitting the walls around me. I zig zag as I run to make it harder to get a lock on me. I reach an opening and dive headlong without looking. Rolling out of the dive I push off the ground and am back on my feet. Energy blasts fly from the alley I was just in as the soldiers keep firing as they chase me.

Three streets over, no time to be cautious. I sprint as fast as I can, driving my feet into the ground like I'm trying to shove the world down with each step. Three blocks and I'm there. If I can reach the alley, before they make it to the street, I can disappear from view and they won't find me.

"Jett," Not now Victor, Jett's busy. "Olivia's clear. Just you and Jensen." One block clear, two to go. I don't dare look back. All I can do is hope that stepping over their dead comrades slows them down enough. I pass the opening to another alley, one block to go. My lungs are on fire. My feet scream in rage. Just a few more steps and I'm clear.

I swing my body around the corner and slam by back against the wall so hard my head starts ringing.

"Where'd he go?" I hear a soldier shout. I glance around the corner carefully. A group of six soldiers rushed into the street from the alley. They started looking around for any sign of where I had gone. I rested my head against the wall to catch my breath, letting my heart slow down.

"Jett," I really got to turn that off, it's freaking me out. "Jensen's clear. It's all you now. Get your rod placed and get back here."

I took a long slow breath. Haste never leads to good decisions. I peek out to the street. My pursuers have circled up in the middle of the street looking in each direction. They are relentless. Then I see it, the perfect place for the rod. Next to the door of the shop is an empty metal bracket for holding a decorative flag. All I have to do is turn it on and drop it in there and we're set. Time is running out. The way the soldiers were advancing, it wouldn't be long before the surrounded the warehouse and all this was for naught.

I can't wait any longer. I press the button on the bottom of the rod. The soldiers will see me. I'll just have to outrun them. I take another deep breath and prepare to make my move.

"There!" They shout. No way they could have seen me. I glance into the street to see the soldiers turning and lifting their guns. One of them was sitting on his butt having apparently been knocked over. I see her running, she must have charged into them to draw their attention. I shake my head, Becka you are absolutely crazy.

"Jett, we are running out of time," Victor's voice rings in my ears again.

The rod drops into the bracket with a crnnck. I glance to make sure the circle turned green. It did. I sprint back towards the building across the street. The alley was empty again, save for the bodies of the soldiers. I run without looking, without ensuring the route is safe. I don't have time to be careful. Getting back to the building across from the warehouse I slide to a stop. From here I can get to the rooftop where Victor told us to meet. I climb the stairs as fast as I can. I push my way out onto the roof and hit my data-pad to send him the message I am clear.

I make my way to the edge, looking at the endless black of the PDF forces packed in around the warehouse. Where is Victor? Why hasn't he activated the device?

"Jett," I hear a whisper behind me. Olivia and Spike are crawling across the roof towards me, keeping their heads down. A moment later the door to the stairs swings open. I raise my rifle to fire. Victor holds up his hands, a remote device in his right hand. Becka pushes out from behind him, motioning for me to lower the gun.

"What happened?" I whisper as Victor slides up next to me.

"Had to make sure everyone was clear," he smiles, "you ready?"

We look over the half wall of the roof together. Walking out of the warehouse is the unmistakable Commander Stone. We are close enough I can see a smile on his face.

"Push it Vic," I blurt out excitedly. I look at the crowd with eager expectation.

Nothing. I turn to Victor, who is hitting the bottom of the remote. He pushes the button again. Nothing happens.

"Hahaha, oh rodents...are you looking for this?" Stone lifts his arm, revealing one of the rods. He laughs and snaps the device between his hands before discarding it. "Don't worry, I picked it up for you. Also, found something else you might be interested in." He snaps his fingers. Two soldiers drag out a straggly young man with a hood over his head.

Stone smiles and pulls the hood off. "Did you misplace one of your little friends?" He asks a sinister satisfaction in his voice. It's Jensen. Stone captured Jensen. How did this happen? What do we do now?

"Out the back, to the tunnels," Victor says, pointing in the direction he wants us to go. "We can't do anything else here." Without a word we run. We run like we've never run before. All our anger, our disappointment, our frustration fuels our steps. By some strange luck, the one route the PDF soldiers hadn't used to converge on the warehouse is the route we needed to reach the tunnels. The tunnel entrance is in the opposite direction of the advancing enemy soldiers, which gives us time. We reach the ivy-covered walls of the floral shop. Next to the floral shop is our secret passage down to the tunnels.

Spike takes two silver cylinders and places them just under the door, wedging them into place. "First person tries to follow us will be in for a wee surprise." He smiles. "Nobody's sneaking up on us today."

Our journey through the tunnels is a long, solemn one. Fleeing the Market is a strange feeling. Our home for many years is burnt to the ground. There are a lot of places we can go, but only one where we can really hide—the Rim. The Rim is the circle of slums just inside the city walls where the Patriarch tries to contain all Undesirables. It's a crowded, festering community of people that society forgot. The downside is, it's a miserable existence. The upside, the Patriarch will have a hard time finding us there. First, we will stop at the Lazy Loafer. It's a safe place where we can rest and lick our wounds before deciding our future.

It's hard to believe things got heaped so quickly. With the data-pads we had the intel. Trying and failing so spectacularly may actually be more frustrating than not trying at all. For all the effort, all the death, what have we really accomplished? The Patriarch still wiped us off the map like we were little more than a bug on a windshield.

We exit the tunnels, checking the area carefully before making our way to the Lazy Loafer. The pub is completely abandoned. Didn't even bother to activate a forceshield. We slip inside and make our way down to the bottom floor. One last burst of nostalgia. Our army of thousands has been reduced to Spike, Victor, Olivia, Becka, Grent, myself, and two others I don't recognize.

The screens show images of the Market. The battle is over. All that's left of the conflict are the smoking embers, debris, and unclaimed corpses. Cam Drones zoom in and out giving an aerial perspective. Holes have been blown into buildings and walls. Several buildings are on fire; a few are completely decimated. No resistance. No defiant gunshots. Just death and defeat for all who oppose the Patriarch. It doesn't make sense that we lost so quickly. With all the plans and preparation, with the troops we had ready to fight, it shouldn't have been so easy for them.

PDF soldiers line the streets as the lower text on the screen celebrates the Patriarch's triumphant victory over terrorism. The camera cuts to a shot of the Market Square. A group of rebel soldiers are lined up in rows on their knees with their hands bound behind their heads. This is all that's left of the rebellion. Apparently, the masses of Dios are not as against the Patriarch as I thought. In the end, not enough people were willing to fight for a change. This small cluster of captured rebels is all that remains of our dream of a better city.

After all that we fought for and all those who died, we didn't change a thing. Lilly's family is in the Outlands. Lilly, Jensen, Telmen, Gibbs are all captured or worse. It's all my fault. My stupid desire to resist, to prove myself, to stand up, succeeded only in getting so many people killed.

The screens shift to another street. Another line of rebels are on their knees, facing the shops, soldiers standing behind them with rifles at the ready. That's weird. Why are there rifles? I realize what's happening moments before it does. Twelve guns fire at once. Twelve bodies collapse to the ground. The cameras zoom in for it to ensure everyone sees it clearly. The message is simple: this is what happens to those who oppose the Patriarch. Fall in line or this will happen to you. Disbelief covers my face. How could they do this? These men surrendered and they are just executing them? There is no mercy today, only justice at the end of a gun.

I slam my fist down on the table, scattering the utensils left on it. "This is Kane's doing! He's going to pay," I declare boldly. No one says a word. We just sit in uncomfortable silence. In the end, it's Victor who breaks it.

"We aren't out of this yet. There's still a way."

"I've been fighting the Patriarch for years," Grent growls. "You haven't been paying attention. You saw what they did to our army. We were prepared. We had the strategic position. We had weapons. They wiped us out like it was nothing. What could we possibly do to defeat them? It's hopeless."

"That wasn't the end of our effort," Victor counters. "It was the beginning. We were never going to win that way."

"Never going to—" Becka catches herself. "Vic, what were we doing if we couldn't win? So many people died."

"I know. There is only one way to win this war. The price is high, and it's time to pay it."

"What are you talking about?" she asks.

Victor shrugs. "I found something on Stone's cloned data-pad." He pauses to let the statement sink in. For some reason, it feels like he's changing the subject. "It may help us." All eyes are on Victor, waiting for him to continue. "Commander Stone was commissioned by the Patriarch to initiate a rebellion."

"What?" I ask, dumbfounded by the statement. "What does that mean?"

"He provided money, information, and ideas to groups of people with the intention of stirring up dissent. He's been working on it for months."

"What are ye saying, brotha? That the Patriarch intentionally started a rebellion just so they could squash it?" Spike asks.

"That's exactly what I'm saying."

"Why?" I ask. "That doesn't make any sense."

"The class system, where the impoverished masses suffer while the elite few live in excess, is unsustainable. Add to it a highly controlling government filled with rampant corruption, and it's a powder keg. As the masses grow, so does unrest. If unrest becomes greater than the fear of reprisal, you have a rebellion," Victor explains.

"Okay, but that doesn't explain why they would try to start one."

"Control," Victor says. "It's all about control. If they waited until an uprising began, they may not be able to contain it. If, however, they incite rebellion themselves before there is enough unrest, they can do two things. First, they can control the population. Fewer people means greater portions for those who remain. Second, and more importantly, they eliminate all insurgents, driving any remaining unrest out." Everyone begins exchanging confused looks. Sometimes the challenge with Victor is tracking with his reasoning. He's smarter than the rest of us—so much so that he can't always explain things clearly.

"You lost me." Grent looks confused and frustrated.

"It's like a controlled burn, right?" I ask. Victor smiles and nods. "Sometimes when a fire is burning out of control, the best way to stop it is to use smaller fires. The small fires burn away the fuel the larger fire needs. It keeps the larger fire contained, and it will ultimately burn itself out. The idea is, you do a little damage to prevent much greater damage. That's what you're saying right, Vic?" Victor nods again. Thinking about it makes me nauseous. Rather than changing, making some sacrifices, striving to make the city better, the Patriarch would rather slaughter tens of thousands of people just to ensure its position of power remains unblemished.

"What's going to happen now?" Olivia asks.

"Likely, the Patriarch will use the public outcry from this rebellion to add more laws and give themselves more control in the name of preventing terrorists from attacking the city again," Victor says.

"The people won't just accept that," I protest.

"Not only will they, they will be grateful for it. Jett, we lost. We lost in the worst kind of way. We wanted things to be different. They will be. They will be worse."

"How does any of this help us?" Grent asks, scoffing.

"Leverage. The information makes it appear as if Stone acted alone. If this information were to get out, the people would demand Stone's head. The Patriarch has already labelled us terrorists. He supported us. Even if he did so at the Patriarch's behest, they'd have to hang him out to dry. If they didn't, they would risk a full-on rebellion."

As much as I love the idea of bringing Stone down, I don't see how this helps us. The Patriarch still won. We still lost. I guess it's a great consolation prize though. It's comforting to think that, if nothing else, we took out that monster.

"Yer not thinking leverage. Yer thinking ransom, aren't ye?"

Victor smiles. "Stone has our friends. We may not be able to bring down the Patriarch, but we can still rescue them."

"You want to blackmail a commander in the PDF?" Grent asks.

"What's to stop him from killing us the moment he sees us?" I ask.

"I have the file loaded onto a server. Something happens to me, the file gets sent to every data-pad and every screen in Dios."

The idea of rescuing our friends lifts my spirits a little. It doesn't undo the damage we've done, but at least it's a start.

"Let's say he agrees. Gives us our friends, we give him the information. What's to stop him from killing us then?" I ask.

Victor just smiles a cocky smile.

"Oh, great. I know that look brotha."

"Do you trust me?" Victor looks straight at me. Why? No one trusts him like I do. I trust him more than I trust myself. So, why is he giving me this look? I don't hesitate for a moment.

"You managed to keep us alive this long, which is pretty amazing considering. No reason to start doubting you now. I'm in," I declare boldly. "Let's do it." Victor almost seems disappointed in my response. I don't get it.

"That's right, brotha," Spike agrees. "We're all in."

"Of course we are in," Olivia declares.

"When do we start?" Becka asks.

"It's going to be challenging. There will be sacrifices. You need to be sure. It'll be easier to run. To hide," Victor warns.

"Enough running," I say. "We've come this far. Let's finish it. We don't leave our friends behind. We may be down, but we aren't out yet!" The others cheer in response. "For those brave men and women who fought against tyranny, who died in the Market. For our friends, our family, our loved ones who suffered under the Patriarch. For Brelar!" Everyone cheers again.

Victor exhales heavily. "There's nothing we can do tonight. Go get some rest, some food. I'll get word to Stone and set up our meeting. By this time tomorrow, we should have our friends back." Victor smiles, but something seems off about it. His shoulders are drooping; his eyes look heavy. He disappears up the Lazy Loafer steps. A minute later, I hear the front door open and then click closed.

Recent events have taken their toll on me. I find a booth away from the others and curl up inside it. My body is still sore from my fall. The forceshield may have saved me, but I still hit the ground hard. My legs are tight and throbbing. I lean back on the padded seat of the booth. My head hits the padding, and I collapse into sleep.

I am the first to wake. Slowly, I pry myself off the booth, my face and skin having stuck to it overnight. It takes me a minute to wake up; my eyes don't want to focus. I force myself to my feet. Jensen and Spike crashed on opposite sides of the same booth. Becka is lying on the floor in the corner under the stairs. Olivia is passed out leaning against the bar. Grent fell asleep on a table and is roaring like a slumbering bear.

I slide behind the bar, looking in the small refrigerator unit to see if there's anything to eat. Not much: a partially eaten sandwich, clumsily rewrapped in some sort of clear film and some fruit. I grab an apple and close the door. It clicks loudly and seals shut. Olivia jolts up and, for a moment, her head slides back and forth like a sprinkler watering the grass.

"Sorry," I whisper to avoid waking anyone else. I show her the apple and shrug.

Olivia smiles and shakes her head. "Don't worry about it. It's okay." I don't know how she wakes up in such a good mood. She's always friendly like she's immune to being annoyed. Maybe that's why she never gave up on Jensen. She has a high tolerance for frustration. "How are you?" She smiles looking very concerned. "It has to be hard not knowing about Lilly."

"It is. It just seems like everything I do makes it worse for her. She gets caught. I rescue her. Then it's not just her, they take her whole family. Now who knows what they are doing to her. I try to help, but it just messes things up for her." I unload more than I should. It's early.

"You know, Jett, most guys—they just go after what they want, whatever makes them happy. They don't care what happens to anyone else. You are trying to help. You can't blame yourself for what others do. It's not your fault. If she doesn't know how much you care, if she doesn't appreciate how much you have gone through to try and help her and others, well, sweetie, she doesn't deserve you."

My face feels warm. I'm sure I'm blushing. I don't know how to respond to that. I hope she's right. Maybe she is. I just can't shake the fact that I promised Lilly I would help her family, and I didn't. I can't let myself off the hook for that.

"You're always so supportive," I smile at her.

Olivia shrug, "That's what family does. You look out for each other no matter what." There is an odd somberness to Olivia's tone. Why do I get the feeling we are nearing a sore subject?

Our conversation is cut short by the sound of the sliding door upstairs. Victor is back. It took him a long time to set that up. Olivia and I wake the others as Victor descends the stairs.

"Stone agreed to my demands. He will return our friends in exchange for the codes to delete the incriminating information on him."

"That's great, brotha," Spike replies. "Let's go get our friends."

"Here's what we do: in two hours we will meet him at our old home. We know the woods. He doesn't. That gives us an advantage should he break his promise. He swears he will come alone. We know he has no intention of doing that. I will meet with him. Once he releases them, Spike, you will escort them back to the woods for safety. Becka, you and Olivia will be standing by with smoke discs ready. If anything goes wrong, you toss those. We'll use the distraction to get away. Jett, your job is simple. You have the trigger. If he doesn't honor his deal, you push the button and the file uploads."

"Give it to Grent," I interrupt. Spike and Victor both look at me, confused. "He's one of us now. We're going to have to start working with him if we are going to survive, right? Give him the switch." Victor's gives me a sour look. Finally, he shrugs and hands a small device to Grent. I slide my hand in my pocket, my finger sliding over the smooth handle of my energy knife. I can't take the device. It would get in the way. As soon as Lilly is safe, I'm going to kill Commander Stone.

CHAPTER TWENTY-ONE

It's time. Victor stands in front of the ashes of our old home. Olivia and Becka are hiding just behind the tree line, smoke discs ready should we need them. The two rebel soldiers who escaped with us, Hal and Markus, are across the street with their rifles ready. The rest of us are lined up a few yards behind Victor, ready for his signal. It's nerve wracking. I feel exposed just standing out in the open, waiting for the man I hate most to arrive. I look at the charred remains of what was home for many years. It, like our lives, is reduced to ash and ruin. I pace back and forth, my body jittering as I try to control myself without success.

Time passes slowly. Stone is late. Every second, makes my anxiety grow. I cover my face with my hand before running my fingers through my hair. What is taking so long? He should be here by now. Is he playing with us?

As if to answer my question, a single vehicle pulls into view. Rumbling along, the black van comes to a stop a few yards away. Commander Stone slides out of the driver's seat and walks around the back of the van slowly. The doors open with a click and a squeaky slide. A pair of feet appear under the bumper of the van.

Telmen is the first to emerge from behind the truck. He's alive. Remarkably, he looks good—no bruises, no bleeding. That's a relief.

He clutches his side as he walks. Maybe they did work him over after all. Gibbs appears next. Gibbs doesn't seem to have any problems walking. Gibbs is followed by Jensen. Three out of four are okay. My heartrate rises. I try to control my breathing, keep myself calm.

Lilly steps out last. Her hair is a mess, and she looks disoriented and confused, the way I felt in the tower prison. Maybe she was there, and I missed her? Couldn't be, I checked every screen I passed. Even if she was there, and I had found her, would I have thrown her out the window with me? No, it's better this way. She's safe. She looks unharmed. That's more than enough for now.

Our four friends are bound together by a rope held by Commander Stone. Surprisingly, he did come alone. No tricks? Maybe he knows he won and doesn't need them? Stone stops a few feet from Victor.

"All right, I got your friends, rodent. Now, give me what's mine and I let them go."

"No." Victor holds up the data-pad with the codes Stone wants. "I walk, they walk, same time."

Stone grins and nods. They walk toward each other slowly. Every step is agonizingly slow—wishing, hoping with everything I am nothing goes wrong. Telmen reaches Spike first. Gibbs and Jensen follow. Lilly moves after them. Spike escorts them back to the tree line. Victor did it, as expected. He rescued everyone. Lilly is finally safe, thanks to Victor. Focus, I have my own mission. I slowly pull the energy blade free, gripping the handle in my hand. I just need a slight opening.

Stone drops the data-pad as Victor starts to walk away. The data-pad cracks, but Stone stomps on it, grinding it into the street for good measure.

"One moment, before you go." Stone reaches behind his back and pulls out a handgun. "See, I've decided to renegotiate our deal." Predictable, as Victor said he would be.

"As I imagined you would," Victor says calmly. "What good is the word of a man who lies to everyone? It takes a considerable amount of duplicity, starting rebellions and putting them down over and over again."

"A regretful necessity in order to keep the flames disorder from burning away at our great society," Stone growls back.

"I had hoped you would be a bit cleverer. There's no joy in outsmarting a fool." Victor grins. "I took the liberty of maintaining remote access. My compatriot here has a switch. If anything happens to us, all your secrets become household knowledge. You may kill us, but you'll be joining us not long after." Victor turns around and smiles. This is almost better than killing him. Emasculating him, stealing the power he's so proud of. It's perfect. "So, not only are you going to let us leave. You're going to make sure we don't get caught by anyone else."

Stone nods, lowering his gun. "Well, you have to be the cleverest rodent I've ever encountered." Victor smiles. This is it. This is my moment. I step forward, inching my way closer. When his guard drops, I will end him. Stone laughs. I freeze. Why is he laughing. Something is wrong. He shouldn't be laughing. "But at the end of the day, the world's cleverest rodent is still just a rodent. Your friend isn't your friend." He smiles slowly looking at Grent. It takes me a minute to process. Grent tosses the switch to Stone who catches it and places it under his boot, stomping on it the same way he did the data-pad. "Sorry about that."

Grent walks over and stands next to Commander Stone, folding his treacherous bear arms over his treacherous bear chest. "Didn't see that one coming, did you?" Grent asks.

My whole body suddenly tremors. Grent is working with Commander Stone?

"Wait," I protest. "Grent what you are doing?"

"He's betraying us," Victor states in an oddly matter of fact tone. I glance over, Victor doesn't seem all that surprised. Why is not surprised?

"No. No that doesn't make any sense. Grent rescued me when I escaped from Stone."

"Did he?" Victor asks.

"Kane...is..."

"I told you it was too perfect. Kane did not betray us Jett. All the things it looked like Kane did, they were all Grent," Victor explains. "Kane was his fall guy. That's why it was neat and tidy."

Grent seems annoyed that we aren't focused on him, "Enough of this! I've won! I've beaten you!" He turns his attention to Victor, ""All your great strategies and schemes and you missed what was right in front of you. Did you really think this was the first time we've done this? My legend, my reputation, they draw malcontents out. I lure them to me with the promise of freedom and a new world. Then we kill them all." Stone and Grent begin to laugh. Not again. Victor wanted to give me the switch. I told him to give it to Grent. This is my fault. If I hadn't been so set on revenge, none of this would be happening. Once again, I have failed my friends.

Spike rushes out of the woods, sprinting toward Grent. Jensen rushes after him, but he's too slow. Victor cuts him off, standing in front of him, shaking his head.

Spike looks over Victor's shoulders. "I knew ye were a piece of filth. Tell me this: Talia—did ye set her up to die on purpose?"

Grent gasps, holding his hand over his heart as if wounded. "Spike, my dear friend, no. Of course not. I would never have set sweet Talia up to die. No. No, I killed her myself." He might as well have thrust a blade into Spike's heart. My friend drops to his knees, hands holding his head as he screams in rage. "You were supposed to join us. We intended to kill you together. You never showed." Something breaks in Spike. His normal, calm, cool-headed demeanor is replaced with a savage, wild beast. He pushes past Victor in a single movement and bounds toward Grent, crossing the distance between them with alarming speed. Grent has a hundred pounds on Spike easy, but it may not matter.

Spike drives one fist hard and fast into Grent's chest. The other hooks into Grent's jaw. Grent stumbles back trying to regain his footing. Spike presses in. He strikes again and again in rapid succession, landing blows on Grent's chest and face, each strike keeping his opponent off balance. He can't even get his hands up to defend himself. Spike is so fast. A rifle shot zips past Spike's shoulder, and Hal and Markus come running toward us. Guess we know which side they are on. Spike side-steps and dives into Grent, chain punching him. The ogre man collapses to one knee. Spike has him.

Stone lifts his gun, aiming it toward Spike. I yell, charging toward Stone. My energy blade sings to life. Stone turns, whirling around. He aims his gun at me. I'm too slow, he's got me by a step or two. I see his finger pull back the trigger. My eyes close as I brace for the shot.

I feel nothing. I open my eyes. Standing between me and Stone is Gibbs. What just happened?

Gibbs drops to his knees in front of me. I drop my knife and catch him, trying to hold him up as blood soaks through the back of his shirt.

"Gibbs!" I shout, trying to hold his body up. Screams come from the woods. I look up at Stone and then down at my friend. He coughs up blood. His eyes look foggy. "Hey, look at me, you're going to be okay, it's just a scratch," I lie.

"It's...okay. The last...few years—" he struggles to talk.

"Don't talk. You'll be fine. We will get you help," I lie again.

"You guys... have been the only family...I've ever known... Tell Telmen—" Gibbs' words are broken up by a series of coughs. "Tell him...I'm Thief King... forever."

I laugh, trying to fight back tears. "Tell him yourself, you'll be just—"

Gibbs smiles. "You're not fooling... anyone, Jett... but I appreciate... the effort."

"No, no, no, stay with me. Who's going to steal us desserts? Who's going to—"

"You'll have to... step up your game... Do one thing... for me—"

"Anything," I say, trying to pull my emotion from my voice.

"Don't waste it," Gibbs says before his eyes close for the last time.

"Awww, so touching," Stone taunts. "You rabid beasts have your moments, don't you? You almost remind me of actual humans."

I stare into his eyes, his monstrous, wild eyes—eyes like a beast. Then it hits me. In that moment, at the worst of times, realization strikes me like a bat to the chest, knocking the wind from my body. I've seen those eyes before. It's been so long. He's aged so much I almost didn't recognize them. They are the eyes I see in my dreams every night, the eyes of the man standing over my parents. I grit my teeth. Rage courses through me like lightning. My body is a roaring inferno.

I lower Gibbs' body to the ground slowly. Scooping up my knife, I look up at Commander Stone, hatred overwhelming me, "I am going to kill you."

"Do you know what you've done, Stone?" Victor cries out.

Stone shrugs apathetically. "Put down another rabid dog. Just an average day at work."

"He wasn't an Undesirable," Victor says. A calmness to his tone covers a deep angry rage. "Gibbs was a Prime. You just murdered a Class A citizen of Dios." Stone's eyes go wide, as do mine. This isn't possible. Gibbs lived with us in a run-down house. He went hungry. He struggled like we all did. He wasn't Class A. No one would choose to live this if they didn't have to. This is a trick, some ploy of Victor's to get in Stone's head. It can't be true. Not Gibbs. Gibbs lived with us for years. He stole with us. Though he did disappear for days at a time. And he always managed to steal things the rest of us couldn't even dream of. And, now that I think about it, I never saw him steal anything.

"You're lying. Just look at how he's dressed. He even smells like one of you." Stone's having as hard a time believing this as I am.

"Scan his data-pad. You'll see. His name is Dr. Jacob Olander. He is one of the most esteemed minds in the city. He dresses and smells like we do because he was doing research for a project he was working on. In order to complete it, he felt he had to properly understand the life of an Undesirable." Victor pauses to let the information sink in. "Do you know what the penalty is for murdering a Class A citizen?"

Stone looks terrified. His hands are shaking, and his eyes dart wildly back and forth, "This is a trick, another one of your little-"

"The penalty is exile to the Outlands, even for a high-ranking officer. You have just sealed your fate."

Stone's hand stabilizes. "Well, I guess I'll just have to kill all of you right here. No witnesses. Guards!"

Hal and Markus raise their rifles. I close my eyes on instinct, bracing myself for what's to come. Zpph. Zpph. Zpph. Three gunshots ring out. I feel nothing. No pain. No heat from a blast. Nothing. I open my eyes and see Hal and Markus drop to the ground, their rifles bouncing away from their bodies.

Grent freaks out. He rushes over to Stone, grabbing for the Commander's gun. Stone resists. They wrestle for the weapon, each trying to pull it from the other's grasp. Stone is a trained soldier, but Grent's size gives him an advantage. Grent pulls the gun from Stone's hand and shoves the Commander over. He turns toward the woods, firing wildly, hitting nothing but air.

"Grent!" Spike's voice rings out. Grent turns around. Zpph. A green burst of energy crashes into Grent's chest. I look over and see Spike kneeling over Hal's body, rifle in hand. Grent staggers back, trying to regain his balance. He's a big man. Spike raises the barrel of his rifle.

Zpph. The blast hit Grent in the forehead. The great bear of a man falls to the ground dead. Talia's death is finally avenged.

A rustling sound comes from the woods. Stepping from the wooded cover, rifle resting against his shoulder, is the last person I expected to see. Emotions collide. I ready my knife as the man who just saved us is none other than Kane, the traitor who sold us out. Kane smiles warmly as he walks toward us.

"When are you going to learn, it's not a party until I get here." Kane chuckles. "Everybody stocked?" His voice sounds oddly genuine like he really cares. That makes me want to kill him more. I lunge for him, activating my knife, I pull the blade toward his neck.

"Jett, stop!" Victor shouts. I freeze, my blade an inch from Kane's exposed neck. Kane smiles, as if amused. He looks down at the blade and then up at me, playfully lifting his hands in surrender.

"Sorry I asked. Next time I'll pretend not to care," he says.

"What are you doing?" Victor scolds.

"He tried to kill me?"

Kane laughs, "That's a lie!"

"I saw you!" I object.

"Course you did. But I wasn't trying to kill you, if I was you wouldn't still be breathing."

"You shot at me."

"I shot at Grent. He set me up. I don't like being set up. Feels personal."

"Think about it Jett. It was Grent. It was all Grent," Victor says.

"Why would he rescue me then?" I counter.

"I wondered that myself for a moment. Then the wall exploded, and it became clear," Victor explains.

"What are you talking about?" I ask still not moving my knife from Kane's neck.

"You were a decoy. After you were captured, I put Market on lockdown. Grent used your rescue operation as an opportunity. While Olivia and Becka were working their parts, he acquired a truck filled with explosives. Bringing back the leader of the rebellion was enough of a distraction that no one would think twice about him parking a massive truck right next to the wall. That's how the PDF was able to re-take the Market."

My hand drops. Could this be true? Did we have it all wrong? Was Kane just a fall guy? How can Victor be so sure Kane isn't involved? Grent was a traitor, that doesn't mean Kane isn't one too. Something about this is off. Victor seems off. Even though he's talking to me, it's like, he's not really talking to me.

"Hold on," I shake my head. "There's one thing that doesn't make sense."

"There's no way Grent could have known about the warehouse though. Grent was with you. Spike picked that route on the way. If Kane didn't betray us, how did Stone know about the warehouse?" I ask.

"Are you satisfied yet? Victor asks.

"Satisfied?" Why is he asking that?

A loud slow clap erupts as a middle-aged man steps out of the trees and into view. He carries himself like a man of great importance.

"We've been doing this a long time. No one has ever figured it out before. You are as clever as advertised." The man's uniform is similar to the standard Levite garb, white robe trimmed with gold, but it is much more unique. The shoulders of his robes are much thicker, and the gold fabric extends just past the edge of his shoulders with thin golden strings hanging down. On his head, he wears a short, cone-shaped turban also white with gold accents.

Before I can blink a surge of white uniforms surrounds us, pouring in from across the street and coming out of the woods. I see Olivia and Becka getting dragged into the open. In less than a minute, we are completely surrounded by Levites.

"Every last rebel, as promised," Victor says turning to the mysterious Levite standing next to him.

"Very impressive, Mr. Karr," the strange man says, putting his hand softly on Victor's shoulder. He reaches into his robe and retrieves what appears to be a golden Levite officer badge. It looks like a keycard and is used to identify high ranking members of the Levite order. Why is he giving it to Victor? What's going on here? "You have proven yourself quite useful. Welcome to the Order." Victor bows his head to the man.

"What is going on?" I demand anger and confusion boiling together in my mind.

The strange Levite smiles and turns to me, "Of course, where are my manners? You asked a question. Seeing you've just been utterly defeated, the hospitable thing to do would be answer it. You're right Jett, Grent is not the reason we caught you in the warehouse. That was all Victor's doing."

I look back and forth between Victor and the Levite leader as if repeated looks would somehow help me make sense of all of this, "No, Victor wouldn't..."

The Levite holds up his hand, "I'm a big enough man to admit when I am wrong. When your friends contacted us, I had my doubts. He was convincing. Even offered to help us capture you, so long as we didn't kill you. Normally, that's a red flag for me. But when he explained his plan, oh, let me tell you, I had chills. So, I decided to play along. See what would happen."

"Play along?" Rage consumes any reason left in my mind. "Victor, tell me this is some sort of trick."

Victor shakes his head, "No a trick Jett. A test."

"A test?" I ask more confused than ever.

"Think of it as a final exam," the Levite leader interrupts. "Taking the Market got my attention. I wanted to see if your friend was as smart as he seemed."

"Join you? Who are you?"

The Levite smiles before taking an exaggerated bow, "My name is Gaius Despreaux. I am the Warden of Law. One of my many jobs is to identify and recruit exceptional people to join the Ruling Counseling. Now that I know how truly brilliant your friend is, I am delighted to have him join us."

"Join you," I growl.

"You may take them," Gaius orders the others.

The Levites converge on us. I try to pull my knife, but there's no time. Two Levites grab me by my arms. I struggle against them but to no avail.

"Wait," Victor says.

Gaius holds up his hand, and the Levites stop.

"Could I have a moment with them before you take them away?" Victor asks.

The Levite leader ponders for a moment.

Gaius sighs, "Very well, but make it quick. My time is valuable. I've spent enough of it on this."

The Levites line Olivia, Telmen, Becka, Jensen, Spike, Kane, Lilly, and me up in a row, fastening our hands behind our backs.

Victor walks over to us, pacing in front of us, "I hoped to avoid this, but there is no other way. Sacrifices must be made. I take no pleasure—"

"No pleasure?" I blurt out. "In selling out your friends to the Levites? Crash off, Vic. You betrayed us."

Victor sighs. Even the sound of his breathing is suddenly patronizing. Of all the people in all the world, the one who I thought would never betray me is Victor. My heart feels hollow; it doesn't want to believe what my eyes are telling me.

"Hold on, brotha. Ye know that's not true," Spike objects. "Victor wouldn't do that to us. He wouldn't sell us out for anything. This is all a ruse," Spike says looking to Victor for confirmation

Victor shakes his head, "Not a ruse, Spike. This is reality. I warned you. I warned you this was a fight we couldn't win. I tried. I tried to make the best of it, to do what I could, but in the end, it was clear the Patriarch will always win. You may be willing to gamble with your lives. I am not. I don't take stupid risks. Soon as you started this, soon as you jumped into this war, there was only one choice. I've made it."

"That's how you knew Kane wasn't the traitor?" I ask. "You knew he wasn't the traitor because you were. How long, Vic? How long were you planning for this, to lead us into this trap?"

Victor shrugs. "I told you that you wouldn't understand. How could you? You are blinded by idealism and anger. You could never see the truth, that only fools fight in a war they cannot win. I'm not a fool. So yes, I traded our friendship for a future." Victor holds up his badge. "Now, I have real power. No more scraps. No more disrespect. You know the old saying, if you can't beat 'em, join 'em."

"A coward's slogan," I spit back. "You were our friend. We trusted you. Put our lives in your hands. You gave us up for a title and a position? You're the worst. It's a good thing your parents are dead. If they saw what you've become, they'd be ashamed!"

Pain flashes through Victor's eyes. That gives me some satisfaction. I turn my head. I don't even want to look at him. Behind Victor I see Stone, struggling against three Levites who are holding him down, shackling his wrists. Are they arresting Stone? That seems odd. The leader of the Levites forces a coughing sound.

"I am sorry it came to this. I hope one day you see that," Victor says, his voice sounding genuine. He doesn't even process how deep his betrayal goes. "If it's any comfort, part of the deal I made with them was that you not be killed or tortured. You will be made Outlands Officers but not publicly. Your exile will be secret. You will live, just not in Dios." This can't be happening. It's a bad dream, the worst of all dreams. Any minute, I'll wake up. Victor looks down to his feet, and under his breath he utters, "I'm sorry."

Everyone starts yelling and cursing at once. It's hard to understand what anyone is saying. They all start pulling and tugging, trying to break free from their captors. Victor says nothing else. He turns and walks away, following the Levite leader to an unmarked vehicle parked a few yards away. Sound becomes muffled like I'm underwater. I can hear everyone speaking, but their words sound alien and unrecognizable.

The next day is a blur. The Levites brought us to some holding station, and we are led down white hallways with bright white lights hanging from the ceiling. We're thrown into separate white rooms, guards positioned everywhere. There's no escaping this prison. At least the walls are thin. I can hear the others talking with each other through them. Our rooms each have a large window to see out into the hallway. The window is protected by a forceshield so it's not a potential means for escape, but at least it provides a view.

Lilly is in the room across from mine. She's sitting on the white mattress, idly sliding a small piece of white and light blue fabric through her fingers. She's slouched over and looks miserable. Who could blame her? She didn't deserve this. I stand in front of the window looking into her cell. No matter how I think of it, she is here because of me. All that she is going through is my fault. She looks up and sees me. Getting out of her bed, she walks over to the glass. I half expect her to yell, to tell me she hates me. She doesn't yell. She doesn't look angry. She looks sad.

Lilly holds the fabric up to the window, a white and light blue lacey design that looks like springtime. "My mother made me this dress," she says softly, almost absently. She must be in shock. That's not a dress, it's a piece of fabric. "I love this dress. I used to wear it around the house all the time. I wasn't allowed to wear it outside, because it's not a uniform, but one day I decided I didn't want to wear my uniform. I went outside in the beautiful dress my mother made me. I felt so free, so alive running around in my favorite dress. Well, a guard happened to be walking by. My mother was punished for letting me out of the house dressed in such a way. She tried to take the dress away from me. I wouldn't let go. The dress ripped. This is the piece that's left. Every time I look at it, it reminds me of when I was little girl. Of that feeling of twirling around in my pretty dress, happy and free. Now, this is the only thing I have left of my mother." Lilly starts to look up but stops before her eyes reach mine. That's my fault too. Her mother was fine before she met me.

"Lilly, I'm," I manage to get out. It's a pretty inadequate apology considering what I've cost her. The only thing left of her family is a piece of fabric. I know all too well what it's like to see the people you love taken away. The Patriarch was responsible for my loss. I am the one responsible for hers.

"Do you know how we became Artisans?" She asks staring off at nothing in particular. I shake my head. "My father enlisted and served in the military. He gave them twenty years of his life, missed the first few years of mine so that his family could have a better life." She inhales slowly, eyes closing, "he wanted to live a quiet life. My brothers and I, we begged him to train us. We wanted to learn to fight so we could be tough like our dad. We promised we wouldn't use it, unless it was to defend ourselves. Finally, he agreed. We trained every night for years. When I saw them, using people as hostages, I couldn't stop myself. I just, I had to do something." She shakes her head. "Now, everything my dad worked for, is ruined."

"I'm so sorry Lilly."

"Why are you sorry?" Her voice sounds soft and sweet.

"It's not your fault, it's mine." I explain. "I'm the reason they came after you, came after your family. I should have known better, should have been more careful. Your family, you, all of this, it's my fault."

"Jett, shut up," she says firmly. "You are not Bealz. You can't control everything. You are not responsible for the actions of others. You think I'm mad at you for rescuing me? For helping innocent people? You think I blame you for what they did? Don't be stupid. You are brave. You are strong. You made me feel that freedom again, just for a moment. I remembered what it was like to dance and play. I'm not mad at you, Jett. I'm grateful."

The door to her room slides open with a whoosh, cutting her off. Several Levites step into the room.

"Lilly Moonslight," one calls out. Lilly looks at me, eyes wide with fear, and then over to the Levites in her cell. She swallows forcefully and nods. I can see her legs shake a little through the window. Like a heartless robot, the Levite glares down at her. "Come with us." They grab her arms and pull her out of the room. She doesn't resist. How could she anyway? They are both much larger than she is.

"No! Where are you taking her? Stop!" I shout. I bang my hands on the glass window of my room. The purple hum of the forceshield activates and propels me back. I land on the floor with a thud. I push myself back up and run back to the window.

"Return to your bed," a voice says. "You will be brought out soon enough." I slam my hands against the window again, defiance over brains. This time I'm blasted even further back.

"Jett, it's okay. Save your energy," Lilly says as they guide her out of view.

"Lilly!" I shout, raging and pacing back and forth. Watching her get taken away makes me long for the days I was invisible. This is why people blend in. This is why they don't draw attention to themselves. What the Patriarch sees, they destroy. So much for making a difference. All I made was a mess.

Days begin to blur together. The bright lights never shut off, which is very disorienting. We are fed and taken care of, but apart from counting our meals, it's difficult to keep track of time. After what I guess is a week, the two Levites come back. This time they take Kane. Why are they taking us one at a time? Where is Lilly? What is going on? Victor said we'd be exiled. Why not just exile us all and get it over with? What's the point of dragging this out?

"I'm going to kill him!" I shout kicking the wall of my cell.

"Jett, I know you're upset. You have every right to be. But right now, we have to remain calm," Becka says from her cell. Just hearing her voice calms me down.

"There's more to this," Olivia says. "There has to be."

"Are you defending him?" I snap at her.

"I'm just saying, remember who we are talking about. Victor is our friend. He's always looked out for us. I get that this looks bad. We have to trust him," Olivia's tone is almost pleading.

"How can you even say that?" I shout anger boiling up in me.

"Jett, she's right. We have to remember the weight he carried. It couldn't have been easy looking out for us for so long. We think because he's so smart that he's not afraid, but maybe he is. It has to be lonely being the one who outthinks everyone else. I can't imagine the pressure he was under. We relied on him for all of it. Maybe we just asked too much of him.I don't like what he did... I think, to honor the friend we had for so long, we should remember more than just his betrayal," Becka, ever the peacemaker.

Two days go by, and the Levites come for Becka. Olivia is taken a week later. Then Jensen a few days after her. When they come for Telmen, our time in the cells gets much quieter. Spike and I are the last two remaining. Thankfully, our cells are next to each other. We can't see each other, but at least we can talk. Anything to pass the time.

"You're oddly quiet Spike, what do you think? How could he betray us all after everything we've been through?"

"I dunna know, brotha. I can't imagine what he was thinking. Betraying yer friends is the worst sin any man can commit. I'll never forgive him for that."

"I just don't understand. Victor and I grew up together. His parents took me in when mine were killed. I was there when his were killed. We were bonded together. I never thought he'd break that bond, especially not for a title and position with the people who killed our parents."

"Aye, it's definitely a shock. Vic's a complicated man. Complicated men dunna always react the way ye expect them to."

This whole time I was fighting against a cruel government when, the real enemy was my best friend. All the lives lost in the rebellion, Brelar, Gibbs, they are on his hands. One day, I will find a way to make him pay for what he has done.

Our conversation is cut short by the door to my cell opening. The two Levites accompanied by a dozen Red Caps enter my room and pull me toward the door. They lead me past Spike's room. He smiles at me as I look over my shoulder.

"Be seeing ye soon, brotha. Stay alive til then," he says with a nod. The door slams behind me. The two Levites on either side push and guide me down a long series of well-lit, poorly decorated hallways. It feels like being underground and yet bathed in bright white light. The hallways lead to what appears to be a massive loading dock. Machines drive around, moving large containers of unknown supplies. We walk through the middle of the room, a path between the two supply areas. There are two towers on either side of the central path. Each appears to be a sort of defensive position. I look over as we pass them. There are two turrets on each tower as well as a roost on the top where several soldiers could fire down if needed. In front of me is the largest automated door I have ever seen. It's taller than any of the buildings in the Market. Two more towers line either side of its opening. I can only imagine what's outside those giant doors.

A Red Cap steps in front of me and shoves a pack into my chest. My arms wrap around it, hugging it instinctively. The bag is heavy and bulky with a zipper to close up the contents. Sticking out of gap in the zipper are the ends of several arrows. I've seen these packs before. They are given to Outlands Officers to help protect the fiction that it's anything more than what it is: a death sentence.

"Time to go, convict." The Levite behind me shoves the back of my shoulder. I step forward, my legs slowly moving me toward the door. This is it. It's really happening. My heart pounds. My stomach lurches. Fear overwhelms me. My mind holds onto some absent hope that this is all just a trick, that Victor didn't really betray us and he will swoop in any moment and rescue me.

What I get is the grinding of gears and metal groaning as the massive doors part. The white cement floor seems to slope up, making every step feel just a little heavier. As the large door opens, a strange orange-red light pours through the crack. Running is pointless. There is a catwalk circling all the way around the building, lined with rifle-ready soldiers. Resistance will get me nowhere.

I follow the path lined out for me. Stepping through the massive tower doors, the red-orange light engulfs me. The texture of the ground shifts from smooth, hard cement to shifting, squishy sand. The sand gives way under my feet. It's firm but still unstable. I look back. I'm about ten yards past the entry when the grinding metal sounds resumes, and the massive doors slide closed behind me. They bang together with a locking, clicking thump. No way back. Then comes the slight hum of the energy field, brighter, louder than I'm used to, not the forceshield that covers the windows and screens of the city. This is the dome of Dios, and I am outside it.

I take a deep breath and turn around, my eyes squinting to adjust to the light. I climb the brown, sandy slope up and away from the city and look out over the horizon. As far as my eyes can see, in every direction there is nothing but arid desert. Terror grips me. This is the place that haunts every person living in the city. It's the horror we are conditioned to fear when we are children. This is the Outlands.

END OF BOOK ONE

The Saga continues with book two: The Tides of Reckoning

Printed in Great Britain
by Amazon

67959942R10197